I0535458

"Reloaded version 2013"

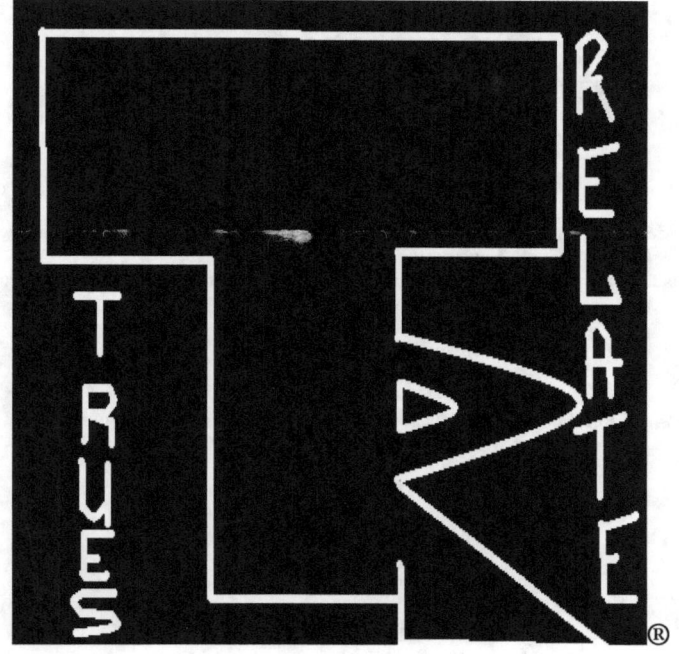

TIME TO GROW-RELOADED
TIME WILL REVEAL PART 2
BY
BLACK COFFEE

TIME TO GROW-RELOADED-TIME WILL REVEAL 2

Published by True's Relate Publishing
Time to Grow -RELOADED-(Time will reveal: Part 2)
Library of Congress Control Number: TX 7-140-118
Copyright ©2003, 2009 True's Relate publishing/LTBROWN
All rights reserved

®REGISTERED TRADEMARK-MARCA REGISTRADA
ISBN:978-0-9844701-1-2
Printed in the United States of America
Set by Createspace
Cover design by Gregory Spencer of Misvision Graphics info@misvisiongraphics.com
Logo design by: JayRocOne [age 15]
Requests for information on ordering, scheduling the author for signings and appearances
should be addressed to: blackdollone@att.net
[Black Coffee's websites]
http://www.blackdollone.com
www.truesrelatepublishing.com
On Facebook; Black Coffee Fan Page
Facebook Group: Black Coffee's Crew Nation-The Movement
www.Twitter. com/AUTHORBLKCOFFEE

Manuscript Preparation: Black Coffee

True's Relate publishing company
P.O. Box 2911
Gulfport, Ms. 39505

[PUBLISHER'S NOTES]

This is a work of fiction. Names, Characters, places and incidents either are the product of the author's imagination or are used fictitiously and any resemblance to actual persons, living or dead, business establishments, events, or locales is entirely coincidental. Any references or similarities to actual events or to real locales are intended to give the novel a sense of reality.

Without limiting the rights under copyright reserved above, no part of this publication may be reproduced, stored in or introduced into a retrieval system or transmitted, in any form or by any means [electronic, mechanical, photocopying, recording or otherwise], without the prior written permission of both the copyright owner and the above publisher of this book.

The scanning, uploading and distribution of this book via the internet or via any other means without the permission of the publisher is illegal and punishable by law. Please purchase only authorized electronic editions and do not participate in or encourage electronic piracy of copyrighted materials. Your support of the author's sons is appreciated.

[Quotes and Reviews]

"The best way you can tell if a young man cares about you, is when he knows he's in trouble with you. If he lets it linger and don't bother to handle it, with you, right away. Keep moving. But if he doesn't let the sun set on it. Meaning, if he comes to straighten it out, as soon as possible. Then he's a keeper. But you still have to let him sweat, even if he does come to you right away. That's so he'll remember, if he gets another chance, not to hurt you again."- {Poppa Jones-from "Time To Learn-part 1"}

"If a man can't fuck his girl after reading this book, he needs to kill himself. [lol]-Tony "Fam" Bass- Houston, TX

"I read it about 4 times, Lol since I got it. I absolutely love it. You did a wonderful job. I like the whole story line. And I LOVE Ajay & Ebony. They bring back a lot of memories. The whole crew is off the chain though. Can't wait for part 2."- Christina "Chrissie" Hall-Detroit, MI

"I'm ready for your next book-great read-I felt like I knew everyone in the story-I don't know how many times I cried-Wow is all I can say! You are indeed a talented writer! Thanks for the excellent novel!"-Trina Hall-Willis

"This is a Really good book. It actually teaches you about the obstacles that a teenage child has during her teen years and I can't wait to read the next book."-Taylor Scaife-Gulfport, MS

"This book was very good! I wish you much success and God Bless."-Harvey Goudeau, pastor-Gulfport, MS

"I didn't want to put it down, a page-turner with characters you'll never forget. Family, love, hate, trust, betrayal it is all there."- Linda Scarborough-Sanders-Biloxi, MS

"It's truly a Time to Learn- Time to Reveal. Each of us can find ourselves or someone we know in the characters from the book. I got so involved in the book that I could hear the old school songs playing in the background as I became engrossed in this story of love, family, friends and memories. Thanks, Black Coffee. I look forward to reading all of your books and hopefully seeing your movies."- Angie P. Owner T.R.U.E. M.O.B. Recordz

III

TIME TO GROW-RELOADED-TIME WILL REVEAL 2

"Let's just say Time To Learn Part 1 is the bomb!!! I have read this book more times than I have read any other book back to back. With that said, you know I absolutely love the book and I cannot wait until you get the set completed. Now Ajay and Ebony brings back sooooo many memories. I love how the crew sticks together throughout the good and the bad.....That is a Love that I hope will grow to the end. Keep doing a GREAT job. You are doing what you are suppose to be doing, as long as you keep God first, your Blessings will follow. Do Not give up. If no one else has your back, I know I do but most importantly GOD has your back no matter what!!!!! Much love and blessings."- Venitia Crawford-Aisola (Admin), Gulfport, MS and Atlanta, GA

"That book was so good I loved it I'm definitely buying part 2. I cant wait for it to come out!"- Michelle Karim-Poet- Marietta, GA

"In the beginning, the introduction of characters had me confused. I feel there could have been a better way to present the "main characters." As I continued to read, I fell in love with the storyline; it kept me on my toes. The characters felt real, which I believe every author should aim for. Definitely a great read. Can't wait to see what the next book holds...keep it up!" -Deb M. On Deck Multimedia and Magazine, Hyde Park, MA

"TIME TO LEARN is a great book. It takes me back to where I'm from and brings me to the place where I am now. Great book and I highly recommend it!"-10 Karat/CEO- Lo Down Entertainment. (706) 617-3563

"You're a great writer. I love the book, cant wait for MORE!"- Roberta Nicole-D'Iberville,   MS

"Time to Learn was captivating to read. This book kept my attention for a full day, I finished it that quickly. For me to do this, I had to really enjoy what I was reading and I must say that I thoroughly enjoyed this book. It gives you a true outlook on family, friends, love and life overall. I believe it is a great read for any man, woman, boy or girl, as it speaks on how life truly is for some people and there's no sugar coating anything. I almost felt as if I was there starring in a role because it was so intriguing. Overall, Black Coffee, has really impressed me and I can't wait to read part 2. Keep up the great work!"- S. Stewart-Emerge Tradeshow/FunkeyFlashBack gear

TIME TO GROW-RELOADED-TIME WILL REVEAL 2

Time To Grow-Time Will Reveal part 2
is dedicated to me,
Lovely T. aka Black Coffee,
for all my time, effort and hard work.
The Time Will Reveal series of books are my babies
and I love my first novels.
All the best, Black Coffee.

Dedicated to the memory of; Patricia Layton of Detroit, Michigan
To the members of "Black Coffee's Crew Nation" she was Mama Pat!
WE MISS YOU, MAMA PAT!

V

CHAPTER 12

LOVE TAKES TIME

TIME TO GROW-RELOADED-Time Will Reveal-part 2

Snow covers the grounds, driveways, streets and cars by early Thursday morning. At granny's house, her, big mama, poppa and papa get up early. They sit around the living room, drinking coffee, reading the newspapers and watching the morning news. That's their usual morning routine. A snow advisory, scrawling across the bottom of the TV screen, gets their attention. Cleveland is due to catch the brunt of a snow storm within the next 24 to 48 hours.

"When it rains, it pours. Doesn't it?" granny asks.

"Looks like that storm's moving in here," says papa.

He's been watching this system since a week before Christmas, when it was over Alaska.

"I'll call the airline and check on our Saturday flight," poppa says as he picks up the phone to call *Southwest Airlines.*

He has to enter his flight information. Then he's connected to an automated agent, where there's a recorded update for all passengers. It goes:

As of now, there has been no cancellation of any flights. If the storm system does progress to severe in our area, your flight will be postponed. Further, the airline will try to put you on an earlier flight, if you desire. But you may be required to leave within the next few hours. We are not booking flights for tomorrow through Saturday, in lieu of the weather. We will not resume until we have further details about the storm system. Thank you for choosing, Southwest Airlines.

"Eloise, do you wanna get on one of those earlier flights or not?" poppa asks, knowing she won't even try to leave today.

"*Today?* That's impossible!" big mama shouts, "There's no way we can get everything ready to make a *noon* flight."

"Percy, there's three feet of snow outside," granny says and laughs, "Are you two able to shovel *three* feet of snow, in a couple of hours?"

"I see that," he says as he laughs too. Then he asks, "Are you trying to call me and Jackson, *old*? Is that what you're *trying* to say?"

"She may be old," papa Jackson Brown says, "But me, I'm better.

I'm fifty seven years, *young*. I'm still vibrant and she knows it," he laughs and says, "Ask her. She'll tell you. I'm as vibrant as a teenager."

"I'm not answering that foolishness, Jack," granny says as she blushes, "You're the reason we got these children and grandchildren, around here *now*, *always* in heat."

"That may be some of my fault too, *on some of* the grandchildren," poppa says, "I can't let you put all that on Jackson." He laughs again.

"I'd say it's, *all* of our faults," big mama adds, "We haven't lost our spunk. I was just thinking. I hope we can get to the *drug store*, at least."

"Ella are you gonna get some *happy* pills?" granny asks, as she still laughs and adds, "Because I *think* that might be the only way to relieve the tension in this house."

"Or a girlie magazine, one," big mama answers, as she chuckles, "With all of this snow, we're gonna be stranded up in here. *Shucks*. We might as well make good on it." They have a good laugh at their own expense as she continues, "Percy, if we can't leave on Saturday, then so be it. We'll leave *whenever* they tell us we can."

"I don't believe we're gonna be able to leave Saturday," he says, "Unless this storm let's up on us or changes it's course. And it doesn't seem likely that it'll do either one. And for *all of y'all* information, I don't have to go *get* a magazine, from the drugstore. I brought two magazines *with* me. I don't understand why Eloise is acting like she don't know that I *always* come prepared." They all laugh again.

"Baby, you know baby girl starts back to school on Monday," big mama says to poppa Percy, as she picks up the phone to call Pearl's home.

"She can't go, if she can't get there. Now can she?" he asks.

"No. I guess not, *Percy*," she answers, slightly perturbed at his facetious remark.

Granny stays out of it but papa Brown can't. He has to add his 2 cents.

"Sounds like Eloise needs you to get one of those magazines out and stop talking, Percy," he says as they all crack up laughing again.

Pearl answers the phone, to a roar of laughter. She asks what's so funny. But then, declines to hear it after her mother begins to tell her about the conversation, they were just having. She's never been able to discuss her parents *sex* lives. Though that's never stopped big mama from trying to share it with her. After Pearl becomes aware of the weather conditions, she hangs up and tells John to turn on the TV. They need to get an update, as well. John clicks the remote control, turning on the TV in their bedroom.

When John learns the severity of the pending snow storm, he know he has to check in with his company, for an updated schedule.

7

"Honey, if they can't fly out of here," Pearl says, "Then *surely*, you can't be expected to drive out. Not in *severe* conditions."

"I know, baby," John says, "But I still have to call in and get things verified. *You* know that."

He gives her a kiss. She hands him the phone and waits, right next to him, while he gets his update.

At Chill's house, everyone in the living room are waking up. Renee and Chill had slept in their room and haven't come downstairs to join the others yet. Jr and Tonya are asleep in Ajay's room and haven't come down either. Lil Kenny slept in the living room with the crew. They're camped out. All over the floor, the couch, the loveseat and the chairs. There are many quilts, comforters and blankets, all over. It looks like a huge, co-ed slumber party. Tank and Nina slept together, on the couch. Rob and Jan had taken the loveseat. Bre slept in the recliner while her brother Bruce, slept on the floor, next to her chair. Jb and Lynn are on the floor, on the other side of Bre. Rebbie and June are in front of the couch. T-baby and Rich are on the floor in front of the loveseat. While Ebony and Ajay are on the floor between the couch and the loveseat.

During the night, Ajay had pulled Ebony over, next to the wall and tried to get a little privacy. Ebony wasn't going for it. Not with *all* of those people in the room. They did manage to slip into the upstairs bathroom and get closer. Throughout the night, in the pitch dark living room, as the stereo played loudly, Ebony heard sounds from several of her crew. It was the sounds of people engaging in *some sort* of sexual activity. She couldn't be certain if that's what it was. Because she was moaning and breathing heavily herself, from time to time. Before their *bathroom break*. And that was just from all of the kissing. She didn't allowed Ajay to take her, all the way. Not in the living room. But his hands always have a mind of their own. He can get her aroused without even concentrating. He didn't really want her to give in. Not with others in the room. He would never do that with her. Because sharing her, *in anyway*, has never been a part his plan.

Bre wakes up with Ebony's flight on her mind. She stretches her body and legs. Then she inquires about the trip.

"Ebony, do you know what time y'all leave tomorrow?" she asks.

"We're not suppose to leave until Saturday, at four," she answers, "Don't even remind me."

"I wish you didn't have to go back, *at all*," Rebbie says, "It's really not the same, without you around here."

The rest of the crew agree and no one, as loudly as Ajay. Ebony smiles.

"I wish I didn't have to go back either" Ebony says, "But you know

8

how I'm trying to look at it? The sooner I go back and finish this semester, the sooner I can come back home, for *good*."

"I'm *so* glad big mama is getting better. Then you won't have to go back and stay, for this long again," T-baby says.

"Knock on wood," Ebony says, "She's been telling me, *her and poppa,* that they're gonna see to it that I go to high school, *here*."

"She was telling me, the other day at my birthday dinner, that she knows we're happy she's in remission," Nina says, "Because we can finally get our sidekick back home with us." She laughs.

"Uh huh. Her and poppa said this *will* be my last year in the Houston school system," Ebony says, *"And* she said, if she gets sick again, it'll be Brittany's turn to go. Or she'll move back here. So either way, when I get to the tenth grade, I'll be at MLK. *Not* Smiley high school," she says as she smiles.

She has that matter-of-fact tone and expression, as she looks at Ajay. He looks her up and down before speaking.

Then he raises his eyebrows and says, "You're not gonna make it."

He smiles because he realizes he'll have access to her on a daily basis, once she's in school here in Cleveland. It's obvious that he is walking hormones. He's *ever ready,* as the guys in the crew say it. They even recall the day Stoney had given him the name. It was because he was always somewhere with a female or about to go and get with one. He has always been ready to handle his business or his personal, at any time. That has changed slightly, now that Ebony is his girl. He's always ready *for her.* The others, not so much. They can be fill-ins but never anything more than a fuck.

Ebony smiles back at him, in her usual shy manner. She fully understands what he means. They're becoming more aware and acute, whenever sexual overtures are hinted on by the other. She looks at Nina, who had observed the suggestive look she'd received from Ajay. Nina just smiles and shakes her head. Her and Ebony *are* best friends. Plus Nina knows how horny her brother is known to be. Some say, always being ready for sex is a Jackson family trademark and the girls have it too. Tank and Jb agree that *their girls* love sex. Even mama Jo and big Al admit to being freaky and highly sexual. But all of the above, say Ajay got it from both sides of the family, where the girls only got it from 1 side.

They hear Tonya go to the bathroom. She goes a lot, now that she's pregnant. Renee comes downstairs while Tonya's still in the bathroom.

Renee asks, "Do y'all know there's a big snow storm coming our way?"

"No, girl," Lynn says, "We've been down here playing Rob's party tapes, all night and morning. The TV hasn't *even* been on. Is it on the news,
9

right now?" She asks, as she grabs the remote and clicks on the TV.

Rob stops the tape. An advisory runs across the screen. Nina and T-baby read it, aloud. Then Tank smiles, as he learns the flight has been postponed.

"You know if we get enough snow, there won't be *shit* moving around here, twin," Tank says, "That'll shut down everything."

"Damn right!" Jb says as he laughs loudly, "No *planes, trains or automobiles.*"

They all laugh at his comment. Ajay seems to appreciate the advisory, more than any of them.

"Baby girl, you're gonna be stuck here with me until *spring*," he says as everyone laughs. He adds, "There won't be enough of you left to go back to Houston, after that."

"I wouldn't even care," she says as she gets up to get the phone, "But I'd better call big mama and see if they know anything else."

"Oh, you'll care by next *month*," Ajay teases, "When you're not able to walk," he's laughing even more.

He loves to tease her with sex talk. Then watch her try to squirm out of it.

She smiles as she's dialing granny's house. She finds out their flight has been postponed and they'll get day-to-day updates, from the airline. She hangs up and shares the news with her crew. They're excited about her leaving, a bit later. But they know nothing is definite.

"*See*? What did I tell you?" Ajay asks, continuing to tease her as they laugh, "I'll get my coach to let you get some physical therapy at MLK."

Then 1 by 1, all they check in with their families. They have plans of staying at Chill's until the storm lets up. They make arrangements to get clothes and their toiletries, so they can stay another night. Their parents allow them stay. Today is the 1 week anniversary of Stoney's death. They know they're determined to spend, as much time together, as they can. Before Ebony has to leave. They all stay at Chill's, again tonight.

By Friday morning, the guys find out, through Arthur, *the money shot*, who the 3rd guy was that helped to kill Stoney. His name: *Greg Harrison*.

"Man, is that that nigga, Eddie's brother too?" Tank asks.

"Who's Eddie?" Ebony asks.

"Who *was* Eddie, you mean?" Jb corrects her.

"Yea, that bitch *been* maggot food," Rich says and laughs.

"Yea and his bitch ass brother's about to join him," Ajay says.

"Believe that!" June adds.

"Who *was* he, then?" Ebony pries.

10

TIME TO GROW-RELOADED-TIME WILL REVEAL 2

"Eddie was a stupid muafucka, who was trying to fuck wit our money. Before we left for H-town, twin," Tank says in 1 breath.

"He won't be trying *that* shit, no more," Jr says as he chuckles.

Foolishly, Ebony asks, "What happened to him?"

The look she receives from Ajay convinces her not to ask anymore questions. And she doesn't. At least, not right away. By the look on his face, she knows Eddie's dead. And it *seems* to her, judging by her crew's lack of concern, he must've died at their hands. She stares at Ajay for a few more seconds. As if he knows what she's thinking, he looks into her eyes and replies, "Yea. The same day you and Tank left for H-town. Now let it go."

Tank changes the subject, to spare Ebony from seeking further clarity on the Eddie matter. This leaves her sitting in silence, as her crew continues talking on past experiences. She can't shake her curiosity about Eddie's death. It's something about the look on Ajay's face that makes her curious about how Eddie died. And just how directly responsible for it, *her man is*.

The phone rings. It's Andre. He's at Joe's house and they've just received positive word that Jake, Danny and Greg are the guys who killed Stoney. Andre had called Arthur and told him the latest revelation. Arthur, in turn, called Chill and told him, Andre was about to call him with more info. So when Andre calls, he makes sure to ask Chill to remember who delivered this useful and pertinent information about Jake and Greg. He tells Chill where they've been hiding out. Then he reiterates that *he* was the person who told Arthur and Arthur had told him to call, while Arthur kept his eyes on the perpetrators. Chill acknowledges him as he takes the phone upstairs to hear him, more clearly.

When Chill comes back downstairs, he calls the guys into the kitchen. Bre goes in with them. She's been waiting on this information, every since the day Stoney was pronounced dead.

Chill says, "Look here, brothers and sister. If we can get to the U, we can roll on them muthafuckaz, *today*."

"Word, man? That's where they at?" Ajay asks quickly.

"They're at some female's apartment, out by money shot," Chill says, "I've already talk to him. The niggaz is there, right now. They've been there since it happened. Or at least, that's the way it looks to Arthur. He said their car is snowed in, worse than his."

"Our shit is snowed in too," Jr offers.

"We need to shovel this damn snow out the driveway and try to get to them niggaz," June says, "Before they go on the run."

"I'm wit you, brother" Rob and Jb say, simultaneously.

"Let's do it," Jr adds as they get up and go get dressed.

11

They get shovels from their sheds and begin to clear the driveways.

Two and a half hours later, they've cleared Chill's driveway and all of the vehicles in it. They cleared Pearl and Jo's too. Then they promised to do all of the others, as soon as they warm up. The snow trucks have plowed the streets and things *look* clear. They get in the Blazer and Cutlass and leave for the U.

They only manage to get a couple of blocks away, before the police, who are directing traffic, turn them around and make they head back. They're told the streets aren't safe enough for travel, at this time. Only snow plows and emergency vehicles are being allowed to pass. They turn back towards the house, disappointed. But they're going to try later.

"If we can't move, then they can't move either," Rich says and the others agree.

When they get back to Chill's house, the females are preparing to go home. Their parents have insisted they come home because the storm will be at it's *most severe,* tonight. Rich and June's parents have called. So have Jan, Bre, Rebbie and T-baby's parents. They all live a block or 2 away. But in these temperatures, even walking is dangerous.

By 4:00pm, everyone has been picked up. The only crew who remain at Chill's house are Tonya, Jr, Rob and Ajay. Lil Kenny is playing with his toys, when Arthur calls back. He tells them, Jake and Greg are still there but may be planning a move soon.

"They just walked outside to check on the condition of the car," he says, "They look like they might try to make a move. But they're gonna have to shovel out, before they do. They can't hide, *in my area.* No way."

"We've been trying to get out there, money shot," Jr says, "But these fucking folks still got the streets closed. We're gonna keep trying until they let us through. We're too close to stop now and we won't."

"We're dug in worse than y'all are," Arthur says, "Being college apartments and all. It's no rush to plow us out because campus is closed until the new semester. I'll keep you posted, though. When y'all can, just come on. If I haven't called back, then these bitches are still here."

"Word," Jr says and they hang up.
He informs the others that the enemies are still there and the hit is still on, as soon as they can get there.

Ebony is in her room. Nina is with her. They're talking to Rebbie and T-baby, on the phone. They call granny's house, so Ebony can get the latest update on their flight information.

12

"Big mama, have you heard any more from Southwest?" Ebony asks.

She's been calling, every hour, to find out if they'll be leaving the next day.

"Still no change yet, baby. But we're all packed up and ready to go. Just in case our flight does leave as scheduled. Are you finished packing, yet?"

"Yes ma'am. Nina helped me get my things together," she says, "My bags are already in the living room."

"As soon as we know something, we'll call you," big mama says, "They've been clearing the streets. But the snow hasn't let up. Not for driving, it hasn't."

"I'll just wait for your call," Ebony says, "I love you, a lot. But you already know, I'm not in a hurry to leave."

"I'm not in hurry to make you leave, either," she says, with a chuckle, "Poor Ajay. He's gotta be without his heart."

"I will too," she says.

"I know, baby girl," big mama says, "But I'll let you know, when I know something." They hang up.

By early nightfall, the streets open up and the guys are on their way to the University apartments. Tank and Jb join them. The 6 of them head out in the Blazer. When they arrive, just outside of the complex Arthur had told them about, they spot Greg and Jake, shoveling snow. Chill parks the Blazer in back of Arthur's building and they load their weapons.

Ajay and Chill get out and go around 1 side of the building. While Tank, Jr and Jb take the other side. Rob gets out last. He runs across the street and goes behind the females building, where the 2 murderers have been staying. Greg and Jake don't even notice him. Probably because he's wearing a parka jacket with his hood on. Everything else is clear, as far as potential witnesses are concerned. There's no one else outside, other then the 2 murderers and the crew, who have come to murder them. Rob pulls down his ski mask and makes his way to the side corner of the building. From there, he signals for Chill and Ajay to proceed. Then Chill signals Jr, Tank and Jb, on the far side and they make their approach.

Jake, Danny and Greg are known gang members. The crew aren't *openly* affiliated with any particular gang. But they have business and links with all of them. Initially, the police worked a gang lead but couldn't tie it to Stoney nor his crew. The crew haven't received any updates on Stoney's case. At least, not any leads that named suspects. There's nothing linking these guys to Stoney's murder. Which means, there will be nothing to link the crew to these 2 *murderers* murder.

13

Greg and Jake are caught off guard as the crew attack. They fire a blaze of gunshots into both of them. They riddle their black and white Impala with bullet holes, to make it look like a gang retaliation. Jake and Greg are dead, in seconds. The females inside have their stereo playing, so loudly, they don't hear anything. The crew hurry back to the Blazer, jump in and stash their weapons. They remove their hoods, gloves and ski mask. They had shown up quietly and that's the same way they drive away.
No witnesses! No crime!

As soon as they arrive back at the house, Renee hands Chill the phone. It's Arthur, with an update on the actions at the U.

"Yea," Chill says.

"Hey, they just found two guys dead, out here," Arthur calmly says, "Some gang shit, most likely. They was shot the fuck up."

"What?" Chill asks, "At the college? I thought college life was suppose to be safe."

"Apparently not, man," Arthur answers, "And these ho's is outside screaming and carrying on, like some drama queens. The police still haven't even gotten here yet. You know how slow they move when it's black folks dead. But I've gotta go find out what the hell happened, since people are coming outside. I'll get back to you."

"In a minute, man," Chill says.

"See ya," Arthur replies.

That lets the crew know they had been successful on their caper and they only have 1 murderer left to stuff out.

At Pearl's house, John has gotten word that his trip is postponed until further notice. Which makes Pearl, very happy. She tries to arrange a family game night while it's still early and John is home. But their 2 oldest sons aren't. It seems someone is always out of the house.

"Ebony, where are your brothers?" Pearl asks.

"They went over to Renee's," she answers.

"Lord knows, y'all can't even go to the bathroom without crossing that street," Pearl says, "Call over there and tell them, *I said,* they *will* stay at home tonight. And they need to get here *soon*."

"Yes ma'am," she says and dials the number to Chill's house.

Renee passes the phone to Tank. Ebony relays the order from their mother. Tank says, "Alright. Tell her we're watching the game. We'll be there when its over."

They hang up and Ebony relays Tank's message to their mother, who doesn't seem thrilled that a family game night, isn't going to happen.

14

"Well, alright. As long as they know, *all of you* are staying at home tonight!" she yells from the kitchen.

Nina is planning to spend the night with Ebony. They stay on the phone with T-baby and Rebbie until Jb and Tank come home, several hours later.

"Ebony, you been on that phone, all night, haven't you?" Jb asks.

"Not really," she says.

"Just a few hours?" Tank asks sarcastically.

"Maybe two," Nina says to Tank, as she sticks her tongue out.

"That's for me?" Tank asks, before kissing her.

Ebony reminds them that Pearl and John are still downstairs.

"Where's Lynn?" Jb asks Nina.

"At home," she answers.

He takes the cordless phone from Ebony and heads out of her room. Then he remembers and tells her, big mama called Chill's house for her, "Because she couldn't get through, over here!" he yells from the hallway.

"What did she say!?" Ebony asks, yelling back.

"The flight for tomorrow is postponed until Sunday, at three!" he answers before going into his room.

"Ajay was trying to call you, just before we left Chill's house," Tank says.

"Everybody must've been trying to call while we was on the phone," Nina says to Ebony, as Ebony smiles.

She's happy Ajay has tried to reach her. That leaves her feeling good. However, the call from big mama makes her feel a little sad. Sunday, just a day and a half from now, she'll be leaving her crew and *her Anthony,* again.

Suddenly, Jb comes back with the phone and whispers,

"Here you go and I'm going to see Lynn, as soon as mom and pop go to bed. Cover for me, alright?"

"Hey man, check the knob before you come in," Tank says.

He's already plotting a rendezvous with Nina, in their room. While Jb visits Lynn. Nina smiles at Ebony because she's thinking the same thing.

"Hey, bro. It'll be before daylight, though," Jb whispers and they all giggle.

"Oh, baby girl. Call Ajay back. He just called again while I was on the phone," Jb says as he heads back to his room.

Nina and Tank look through Ebony's song notebook while she dial Renee's number.

"Yea," Ajay answers.

"Hey, did you call for me?" she asks with a smile.

15

"Hell yea. You and them girls been on the phone, ha?" he asks in an almost whisper.

"Yes but you know we have to talk on the phone, *at least.* Since we can't be *together*," she says with a smile.

"But you never know who else might need to talk to you," he says, "While you're giving all of your time away."

"Yea, you're right. So who else would that *be*? Do you *know*?" she asks, sarcastically.

"Uh huh," he mumbles.

"Who?"

"That's *my* time you're giving away," he says with a chuckle.

"Okay. I'm listening," she says.

"I wanna see you."

"I wanna see you too, baby," she says.

"Lets make it happen, then."

"Tell me how. You know I have to stay home, tonight," she says.

"Uh huh but I don't," he says.

"So, you're gonna come over here?" she asks.

"I might. It's not like I don't know the way over there," he says with a chuckle.

She blushes. When she does, she notice Nina and Tank watching her. They're smiling at her. What she doesn't see is her parents approaching her doorway. If she had, she probably wouldn't have been so sassy with her next comment.

"Take a picture," she says, "It'll last longer. And mind y'all business and not ours. Thank you."

Pearl and John had just stopped in front of the doorway.

Pearl asks, *"Who are you talking too, like that, young lady?"*

"I wasn't talking to you, ma. I was talking to Tank and Nina. They keep staring down my throat," Ebony says quickly.

"Alright, then. I thought, for a minute, you was loosing your mind. Talking like that. And don't you be on that phone, all night, either. Do you hear me?" She yells back, as her and John head to their bedroom.

"Yes ma'am!" she answers, before she turns to Nina and Tank and says, "Y'all could've told me she was there. Y'all gonna get me busted, up in *here*?"

"She just stopped there, when you said that shit," Tank whispers.

Ebony still has Ajay on the phone and he's impatient.

"Hey! Are you gonna talk to me or what?" he asks.

"Oh yes. I wonder if ma heard what I said?" she asks, now talking

16

to Ajay, as well as Tank and Nina, while hoping her mother doesn't return.

"No, kid. You was talking too low. But she saw you blushing, though," Nina whispers.

"If she had heard you, she would've said something. Don't you think?" Ajay asks.

"Yes, probably," she answers.

"Shit, definitely," Ajay adds as he laughs.

"So when are you coming over here?" she asks.

"Call me back when your mom go to sleep, alright? I'll work it out. Is that cool?" he asks, sounding very sexy to her.

"Cool," she says and laughs.

"What's so funny?" he asks.

"You sounded so sexy when you said that," she whispers.

"Uh huh. Well I got some more sounds, for later on. You should really like those," he says confidently.

"I'm sure I will."

"Oh yea, you will. I got it for you," he says.

"I know you do."

"You'd better hang up this phone. Talking all sexy and shit. Make me run up over there, right now," he says with a chuckle, "You don't know what hearing your voice, does to me yet. But you will. You'll learn soon."

"Uh huh. Okay. I'm gonna call you as soon as things quiet down."

"Alright, cool. I'll chill until I get that call," he says.

"Alright, baby. See ya," she says.

"In a minute, baby girl." he says and they hang up.

As soon as their parents room is quiet, Jb goes to Jo's house, while her and Al are gone to work. Ebony, Tank and Nina have been talking since she'd gotten off the phone with Ajay. Now Tank and Nina are making their move to the boys room. They head quietly down the hall, enter the room, then lock the door behind them. That's when Ebony calls Ajay back.

"Fred's pool hall!" he answers, "Eight ball speaking."
She giggles softly, at first. Then she erupts in laughter.

"Hey, what's up, baby?" he asks, chuckling at himself.

"My parents are asleep," she says.

"You ready to do this?" he asks.

"Yes."

"Alright. But look here. I'm gonna come and meet you at the door. You can come over here, alright?" he says.

"Alright."

17

"See ya," he says.

"In a *New York* minute," she says and they hang up.

She gets up and dresses quickly. She grabs her jacket, cap and gloves and puts them on. She gets her house key. Then she calls Ajay right back. He meets her at her side door.

Together, they wade across the street in the snow. The temperature is only 14 degrees. The wind chill factor is 20 below zero. They hurry inside and go directly upstairs to his room. She's chilled to the bone, just from the walk over.

"Let me get you out of these clothes, first," he says.

"But I'm still *freezing*," she tries.

"That's okay. I'll warm you up. I promise," he says as he removes her jacket, gloves and cap.

He removes her outer clothing, then her bra and panties. He even takes the ponytail holder out of her hair. He wants her completely naked.

"Lay down on the bed," he instructs, as he walks her over to the bed.

She does as she's told. He starts his *Isleys* tape which has some Prince songs on it now. Then he removes his clothes and joins her in bed. He begins kissing her face as his eyes search for hers in his room, dimly lit by the night stand lamp. He's halted by her reserve. She has a question that won't wait.

"Anthony, can I ask you something?" she asks softly.

"Uh huh," he answers, still kissing on her.

"You know today, when we was talking about Eddie. I wanted to know how did he die?" she asks.

"Real quick," he says as he continues kissing her.

"I mean, *how* though?" she persists.

"Baby you wanna talk about that fake ass nigga, *right now*?" he asks and he's very impatient about discussing his bad deeds.

"I just wanted to know what happened to him. And if you, you know?"

"What did I tell you, today?" he asks.

"You just said yes. But I didn't know if you *knew* what I was thinking about when I-"

"You're wondering if I did him, right?" he asks.

"Right."

"And what did I say?" he asks again.

"Baby, *you* did it?!!" she asks, in shock.

"Uh huh."

"Anthony, are you telling me you *killed him*? I mean, you're so calm about it. Like it's nothing. How can you-"

18

"It ain't nothing, alright," he says and starts kissing her again, "It's nothing."

"Wait Anthony. I don't understand how you can be so, *I don't know*, just like nothing *even* happened," she says.

"Look, baby. This is how it is. If a nigga violate the crew, then *that* muthafucka is gonna get his or hers. You know what I'm saying? And it ain't shit to it. But to do it. Its just part of the job," he says bluntly.

"Anthony, I really don't even know you, do I?" she asks.

"Yea, you know me."

"Not *like that,* I don't," she says.

"And you don't wanna know me, *like that,* either," he says. Then he composes himself and continues, "Hey, look here, baby. Can we get on with us now? I'm not thinking about *that* nigga nor any other nigga who had to go out for fucking with me or mine. Understand?"

"Is he the only one?" she asks.

"No," he answers, still calm like usual. She lays there trying to think of what else to say. He starts kissing on her neck, face and breast again. But he can tell she still isn't into it. She can't get his revelation out of her mind. The fact that the man she knows and loves, as a gentle caring person *to her,* most of the time. Can actually kill someone. "You're not feeling this, are you?" he asks, noticing she's in another zone.

"I was still thinking, that's all."

"Why do you want to talk about that old shit?" he asks, "It's over Ebony. That happened before you moved to Houston. It hasn't changed anything about you and me. Or nothing else with our family and crew. We're here now and we don't have that much time to be together. All I wanna do is to get into you," he says as he looks into her eyes, "I just wanna have some private time with you, baby girl."

"I know," she continues, "But all I'm saying is, I could *never* kill someone. It would probably drive me crazy."

"You never know," he says, "So don't say what you won't do. You never know until the time comes. Once you do it one time and it don't take your mind, then it's on. It ain't shit to do it, again and again. If you're put in that situation."

"How many-?"

"I don't know. And baby girl, I don't even try to keep up," he says, "That's nothing to come between me and you. That shit ain't got nothing to do with how we are. So let it go," he insists but she's on a roll.

"I *can* say never because I know-"

19

"How the fuck do you know?" he ask, losing patience.

"I just do, that's all," she says, a bit less aggressively.

"Alright. What about that night at my fifteenth birthday party? When you was beating the hell out of *Anita?*" he asks, "What did you want a bottle for? What was you *gonna* do wit it?"

"I was gonna beat her.., with it," she says as she pauses to keep from using a curse word.

She catches herself and then says, "Beat her across her head with it."

"One good lick and that muafucka would've broke," he says, "What then? What was you gonna do then? Throw it down? *Hell* no. You was gonna keep jabbing at her ass. What do you think was gonna happen? What do you think was gonna happen with that jagged bottle? Baby girl, a muafucka is not gonna walk away from that type of shit. Besides, you had a lock on that bitch throat like you was trying to take her last breath. If I wouldn't have stopped you, when I did, you would've *choked* her ass out. So don't tell me what you won't do. It just depends on the situation."

"But she started that," she tries.

"So did Eddie. I just finished it. Just like them niggaz that got Stoney," he says, admitting more than he intended too. But she's got him worked up, as only she can. He goes on, "What am I suppose to do? Let a muthafucka think they can fuck with my crew and a gee ain't gonna get in that ass? Shit if that's so. I'm always down for whatever, when it comes to my family. And you'd better know that." He gives her a serious look.

"So y'all got 'em?" she asks, realizing he's killed someone, *today.*

"A couple of 'em. Yea," he says impatiently.

"I knew it. I *knew* it. When I saw y'all leaving-"

"Ebony don't be so naive about certain shit," he says, "You damn right! I'm going out in a blaze for my brother Stoney, if I need too. Damn right. And any of the rest of my crew. Point blank. That includes you too. If a nigga fuck with you wrong, I got his ass or her ass. I don't give a fuck who it is," he says, "You wouldn't do the same for me?"

She thinks for a moment. Then she looks at him.

She says, "If somebody was to hurt you, in any way. Or anybody in my family, then I would want to hurt them back the same way. You know *that's* how me and my girls are. One for one and all for all."

"They *killed* Stoney, baby. That's your crew. You should've been on that hoot ride too. All o' y'all!" he says with his voice rising, as his eyes well up with tears but he doesn't let 1 fall.

She can see the passion in his eyes as he talks about her and their crew.

"I know what you're saying. I kind of knew it, all the time. But I

20

wasn't sure if *you had* ever done it," she says, "And as long as it wasn't put, right there in my face, I just tried to believe that you hadn't. Because that makes it easier for me *not* to be afraid of you."

"You have *no* reason to be afraid of me. I'm not gonna hurt you. Not unless you hurt me. Are you planning on hurting me, baby?" he asks.

"No. I would never hurt you. I never wanna do that, ever in my life," she says as she looks into his eyes, "I still feel bad about that letter. I know that hurt you. Which ended up hurting me too. I never wanna do that again and *I can* say never, on that."

"Listen," he says as he gathers himself, "I do what I have to do to survive in them streets. But when I'm with you, it's not like that. This is my cool out time. This is the real shit I'm trying to stay alive, *in those streets,* for. Do you feel me?"

"Yes," she answers, remembering what Chill said to her last year, about her being his sanity and the only female he can feel comfortable with.

"I need to be able to relax sometimes. I can do that with you, Ebony," he says, "You bring out the good in me. When you look at me, I can see it in your eyes. You don't see no wrong. That gives me confidence, rather you know it or not. I stopped looking for good in other folks, a long time ago. But you changed that. You need to stay focused on the good when it comes to me. Because I'm not with the dumb shit. No lying letters, to get my attention. Just talk to me. I don't have trouble understanding you. You can talk to me about whatever's on your mind and tell the truth, when you do. I don't have a lot of patience, with a lot of people. And the little patience I do seem to have, is with you."

She smiles and says, "Other than that letter, I do keep it real with you."

"Well bring me the real," he demands, "Let that street shit stay out there. I wanna get into your world. Fuck the other."

He starts kissing her again. She puts her arms around him and kisses him back, very passionately.

"Mmm. That's what I'm talking about, baby," he whispers, "This is what I need. *Our* thing."

"Uh huh. Well I got it for you," she says while blushing.

"Come on wit it, then," he insists.

They smile, then he lets his hands probe her body. She lets her hands probe his too. But she's always been shy about touching his penis. Every time her hand ventures near it, she always pulls it back. Tonight, he wants her to open up, a little more. He needs his stress reliever.

"Grab it," he instructs, again knowing her thoughts.

She looks at him. "Go on," he says, "Don't be scared to touch me, Ebony."

21

She grabs it, gently. He closes his eyes and whispers his instructions, "Uh huh. That's it. Play wit it."
She begins to rub it up and down, gently with 1 hand. Then she uses 2 hands. He raises his body up to look down at her work. He smiles slightly and looks into her eyes. She feels shy, all of sudden. But he feels ready.
"Put it in for me," he whispers.
She does as she's told and they both moan. He starts to churn inside of her, slowly, as he whispers, "Damn. I missed this. Seems like its been so long."

"Since my birthday," she whispers, "Christmas night."

"That's *too* long," he whispers as he kisses her gently.

"I missed you too," she whispers in his ear.

"Uh huh. Show me," he demands, "Show me you missed me."
What she said must've turned him on, more. He begins to stroke her with force. It's too much for her, this soon into the session. Still, she tries to move with him, initially. But some of his strokes are just to painful. He's being overly aggressive from the onset. Something he has only done, once. The night of his 15th birthday. She wonders if he's upset with her for mentioning the stuff about Eddie. Or if he's thinking about the fact that she has to leave in a couple of days. That was the reason he'd given her for his aggressive behavior on the night of his 15th birthday. When the truth was, he was actually high off of cocaine. Same as tonight. She still doesn't know anything about his *usage*. She tries to remain calm as his strokes become more and more aggressive. She scoots away from him. He pulls her back under him, to the spot where she has to take the brunt of his girth. She begins to pant and gasp, like a woman in labor. He's way to aggressive. She tries again to slide up and away. Again, he pulls her back. This time he orders, "Don't run from me."

"It hurts me," she tries.

"It hurts good, though baby," he whispers as he continues to stroke her forcefully, "I need this, baby. I need you."
She can't help but be loud. Because his force is more than she can handle.
"See. That's why I brought you over here. I knew you would've got us busted," he whispers, "I don't want a Jb and Lynn moment. I'm still hearing it about the motel."
He doesn't seem to have the ability to hear her and she's screaming.

"Baby! You're hurting me! *Anthony*, wait a minute!" she screams.
His behavior is different and his chatter is a bit bizarre. He's in the zone.
He's gone deaf again.

"This is *my* pussy and you know that," he says arrogantly, as he

22

continues with the same force. As though he can't hear her voice, at all. All she can do is plead and scream because getting away isn't even an option. He's holding her firmly in place. She's not able to handle him, like this. She continues to plead. Telling him it hurts. But he isn't letting up, not one bit. Suddenly, there's banging at the door and Chill is yelling outside of it.

"*Ajay!!*" he yells as he beats on the door, continuously.
Pausing in mid stroke and nearly out of breath, Ajay answers, "Yea!"
Oh, he can hear Chill but not me?

    "*Come here, man! Come here, right now! Open the door!*"
    "Hold up, man!" Ajay tries.
    "*Nah, bro! Come here now, man!*" Chill insists.
    "Damn. Alright," he says as he pulls out and slides off of Ebony.
He stands and puts on his t-shirt and boxers. He looks down at Ebony, who's already covering herself with the comforter before he can suggest it. He winks his eye at her and smiles, just slightly, before going to the door. He's letting her know, he likes that she knew what he expected. He peeks his head around the door and asks Chill, "What's up?"
    "Come out here for a minute," Chill says sternly.
Ajay steps into the hallway and pulls the door closed behind him.
"Brother, what *the hell* are you doing up here?" Chill asks in a very serious and agitated tone, with a deep frown on his face.
    "That's me and Ebony," he answers, thinking Chill believes he has brought a non-crew female into his house.
    "I know that's baby girl, brother. I can hear *that much*. But what are you doing to her? Sounds like you're beating her ass."
    "Oh nah, man. You know better. We're just getting our thing on."
    "Lil bro. We can hear her downstairs. Over *Marvin Gaye*. It don't sound to me like she's having a good time," he says very seriously.
    "She do that, sometimes. It ain't no thing, though."
    "Ajay, look here. Don't take out your frustrations on your girl, bro. You can't do it that way either" he says as he smiles for the 1st time, "I know you're uptight about the work. But don't do it like that."
Chill has a feeling it's more than their actions out at the U, that's causing Ajay's aggression. But rather then accuse him of dabbling in his stash again, he focuses on making sure he knows that him and Renee are downstairs. And they don't want to hear another peep from Ebony, where she sounds like she's in distress.
    "Alright, man. Alright," Ajay says, realizing his faults.
He's still a bit wound up over everything that has happened in the last
23

week. For him to not have even had sex for days, with Ebony in town, should've been his 1st clue. But he hadn't thought things out, *that* far.

"Chill out, Ajay," Chill says, "Don't treat your lady like that. Calm your ass down, homie. Everything will be everything," he's whispering now. Then he laughs and starts back down the stairs.

"Cool. I got ya," Ajay says as he turns to go back into the room.

"Hey. Seriously. If we hear some more noise like that," Chill says, "Renee's gonna come up here and you don't even wanna *see* that."

"I know that's right!" Renee yells from downstairs, just as Chill makes it to the bottom.

Ajay smiles as he closes the door behind him. He looks at Ebony. She's still in bed, covered up. He can see that she's been crying. He goes back to the bed and lays down beside her.

"Hey. My bad, baby. I'm sorry. I'm *so* sorry. I don't even know where the fuck I was," he says as he's mellowing out and calming down now, "I ain't trying to treat my lady like that."

"You're like two different people sometimes," she says.

"Anthony and Ajay," he says and smiles, "I'm sorry. Really I am."

"I accept your apology, okay? I could tell you was in another world, so that must've been Ajay?" she asks, "I don't *want* to meet Ajay, remember? You said it, yourself. I can't even call you that. So I'll just stick with Anthony," she says as she smiles.

"That sounds cool. Stick with Anthony," he says as he takes off his t-shirt and boxers again and slides underneath the comforter.
He kisses her gently, this time. He sucks on her nipples and she lets out a sigh of pleasure. Her body's relaxing again. He likes and needs that action.

"Hello, Anthony," she whispers as she giggles.
He smiles and says, "I'm sorry, baby. I was just caught up in the moment, earlier. But I'll make it up to you."
He enters her again and says, "I wanna feel you tremble in a good way."

"Uh huh and I *wanna* tremble in a good way," she says as she moans in a way that sounds very sexy to him.
He's much more gentle this time and she likes it. She likes it, a lot.

"Come here, baby," he says, "I can do better than that."
He holds her tight and puts his tongue in her mouth.

"Mmm," she moans.

"I got to feel you cum. I have too," he whispers as he positions himself in that familiar spot.
She can feel the tickling action, her clitoris loves. Her body's quaking like the *Prince* song, her mama plays. But the song is, most likely, about a dance.
24

"Oh yes. Do it like that," she whispers her instructions.

"Yes, baby," he says, ready to obey *her* commands now.

She feels her body tightening up.

"I know this body," he whispers confidently, "You're feeling it."

He sticks his tongue in her ear. He's right. He knows exactly what to do to take her to ecstasy. She can't believe how he always seems to know when it's good to her. But doesn't seem to recognize when it hurts her. Doesn't matter. *It's good now.* It's good to the point where she loses control. He commands her G-spot. It's something he had made an effort to learn, back during their sessions, long before the penetration. That is most *definitely* the reason why he knows how to make it good to her, during sex. He took the *time to learn,* what *she* likes. Now they can grow together and into each other. She's still unaware of the pleasure he gets from pleasing her and from watching her cum. He feels it's his duty to bring her pleasure, each and every time they make love and he's always on his job.

"Oh I like it, Anthony!"

"Tell me who makes you cum, baby."

"You do, baby! Oh Anthony! Oh Anthony! Yes! Yes, baby! Yes! Oh this is *so good!*" she screams.

He loves the sounds, she's making now and the way her eyes roll back in her head, then become very intense. How her lips quiver, like she's standing outside in the frigid temperatures they'd just walked over here in.

"Mmm, yes. Get it, baby," he demands, directly in her ear, "Get this pussy wet for me."

"Uh huh! I'm doing it," she oozes.

"What you doing, baby. Ha? Tell me," he whispers in her ear, in a demanding tone and wanting to hear her declare it.

"I'm cumming, baby! Yes! Oh!" she manages.

It drives her crazy to talk dirty but she's so crazy about his pillow talk. He urges her to purge herself of all the words in her head. She does so, while kissing his shoulders and chest, which drives him nuts.

"Oh! Oh! Uh huh. You're so muthafuckin hot, baby," he says, "Damn! You turn me on, Ebony," he whispers as he kisses her with fervor, "Can I get some of that action? Ha?" he asks as he raises her bottom up off of the bed.

"Mmm. Go head, baby," she instructs and he begins to grind deep inside of her slippery wet hole while she's rolling her hips for him.

"I don't wanna hurt it, baby," he whispers as his strokes get harder, "Tell me if I'm hurting you, alright?"

"Okay," she says, "I just hope you *heart* me."

25

She feels a little pain but she wants him to experience the same pleasures, he had just given to her. For him to show that he's concerned for her comfort, is all she demands. But she's going to allow him to be pleased by her, just as she allows him to please her. She simply holds her breath and lets him work it out.

"Oh baby girl. Give me my pussy, baby," he whispers, feeling his climax nearing, "I love when you let me have all of my pussy. Uh huh. Baby. Pussy good. *Damn*. Oh shit," he starts to mumble, incoherently.

He's passed the point of forming sentences. He can't hold it any longer. He cums hard, thrusting in and out of her until he can't move a muscle.

"Oh yea, baby," he whispers as he flops down on top of her.

They're both exhausted. She's kissing his face. He's kissing hers. Then they lay covered in sweat as their steaming bodies glisten in the dimly lit room. They're done. Tonight, it only took 1 episode. She's thoroughly satisfied and so is he. They start to drift into a deep sleep. Both naked but warm. He remains on top of her. His penis is softer but still inside of her. This is a peaceful sleep. The 1 thing he needs more than anything else, is rest and time to think things through. He knows that too, as he drifts off to sleep.

I can only do this with you, baby girl. That's why I need you and love you, so much.

Nina makes it back to Ebony's room and locks the door. She discovers Ebony isn't in there and figures she must've gone to Chill's house.

"She's with Ajay," she says to herself and smiles.

She puts on her nightgown, gets in bed and falls fast asleep.

Lynn kisses Jb, long and hard. Then they say goodnight. She locks the door after he leaves and goes to bed.

After making it home and up the stairs, Jb checks the knob. It's unlocked. He goes in, gets into his bed and goes to sleep.

Over at Chill's, him and Renee have gone to bed. Besides the noise their stimulating sex sends from their room, for the next several minutes, everything else is quiet. Even in the neighborhood, everything is quiet and peaceful, for a change. The streets are still very icy and dangerous. Driving is prohibited throughout the night. The snow is falling again. In the spare room, Ebony and Ajay are still sleeping peacefully.

****

Saturday morning, Pearl goes upstairs to wake everyone after she finishes making breakfast. She knocks at the boys room, then at Ebony's

26

door, before heading back to her room to wake John up, for breakfast.

Nina awakes from a deep sleep and realizes Ebony still isn't home. She pretends she doesn't hear Pearl at the door. So Pearl goes on into her room and wakes John. She returns to Ebony's door, because it's the only 1 that still hasn't opened. Nina pretends to be still asleep when she knocks again. Pearl goes back to her room again. This time she gets the key so she can wake girls. Nina continues to pretend she's asleep, even after Pearl opens the door and comes in.

Pearl asks, "Nina, where is Ebony?"

Nina tries to cover for Ebony by saying, "She must've got up early and left already."

But Pearl knows better. She leaves the room and heads back to her room to get dressed, this time. She knows exactly where to find Ebony.

While Pearl is dressing, Ebony, who had awaken at Chill's with Ajay, gotten dressed and hurried home, creeps quietly up the stairs. She goes into her room where Nina tells her, her mother has been in there and knows she wasn't home. They hear Pearl ranting and raving from her bedroom, while she's dressing. She's telling John, she's going across the street to get Ebony. Not wanting to hear her mother, Ebony closes her door and locks it again. She gets out of her clothes, climbs into bed, as Pearl comes back down the hall. She doesn't even stop at Ebony's door, this time. She's fully dressed as she heads downstairs, out the door and across the street.

She knocks on Chill's door, very loudly. Renee, still winded from her and Chill's morning *activity*, answers the door.

"Good morning, mama P," Renee says with a smile.

"Good morning and where's Ebony?" Pearl asks, without smiling.

"I thought she was at home," Renee tries.

"Well she's not home! Where is Ajay?!" Pearl asks loudly.

"I think he's still sleeping," Renee answers.

"Tell him to come down here, for a minute, please."

"Sure, mama P. Come on in," Renee says.

She invites Pearl into the living room while she goes upstairs to wake Ajay. Renee knows Ebony has gone home. She saw her leave and they said goodbye to each other. But she knows Pearl isn't going to leave until she can see for herself. Renee arrives at Ajay's door with company. Pearl had followed her upstairs.

"Ajay, open the door," Renee says from the hallway.

Ajay gets up, opens the door and is thrown off when he sees Renee and Pearl standing there, looking at him.

27

"Ajay, where is Ebony?" Pearl barks.

"She's not here," he answers.

"She's not home either, Ajay," Pearl says with a desperate look in her eyes. "I know you know where she is. She's in there somewhere, so open this door."

Ajay opens the door wide, giving her a full view of the room. Pearl walks in and looks behind the door, in the closet and under the bed. Ajay looks at Renee with a confused look. Renee shakes her head and signals for him to play it cool and let her do whatever she wants.

Suddenly, Pearl says to Renee, "I know she stayed with you, last night. Didn't she?"

"I thought everybody went home, mama P," Renee tries.

"Oh, she was home when I went to bed. But she certainly wasn't home when I got up," Pearl says, "I know she slipped out, sometime last night, to come and see you," she says to Ajay, "I'm not crazy."

Ajay looks at her, for a second. Then he looks at the floor. He's not going to deny it if she demands an answer but she doesn't. After seeing that neither of them are going to tell her what she wants to hear, Pearl walks out of the room and down the stairs. Ajay throws on a t-shirt, with his shorts and follows Pearl and Renee downstairs.

"Mama P, I'm sure she's not here," Renee tries, still.

"Renee, I know you're gonna say that," Pearl says, "You're *suppose* to say that. I'm familiar with the whole, *hold up for each other until the end,* routine. I'm in this crew too, you know? I don't want y'all to make a baby, Ajay. Don't you get it?"

She doesn't wait for either of them to say anything else. She leaves the house, goes back home and heads back upstairs.

When she checks Ebony's door, this time, she finds that it's locked again.

"Yea right," Pearl says and uses her key again.

She finds Ebony laying in bed, pretending to be asleep. She goes back to her room. She grabs a belt and heads back to Ebony's room. She barges in and storms toward the bed. Nina flinches.

"I know you're not sleep, baby girl. Get your ass up!" she yells.

Ebony rises slowly, pretending to be just waking up from a deep sleep.

"Where the hell were you when I came in here earlier?"

"Ma'am?"

"Don't ma'am me, Ebony! Where were you? And don't you even think of lying. I just came from Renee's house, talking to her *and* Ajay."

Ebony doesn't say a word. Pearl is determined to get a confession out of
28

her. Pearl acts like Ajay and Renee told her, Ebony stayed over. But Ebony knows no one at Chill's house or any of her crew would rat her out. But to protect her crew from any further interrogation, she decides to tell the truth and see if that'll satisfy her mother.

"Yes ma'am, I stayed over there," she confesses.
Without another word, Pearl begins lashing her with the belt. Ebony tries to move. But Pearl has her cornered, while striking her hard for 3 straight minutes. This whipping seems to know, no end. Exhausted from trying to evade Pearl, Ebony finally grabs the belt. She tries to pull it away. That only makes Pearl angrier. She demands Ebony, "Let go!"
As Pearl yells, Ebony cries and begs her not to whip her anymore. All the commotion brings John, Tank, Jb and Jesse from their rooms. Nina is witnessing the whole ordeal and begging Pearl, along with Ebony, not to hit her anymore. Pearl screams and curses but she can't make Ebony let go of the belt. She loses patience and lets go of the belt, herself. She begins to use her hands. Just as she'd done at the motel. She's screaming like a woman. She's slapping and punching any part of Ebony's body, her fist and hands connect too. Ebony reflects back to motel room 111 and how Ajay had come to her rescue. He wouldn't stand for Pearl to beat her that night. He wouldn't like it today either. But he isn't here. So this time, Ebony fights back. She isn't going to allow her mother to beat her unchallenged. They tie up like 2 rams on an open range. Ebony is on the defensive. She doesn't swing at her mother. Instead, she grabs and holds her arms, each time Pearl tries to swing at her. That angers Pearl more. Eventually, Ebony grabs hold of her mother and locks her legs around her to keep her from swinging or kicking. Pearl is both angry, exhausted and now, she's tied up in Ebony's *Sioux-flex*. She continues her struggle to get free. Ebony holds her down easily, making her mother livid. They are so entangled, it takes John, Jb and Tank to separate them. Nina cries as she tries to comfort nearly 10 year-old Jesse. He's very upset at seeing his sister and his mother fighting. The men finally split them apart. Pearl is in a rage as she shouts at Ebony. John pulls Pearl until they reach the bedroom door. He holds her there. Ebony is shouting back, equally as loud from her bed, where Jb is holding her. John doesn't like his daughter's tone.

"Watch your mouth, baby girl," John says calmly, as he continues to struggle with Pearl.

"Let me go, John! I'll be damned if my child is gonna hit me! Instead of holding me, you should be whipping her ass! She's getting to damn grown!" Pearl shouts as John throws her over his shoulder and carries her to their room.
29

"I didn't hit you! *You* hit *me!* All I did was hold the belt and your arms and legs, so you couldn't keep punching me!" Ebony screams, "Who you think wanna keep getting hit on, all the time!? Not me!"

Jb and Tank tell Ebony to stop shouting and be quiet.

"It's over, twin," Tank says, "Be quiet. Don't yell at mama. Stop it, girl. Stop it, right now."

John finally gets Pearl into their bedroom and closes the door. Jb and Tank have Ebony in her room. They close her door.

"Ebony, what the hell *happened*?" Jb whispers.

"I'm tired of her jumping on me! Shit! She's not gonna hit on me, all the time! I'm not even going for that no more!"

Jb lets her up off of her bed, while Tank continues talking to her and trying to calm her down. Jb makes her calm down, whether she wants to or not and tell them what happened. She calms down, grasps the situation, then tells them the details. After hearing what happened, they know it's a wrap.

"Oh shit," Jb says, "Here we go with this shit again."

"Calm down, twin. It's gonna be alright. Just stop talking so loud," Tank says, "As long as you didn't swing on mama, you're good wit me."

"I didn't. I just kept her from hitting me," Ebony says, "I tied her up like the wrestlers do. That was after she slapped me in my mouth. I could've lost it but I didn't. I didn't wanna hit her. I just wanted to stop her from hitting me. It feels like my lip is swelling. Twin, Nina was here the whole time. She can tell you I didn't hit her. Not even *once*."

"She didn't," Nina says as she sniffles, "She just held her hands and legs. She never even tried to hit her, baby."

They stay in her room and discuss the fight until Ebony is completely calm. Then there's a knock on her door. It's John. He's comes to her room, looking as though he's been through a storm. After getting Pearl's side of the story, he's come back to hear Ebony's. He sends the boys to their room and sends Nina home. He wants the room cleared so he can speak to his only daughter, alone. Once the others are gone, he gets right to the point.

"Baby girl, tell me what happened," he says calmly.

She cries as she tells him what her mother had done and how she had only defended herself, because she didn't want to be battered and bruised. She even shows him the whelps on her legs, arms and back. He's sympathetic to her pain but she has to answer for her actions, the night before.

"Did you sneak out of my house to go see Ajay? That's what I wanna know."

"Yes sir."

"Why did you do it ?" he asks as he shakes his head.

30

"I wanted to see him before I leave, that's all. I just wanted to see him," she answers as she wipes her tears away.

She's trying for that *daddy's girl* sympathy, she usually gets when she's upset. But her father isn't babying her, like his *little girl*, this time. He makes her face him and look into his eyes.

"Ebony you're not grown and you're not allowed to leave out of *my house* whenever you get ready too. You *know* it was wrong. I know you knew better. I know, you knew it was wrong because if you thought it was alright, then you would've asks your mother or me, if you could go. And you *didn't* do that. You just left out of my home and stayed out, *all night*. Now we've told you before, you're not suppose to see Ajay. Not without our permission. We allowed you two to go to the movies. We was trying to see if you could do right. But it seems like, *one* of you can't. And I think that one who *can't*, is you. Ajay isn't gonna tell you no, baby girl. I believe you know that already too."

She doesn't understand what he's saying, fully. She tries to argue her point.

"Daddy, its not like y'all think it is," she tries, "He *loves* me."

"It's not suppose to be like *anything*, right now. Baby girl, you're fifteen years old. You just *made* that. Now I don't agree with your mama putting her hands on you like that. Not at all. I let her know that too. But *I can* understand her anger. When she gives you rules to abide by, those are from me. She's in charge of my house, when I'm on the road. Even if I'm home and she tells you to do something, you have to do it. And you haven't been, young lady. You're disobeying the rules of my house and bottom line, it's gonna stop today. Do you understand?"

"No, daddy. I don't. Why do y'all act like Anthony is a grown man? He's only one year older than me. I don't understand why *we* can't see each other. But Jb and Lynn can. Tank and Nina can. We're all the same age, " she says, making waste of the double standards her family uses. Actually the whole crew uses them. Big John isn't trying to hear it. His mind is made up.

"I haven't told *any* of you girls it's okay to date, *any* boy," he says for clarity, "Your brothers aren't an issue here, as long as they do what I tell them to do. But you are, baby girl. To your mother and I, *you are*. This isn't about the crew, right now. This is about our daughter. You and your wrongdoings."

He supports Pearl. Ebony was wrong for sneaking out, for any reason. But they know her ultimate reason for wanting to see Ajay, last night, was to have sex. Her parents love Ajay like a son. One day, they would love to see him marry their only daughter. But John won't entertain the thought of his

31

baby girl having sex. Not at any age. And definitely not at 15. Ebony is up a creek with no paddle, on this argument. They're never going to see things her way, at fifteen. No matter what she says. She feels they're never going to allow her to date Ajay, which is wrong. But her thoughts leave her feeling desperate.

"It has nothing to do with his age, baby girl," her father says, "It's *your age* that I'm concerned with and the fact that you're *my* daughter."

"Jb and Tank was dating at fifteen, daddy," she tries.

"In this family, it's a little bit different for boys. In the world, it's different for males. Different than it is for females," he tries, "But you're going to do whatever I tell you to do. No matter what your age is."

"That's not fair, daddy," she says.

"Maybe not," he says, "But those are my rules. Your mother follows the rules *I set* and dictates them to you and *you will* follow them."

Suddenly her mother comes back into the room. She's calmer now but still visibly upset. Ebony doesn't look at her.

"What do you have to say for yourself?" Pearl asks.

Ebony says nothing. She tries not to even acknowledge her mother's presence.

"Do you hear me talking to you?" Pearl asks but Ebony still doesn't say a word.

"Ebony, do you hear your mother talking to you?" John asks.

"Uh huh," she says defiantly.

"*What?*" John asks, of her ill mannered retort.

"Yes sir," Ebony says, correcting herself.

"Then answer me," Pearl demands but Ebony still says nothing.

Pearl rants, "You can sit your behind there and not open your mouth. But I tell you this. Don't even think about dotting that door before you fly out of here. Do you hear that? You need to get on back to Houston, anyway. Before you end up pregnant, while you're laying up with Ajay! That's all he wants to do. Or any boy wants to do, at that age. You're just too blind to see it. I can't tell you *anything* anymore. You've gotten too fast for your own good. I hope you don't have to find that out the hard way."

Ebony pouts and turns her head away from her.

"Seeing the way you're acting now, I have a good mind to let you stay in Houston until you're eighteen. Then you can make your own decisions about what it is you wanna do! John, I think she needs to stay down there until she finishes high school. Because I can't deal with this. Not all by myself," Pearl says as she walks out of the room.

Ebony looks up at her and rolls her eyes. She gets angry and yells behind

32

her mother, while her father is *still* sitting in her room.

"That's all you wanna do, anyway!" she yells, "You don't want me here! That's why I try to see my friends while I'm can! I know all you're gonna do is keep sending me away!" she yells and cries as her father demands that she stop talking back.

"What has gotten into you, baby girl?" John asks, "You never use to be this hard headed. Young lady, this is gonna stop or I'll have to agree with your mother. Right now, you're not leaving me any other choice."

She says nothing as she looks at her father with sad eyes. She had hoped he would be the arbitrator. Or at least, marginalize her mother. But he isn't interested in spoiling her, at this point. He's angry that she disobeyed the rules of his house. That's where his focus stays. He gets up and leaves her room, closing the door behind him while shaking his head.

She can hear her mother yelling from the kitchen. She puts on her walkman headphones and presses play. Her *Mariah Carey* tape is still in it. As she listens to, *Sent from up Above*, she lays across her bed, thinking only of Ajay.

Why can't my parents understand that you love me? They found love with each other, same as us. But they want to stop us from loving each other.

She knows Ajay loves her. Even if he doesn't say it, a lot, like Tank does. Or if he hadn't *ever* said it. For her, it isn't the things he says, it's the things he does to her and for her, that assures her. And the way he does it. He's in love with her too and there's no way she's going back to Houston, for 3 more years and leave her man behind. She's definitely not going to leave without seeing him again. She gets up, gets some clothes and goes to take a bath, while her parents aren't in their room. The arguments with her mother will make it awkward for her to use the master bathroom. Because if her mother is in her room, Ebony will have to pass her. Or she'll have to knock on the door and have Pearl open it. Seeing her mother isn't something she wants to do, at the moment. Pearl is downstairs with John, so Ebony runs her bath and gets in. She listens to her Mariah tape, in it's entirety, as she soaks in the tub. She's trying to ease the sting of the whelps from the ass whooping her mother had put on her.

Next door, Nina calls Ajay and tells him what happened. Immediately he comes across the street and knocks on John and Pearl's door. They answer and invite him in. He apologizes and accepts *his part* in her disobedience. He lets them know he does love Ebony and that gets in the way of him abiding by the rules the crew set for the guys, as opposed to the girls. Especially with her. John tells him, he knows that and had just tried

33

to explain that to Ebony. Ajay tells them he wants to marry Ebony and he isn't trying to use her. Nor disrespect them. John and Pearl tell him, they understand and they love him too. Then they tell him they need for him to help Ebony understand why they're taking the position they are. Further, they need him to make sure she stays safe, doesn't get pregnant and doesn't do something that could ruin her life. He promises he'll never take her there and he'll try to help her understand why *their parents* aren't allowing this relationship, at this time. Nor Lynn and Nina's. They finish they're talk and Ajay returns to Chill's house. Now he wants to hear from Ebony, so he'll know if she's okay.

After her bath, Ebony grabs the cordless phone, goes back into her room, locks her door and calls Ajay.

"Hello," he says, picking up on the 1st ring.

"Hey, baby. What are you doing?" she asks.

"Hey, baby girl. I'm not doing anything, right now. But worrying about you. Nina told me what went down. Are you alright?" he asks.
It's obvious he's been waiting on her phone call, since he left her house and returned to Chill's home.

"I'm alright but I'm sore. I'm tired of her always on me. She hit me again. This time I just lost it. I can't just sit there and let her punch me. No way," she says sadly.

"You know I don't like nobody to hit you," he says, "But you still can't fight with your mom. I know she hit you but it's still not right."

"I didn't hit her. I just held her off of me," she says.

"It's not gonna make things any easier for you and me," he says.

"They're talking about making me move back and stay in Houston until I'm eighteen," she says.

"What? Oh no. Oh hell no. Not that shit, baby. That would be the worst thing that could happen. Are they really stressing it?" he asks.

"Mama said it. And then daddy said, *'with the way I was acting, when I wouldn't answer her, that I wasn't leaving him no other choice but to take her side'*," she says, "So I don't know."

"They can't send you down there for that damn long," he says, "That would be fucked up, baby. Because then I'd have to leave MLK and transfer to Smiley and put them on the map."

"I wish you could but you would lose a year of eligibility," she says, "I checked into that when I had to stay for this season."

"Once you pass tenth grade and transfer, you lose a year, right?" he asks, for clarity.

"Yes, that's right. That's why poppa said I will start tenth grade

34

here," she says, "So I won't lose a year. Plus they know I wanna graduate with my girls."

"Everybody knows that," he says with a chuckle, "But I'll move if you don't come back. I've got the recruiters attention already, baby girl. They'll follow me. They'll keep up with me. I'm a diaper dandy player."

"You and that punk, *Raymond White,* on the same team?"

"I'll kill his ass before the season starts," he says and laughs, "But I'll bet you he wouldn't fuck with you, with me there everyday. I would gut that bitch."

"My mama thinks you're just using me for sex and that you don't care about me. Please tell me she don't know what she's talking about," she says as she listens for reassurance from him.

"Baby, your mama don't think that. She's just trying to get her point across to you. I love having sex with you. *That's true.* But I love every minute I spend with you, though. If you think that's all it is, then you shouldn't be fucking wit me. But I know you don't. I try to show you things, better than I can say it. It's never just about sex with you. Never has been. It's way more than that," he says confidently, "We've got history, baby girl. A whole lot of history. It's my job to make sure you don't break the rules. I have to do better with that, from now on."

"True that but she also said, I can't leave out of this house before it's time for me to go to the airport. She can forget about that too. There's no way I'm leaving here without seeing the crew and going to Stoney's grave."

"Baby, you're in enough trouble, already. Don't mess it up worse."

"It can't get worse than not seeing you before I leave," she says.

"Yea I hear you but I don't want you trying to go up against mama P, anymore. Alright? Do that for me," he says calmly.

"Okay. I have to clean my room now," she says, "I'll call you later. If I can."

"Okay, baby. See ya," he says.

"In a minute."

They hang up and he lays back on his bed, thinking of her. He wants to see her just as bad as she wants to see him. He genuinely cares about, not only Ebony but also her family and her relationship with her mother. He understands how Ebony feels and he can see her parents point too. He's a thug type and he's not even the 1st thug of this clan. He grew up under this family's male tutelage, so his pedigree isn't in question. *Her parents* know *his history*. It's not about whether he came from a good family or not. It has to be about the *girl/boy rule* of their family. The double standard which he
35

learned to live by, himself. As a father, he'll abide by those same rules. But for now, he has to show he's committed to her and not to glorifying some lifestyle. Her parents need to see that he has deep feelings for her. Not just for now but for the future of their relationship. Because now, her age limits what they'll allow her to do. He has to have her parents approval, to date her. He needs to make her understand, this is about their future and not just today. Having their parents approval will do 2 things. Show her that he sees her in his future and help her understand that is what both their mothers *need* to see. He has to show that he'll never use her or intentionally hurt her. His love and respect for her, stems from the fact that he loves and respects her family as his own. No matter what Ebony feels about what her parents said, he knows they love him. That will help him, help her to understand. It isn't about him. It's about her virtue. She won't stop having sex with him to please anyone. He doesn't want her too either. This is another phase of growing up. Something they're both still doing. One day, he'll prove to be exactly the man they seek for their baby girl. In time, he'll learn the civil way of handling life's situations, instead of acting on impulse. Including situations with her. He loves her. There's no doubt in his mind. He just has to grow into the man who can and will take care of her, like her father does and then some. He knows John wants him to slow things down with Ebony. He has to figure out how. Her grandparents have assured him that he's on the right track with the courtship. He just needs the *Time To Grow*.

Later in the afternoon, Tank comes in from Chill's house. The storm has let up and the streets are a lot safer for driving. Ebony has received word from big mama. They're definitely leaving at 3:00pm, tomorrow. Tank comes into her room to check on her. He tells her, he's about to go with Jr, Tonya and Ajay, out to Arthur's apartment. He wants her to go and he's willing to help her sneak out. He calls Nina, from her room. He asks her to go with them. She's going. He tells Ebony to call Bre. Ebony wants to go but Pearl is getting dressed for work and she's suppose to be responsible for Jesse, even though John will be home. Still she calls Bre to see if she'll pick her up.

"What's up sis? How are you doing today?" she asks when Bre answers the phone.

"I'm doing okay. Just one day at a time, kid," Bre says softly.

"Are you going over to Arthur's?"

"I was thinking about it but I don't know if I'm ready for all of that yet," Bre says.

36

"If you do. Will you come by and get me?"

"No doubt," Bre says, "But I thought Lynn said you was on punishment?"

"I am. But Bre they're talking about not letting me come back until I'm *eighteen*. How am I suppose to just sit here and wait to leave, when I know I might not see y'all for *three more years*? I can't do that."

"I know how you feel. In a way, I do. I went through this same thing when me and Stoney first got together. Because of our age difference, his mama didn't want us to date. But we just wouldn't give up. I'm so glad we didn't. I miss him, so much."

"You know what I've been thinking?" Ebony asks.

"What?"

"What if something happens to Anthony after I'm gone and I didn't even get the chance to see him and say how much I love him. Or even tell him goodbye."

"I feel you," Bre says.

"When we was at the hospital, viewing Stoney, I didn't even know how to feel. Until I put myself in your place," she says, "I imagined that was Anthony laying there. It tore me up, just to think it."

"You don't wanna know this lonesome feeling, baby girl," she says, "I wouldn't wish it on anyone."

"That would tear me up, for life," Ebony says, "So you see why I gotta see him while I'm here? Because you never know what the next day will bring."

Her and Bre talk for a long time. Bre agrees to pick her up, on her way to Arthur's, before they hang up.

Pearl leaves for work, just after Tank and Nina leave with Jr. Jesse is in his room playing video games with John.

Later, Bre pulls up and Ebony sneaks out the door and jumps into the van with her. Ebony had brought her suitcases outside after her and Bre hung up. She'd hid them behind the shrubs in their yard. Her and Bre drive to Arthur's and join the rest of the crew.

Ajay is shocked to see her come in the door but he's glad to see her. What he doesn't know is she's not planning to go to the airport. She wants to discuss it with him, first and she does. Chill and Renee are there. They all find out she left home without permission, after John calls. No matter how much each of them disagree, she isn't going back home. Not right away. She's determined to see Ajay and she's determined she isn't going to be on that flight to Houston, when big mama and poppa leave at three o'clock,

37

tomorrow afternoon. Ebony had started to feel more defiant by the hour.

Everyone leaves Arthur's before nine. Chill and Renee leave early, primarily to persuade Ebony that she has no other choice but to go back home. Since she wouldn't listen to them or take their advice. Her and Ajay ride back with Bre. As does Tank, Nina, Jb and Lynn. Ebony reminds Ajay that they're suppose to go to the movies together, before she leaves.

They go pick up Rich, June, T-baby and Rebbie. Then they all go and see *New Jack City* together.

Bre isn't feeling well when they're ready to leave the movie. She plans to drop everyone off and go home. But Ebony convinces Ajay to ask for the van so the 2 of them can go back to Arthur's. He does. And even though he knows she's being defiant, he doesn't want her out of his sight. She said she's going to run away if she can't be with him. He figures if she's with him, her parents will know where to find her and he won't be worried that she's come to any harm. Of course, he wants to spend time with her before she has to leave too. Bre loans them the van and Ajay takes the 5 of them home.

When they drop Nina, Tank, Jb and Lynn off, Ebony jumps out and grabs her bags. Tank or Jb say anything because they understand how she feels. They know where she'll be. They aren't going to tell their parents. They know Ajay will make sure she's back on time to catch her flight. And if their parents make her stay in Houston until age 18, Ajay will make sure they see each other. Even if he has to move to Houston. Tank and Jb don't worry about her as long as she's with him. They worry more about her being without him and the crew, when she gets back to Houston.

Ajay and Ebony leave before John has a chance to come to the door. They go back to Arthur's apartment and hang out for the rest of the night. John doesn't come after them. Pearl is at work and isn't in his ear or in his face, insisting that he do. But she calls many times. John tells her, he has no idea where Ebony is. He feels confident Ajay will see to it she makes her flight. John is no longer willing to be a hypocrite.

Meanwhile at Arthur's, Ajay talks to Ebony about her plans. In the beginning, she's determined not to go back. He stays on her until she gives in. First, she makes him promise he won't take her home until the next day. Even then, she wants to go to granny's house to meet big mama and poppa. He tells her to call big mama and let her know she's okay. Since she refuses to call her parents. She calls big mama and tells her she's okay. Ebony knows, full well, her parents are aware that she has left the house with her bags. And they've probably called every house on the set. She tells big mama she'll be there in time to leave. But there's no way she's leaving Ajay,

38

tonight. Big mama is always understanding and so is granny. Her grandfathers are too. But they do tell her they wish she had done things another way. She tells them she didn't know any other way. They hang up and her grandparents talk amongst themselves. They reminisce on how this is *Déjà vu. H*ow this is very similar to what they had experienced with John and Pearl, 18 years ago.

"Well you know, it's like that old saying. W*hat goes around, comes around*," big mama says and the others agree.

They call John and request that he get Pearl on 3-way. He does. Papa and poppa each get an extension of the phone line, so they can do the talking to their son and daughter. They tell them Ebony has called them, she's safe and she will be there on time, to make the trip. Then all 4 grandparents encourage them to leave well enough alone, for the time being. Because she has called and she is coming back.

"Ebony is specifically going against what we told her," Pearl says.

"And that sounds *very* familiar to me," poppa retorts.

"Look, I'm not gonna be okay with her laying up with Ajay," John says, "She's only fifteen."

"Give me *your remedy* for stopping it," his father, Jackson Brown says, "And then us, *over here*, we'll reverse life back about twenty years, so we can see if it works on the two of you."

Big mama and granny share an extension and have some input, as well.

"At least she *has* called someone and let them know that she's okay. You two didn't do that. Y'all was in hiding. *Remember John*? We had to hunt the two of you down. Y'all didn't call either one of your parents and you definitely wasn't doing what *we told you* to do. The both of you *still refused* to come out of that house. Even when we did find you," granny says, "Ajay made sure she called us, son. He's not using her and okay, I know she's a fifteen year old girl, *in this crew. B*ut Ajay is doing exactly what we raised him to do. Making certain she knows that she's loved and protected. No matter what or who. He's doing what he was taught to do. With the girl that he's chosen for his future."

"And so is she," papa adds, "We all knew these grandkids was going to settle with each other, just like we knew our kids would."

"It's what we planned," poppa says, "And so did you all. But you don't get to say, *at what age* it starts. That's what's bothering you. Oh you can try too. But it never works out the way you plan it. You're just lucky if they get with good family. And in this case, they both have."

"Ajay loves her, John and Pearlie," granny says, "He wouldn't encourage her to do something that would drive a wedge between her and
39

any of us. This is *Ebony's* defiance. Not his. I wanna make sure we're all clear on that. If he didn't let her stay near him, she was going to run off somewhere and not even make the trip."

"And if she did that, she *would be* following in your footsteps," papa adds, "But she's not. She just wants to see him while she can. And we're not gonna stand in the way because we love *the idea* of that kind of love. It's what we all expect and it's what we've reared them on."

"And we'll have a talk with her, about this, when we get back to Houston," big mama adds, "Pearl, you've never had a Houston address. Do you remember? Me and your daddy allowed you to stay here with Pearline and Jackson because we believed in the love you two have."
The grandparents remind them that these are the same things they had done when all they wanted to do was to be together. And at least, Ebony *is* going to return. That's the most important thing. Pearl never even went to Houston when her and John rebelled. Granny and big mama don't leave out any of those points either.

"You can't stop real love so you shouldn't try. That's what y'all told us," granny reminds them, "We didn't and you two shouldn't either."
Pearl still tries to protest but John cuts in and says,
"Fine. We'll take the advice our parents are giving to us. Since we didn't listen, back then. I refuse to be a hypocrite. No matter how hard it is to allow my fifteen year old daughter to stay out, *all night,* with a boy. I never realized how hard it was on you all, until right now. We see what you mean and we're not gonna say anything else about it."
He convinces Pearl to let it go and soon, they all hang up. Pearl goes back to her shift while John sits in the boys room and talks with Jesse.

"I'm glad you only have one sister," he says.

"I love my sister," Jesse says, "My sister's pretty."

"I love her too, Jesse," John says, "And yes, she is pretty. She's also growing up now, Whether your mother and I, like it or not."
Him and his youngest son get back to their video game. He thinks about what their parents said. He agrees and he always did agree. He has only 1 problem with their relationship, at this point. It's Ebony's age. He's a father, so that's a natural thing. But he knows poppa loved and accepted him when him and Pearl went through this same thing. He also knows that Al's only son *is going to marry* his only daughter. That has been set in stone since their births. Just like him and Al thought. The only trouble him and Al have is convincing Pearl and Jo. They want them to marry, one day too. They didn't add in having to deal with the growing years. John and Al had counted on Ebony being slower to move to Ajay. They had figured on her
40

TIME TO GROW-RELOADED-TIME WILL REVEAL 2

being out of high school and more like 18, before she chose him. But like his parents had just said, *"You don't get to pick the age when it starts. You're just lucky if she gets with good family."*
He's satisfied that she has done that. He'll get with Al and they're going to work on bringing Pearl and Jo to the light. Their own light.

Love will find away to happen, if it's meant to be. There is no set formula. No blueprint. No guidelines to follow. It simply takes perseverance. Despite all opposition and discouragement. If it's true love, it will prevail. If your heart, soul and mind are all in it. Love takes time to happen. And when it does. It is it's own reward.

Ebony and Ajay spend tonight at Arthur's apartment. Arthur visits a lady friend, in a neighboring apartment, to give them privacy. Ebony thinks it's a beautiful gesture for him to leave his *own* apartment to allow them to have alone time and she says as much.

"If everybody else can see that we belong together. Why can't our parents see it?" she asks as they lay in each others arms.

"They *do* see it, baby. They've always seen it. They're just not ready for it, because they think we're not. One day, they'll be ready to accept it, if we hang in there. Either way. I'm not gonna leave you, baby. I've put *too much* time into you to stop now," he says as they both laugh.

"I'm gonna miss you, too much, Anthony. I am so tired of saying that. Y*ou know that?*" she asks as she looks into his eyes, "The summer is a long ways away."

"Check this out. I'm coming down there on my spring break, alright?" he says, "I wasn't gonna tell you until later. But I figure now is as good of a time as any. So you can stop looking so sad. You know I can't stand that, right?"

"I know and I'm sorry."
They kiss. She smiles. After laying her head on his chest, they fall asleep.

They spend the next day together. He takes her to the mall, where he buys her some clothes and earrings. He also buys 4 matching shirts with their names airbrushed on each, at her request. A set for him and a set for her. He even buys a small suitcase for her to pack her new things in.

"We'll wear these when I come down there, okay?" he says of their matching shirts.

"Okay," she says and smiles, "I'll save them, for sure. Baby, that gives me something else to look forward too."

At 1:30pm, as promised, he takes her to granny's house. John, Al,

41

Jo and Pearl are there. The mothers look visibly agitated. Ajay stays until poppa and big mama are ready to leave. He drives them to the airport while both set of their parents plus granny and papa follow in Jo's van.

Ebony is very emotional at the airport. She stays with Ajay until the last possible second. She's holding onto him and he's holding her, just as tight. Their parents watch as Ebony cries while they hold onto each other. It's evident to them that he's shaken too.

"Anthony, please make them understand that we need each other," Ebony cries, "I don't wanna stay three more years. I can't."

"I will, baby. Don't cry. I'll do that," he says.

"I love you, Anthony."

"I love you too, Ebony," he says, "I'm coming to see you soon."

Then her, big mama and poppa board their flight. Ajay, granny, papa and their parents stay until the flight departs.

Afterwards, Pearl and Jo stand with such a posture, like they're waiting to talk to Ajay. He stops and stands before them, waiting for what he thinks will be a verbal assault. But neither parent say anything. Neither does he. Eventually, he excuses himself and walks around them. He goes to the parking lot. In the van, with granny and papa by his side as comfort, he fights back his own tears. They leave the airport and he drops them off in *The Point*.

He turns on the stereo, for his ride to Shaker Heights and finds himself listening to Ebony's *Mariah Carey* tape. She had left it in the tape deck. He thinks of how disappointed she'll be when she discovers she'd left it behind. He knows how much she loves Mariah's music.

In flight, after a brief talk with big mama and poppa, Ebony puts on her headphones and turns on her walkman. She turns the volume up to the maximum and presses play. She smiles as *Voyage To Atlantis* plays. She had put Ajay's *Isley Brothers* tape in her walkman, at Arthur's and never thought to switch it back, after they'd left the mall. As they sing, *I'll always come back to you,* she smiles. Big mama can hear the song playing. She looks at Ebony and smiles too.

42

CHAPTER 13

ONE TO GROW ON

It's 3 weeks into January and schools are back in session. The crew announce Tank's 16th birthday party, which will be in a few days. Bre, Jr and Tonya have done the necessary paperwork and taken possession of Stoney's house. Bre has had some work done and scheduled even more upgrades to be done to the home, in the future. Her, Jr and Tonya are living in the house now. But Bre finds it hard to sleep without Stoney being there. At the same time, there's no other place she'd rather be. Even with the upgrades, she didn't make any drastic changes to the house. She wants to leave it as original as possible, to preserve the beautiful memories they shared. Bre and the crew felt the need to have another party at the house, in order to get past the fatal memories of the last one. Tank's birthday party will be the re-christening of the house. The party is Saturday night.

Rob and Jan get a lease at the U. Ajay moves some of his things in too. Since Jr and Tonya moved into Stoney's house, Ajay asked Rob to get the lease in order to keep his word to Ebony. Still he has plans of leasing his own apartment, in a few months. He wants his own apartment so him and Ebony can have private time, whenever they desire it.

During the winter semester at MLK, the crew are superstars. Not only because they're crew but because all of them are top athletes too. Jb is the senior captain of the basketball team. Ajay is a junior captain, All-American, top recruited shooting guard, ranked in the national top 10 polls. He's also a *Dick Vitale's diaper dandy*. June and Rich are co-captains of the state champion football team. They're expected to compete for the state title for the next 3 years. Tank is the captain of the boys track team.

The girls are prime, as well. Lynn is already All-state for track and ranked in the top 10 polls, in the nation. Jan is on the All-Ohio state softball roster. Bre is a stand out point guard and T-baby is soon-to-be All-State, as a shooting guard for basketball. Nina and Rebbie's dance and cheering teams are ranked nationally. The crew are celebrities and receive a lot of attention. For the guys, this means many more girls at their beck and call. But for the girls, there are guys who come-a-calling. But it changes nothing.

At the start of the winter semester, Rich meets a new transfer named Tameka Robinson. He's determined to get with her. Only he needs to do it without T-baby finding out. That's going to prove difficult because, just like him, T-baby is a celebrity at MLK high school and all the students, know they date. Rich has been flirting with Tameka. The word just hasn't gotten back to T-baby. Tameka finds out about Tank's party, through other students. She asks Rich if it's for real and why he hadn't told her about it.

"Yea my crew having his sixteenth birthday party. Saturday night on Union avenue," he says, "Why? Are you coming?"

"Yea I'm coming," she says enthusiastically, "What time it start?"

"Nine o'clock."

"Okay and I called you, last night. Did your mom tell you?"

"No she didn't. But she was already gone to bed when I got in," he lies.

Anna was up when he got home but she favors T-baby. She didn't pass the message along because she didn't care for him to know she'd called.

"I sure called," Tameka says.

"Uh huh. So what's up wit that? Are you down to do the nasty or what?" he asks.

"That's all you think about. You're a trip," she says as she smiles but she's all for it.

They make plans to hook up, after the party. She knows he has a girlfriend. But Rich, being the player that *he thinks he is*, has convinced her, he'll be able to handle T-baby. He tells her the 2 of them *will* hook up. He's planning to ask Arthur if they can use his apartment during the party, so he can do Tameka and return to the party after sending her home. Then finish his night off with T-baby. Again, at Arthur's place. He thinks his plan is fool proof. But he has underestimated T-baby's intelligence. Saturday night is Tank's party but Rich may be the 1 who gets the biggest surprise.

Ebony is into her 2nd semester of classes and basketball. Things between her, Sonya and Shuntay are even more tense, since she returned. The girls hadn't told the story of their assault, to the people or the students in Houston, *correctly*. The students at their school are under the impression that *the crew* had done the deed. Ebony corrects every person who comes at her, blaming her crew. She tells them it had to be some other guys from Cleveland, who was at their party. Guys whom the 2 girls had met and rode home with. And her crew had nothing to do with the assault. Nor did they know whom they'd left with. She'll find out later, this was the same story the 2 rats had given to Raymond White. And he now wants revenge of his own, for his girls being taken by someone other than him.

44

TIME TO GROW-RELOADED-TIME WILL REVEAL 2

It's Saturday night and all of the crew are at Jr's house, formerly Stoney's house, for Tank's party. Though everybody is still missing Stoney, they eventually relax and try to have a good time.

Ajay shows up in his newly purchased, *1964 Chevy Impala* convertible with pearling royal blue paint, platinum trim and white wall tires. The fathers in the crew have told him, that was the car of many of their dreams during their school days. Chill calls him, *The Fonz,* as in *Fonzie* from *Happy Days.* A show they use to watch as small children.

His father teases him, saying, "You don't know nothing about those times, son. That car is ten years older than you."

Ajay got his car the week after Ebony left and had it accessorized at their detail shop.

Tonight, he's rather withdrawn at the party, to say the least. Nonetheless, he's going to make good on his promise to help Tank have a good time. Him and Chill stay in the background, all night. They watch the grounds and the door. And everybody who comes and goes through it.

Tameka shows up around 10pm, with 2 of her friend girls, *Angel* and Michelle. Rich is pretending not to notice her, while T-baby is in the room. She has no idea Tameka is there to meet, *her* man. The party is going well. Nina and Tank are together and enjoying each other, as usual. Rebbie and June are kicking it as well. Rich is with T-baby, for the most part. But he sneaks over and talks to Tameka, whenever no one's paying attention. He's going to be with T-baby, if he can. She's his 1st option. But in case she has to go home early, he's keeping Tameka around, for a back up piece.

As the party starts to wind down, T-baby tells Rich she's staying out with him. Now he has to figure out how to get Tameka to leave without alerting T-baby. He still wants to sex Tameka but he'll have to do it later. He goes to Arthur and asks if he can still use his apartment.

"You and T-baby are alright, man," Arthur says, "You know it's not a thing for crew to chill at the crib. I told you that before."

He doesn't know that on Wednesday, when Rich 1st ask to come over, he was asking for him and Tameka. What Rich doesn't know, is Arthur is vaguely familiar with 1 of the girls who's with Tameka. The 1 named Michelle. The things that Rich doesn't know is about to get him caught up. But he's so convinced that he has T-Baby, so blindly in love, that he believes she won't have her guard up. He's sadly mistaken.

Ajay drives him and T-baby to Arthur's spot and returns to the party. Tank and Nina are going to the motel. Rebbie and June are staying at Jr and Tonya's house. Tameka is still at the party when Rich leaves. She still thinks they're on, for later and he has only left to take T-baby home. So

45

they can hook up, after he's gotten rid of his girlfriend. She doesn't know where they're suppose to meet because he didn't tell her, before he left. She discusses this with Angel.

"He forgot to tell me where he was going," she says to Angel.

"I heard Rich talking to that Q dog, earlier," Angel says, "He was talking about going to his apartment." Angel is pointing at Arthur.

"Do you know where he lives?" Tameka asks.

"No," Angel answers, "But Michelle might. She attends all the frat parties, at the U. She's talking to them now. Let's ask her."

The 2 of them join Michelle, who's talking to Arthur, Kilo and Wayne. All 3 guys are Omegas at Cleveland state. As soon as the guys walk away, Tameka and Angel asks Michelle if she knows where Arthur lives.

"Yea I know where he lives but why do *you* wanna know?" she asks, wondering why they're inquiring about a man, *she's* interested in. She knows their reputations. She asks, "What's up with that?"

"I was suppose to hook up with Rich, over there," Tameka lies.

"Oh okay. Is that where he went?" Michelle asks.

"I guess so," Tameka says.

"He didn't tell you?" Michelle asks, looking doubtful.

"No he didn't say nothing when he left. But earlier tonight, and all this week, he's been telling me we was gonna get together over there," Tameka lies more, "He must've went to get rid of T-baby and then just went straight there."

Then she asks, "So what's up? Are you gonna take me by there or what?"

"Yea, girl. We can check it out," Michelle says, "Arthur wants me to come over there, anyway. Y'all can just roll with me."

"Is Ajay going over there?" Angel asks.

She's been admiring him from afar, at school, at his basketball games and everywhere else she's seen him. She's been nervous about saying anything to him because of his celebrity status. She's just a freshman with no extra curricular activities.

"Why don't you ask him," Tameka says, "He ain't wit nobody, wit his *fine* ass. He's *way* to fly to be alone. He's been chilling in the background, by himself, all night."

"Call him over here," Angel says, "I'll talk to him, if he comes."

Michelle approaches Ajay and tells him, Angel wants to speak with him. He comes over, right away, to see what she wants. That's when she tells him, she's been wanting to talk to him. But she has been afraid to say anything at school. She tells him how fly she thinks he is and she wants to hook up with him, tonight. He's only mildly interested but he's down to *hit it,* if she has

46

some place where they can go. He's thinking it's too cold for the baseball field. Besides, he isn't about to break in his *"six foe"* with her. He isn't even down for letting her ride in it. After all, Ebony hasn't ridden in it yet.

"You wanna go out to the U? That's where my girls are going, with Arthur," Angel tries.

"No we can't hook up over there. That's not cool," he tells her, "I thought you had a spot. Arthur needs his own place."

"We can go to my cousin's house. She lives in the Grove, though. You wanna go over there?" she asks, desperate to get a yes out of him.

"I'll get back with you on that, alright?" he says and walks away, leaving her to think about it.

If she wants to get it on with him, then she'll have to do all the work and come up with a better game plan. He's never been excited about these groupie types. They try to act like they're all about him. They always have fuck history but play like virgins. He *has* a virgin girl. That cousin move, he doesn't trust. Crew have to be careful about the spots they occupy.

It's ten o'clock when Ebony gets home from her game. Her team played a road game. Tonight, she had the best game of her basketball career. She scored a career high; 37 points. She can't wait to tell her crew. She takes her bath. Then she grabs the phone in her room, which had been installed once she moved back. She has permission to call Cleveland, after her games. As long as she doesn't run up the phone bill. She has to wish Tank a happy birthday and talk to *her man*. She knows Tank and Nina are suppose to go to the motel. She's trying to catch them before they leave. She calls the house on Union avenue and Tonya answers the phone.

"Hello," Tonya says.

"What's up, big sis?," Ebony asks, "How's the pregnancy? How's everybody?"

Tonya tells her she's managing. And that all of her crew are cool. She also tells her, Nina and Tank have already left for the motel and T-baby has left with Rich, going to Arthur's apartment.

She says, "Ree Ree and June are still here."

Her and Ebony talk for a while before she gives the phone to Rebbie.

"What up, kid?!" Rebbie asks.

"Hey! What's up?!" Ebony asks, excited to hear her girl's voice.

"It's on, girl," Rebbie says, "We're getting our party on. You know how crew do it."

"Yes I do and I wish I was there so I could do it too," she says, "Nina and T-baby already *caught out*? They're gone already?"

47

"Yes, they're already being fast. You know that," Rebbie says as she giggles, "They left here about an hour ago."
She tells her, T-baby and Rich are gone to Arthur's place and she's staying at Jr, Tonya and Bre's tonight, with June.

"Where's my baby?" Ebony asks, "I've got to hear his voice, so I can sleep tonight."

"He's in the kitchen," she says, "He's been looking so sad. I don't know what the deal is. But I know everybody is missing Stoney, though. It just seems like Ajay ain't really here, tonight."

"He might be missing his baby. *Hello*? Did you even think of that?" Ebony asks as she laughs.

"If that's it. Then you need to cheer his ass up. Because he's out there, girl," Rebbie says and laughs too.

"Fuck you," Ebony says, as they continue to laugh.

"Really though. *He is*. You know how he can just zone out and get *weird* on our ass?"

"Like I said, *fuck you*. Alright? My baby's not weird. Y'all just don't have the game to change his spirits. Only I have it like that!" she says confidently, as they both laugh more.

"Well here he is. Why don't you go on and work your magic spell or whatever it is you do. I love you and I'll see ya."
Rebbie gives Ajay the phone. Then she joins June on the dance floor, for a slow dance.

"In a minute," Ebony says before Rebbie gets off the phone.
She's still laughing, as Ajay says, "Yea. Who is this?"

"You don't know me anymore?" she asks, as she speaks softly.

"*Oh man*! What's up, baby?" he asks, smiling for the 1st time tonight, as he takes the phone down the hall, so he can hear her better.

"You, baby and that's it," she says.

"I got it like that?"

"Uh huh. Its just like that," she says.

"Uh. Damn, baby girl. You sound so good," he says.

"I am good."

"I know that, Ebony," he says, "Don't be trying to shoot no game to me, from way down there, alright? You know how your man is. I'll be up all night trying to clear my head."
His voice is sweet, seductive and very heavy.

"Huh. I guess I got it like that too," she says.

"I'm telling you. We need to change the subject, baby. Don't have me getting hard, on the phone," he says, "Talk about something else."

48

"Mmm. We won. I got my career high," she says as she laughs.
He laughs too. Then he sighs, as he say, "You're a trip, girl."

"Too late, ha?" she asks as she smiles and he laughs. "My bad, baby. I didn't know I had it like that!" she says, "But that *is* good to know."

"It's not good when you can't do nothing about it, though," he says in a more serious tone.

"I know," she agrees, in a soft voice.

"Do you miss me yet?" he asks.

"I missed you when I got on the plane," she says, her eyes welling up with tears. She continues, "Really, as soon as I walked down to the tarmac. I was already in tears because I knew you was still standing at the other end. I wanted to turn around, so bad and run back to you. But you told me to be strong, so I just kept walking."
She's tearing up just thinking about the day she last saw him.

"Our mothers are still not really speaking to me. Plus mama is mad because I bought the car," he says.

"I got the pictures of your drop top," she says, "It's *so* fly. Nina told me, mama Jo was mad at you. She doesn't want the NCAA to think you're getting gifts."

"Mama will be alright. So will I. I can show how I paid for it."

"I'm not speaking to mama," she says, "She be calling down here but I won't talk to her. I don't even wanna talk to her."
He says, "Now you know how I feel about you and mama P. I don't like that y'all are not speaking. You're gonna fix that."

"Baby, it's not my fault. She started this stuff, last summer."

"I really don't care who started it," he says, "Y'all use to be close. Now its like you hate her guts. Baby, that's your mom and you're gonna make it right. That's all it is to it, alright?" he demands. She says nothing. "Did you hear me?" he reiterates, after he notices she didn't answer.

"Uh huh."

"Alright, then. Make it right," he says, "I don't care what you have to do to start talking to her. Just do it and do it soon, okay?"

"Uh huh," she says reluctantly.

"Don't be lying to me," he says as he smiles, "I'll get you for that."

"I'll try but I don't like how you be fussing at me, about her," she says, "She's the one that starts all the stuff because she knows I love you. Then you fuss at me because I don't like it."
She's using her whinny little girl voice and playing for his sympathy but he isn't bending.

"Stop acting like a baby," he demands, "You want to be treated

49

grown up. But then, every time its time to show your stuff, you wanna be a lil girl again. You can't have it both ways, Ebony. Show your stuff."

"I *know* that," Ebony says in a sassy tone.

"You need to check your tone with me," he says calmly.

"My bad, Anthony. God!" she says, still in an uncooperative tone.

"You act like I can't get to you, down there," he says suddenly.

"I wish you would," she says in her usual shy voice.

"You keep clowning me, I will. It's not gonna be nice, though."

"Okay, Anthony. I got it, baby. Come on now. I don't want you to fuss at me. I miss you, too much."

"Okay. Then you understand what you have to do, right?"

"Yes I do."

"Cool," he says, "See how simple that is."

She laughs, "Uh huh. I see."

"Good but I'm still gonna get you," he says and they both laugh.

He feels it's important to their relationship and their mothers approval of it, if she opens up dialogue with her mother again.

"You know you got me, already," she says as she smiles.

"That's my blessing," he says. Then he changes the subject, "So you had your career game, *tonight*?"

"Yes. Thirty seven points. Fourteen boards. Six blocks. Four steals and four assists," she says.

"Damn! Did anybody *else* play?" he asks with a chuckle.

She laughs. He says, "It sounds like you got up good, for the game. You still sound hyped."

"That's because of you," she smiles, "And *Public Enemy*."

"You listening to that *Do The Right Thing* soundtrack, for pre-game?" he asks.

"Yes and that song, *Fight the Power*," she says, "Baby, that song gets me so hyped up and in the groove. It's got the lyrics and that bass line is awesome. It makes me wanna organize a sit-in or a rally or something."

They laugh hard.

"*Chuck D* got the motivational lyrics, for sho," he says, "My pops feeling them too. He plays them, all the time."

"I put that song on and I can see radio Raheem getting choked out. Plus *Rosie Perez* dancing," she says, "That gets me fired up."

"I'm gonna bump that, this Tuesday," he says, "See what I can do with it."

"You'll get seventy five, baby. Easy," she says and they laugh again.

50

They talk for over an hour before they finally hang up.

Tameka, Angel and Michelle had left, following Arthur to his spot. Angel had given up on trying to get Ajay's attention. He was preoccupied with the phone, for so long. He hadn't even glanced her way, the entire time. But when he finds out they're gone to Arthur's apartment, he finds June and tells him, Rich and T-baby are over there. He reminds him that Rich had been trying to make a play on Tameka, all week. Now she's gone over there, probably thinking he's there waiting for her. Ajay and June rush out to his car and get in. Rebbie rushes out and gets in too, sensing that something's going on with her girl. The guys try to deny it, initially. Then they finally admit there *is* something wrong but won't say what it is. She stays in the car and refuses to get out. They have to bring her along or not go, themselves. They all leave for the U.

When Arthur arrives home, Rich is already in the guest bedroom with T-baby. Arthur had no idea Tameka was even interested in Rich, when he'd told Michelle they could all come over and chill. It isn't until they get inside and she asks where Rich is, that alerts him. Now he knows he's made a mistake by bringing her. But he's going to keep things cool and play it off. He pretends Rich isn't there. Tameka chills on the couch with Angel. Arthur turns the music up to signal to Rich that he's there. He plans to watch the room door and wait for him to come out, so he can pull him aside and warn him about Tameka, before she sees him.

Inside the room, Rich and T-baby are into each other. They've been together, many times, by now. They've discovered they both like wild and crazy sex. At times, they can be very loud. When Tameka goes into the bathroom, she can hear noises coming from the bedroom but she doesn't know it's Rich. She goes on into the bathroom. When she finishes and opens the door, Rich is exiting the room at the same moment. She sees him come out in his boxers. Arthur hadn't caught him, in time.

"You was here, all the time?" Tameka asks.

"Oh man. What's up?" he asks, obviously surprised but tries to remain cool.

"You're here with T-baby, aren't you?"

"Yea but I didn't know she was coming. Not until the last minute. That's why we left, like that," he lies.

"I thought we was suppose to hook up, over here," she says.

"We can but you have to let me get her home, first," he says.

"Oh it's like *that*? I'm suppose to take her sloppy seconds?"

"She's my girl and you knew that. We haven't done nothing," he lies, "We're just kissing and shit. She don't like to do it, right away. I have

51

to play with her, for awhile," he says, still lying to her and sadly, it's working.

"You need to stop playing with her and take her home. So we can get down to business," Tameka says and heads back toward the living room, believing Rich is about to get rid of T-baby.

Tameka is a junior at MLK, 1 grade higher than Rich. But her game isn't even close to his level. And he has very little, compared to the rest of his crew brothers. He uses the bathroom and goes back into the room with T-baby, who's ready for another round. They begin kissing again.

Suddenly, Tameka turns the knob and walks into the room. The room is dark but she can see them on the bed. She turns on the light. They're startled by the brightness, as they jump up quickly.

"I thought you was taking her home?!" Tameka asks loudly.

"*Who the fuck is this*?" T-baby asks, her voice rising an octave.

"I don't know," Rich tries.

"Bullshit! I bet you don't!" T-baby says in a doubtful tone.

She's no fool. She turns her attention to Tameka and asks, "What do you want, bitch? Ha? You think you're fixing to get with him?!"

"No baby. She's not trying to get-"

"I'm talking to her. Not you!" T-baby yells at Rich, after cutting him off, "You say you don't know her. Let's see if she knows you. I have a feeling somebody is lying or about to lie."

T-baby is putting on her clothes in anticipation of something going down.

"Rich, that's what you said all week and as a matter of fact, at the party. Before you left with her *and* just now, out in the hallway. You was suppose to be telling her it was time for her to leave."

"What?!" T-baby yells as she pounces toward Rich, "Is that what you said, Richard?!!"

She's a tiger with a short temper. She isn't done yelling at him either.

"Did you say that, *nigga*?! Did you tell this bitch you was coming back in here to get rid of me!? Ha?!"

You can see the anguish in her face. She's dangerously close to striking him. He feels like she might, at any second. He tries to restrain her but that only infuriates her more. She starts kicking, slapping, punching him and going after him with everything she has. She's doing a good job of it too.

"Calm down, Trisha. Shit!" he says, "Don't hit me no muthafuckin more, alright?!" He's barely managing to hold her off.

"What are you doing talking to that bitch, Richard?! Answer that, *muthafucka*! You ain't fuckin with no slow bitch! *LaTrisha Nicole Brown* got plenty of damn sense! You'd better recognize that shit, right now!"

52

He tries the truth. He says, "It's not that crucial, Trisha. I was gonna hit it if you had to go home. But after you stayed, I didn't say shit else to her." Tameka has a few comments to the contrary but Rich had been truthful, about that part. In seconds, T-baby and Tameka are both screaming at him. He calms each of them down. They're all talking calmly. Then he blows it when he says, "I don't see what the big deal is anyway. You're here with me now, Trisha. Tameka you wanna get with me. It's only one of me. But both of y'all can get some. I wouldn't give a fuck. Just stop all this screaming."

T-baby punches him in his face. This time he punches her back and they begin to fight. Rich is a bit stronger than her but as a female, T-baby's holding her own. For awhile, at least. Eventually, he gets the best of her. He tries to control her and not hit her anymore. But each time he lets go of her, she hits him again.

Ajay, June and Rebbie arrive. Everyone is in the bedroom when they enter the front door. Rebbie runs straight to the back to find T-baby. She finds Arthur trying to hold T-baby back, while her lip bleeds. Automatically, Rebbie assumes the 3 girls had done it. She pushes Arthur and jumps in his face, demanding he let go of T-baby. He does.

"Come on, crew. We can handle these ho's!" Rebbie screams.

"I'm not even fighting them!" T-baby says, "It's his triflin' ass!"

"What the hell is going on here?" June asks as he enters the room.

"He's trying to get me to fuck him *and her!*" T-baby yells.

"What *crew*? You trippin or what?" Ajay asks as he laughs.

Him and June snatch Rich up and with Arthur's help, they drag him out of the room and out to the front balcony. They need to talk to him in private.

Rebbie helps T-baby fix her clothes and hair. T-baby is crying, very emotional tears, right now. This is her 1st experience with Richard, on the cheating side. She's suspected him but she's never had any proof. Tonight, she has proof. This is her 1st heartbreak. Rebbie cries too, as she tells T-baby it'll be okay. The 3 girls are in the hallway trying to stay clear of everybody. T-baby and Rebbie exit the bedroom and walk pass them.

T-baby looks at Tameka and says, "Oh yea. I do have something for you." She punches her in her face, knocking her to the floor. She's stomping on her before she can even react, while Tameka is trying to crawl away.

"Come on, ho's! What the fuck y'all wanna do!" Rebbie yells to the other two.

She's ready to scrap for her girl but neither girl responds. They don't even say anything, as they help Tameka up off of the floor. She didn't even fight back, after being punched in her face and stomped repeatedly. She just laid there until her girls felt brave enough to reach down and pick her up.

53

"Scared ass, bitches!" T-baby says, "Be down for your shit, like you was when you barged off up in the room on us. You scary, ho!"

"Desperate whores!" Rebbie adds as she walks with T-baby into the front room.

Ajay and June are just outside of the door. They're all over Rich, for hitting T-baby and they still have him by his collar.

"I don't give a fuck if she did hit you first," Ajay says, "Are you a muthafuckin man or not? Real men don't hit ladies, cousin. You need your ass *kicked*, for this shit here."

"A real man, don't hit on a lady, crew," June reiterates, "And definitely not a crew lady. You done violated like a *muthafucka*."

"That's out of bounds, man," Arthur adds, "Chill ain't gone like this, one bit."

They're ready to leave as soon as T-baby and Rebbie joins them.

"Come on. I'm taking y'all to Jr's crib to see Chill," Ajay says.

"I know he's gone wanna see you, homie," June says to Rich.

Rich is quiet as the 5 of them walk out to the Impala. Ajay tells T-baby to sit in the front.

"Good. Cause I'll punch his ass again, if I sit near him," she says, "I don't *believe* this shit."

As they ride to Jr's house, she cries softly and looks through Ajay's music collection. He glances over at her. He notices her face is already beginning to swell and her lip is already swollen. He looks at her tear soaked face and for the 1st time, he can see her resemblance to his Ebony. They're 1st cousins but he had never noticed they favor, some what. He can't help but sympathize with T-baby, while thinking of Ebony and how this news will affect her. She isn't going to accept Rich putting his hands on her cousin. He knows that. He also knows she's going to ask what they'd done about it. Ebony is familiar with crew justice and how violators get handled. Ajay doesn't know what Chill's decision will be. He'll find that out as soon as they get to Jr's house.

"Is this Ebony's?" T-baby asks Ajay, as she holds a *Mariah* tape in her hand.

"Yea. She forgot it. She knows I have it in here, though."

"Can I listen to it, tonight? I'll give it back to you."

"*Yea*, T-baby. You can listen to it for as long as you want too. She's not gonna mind, if one of her girls borrow it."

"I'm gonna call her tomorrow," she says, "You know I'm telling her about this bullshit. I can't believe this shit."

He cringes at her language. That's 1 thing that isn't similar about T-baby
54

and Ebony, for him. Ebony wouldn't dare let him hear her using bad language. But he knows she uses it sometimes, because all 3 of her girl's do.

"Please take me home, Ajay. I don't wanna be nowhere, near his muthafuckin ass," T-baby demands.

He drives her home. Rebbie gets out with her and tells June, she's staying until T-baby is calm. June agrees, she should. They arrange with Ajay to come back and get her later.

Her and T-baby go into the house and go straight to T-baby's room. She locks the door behind them and turns on the light. She checks her face for swelling, in her dresser mirror. Then she asks Rebbie to go and get some ice, for her lip. Rebbie goes to the kitchen, gets some ice and a towel, then returns. T-baby turns on her tape player and puts the *Mariah* tape in. When she hears, *I Don't Wanna Cry,* she breaks down crying, immediately. The song seems to say everything she's feeling, right now. She cries herself to sleep while Rebbie rubs her head.

At Jr's house, things aren't quite as calm. Ajay has made it there with Rich. Arthur has come back by, after sending the 3 girls home from his apartment. Chill and Renee are aware of the situation and Chill is enraged. This is the angriest, many of the crew have ever seen him. Renee is very angry, as well. Just not as animated as her fiancé. The reason for their anger, very simple.

"Crew are never to fight amongst each other!" Chill yells, "No matter *what the fuck* the situation is! Crew are never to fight crew!"
Crew Rule #1: Crew situations must be settled in a peaceful way. Chill has been holding Rich by his collar, since he got the news. Finally, he slams him against the wall and yells, "If you wanna fight a muafucka! Fight a man!"
Rich knows not to retaliate. For if he does, he'll have to fight the entire crew.

"Why you wanna hit on my sister, like that?!" Renee yells.

"She hit me first, y'all," he tries, "A lot of times."

"I don't give a *fuck*!" Chill yells, "That's a lady! You're suppose to be a man!" Then he tells Rich to go to the kitchen so the men can talk,
"Man to boy. I'm calling you a boy because, *right now*, that's what I see."
He's a little calmer as all the males file into the kitchen.

Renee and the females leave, going to check on T-baby. No matter the hour, they have to know how she's doing.

Chill tells Rich to have a seat. As he talks, the other guys stand around him. They're ready for his order to whip Rich's head, if it's given.

"Rich, what the *hell* is wrong with you?" Chill asks.

"Man, I don't know," Rich says.

TIME TO GROW-RELOADED-TIME WILL REVEAL 2

"See brother. This type shit *here*, will not work," Chill says, "And this is how it's gonna go down. You're gonna go to T-baby, whenever she's ready to talk. And you're gonna make it right. You got that? Hear *me*?"
Rich nods his head, as Chill says, "I can remember when your father use to treat your mother like that. Can you?"
"Uh huh," is Rich's response.
"Do you remember how it made you feel?" he asks, "because I do."
"Yea, man," Rich says in a low voice, "It made me feel, real bad."
"Are you planning on being with T-baby *forever*?"
"I was. Yea," he answers, "But she's not wit that, anymore. Not after tonight. I know that."
"Y'all both said things y'all didn't mean. I'm sure. But you was wrong. You can't tell your lady you want her to fuck you and a bitch. I can see why she clocked you," he says with a slight laugh, "Renee's foot would be *permanently* stuck up my ass, if I said something like that. There isn't a female in this family, that wouldn't be ready to kick ass, over that."
He talks to Rich for more than 30 minutes, before telling him the penalty for violating the code of the crew.
"I'm gonna let you make it. Only because this is your first fuck up. But if you ever hurt a muafucka from your family again. Then your family is gonna hurt you. Do you feel me?"
"Yea, man. I got it," Rich answers quickly.
He's relieved that he doesn't have to suffer the consequences of; *The Circle*. The Circle is when all of the crew members stand in a circle and put the violator in the center. The violator has to fight his/her way out or get beat down. Rich remembers the time when Jb had gone in the circle for shoving Lynn, after a basketball game, 2 years ago. That was when they broke up, initially. He also remembers Stoney and Rob going into the circle, when they had an altercation at the detail shop. Rich got off easy. He remembers the damage they'd done to the 3 crew members. Right now, he's happy he gets off with only a warning.
"If it happens again," Chill says, "You're going in the middle."
"Cool," Rich says and they end the discussion.
Chill tells him to go home and think about what he's done. He tells him, he needs to really remember how he felt when he watched his own father, hit his mother. And if he wants that for his own children. He is not to party with the crew until he makes it right with T-baby. The subject is closed.

The next day, T-baby calls Ebony and tells her the whole story. It leaves Ebony, very upset. As soon as they hang up, she calls Ajay and Chill.
56

Ajay tells her what Chill had decided the penalty would be. She knows that's the end of it. And though she wants them to put Rich in the circle, she knows it's not going to happen. So she lets it go.

After she hangs up with them, she thinks about T-baby, a lot. She wonders if her and Rich will ever work this out. Only *Time Will Reveal* if Rich and T-baby ever recover from this night. Or will Tank's 16th birthday become a bookmark for the foursome, just as Stoney's death has been for their entire crew.

The next couple of weeks are uneventful, for Ebony. Her season is going great. They're looking towards post season play. Her problems with Shuntay and Sonya are causing tension below the surface. But she's an athlete, first and foremost. She's willing to let things lay low, as long as the season is going on.

On Valentines Day, she receives cards and a big box from Cleveland. It contains a little something from her entire C-town family. There is something in it for her, big mama and poppa. Renee, Tonya and Bre had mailed it to them. She has candy, clothes, money and earrings from Ajay. He sent big mama some candy. Pearl added some candy plus some money, in a card, for her. She'll find out later, the gifts from Pearl was paid for by Ajay. He had gotten Pearl to sign the card. He's still trying to make peace between them. Ebony and big mama go through the box together, while big mama talks to her about the similarities between their relationships. She tells Ebony that her and Ajay's situation isn't any different than her and poppa's had been. Nor her mother and father's.

"My *and* your mother's relationships, started out just like yours is with Ajay," big mama says, "But I applaud you, because you didn't disobey your parents wishes and stay with him, like your mother and myself. You came on to Houston, *each* time. Just like they told you too. And I know Ajay is a good young man. He encourages you to obey them. It wasn't like that for me or your mama. I left here with Percy, against my parents wishes. I ran away with your poppa. And Pearl never moved here when he and I, moved back from Cleveland in nineteen seventy. She stayed with Pearline and Jackson. And her and John got engaged. They was fifteen and sixteen. The same age you and Ajay are now. That's why she's so afraid to give in to your request. She knows it's the real thing, baby. Why do you think they left you alone, the day before we left to come back down here?"

"We was expecting them to come *drag* us back home," Ebony says, "We even talked about it *that* night."

"They didn't come because we all made it clear to them, that they

57

were being hypocrites," big mama says, as she explains it to Ebony in a way that only big mama can.

It helps Ebony see things from her mothers view, for the 1st time. Big mama tells her the entire story of when her parents was caught at grandparents Charles and Annabelle's house.

"That sounds like me and Anthony, getting caught at the motel," Ebony says after hearing the story, "Except we didn't get caught *in the act.*"

"That's right. I found out they'd been sexually active for over a year. She was in love by then and determined she wasn't gonna leave him," big mama recalls, "On that day, Percy went with me. I was gonna drag her out of that house. We was moving here, the next day. She was hell bent on not coming. She had her mind made up. John was right there by her side, honey. Begging her not to leave him. Ajay never did that with you. But he wanted too. I know he wants you and so do both sets of your parents. I tell you, Pearline and me, we fussed and we cussed. We tried to whip them. No matter what we did, they wouldn't come out of that house. So I let her stay. Pearline and Jackson said they would make sure they got along, okay. I was angry. But Percy, he wasn't even mad and neither was Jackson. They were okay with them being together at that age and at that time. Because they had already planned it. Baby girl, you need to know only one thing. In this family, the men arrange marriages, from your day of birth. I don't think that's ever talked about with the females. If you pay attention, you'll see it. Your daddy isn't mad about you, *loving* Ajay. He just wants you to be older. Because nowadays, folks marry later. His only problem is that you're not eighteen. With your mama, folks married before eighteen. *These* fathers want the girls to be eighteen and they want the best man for their daughters. See, John already knows that Ajay is a good man. He has no other choice *but* to be. Look what he comes from. We all raised each others children, so we know what we're getting. But us women, we can't seem to accept it when it happens. We want to play out whatever fantasy we have in her heads, for our girls. But for our boys, we'll let the husbands go with as much double standard as they want."

"I notice that with my brothers," Ebony says, "And all the guys. I said that to daddy that day when mama was whipping me."

"He already knows what the future holds for you, as far as a husband goes. But he has to set boundaries, baby girl. It was the same for all of the women in this entire crew. This families *double standards,* go way back to the olden days. Females are expected to have and to hold, *one man.* While the males can sew their wild oats and be worldly. So that they are knowledgeable enough to head their households. They're raised to be

58

socially, as well as sexually, dominate to their woman. And to be her protector too. Now they all cheated, at some point. And some, probably *still* cheat. But I see you as being one female in this family, who just might make some changes for the daughters you'll have. And probably for yourself too. Because Ajay will move this earth for you, if he can. You just watch what I tell you. Be good to him. Never let your eyes fix on another man. Even if Ajay does mess up, here and there. They're all good men. But they've all cheated, at some point. Still we fight, *tooth and nail*, to be able to love these men," big mama laughs, "It wasn't until later, when Percy made me realize that John and Pearl was only doing the same things we'd done. Your father and grandfathers want you to marry Ajay. They've reared him to know what they expect of him, when it comes to you. Al has molded him into a fine young man. His personality is just like his grandfathers, Saul and Allen Sr. He's going to be stern with you. He's a disciplinarian, so be aware. But he would never allow you to come to any harm. He just wants you to carry yourself in the way *he* desires. Ajay doesn't give a damn about *too many* people. But he loves you more than his own life, already. And I *like* that."

They laugh as big mama continues, "He doesn't mix with too many folks, it's true. So those he does care about, *oh honey child*, he'll kill for them. He didn't steal that and he's not acting off of no street codes, either. That's what he comes from. *Warriors*. He's willing to kill or die to keep the order he needs for his life to be peaceful."

She reminisces back to the day she ran away with the band.

"See baby. Back when I ran away to be with Percy, all I saw was how he looked at me. He still looks at me like that, today," she says with a sly grin, "But it was different kinds of dangers out there, when we were teenagers. So my parents had other reasons for not wanting me to be out and about. I'll tell it to you in two words. *Jim Crow*! But I knew Percy loved me. I was ready to risk whatever I had too, to be with him. Drove my parents crazy."

"Big mama, Anthony loves me. I know he does. He looks at me the same way my daddy looks at my mama. Just like poppa looks at you. And how papa looks at granny. But big mama, they seem to think it's just about sex. I don't know *why* they can't understand us. *Especially* since they went through the same things," Ebony says, "Anthony said they *do* understand. He said some of the same things, *you're* saying now."

"He's right. They understand. Ebony, they always said their children weren't related by blood but they would be, by marriage. It's the same oath we took about them. So they know exactly where you and Ajay's hearts are. It's just different when you're the parents. Namely, us mothers. See, you don't want to let go of this precious lil baby you brought into this

59

world. You wanna protect it from all harm. Even when it's not facing any harm. A mother just always has that fear. It's her natural instinct, that's all. In her heart, Pearl is protecting you because that's what she promised God, herself and you, that she would do. From the first day she felt you move in her belly. That's what mother's do. And daddy's, they just go along with whatever we're saying. Because they don't truly understand that kind of a bond. They just know this lil person came into their lives and changed it for the better. Made him wanna take on the role as the provider and protector. So his woman, *the mother*, could stay with his child and continue to strengthen that bond. A bond he, himself, couldn't even come between. That's how it's suppose to be. The man is the King, the provider and the protector. The woman is the Queen, the first teacher, the nurturer, the caregiver," big mama says and laughs, "You just let Ajay wear the pants. Don't let anyone else's problems, become yours. You keep his mind free of stress. Then everything you want from him, he'll have to do it. Because you will have earned it and he'll know you deserve it. He'll make it happen for you or die trying."

"Daddy use to say that about me and mama. That we act like girlfriends. Like when she said she wanted me and her to share the master bathroom. That was funny. Anthony talks about it, right now. Because he knows I'm mad with her. He said I have to fix it because he wants us to be close, like we use to be. That seems like a lifetime ago," Ebony says, "I believe what you said about him being stern and a protector. He's already like that. But mama seems like she's mad at me. More than she's trying to protect me. She knows Ajay is from a good family. He's like her son."
She smiles and watches her grandmother's eyes and still she listens.

"This *mother-child* relationship is something you will never *fully* understand, Ebony Eloise. Not until you have children of your own," big mama says, "And then, its *payback* time."
They laugh and after finishing their talk, Ebony takes the initiative to call her mother. They talk for a few minutes. And though, in the beginning, the conversation is filled with tension and awkward silences. They do manage to see eye to eye on some things. Pearl promises she'll try to give her room to grow up. If Ebony promises to give her room to be the mother and try to understand, how all of this is affecting her. Ebony promises she'll try, very hard. They both say, *"I love you,"* before their conversation ends. Big mama is proud of both of them and the progress they made today. She reminds Pearl about the early 70's, when they didn't speak to each other for nearly a year. Pearl admits, she hates to think about it, to this very day. She says that was the loneliest time of her life. Except for now. Big mama asks her to
60

realize, she has a daughter who's walking the same path they had both walked. And please, do not leave her on that path to walk alone. She tells her to remember how young love was, for her and John. Because the only way she was able to understand them, was when her husband forced her to remember their own relationship and how they had to fight to keep it. Pearl vows to open her mind, before they hang up.

As the weeks pass, Ebony's driving skills have improved to the point that she's ready to take her test for a driver's license. She takes the written test in early March and aces it.

By the end of her season, she's ready for the road test. She wanted to focus on the basketball season, first. Unfortunately, her team finished 2nd in the state tournament. She was selected to the All-State and All tournament teams, as a freshman.

On March 26, she takes and passes, the road test. She'll receive her driver's license in 4 weeks. She can't wait to share this news with the crew.

When she calls and tells them she's passed her road test, everyone is happy for her. Renee even adds a joke.

"Alright, kid. The next time you take the Blazer, it'll be okay. Just remember to ask first," she says and they laugh hard.

"I was going after my man, big sis," Ebony says, "I'm sorry."

Then she finds out, Rich and T-baby are still not back together. To make matters worse, Nina and Tank are having problems. She'd read that on the last 2 letters she'd gotten from Nina and T-baby. They're always arguing about, 1 thing or another. In a letter from Bre, she had revealed why she was feeling sick, all the time. Dr. Weston had done a pregnancy test and it was determined that Bre is carrying Stoney's child. She's already 3 months into her pregnancy and due in September. Bre was shocked but still happy. She hadn't even missed a period until last month. Ebony is blown away by that information from Bre. But her, like the rest of the crew, are happy that she's pregnant. They feel this is a 2nd chance to have a part of Stoney, back in their lives. They are going to make certain Bre has everything she needs, to insure that lil Stoney will be born alive, bouncing and healthy. Ebony is elated about the baby. But she's sad and disappointed about her girls, Nina and T-baby. Especially after she's learned from big mama that they were all meant to be together per their forefathers wishes.

The crew gear up for the official opening of their club, *The Chill Spot*. March 30-April 7 is college spring break and the grand opening of their *top-of-the-line* club.

61

TIME TO GROW-RELOADED-TIME WILL REVEAL 2

The opening goes off without a hitch. The Cleveland PD do all they can to close opening week down. But they aren't successful. Chill and the crew have their business permits and plans, in order.

Ajay is still living with Chill and Renee but he sleeps at Jan and Rob's, from time to time. His probation ended a week before spring break. He's free to travel as he pleases. Rob had gotten the apartment. Him and Ajay had discussed sharing the lease. And though Ajay keeps some clothes there, he's yet to make the official move. He spends a lot of time out there and so does Jan. Ajay drives him and Jan to MLK, every morning. He'll decide on moving later. But there's something more pressing that he has to do, first.

April 5-14 is MLK's spring break. Ajay is off probation and he's going to visit his girl. The end of his probation couldn't have come at a better time.

Ebony is very excited, the night before he arrives. He has a room reserved at the motel but big mama will insist that he stays at the house. She wants to keep as close of an eye on them, as she can. And at the same time, give them a little privacy too. Ebony sits on the back deck with poppa, the night before. He gives her a last minute talk about how she is to behave with Ajay in the house. He allows her to drink a beer while they talk.

"No sleeping together under my roof, young lady. Is that clear?"
"Yes sir."

Ajay is keeping the motel room as a back up. They would have no need to have sex in her grandparents home. Besides, her grandparents have been more than understanding with them. And neither of them want to disrespect big mama or poppa Percy.

The next evening, Ajay arrives. Ebony is happy to see that Chill, Tank, Jb and June have come too. Renee wanted to come but she has classes starting back on Monday, at Cleveland State University. So she wasn't able too. She's in the spring semester of her junior year. The guys plane arrives at 10:30pm, Friday night. They rent a car and come to big mama's house. After eating a late supper and talking for a bit, Ron and Charles come by to get them. Ron's having a house party. Ebony goes too.

She's happy to see April and Yolanda. Sonya, Shuntay and Tina are there too and up to their usual tricks. Ebony stays close to her and Ron's crew. She still doesn't know Ajay had slept with Shuntay and Sonya. She won't find that out until later, after her crew are long gone and back in Cleveland.

Later at the motel, Ajay gives her a .25 caliber automatic pistol, for

62

her protection. Ron had gotten it for her, at Ajay and Chill's request. During her crew's visit, they take her to Ron's private shooting range and Ajay teaches her how to use it.

"I don't like guns, Anthony. They scare me," she says.

"It ain't shit to be scared of, baby girl. If a muafucka come at you and they're trying to take you out. Then you have to light their ass up."

"I could never kill anybody. I told you that, before," she says as she looks into his eyes.

"And I told you to never say what you can't do," he responds.

For most of his visit, he practices with her at the range and at the basketball court. She's pretty good at hitting her targets but her basketball game is awesome. He's so proud of her. Still he makes jokes.

"Don't get *too good,* now. You might try to nut up on me, one day. Then I'll have to show you how the master works his," he says and they laugh, "That goes for hoops too."

They spend a lot of time at the motel. He verifies that she's still on the pill before they have sex. He doesn't want her to get pregnant, anytime soon. She shows him her prescription and that she's up to date on taking them. Their week is filled with plenty of partying, lovemaking and business deals. Then on Sunday, April 14, the crew return to Cleveland.

The next day, Ebony goes back to school, only to hear that the 3 Houston hood rats had fooled around with her crew again. She isn't going to stress over it because she knows where her crew guys hearts are.

But by Thursday, a student name Rolanda is talking about the crew and the hood rats, during lunch break. That's when Ebony learns of the incident in C-town which involved Ajay. She overhears Rolanda say, "Sonya and Shuntay was with Ajay."

"What did you say?" Ebony asks.

"Oh, *hey* Ebony. I didn't see you come-"

"Fuck that. What did you say?" Ebony asks again.

"I was just telling them what Tay said," Rolanda says.

"Yea *and*? What did she say?"

"They both said they was with Ajay," Rolanda says.

"Shuntay is a lie. Anthony was with me the whole week. So y'all can run that shit, somewhere else." she says, growing very agitated.

"She said she was with him, in Cleveland. Not here," adds a girl name Tammy, who's seated at the table with Rolanda.

"How? I bust that shit up at the motel," Ebony says, "I cut that shit short. Plus I burst her nose, in the process. Then me and Anthony spent that night together, at his brother Chill's house."

63

"Was that the night that you and your girls had a fight with some girls from there?" Tammy asks.

"No. It was the night before that!"

"Well, they was telling everybody this story," Rolanda says, "They said, one night when you and your crew beat up some ho's for trying to fuck Ajay. And your daddy made you go home but he didn't make them go with you, when y'all left. They said, *on that night,* they was with Ajay, a dude name Rob and another dude name Stoney. And they said you didn't know nothing about it. Plus Ajay told them if they tell you, he was gonna kill both of them."

"And they said Ajay got a big ass dick. They said he got thirteen inches," Tammy adds with a grin.

"Them ho's wanna go there?" Ebony asks, "They telling lies on my homeboy Stoney? He's *dead*! There's no way a ho is gonna disrespect his memory with no shit like this! That's my word!"

She gets up and puts her tray away. Then she heads off looking for Shuntay and Sonya. April goes with her and so does Tammy and Rolanda. She catches up to Sonya and Shuntay as they're changing classes.

"Why the fuck are y'all lying on my crew?" Ebony asks and she's heated.

"What are you talking about?" Sonya asks as she laughs.

"You know what I'm talking about, bitch!" Ebony yells, "Why are y'all ho's trying to run down my crew?! Telling lies on my brother Stoney. When he's not even alive to speak for himself!?"

Sonya, Shuntay and Tina tell her the same story that Rolanda and Tammy had just told her, in the cafeteria. Ebony snaps and grabs Shuntay. She's punching her, repeatedly. Sonya and Tina jump in. There's the 3 of them against Ebony. April drops her books and starts to fight on Ebony's side. Yolanda gets word of the fight and comes tearing up the sidewalk. She joins in on Ebony's side. The fight last another few minutes, before teachers run out and break it up. Sonya and Shuntay together, was getting the best of Ebony before Yolanda jumped in. She had grabbed Sonya and beat her, while Ebony whooped Shuntay good. April held off Tina. But now, with the stopping of the fight, Ebony is out of control. She wants to fight to the death. But the teachers take them to the office. Raymond was a bystander, during the fight and gets the details from Rolanda and Tammy. They hadn't bothered to help Ebony. Even though they had instigated the whole thing. All 6 girls are escorted to the principal's office. Raymond is pissed off to know that the Cleveland crew are still sexing his ho's. He isn't going to go out like a sucker. He wants reciprocity.

Ebony is suspended for a week. The other girls get 3 days.

64

CHAPTER 14

"I COULD DO IT NOW"

Poppa calls Pearl. Ebony talks to Tank and Jb. She tells them the reason she was fighting is because of what was said by Sonya and Shuntay. She didn't like them lying on her crew. Tank and Jb know they need to have Ajay call and tell her what really happened, in his own words.

"I'm going to Chill's house and tell him to call you," Tank says.

"Yes, do that! Tell him to call me, *right* back," she demands.

They hang up and Tank heads to Chill's house.

He tells Ajay about him and Ebony's conversation. And she wants him to call her, right away. He lets him know, him and Jb still have permission to finish their talk with her. And Ebony had asked her mother's permission before they hung up. Ajay follows Tank back to Pearl's house.

He learns Pearl has no problem with Ebony's request. She allows Ajay to call Ebony back, from her phone. She also tells Tank to take the phone into his room, so they can talk privately.

Ebony is pleasantly surprised when Ajay calls her, within minutes, from her mother's phone. She didn't think her mother would allow him to make a long distance call but she has. She had even allowed him to go to Tank and Jb's room. Ajay tells her, that her mother allowing *him to call* her from *her* house, proves she's opening up to their relationship. She agrees. Then gets on with her reason for wanting him to call.

After hearing her reasons, Ajay finally tells her the truth about that night at the dilapidated baseball field. Ebony is royally disturbed by it.

"Why Anthony!?" she asks sadly, "That's all them ho's wanted. So they could rub it in my *damn* face. Now they can brag and say they took something of mine. You shouldn't have ever *fucked* with them!"

"Hold on. Don't start cursing," he says calmly, "This *is* your man you're talking too. I know I fucked up. We all did. But they didn't get nothing but a nut in a condom, from me. I would never fuck neither one of them nasty ass bitches. And I told them both that. So if they're gonna tell you something, then they need to tell you the facts."

"Y'all shouldn't have been with them *period*, Anthony. That's all I have to say on that!"

"You're right. I wish we hadn't. But I can't change history, baby," he says, "All I can do is tell you I regret it. I'm sorry I did it and that you was hurt by it. There's nothing about, either one of them that attracts me.

Shuntay got stretch marks on her breast. She showed it to me, on Chill's porch, the first night y'all got here. While you was at mama's house."

"I wish you didn't too and I know you're not lying about her flashing you. She do that to guys at school. I accept your apology but I'm gonna beat they're asses, every time-"

"What did I *tell you* about *cursing*?" he asks as his voice rises.

Even though he has called to admit that he cheated. He's still the disciplinarian. Still the alpha male. She pouts initially. Not wanting to allow him to control the situation. But he's steadfast, so she calms down on the foul language, quickly. Then allows him to make his plea.

"They can't fuck with what we have. Nobody can," he says, "And you're gonna tell me you know that, before we hang up. Here it is. I fucked with those tramps on a triple up. What kind of a female *brags* on that type of shit? *Especially* when the guys don't? They was use to trains and they got a train. They was never gonna get with me, alone. Like they wanted too. Both of them wanted to fuck me, solo. I told them no. They wanted me, at the same time. I wasn't with that either. I had my mind on that letter you wrote to me. *Not them.* Seeing that they was ho's, I told them they had to do my crew or get the fuck on. Stoney and Rob ran up in both of them while they was giving me head. At the same time. They know I'm large because they was gagging, trying to deep throat my shit. And I tried to choke the fuck out of 'em. Plus I was telling them to handle this thirteen and stop gagging. I didn't put my dick nowhere else. It wasn't like that for me. They sucked my dick with a condom on it. That's it. Period. Over. *End* of that story."

She's speechless. She doesn't know whether to laugh or cry. She had been angry and disappointed, thinking her rivals had been to ecstasy with her man. He has just confirmed that they hadn't. That night had been about him, Stoney and Rob getting a nut and that was it. The same thing she's known her crew guys to do, for all of her life. All of the males in her extended family, for that matter. Her big mama had just told her that, a few weeks ago. There was no glory for Shuntay and Sonya. They're beneath her. But Ajay still has more to reveal about their saga.

"That's the reason Dre and Joe fucked them up, the next night. Because on the night they was getting the train from us, they was suppose to be meeting them. They told them they was gonna asks Stoney to bring them to the *Waffle House* to meet them, so they could go get down. They had already promised Andre and Joe, the pussy. Stoney was just giving them a ride to meet them, before he went home. He asks me and Rob to ride with him to drop them off, then we was gonna stay at his spot, on Union *ave*," he says, "On the way there, they was kicking it to me. Still trying to get with me.

66

I wasn't gonna fuck with them, at all. They kept begging me. So I told Shuntay she had to serve Rob, first. I told Sonya to serve Stoney. I thought that would've killed the noise. But shit, they got right on them. While Stoney was *still driving,* as a matter of fact. So by the time we got to the *Waffle House,* them ho's knew they was going with us so crew could run a train. Still they went inside the *Waffle House* and let Joe and Dre pay for their food. Plus they had already given em money to get some weed and drink, from Chill," he says as he goes on, "They got the weed but they smoked it in the van, on the way. Then they told them they wanted to fuck the crew, not them and they left with us. They had promised them they was gonna give them some pussy, *that* night. The same night you beat Darlene's ass. They didn't hook up with Joe and Dre. And they had already spent the dude's money. So Joe and Dre must've got back at them by doing that dumb shit, the next night. All because they had used them and spent their money. They only rode with Joe and Dre, the next night, because they thought y'all knew what had happened the night before. That's because I told them I was gonna tell you how trifling they was. So when they showed up at Nina's party, that's the first thing they asked us. *Did we tell on them.* Stoney told them we hadn't yet. But he said if they get in his van, he was gonna tell y'all on the way home. So they rode with Andre and Joe, instead. And that's how the whole thing unfolds. I don't have no love for them and there's no disrespect to my brother Stoney or you either. It was a crew thang and that's it."

"I'm shooting them. Excuse me but that's how I feel, right now."

"You'll shoot over me, ha?" he asks and laughs. Then he says, "No, baby. It don't even have to be all that. You can handle it better. Just get a couple of your real partners. April and *what's that other chicks name?*"

"Yolanda," she says.

"Yea. They're down wit you. Y'all get together on them ho's, if they fuck wit you. You can hold up on one of them, at a time. Maybe even two, if they don't be trying to steal on you. You know how to handle your business," he says, "If they fuck wit you again. Put them thangs on 'em."
She laughs for the 1st time, during this conversation. "How *you doing*? I know they ain't fuck with my face, did they?" he asks, "As if they could."

"No. I got some scratches on my chest and my arms. But they didn't hit me in my face. I'm hearing that I broke Sonya's wrist and I know I drew blood from Shuntay's nose again," she says.

"Alright. And it was two against one when you did *that*. You don't need to risk going to jail for shooting no tramps," he says, "If y'all square off again. You know what you have to do, right?"
67

"Uh huh. I know. But I don't ever want you to mess with them again. Not even to get your nut, *as you call it*. No more, Anthony."

"You got my word on that, baby. They can never suck my dick again," he says as he laughs, "Hell, I might kill them ho's for snitching on me. I told them if I heard about it, it wasn't gonna be nice."

"I heard that you told them you was gonna kill them if I found out. Did you?" she asks.

"Yep," he admits, "But it ain't worth, not being with you. I wanna be out here *with you,* when our future unfolds. That'll be worse than death, for them."

They laugh. Then he tells her, her crew have all shown up at mama P's, to find out how she's doing. He had to go downstairs. He shares the phone, so she can talk to the rest of the crew and get their opinions.

By the time her crew are done, she knows it's on her to hold up, like she's always done. Ajay take's the phone back.

"Everybody came over to talk to you," he says, "They knew I was calling. I had to let them all say something. Mama P got a house full and they're eating up her food too."

She says, "I feel better now. I'm glad you called me."

"I am too, baby," he says, "I had to call. I need you, Ebony. I messed up, baby and I'm sorry. But you know I love you, right?"

"Yes. They can't mess with us, like you said. Nobody can."

He's satisfied that she's okay and knows, she's the girl for him. She enjoys hearing from everybody, back at home. She know when she does see Sonya and Shuntay again, it may be round two. Deep down, she really hopes her and her girls get the chance to stomp them out.

It's late April. Ebony is enjoying another fishing trip with poppa and his friend, Mr George. Big mama is there too. It's fun for Ebony. She likes pulling the fish out of the water, then watching them flap around as they try to find their way back into the *Gulf of Mexico*. Poppa and Mr George teach her, not only how to fish but how to clean them too.

"Your granddaughter is a natural born, country girl, Percy," Mr George says, "I thought she would be afraid to even touch the fish. Here she is taking them off the hook and gutting them too." He laughs.

"She's got me and Eloise, in her," poppa Percy brags, "She's not afraid of nothing but God."

Ebony smiles as she cleans all of the fish, they caught today. She'll do this from today, forward. Big mama tells her it's possible to pay someone to do it or buy the fish at the market and have them cleaned.

68

"But you're frugal like your grandparents, on both sides. You'll clean yours, yourself. Unless there isn't enough time," big mama says, "You'll wanna save you and Ajay's money. Anyway you can, dear."

They have good times on their fishing trips to Galveston. April and Yolanda had even started going with them. Ron, Carolyn and their crew join them, on several trips as well.

She hasn't had another altercation with Sonya, Shuntay and Tina since her suspension. Her, April and Yolanda have grown, very tight these days. They go everywhere together. Just like she does in Cleveland, with Nina, T-baby and Rebbie. She remembers when she was preparing to move here with Tank. Her mother *told* her, she would meet friends in Houston. She doubted Pearl and said, all of her friends was in her crew. At the time, she thought she would never learn to love anyone else, the same way she loves her crew. But since meeting April, Yolanda, Ron, Carolyn and their whole crew, she has had to change her view. Her mother was right. She has great friends here. Friends who will be in her life, forever.

Today, her license come by mail. April and Yolanda share this big moment with her. Then, to her surprise, poppa takes her to a few car lots and lets her test drive cars. She's totally excited about the possibility of having her *own* car. She's even more excited that her Houston girls are there to witness it. But it seems the better things get for her in Houston, the worse they are for her girls, back in Cleveland.

Her girls aren't faring well, at all. T-baby and Rich aren't back together and now, Nina and Tank have broken up. On a brighter note, Bre and Tonya are past their morning sickness stages. Also, Renee and Tonya are planning their double wedding. The wedding is, this June. Ebony has talked to her mother a lot, by now. She knows she'll definitely go home this summer. Pearl had told her, they're going to take things 1 day at a time. And if she behaves herself, she may not have to come back to Houston for the fall. But poppa has already told her, she'll go to MLK and play basketball with T-baby for high school. And that him and big mama will make sure of it. Even if papa Jackson and granny have to step in to help handle John and Pearl. She knows she's going to be home for the double wedding. All she's concerned about, *at this moment,* is her Anthony, her crew's 1st wedding and getting her own car.

How am I gonna get my car home? Surely no one is gonna let me drive, all the way to Cleveland, by myself. I'll need someone to help me drive. Anthony can come on the road with me. Now that would be the bomb!

69

"Oh well" she says aloud, "I'll worry about that when the time comes."

She knows if she gets her own car. Her family and crew will make sure it gets to Cleveland. She knows that, for sure. What she doesn't know, is during this spring semester, Ajay and her mother have talked many times. They've discussed his feelings for her and he has sworn Pearl to secrecy. He told her, he had suggested to Ebony that they need her approval or he won't feel comfortable trying to see her, in the future. And that she had to make things right with her mother. He has also told Pearl. Even though he loves Ebony, he still wants her parents to be okay with them being together. Pearl had found that very honorable of Ajay. She is now able to accept him as completely genuine. Ebony will learn about their closeness in the coming weeks.

Jb and Lynn are looking forward to their high school graduation, on June 7th. They have scholarships to *Georgia Tech,* in Atlanta. The double wedding is set for June 28th and all of the crew and their families are a part of it. But family business always comes first.

The crew never leaves a score unsettled. Proof of this comes on April 24th when Danny Washington comes home from West General. Danny is the owner of the black and white impala which was used in Stoney's murder. The crew get the news from their usual sources, on the streets. Danny is still not fully recovered. He's very weak from the waist down but he isn't paralyzed. Chill is determined not to allow him to get a day older. By now, all of the police leads have gone cold. To the crew, it seems the police never really looked for leads. The crew know 2 of the guys are already rotten. The only thing to do now is to get number three.

"Alright. In order to get Danny, we may have to get dirty, right?" Chill says as him and the guys meet up at Jr's house.

Bre sits in on the meeting again because she wants some of this action. She's dreamed of the day that the last of her *1st and only love's* murderers, Danny, meets his maker.

"He's gonna be in the house and his family is gonna be there too. We're not leaving *any* witnesses," Chill says.

"Cool. Dirty me on up, then," Ajay says, always down to do dirt.

Everyone else agrees. They decide to strike on a quiet evening, in the middle of the week, when most of his family are known to be out of the house. That will be next Tuesday. His mother works nights. Usually his lady friend or *bottom bitch,* comes over to look after him while his mother works.

"Her ass is going out too," June says, "Makes no difference to me."

70

"Hell no, it don't," Rich adds as he chuckles, *"Gotta go! Gotta go!"*

On the rainy Tuesday night, of the following week, the crew retaliate on Danny and his girl. Bre goes along on this ride. She wants justice for herself and her unborn child. And she gets it. The crew actually allow her to do Danny in. She didn't hesitate when the time came to fill him with lead. Then they clean the place and vamp.

Bre feels solemn on the ride back. No major feelings are taking over her. No anxiety. She always thought she would freak out but she didn't. They return to Jr's house, after the caper. For the time being, Bre has found closure. She has always felt like she could kill. Tonight, she had. After she shot Danny and headed back to the get away car, she felt her baby move for the very 1st time. She shared that with the guys. They feel vindicated now that all 3 of Stoney's murderers are murdered. It was breaking news before they could get there buzz on. Not 1 of them cared.

The next day, as Ebony is going to her 5th hour class, she's approached by Raymond. She picks up her pace and walks faster, trying to escape him. But he's persistent, so he skips and catches up to her.
He leans in and says, "How are you doing, gorgeous?"
She walks faster. So does he, to stay right next to her. She continues to walk and he continues to talk. She doesn't answer any of his questions but he doesn't give up.
"Hey, why can't we let by *gones*, be by *gones*? I'm not trying to get with you like that, no more. I know about your nigga and all. I was just hoping we could be friends. I don't have no hard feeling's towards you or your family. Can't we be friends, at least?" he lies, sounding like he's begging.
"I don't have a nigga. I have a man," she says, "His name is Ajay. He's a brother. Not a nigga. But you can't relate to that part of life either. So just leave me alone, alright? That's all I want from you. Is for you to leave me alone."
She stops in the hallway, in front of her classroom, to wait for April and Yolanda to catch up. As she waits for them, Raymond keeps talking.
"Can I take you out, sometimes? I'm not talking like a date or nothing. I just wanna go get a meal or something, sometimes?" he asks.
"No. *Never*. I wouldn't be caught dead with you," she says with conviction in her voice, "Catch the hint and leave me alone. *Please*."
"Come on now. You can't be *that* damn cold. I'm trying to be your friend, Ebony. That's all," he tries.
"No way. I am not going *anywhere* with you. Not now and not ever.
71

Understand me when I say that," she says, borrowing a line from her man. "It's not gonna happen. So let it go. If you really wanted the respect I give my friends, you would respect my space and stay away from me."

April and Yolanda are procrastinating about getting to class. She gives up waiting because she doesn't want to wait and be bothered by Raymond. She walks into class and takes her seat. Raymond is still standing outside of the class, making gestures to her, when April and Yolanda finally get there.

"Leave her alone, Ray," April says, "You see she don't want you. You need to go on about your business and forget about getting with my girl."

She finishes by laughing at him and pointing in the direction he should be going. Next, Yolanda has a few choice words for him.

"Dude, my girl know you ain't nothing but a loser," she says, "And if you fuck with her wrong again, the three of us are gonna kick your ass. You see your ho's done got scared to face us, right? Act a fool if you want too and meet yo maker."

Her and April laugh hard as they walk into the classroom, just as the bell rings. Their teacher closes the door while Raymond still stands there, with a shit eating grin on his face. Looking dejected and pissed off.

Who does that bitch think she is? She ain't no better than the rest of these ho's. I'm gonna take her ass down, a peg or two. Watch me.

He goes on to his class. But in his mind, it isn't over until he says it is.

After school, Ebony calls her crew and tells them about the incident with Raymond. Again, Ajay is very angry.

"See that nigga, bitch up when I go down there. But that's alright. I'm gonna get him. He'll have to see me, sooner or later. I'm gonna handle his muthafuckin ass, once and for all. I'm *sick* of this shit. He's gonna have to come see Ajay. That's all it is to it."

He's pacing the floor, using his hands and arms as he talks. He's riled up. Ebony is holding the phone, listening to him rant. He's already saying he's going to fly to Houston. But Chill isn't going to allow it because he has school. Still Ebony holds the phone while he goes on and on.

"What's he saying?" April asks.

Her and Yolanda are at big mama's. Ebony can't answer because Ajay is still going. Chill takes the phone and has Ebony to hook-up Ron, on the 3-way. He tells Ron about today's situation. Ron agrees to *half court* press.

The next day, Raymond is absent from school. He's in the hospital. The rumor around Smiley high is that he'd gotten beat up by drug dealers, 72 which is the truth. But everybody thinks it was about a deal gone bad. Everybody except Ebony, April and Yolanda. They know Ron's crew had whipped his ass and they know why. They aren't going to tell the real reason because Ebony knows the code and she hipped her girls to it too. She's elated to know that her crew can reach out and touch someone, all the way from Cleveland. Raymond will be out of school for 10 days. Her, April and Yolanda refer to these 10 days, as the *Alka-Seltzer* days.

When others asks why, they say, *"Oh what a relief it is,* that he isn't there to bother Ebony."

They get major laughs from all of the students, who hear the joke.

By the second week in May, Ebony knows what day she's going home. June 3rd. April and Yolanda are throwing her a going away party at Ron and Carolyn's house, in the 5th ward. Ron said they can have it at his house and the crew are cool with this plan. They set the party for May 28th.

The next week, poppa and big mama take Ebony to get her car. Poppa had decided to buy a 1990 Honda Accord from a friend of he and big mama's fishing buddy, Mr George. The friend is retiring to Florida, with his wife. They don't want to move a 2nd car and wants someone to take up the notes. Poppa does just that and puts Ebony's name on the title with him and big mama as co-owners.

"Yes! Yes! Thank you, poppa! Thank you, big mama! I have my *own* car! This is the bomb!" she says as she drives it back to the house, "Me and my baby got navy blue cars."

Little does she know, big mama and poppa had gotten this car because it's the same color as Ajay's. They knew the 2 of them would like that.

As soon as she gets home, she calls April and Yolanda. Then poppa lets her go and pick them up. They come back and the 3 of them wash and clean it up. It's Friday evening and they want to go riding. Then she plans to come back and call Ajay and her crew. Poppa says it's alright for them to go riding but they have to be careful. They promise they will. After they're dressed in some riding clothes, they leave.

They go show the car to Ron, who's on the phone with Chill when they arrive. She tells Chill about her car. He tells her the crew will help her get it to Cleveland. She's super excited. She finds out that Jb had gotten a Buick Regal, 2 days ago and it's clean too. She thinks about all of her crew, who have cars now. Chill and Renee's Blazer, Jr's Cutlass, Bre and Stoney's van, Tonya's Sentra, Ajay's six four, Rob's caddy, which he got in February, Jb's Regal and her Honda Accord. Her crew has wheels now.

73

Everyone will have a ride and no one will have to be crowded, ever again. To accessorize her car, Ron has 1 of his homeboys do a custom tag for her. She gets an airbrushed tag for the front of the car, which reads; *Ajay's Girl*. It's navy blue, baby blue and platinum, which matches the navy blue car, perfectly. Ajay wants to finish tricking it out, after she gets it home.

Her, April and Yolanda are inseparable, now that she has a ride and can go pick them up. They furnish all the gas and fast food while she drives. They play basketball at the park, every day. They go riding together, every night and spend a lot of time at Ron's house.

Smiley high school's graduation is the following night. Saturday, May 24th. Big John is in Houston. It's an unscheduled stop, he's been planning since hearing about Ebony's fight with Sonya, Tina and Shuntay. Plus her last encounter with Ray, in the school hallway. Ray is graduating and had signed a scholarship with the University of Ann Arbor Michigan, back in April. He'll be attending school there, in the fall. John is planning to speak to him about him aggravating Ebony. He'll do it after the graduation ceremonies are done.

Ebony, April and Yolanda are going to graduation. John rides with them, in Ebony's car. After the ceremony, he confronts Raymond and as usual, Raymond acts in a respectful way when John confronts him. Only because he's phony. He's always bitching up whenever a man confronts him. He apologizes to John and Ebony but she can tell he isn't sincere. He's visibly embarrassed by John being up in his face but what can he do? He apologizes a 2nd time, then walks away. John doesn't believe 1 word he said but he knows if he hits him, he'll go to jail. Ray walks off, down the way, to where Sonya, Shuntay and Tina are waiting for him. As soon as they walk off, Ebony, John and her friends go to her car and leave. They take John back to big mama's house, then they go riding. There are several parties going on, for graduation. They go to Ron's party because that's where Ebony feels safest. She knows her crew are okay with Ron and he has her back. Her and her girls have a great time and spread the word about their upcoming party. At the end of the night, they come to big mama's house. April and Yolanda are spending the night.

Wednesday, May 28, is a half day of school at Smiley, for the underclassmen. School is finally out for the summer. John wants to drop the girls at school before he leaves out for Arizona. They decline his offer. Poppa is letting Ebony drive her car to school for the last day. The 3 girls look forward to their party tonight, which has been the talk of campus for the last week. Ebony drives her car to school and her girls ride with her.
74

After school, they check in with big mama. Then go to Ron's to set up. But when they arrive, him and his wife Carolyn have everything ready to go. All they have to do is go home and get dressed. April is dating Charles now. Yolanda had introduced the 2 of them, while at 1 of Ron's parties, in March. They're planning to stay the night at Ron's, after the party. Ebony is going to take Yolanda and her boyfriend David to the motel, on her way home. Charles and David was always in Ron's crew. Now April and Yolanda are. Since they're dating in that crew. Ebony loves that. They go get dressed early, then head to Ron's house in South Acres.

The party is on and everybody is having a great time. Sonya, Shuntay and Tina show up. Carolyn tells them they have to leave. Carolyn and her female crew, don't mix with them and never did. It turned out to be true, just as Ebony had figured from the beginning. These 3 girls are backstabbing, *try to fuck your man while pretending to be your friend,* types of girls. She'd pegged them just right, on her big mama's porch, a year and a half ago. They're loose like Anita's crew and not joined by *anyone,* who deems them self respectable.

After they leave, Raymond shows up. He asks Ron if he can chill. He tells him, "hell no," and orders him out. He leaves pissed off. The rest of the partiers are straight. There is no real disorder for the rest of the night.

By party's end, Ebony, April and Yolanda are danced out. They've had such a good time and danced so much, that Ebony is almost sad to be leaving them in less than a week. She wishes they were going back with her. They talk and clown around while the partygoers file out. They help Carolyn clean up, before Ebony, Yolanda and David say goodnight to Ron, Carolyn, April, Charles and their crew. Ebony has to drop Yolanda and David at their motel room. Ron had reserved it, earlier in the week.

On their way, Ebony think she sees Raymond's car in her rearview. But she isn't certain. Eventually, the car turns on a side street and she relaxes. Thinking she was being paranoid. She drops Yolanda and David off and heads on home. She's going to call Ajay, at Rob's, when she gets in.

In Cleveland, Angel has finally hooked up with Ajay. She's very excited to finally get some of his time and dick. They share a brief session at Rob's apartment. That is, until Jan arrives and cuts the scene short. He gets to take Angel home, only after promising Jan he'll come straight back. That only left him time for a little more of Angel's *lip service,* in his car. He heads to her mother's apartment and parks in front of her building. He gets his, then heads back to the U. As soon as he walks back into the apartment, Jan gets all over his case, as he knew she would. He smiles and goes to bed in the
75

spare bedroom. The room which will be his, if he ever decides to *officially* move in. He thinks about calling Ebony to see how her party went. But it's too late to call big mama's house. He knows she'll call him when she gets in. He fluffs his pillows and falls asleep, almost immediately.

Ebony is pulling into big mama's yard. She turns off her car, grabs her bag and keys. She gets out and remotely locks up her Honda Accord.

"It's about time you made it here. I've been waiting on you," comes a startling whisper from directly behind her.

She whips around to see that it's none other than, Raymond White! He *had* been following her, earlier. He had taken a shortcut to big mama's house, parked down the block and waited quietly, near the carport, for her to pull in. He has a pistol in 1 of his hands. She's terrified as she tries to back away. He puts the gun to the nape of her neck, while he has his arm wrapped tightly around her shoulders. He demands that she walk down the street to his car.

"No Raymond," she tries, "Leave me *alone*."

He orders her to shut up. Then he whispers,

"If you try to get loud, I'm gonna shoot your ass. Now, let's go."

She should have told him to shoot her right there on poppa's driveway. Because then, she would've seen that he wasn't gangster at all. He's a punk ass bitch. Just like she'd summed him up to be. But there's something about having a gun to your head that makes you not want to be so bold. What would Ajay do, she wonders. She wishes he was here now. Against her better judgment, she walks slowly away from the house. She looks over her shoulders, hoping her poppa, who sits up and waits until she comes home, looks out the window. But it's late and no one is looking out for her. She has to look out for herself. Her and her alone. Tears form in her eyes. She has no idea of what his plans are. He keeps his arm around her shoulders, so anyone passing will think they're just a couple of teenagers, out on a stroll. He moves the gun to her side. She walks and begs him to *please* let her go home. He just laughs.

When they reach his car, he sits on the drivers side and quickly, snatches her into the car as he's scooting over to the passenger side. This forces her into the driver's seat. He makes her drive up the block, to the park. She starts to think, maybe if she isn't mean to him, then maybe he won't hurt her. But she doesn't know his *entire* reputation. She drives to the park and pulls in under the big tree, as he has instructed. She parks. He reaches over and turns off his engine.

"Bitch, you think you better than me," he says, undoing his pants.

76

She knows she's in trouble now. She starts to scream. All of a sudden, he hits her in her face with his open hand.

"Scream again and I'm gonna hit you with this muthafuckin pistol! Shut the fuck up and take off your shit!" he orders.

She doesn't. She knows she's not going too, either. She's not *that* scared. Not in a million years, will she disrobe for anyone except Ajay. *No way!*

"Did you hear what I said, bitch?!" he yells and punches her in her face, very hard.

Her neck snaps back and she hits her head on the steering wheel. She feels dazed but she's still conscience. He lays the gun on the floorboard and begins to violently tear at her clothes. He rips her shirt apart. She starts to fight him back. She punches him with everything she's got. He's punching her repeatedly while yanking her into his backseat.

"No!" she screams as she continues to fight. She screams, "Just kill me, Raymond! Kill me now! Kill me!"

She's willing to die before allowing him to have her. While he's determined that he's *going* to have her. He has ripped her bra apart and he's trying to feel her breast. She continues to fight him. She's not going to allow him to touch them. He reaches across the seat, quickly and grabs his pistol. He's back on top of her before she can reach for the door. He presses the gun against the center of her forehead and pulls the hammer back. She freezes. *I'm about to die. Do it! Do it!*

"If you don't calm your ass down! You're dead, bitch! Do you hear me?! I'm *sick* of your shit!" he yells, "You always got some muthafucka up in my face, about you! You caused my own homeboys to jump me, because of you! So if I'm gonna have to wear an ass whipping, then I'm gonna get my monies worth! Now lay your ass down and shut the fuck up!"

"Kill me, Raymond!" she screams, "You're gonna have to kill me! What are you waiting for?!"

She's still afraid but she refuses to let him have her, while she's breathing. If she can't beat him, then she's willing to die, this early spring morning. She can feel the pain from what *feels* like a gash on the top of her head. She can feel the warm blood flowing from her head and her lips. She pretends to beg for her life. Raymond is pulling down his pants. He lays on top of her. She still has on her shorts but her blouse is gone. Her bra is barely intact. When he first lays on top of her, she starts to feel helpless and her body is so uncomfortable. Finally, her inner warrior surfaces and kicks in.

Why is he doing this? No way is he gonna do this to me! Fuck that! My body is for Anthony Jackson and Anthony Jackson, only! I'm not trying to eye

77

another man, big mama! I'm not gonna do anything else with one, either. God give me the strength to fight him off of me. Or make him take my life!

He grabs for her breast and tries to suck on them. This disgusts her, so much, that she keeps shifting her back so he can't get a firm grip on them. She does this without alerting him that she's doing it, *purposely*. She feels that would surely set him off. He's fumbling over her breast, like a kid who has no skills whatsoever in the art of lovemaking. He's already aroused. She feels sick, just from feeling his mouth, lips and *even* his teeth, near her breast. He's biting her. He starts to talk to her in a muffled voice, as if it's pillow talk. She can't understand what he's trying to say but she never lies still. She *isn't* going to be had by him. He keeps trying to suck on her nipples and she can't take it anymore. She'll never forgive herself if she doesn't win. Ajay is the only man for her. And she's going to stay true to him. Even if it means loosing her life.

"Oh *God*! Anthony!" she screams, as she starts to punch him with all of her might and continues screaming. "Where are you, baby?! Please God! Anthony! Please, somebody!"

She screams and fights. Still she can't get him off of her. He punches her on the side of her face. She continues to scream. She continues to fight. He continues to hit her. She doesn't care if he hits her, at this point. If he's using his hands to punch. Then he can't be touching her body.

Suddenly, he puts the gun to her head again. She freezes again.

He's still not touching me. That's what I was trying to accomplish.

"Take off your muthafuckin pants, bitch! *Right* now!" he yells.

She isn't going to do it. He's going to *have* to kill her. She thinks about Ajay and how he'd feel about another man penetrating her. Or worse. How would he feel if she lets him take her life and if she didn't risk it all to keep their love true. How can she just lay there and let him ruin her life? Her life has been planned *with Ajay,* not Raymond.

Would he still want me? Would he blame me? What will my crew think? How will Anthony go on without me? Would he want to die too? I would if I couldn't have him next to me. I can't die. I have to kill Raymond.

"Take the muthafuckaz off, *now!*" Raymond screams again.

She's disoriented. But even unconsciously, she feels if she lets Raymond do this to her, Ajay will no longer want her. And if Ajay doesn't want her anymore, then she'd rather be dead.

Suddenly, she remembers the self defense tape she had watched in

78

her 7th grade *Health* class. She remembers the woman's voice on the tape. The voice went as follows;

"If you ever find yourself in a compromising situation. Try to make your attacker feel as though he can trust you. But all the while, look for an escape. And at your first available moment, disorient him by going for his jewels. This gives you a good thirty seconds to get away from him."

"Bitch if you don't get these pants off, I'm gonna shoot your ass. This is the last fuckin time I'm gonna tell you," he says as, this time he hits her in the face with the gun, for good measure.

That hurt her, pretty bad. She knows she has to either kill him or escape. Because he's not giving up.

"Okay," she says calmly, "Okay. Just don't hit me anymore and I'll do it, alright?" she whispers as calmly as she can without vomiting.

She thinks of Ajay and how much he *believes* in her. How much he *needs* her. How much he *loves* her. She thinks of how much they're relationship and love has grown in just this past year.

There is no way I'm gonna let him ruin what we have. He's not who my daddy wants for me and he won't have me. He's gonna have to kill me if this doesn't work. And my crew will kill him because they'll know he did it.

She's already prepared herself to die. But she'd much rather live. She's not ready to leave Ajay. She's not ready to walk away for her beautiful future with the man she loves.

I'm gonna live. And I'm gonna stay true to Anthony and my papa's legacy!

She has located the door handle. Now all she has to do is get him to raise up, just a *little* bit more.

"You're squashing me," she whispers, "I can't even get my hand on my buttons."

She said that so calmly, he thinks she's given up. That's because he doesn't know her, at all. He hasn't learned shit after all of the rejections she has sent his way. Which led him on this very desperate and deadly course. She's a panther at heart and was taught to *never* surrender. Never do anything she doesn't want to do. She coaxes him to ease up off of her, just a little bit more. He raises up onto his knees while still holding the gun to her head. She's able to reach the button on her shorts. She grabs for her button with 1 hand, bringing her knees up, pretending she has to lift her bottom to slide her shorts off. He feels as though he's won her over. He lays the gun down on the floor. *That's* what she had counted on. He starts trying to rub her

79

breast again while attempting to smooth talk her. He thinks he's won.

"It's about time you come on in and stop bullshitting, baby. It didn't even have to be like, *AH GOD!!!!!!*"

He screams after she knees him, as hard as she can, in his *balls*.

He doubles up in pain immediately. This is her chance to get away. She grabs the door handle and pulls it. She discovers he had locked the doors. She can't find the lock release.

Instead of panicking, she springs to the front and releases the locks. She has the presence of mind to grab her bag as she springs from the car.

I'm free! I have to run fast! Which way to big mama's?! This way! This way!

She runs back up the street as fast as she can, screaming and calling for help, the entire way. Just like the lady's voice on the tape said to do it. She's only 2 blocks from big mama's house. She runs hard. She runs for her love of Ajay. To keep it sacred. She runs for her life. She's a block away. She continues to scream as she runs. Several lights are coming on in houses along the street, as she passes them. She doesn't notice. She's trying to make it to big mama and poppa, before Raymond can recover. She can hear his car start up, as she nears the house. His engine races as he tears out of the park, very fast. He's coming up the street behind her. She screams louder and more frantic. He's behind her. She knows he's going to kill her if he gets to her again. Or if he's able to get her back in his car, he'll never trust a word she says. She reaches big mama's yard, just as he closes the gap to 10 yards. She runs onto the porch, screaming and banging on the doors, walls and windows. She's making all the noise she can. Still like the voice in the video said too. If he gets out, someone will see him when he shoots her. Four of her neighbors have made it out to the street. They're calling her name but she can't hear them. The porch light is on. Poppa had heard her before she got to the yard. He's already at the door. He wondered where she was when he looked out and saw her car. He had stayed up in the living room, waiting on her. He had already called the police, just to make sure they didn't have a girl fitting her description or worse.

"Big mama! Help me, Poppa!" she yells and beats on the door.

She isn't about to search for her keys. She needs to make as much noise as possible, beating and banging.

Raymond notices the neighbors running out of their houses and toward big mama's. He wisely accelerates when he gets closer. He decides to speed away as Poppa turns on the living room light and flings their front door open.

"Help me! Help me, please! Please don't let him get to me again, poppa!"

80

"Ebony, what happened to you!?" poppa asks as he hugs her and pulls her inside of the house. "What happened to you, baby girl? Tell poppa who hurt you and I'll go get 'em."

"Raymond tried to hurt me, poppa! Her tore off my shirt. I fought! I fought him! I wouldn't let him hurt me! I wouldn't let him take me!"

Big mama slips on her robe and enters the living room, just as poppa gets Ebony inside and sits her on the couch.

"Oh my *dear Lord*. What's wrong, baby!?! What *happened* to you!" she screams and burst into tears when she see Ebony's shirt is missing.

She grabs Ebony and holds her close, while she imagines the worst.

"Mama got you. Nobody can hurt you now. Mama got you," she says, trying to calm her down and calm herself down too.

Poppa dials 911 while big mama puts a robe around Ebony. She sends him to get a blanket from the living room closet while they wait for the police and ambulance to arrive. Poppa is heated already and he doesn't even know the full story yet. Several of the neighbors are here. They heard Ebony's terrified screams while they witnessed her running home. They have a description of the car and are very willing to help. Big mama and poppa are like family to everyone in this neighborhood. Whether or not to cooperate, isn't even a question. Big mama puts some ice on Ebony's face. Her lips are busted and she's bleeding from her head, nose and forearm. Her body's shivering uncontrollably, from nerves. Her shirt is completely gone and her bra was barely hanging on, before big mama covered her up. She has a robe on and she's still shivering. Poppa gets the blanket and puts it around her.

Five cars from Houston police come immediately, along with an ambulance. Poppa already had them in route, for a routine drive through. Ebony isn't in *any* condition to talk to them, so they get statements from the neighbors. Two squad cars go to the park to look for evidence while the paramedics attend to Ebony. The witnesses give a description of the car.

Eventually Ebony tells them it was Raymond White. She tells them the kind of car he's in. The color, make, model, everything she knows.

"My blouse is still in it or it was when I jumped out," Ebony says, "I didn't try to find it. I just ran for my life."

The police call in the description. The officers at the park, radio back that they've found part of her blouse as several more units arrive. There are even more cars out looking for Raymond White. Ebony tells them the area where he lives is the 5th ward. She isn't sure of *where* he lives, exactly. Big mama and poppa give statements as well. They tell them they have a contact number for Carolyn Banks and she'll, most likely, be able to give them an address for Raymond. Then her and poppa remind them of the previous

81

harassment complaints they've already filed on Raymond White. They tell them to check with Smiley high school officials and security. Because it's well documented. Plus they have police reports at the school for every time he had bothered her. Big mama shows them her copies of each incident and the police get Raymond's address from those. The paramedics say Ebony will need to go to the hospital for further care. Big mama goes to get her purse. Poppa goes and gets his *gun*. They're going to meet Ebony at the hospital. But Ebony becomes hysterical again. She doesn't want to go in the ambulance without big mama and poppa. They agree to let big mama ride inside with her, while poppa follows in his Lincoln. He has his loaded .45 in the car. He's very ready to kill, Raymond White. He's going to make certain his granddaughter is okay, first. Then he's going to seek his own justice, as if he was still on the force.

At the hospital, the emergency room staff attend to Ebony as if she's royalty. Things are all a buzz around her. Mostly because of her grandparents. Big mama worked as an RN and retired after only 15 years, to work at home. Many of the senior staff worked with her and they know Ebony too. She's the All-star freshman from the local high school. Many of them know her as Eloise' granddaughter. They've heard of Raymond and are shocked to know that he had done this. Big mama stays by Ebony's side, the entire time. Poppa is in the hallway, outside the door, pressing the police for information and demanding results. He's upset. He wants Raymond locked up immediately. "Or I'm gonna kill him, *myself*," he warns.
He retired after 15 years too. He was a police captain, so the cops move on his command and with expedience, to get results for his granddaughter.

The staff sedate Ebony after she returns from x-ray. Her left wrist is broken. She had to have 12 stitches for the gash on the top of her head. Her nose had been badly bruised but it isn't broken. She has multiple bruises all over her face, shoulders and chest. There are bite marks on her chest, breast and neck. She received 22 stitches on her right forearm. She cut herself on his drivers door when she bolted from the car. The staff checked her out and gives big mama and poppa the relief they needed. They inform them that she hadn't been raped. They are *very* relieved.

After a few hours, things calm down. Ebony goes to sleep with the help of the anesthesia. She jumps and screams throughout her, otherwise peaceful rest. Poppa leaves after she's about to be moved to her private room. He's going to get Mr. George and they're going to look for Raymond. Ebony's resting now and big mama has to call Pearl. Ebony is admitted into a private room. It's nearly 4am when big mama phones her daughter.
82

"Hello," Pearl answers.

"Hi, Pearlie. How are you?" big mama asks.

"I'm fine, mama. How are you? How's my baby?" she asks.

"We're okay but I need to tell you something."

"What is it, mama? What's wrong?" Pearl asks as she's able to hear in her mothers voice that something's not right.

"Honey. It's baby girl. She was-"

"What, mama?! Is she alive?!" Pearl yells.

"Yes she's very much alive. But I need you to calm down. She's alright," she says.

"What happened?" Pearl asks and her voice is very impatient.

"She was attacked-"

"Oh God! *Oh God! Lord no*! Mama is she okay? Who hurt my *baby*?!" Pearl asks as she starts to cry.

"It was Raymond, messing with her again. He beat her up after her party. He was trying to rape her but he didn't get the chance too. Because she beat him and fought him off of her," big mama says bluntly, "And she bruised him pretty good, in the process."

Pearl cries frantically on the other end of the phone.

"She's got some bruises and stitches and her wrist is broken-"

"Oh my Lord, *God*! How is she, mama?! Please tell me the truth!"

"I'm telling you the truth, Pearl," she says, "She's gonna be okay. She's in the hospital and she's sleeping. They gave her a sedative to help her calm down. She had gotten herself worked up during the process. She's a fighter. She wasn't gonna allow him to take her virtue and he didn't get to do anything under her clothes. I'm in her private room with her. Right next to her bed and she's resting. She's got some scrapes and bruises but that's it. And baby, he's got some scrapes and bruises too. The same thing he did to her. She did to him. The doctors have checked her thoroughly and she's going to be fine. The bruises and cuts will all heal. But listen to me and listen good. The most *important* thing is that she's alive and she *was not* raped. We can get her through this thing if we're strong for her, okay? Baby, calm down and just say a lil prayer. Thank the Lord it wasn't any worse. Thank God. He didn't succeed with what he was trying to do because he had a gun too. And Pearl, he beat her with it. She told me, she was willing to die. But she wasn't gonna allow him to have her. She told me all of this, in the ambulance. It could have been a lot worse."

Big mama tells her this in a calm voice. Still Pearl cries uncontrollably. There's no calming her down. Not right away.

Jb and Tank are just coming in from *The Chill Spot,* when they

83

overhear their mother, in her room, screaming and crying. They rush up the stairs and to her side immediately. They find her sitting on the edge of her bed, leaned over and holding her stomach, as if she's going to be sick.

"Ma, what's wrong with you? What's going on?" Tank asks.

Pearl's in no condition to talk, so Jb grabs the phone. They're both worried instantly. Thinking it's a call about their father.

"Hello? *Who is* this?" Jb asks, expecting to hear big John's boss.

He quickly identifies his big mama's voice and knows right away that it's about his little sister. Ebony was absolutely right with her thinking, when she was in Raymond's car preparing herself to die. She knew her family would know it was him if anything happened to her. Jb knows instantly. Whatever the problem is with his only sister, it has Raymond White's name written all over it. He talks to big mama in a calm voice, just as his father would. She tells him the whole story and from Jb's end of the conversation, his attitude, his gestures and comments, Tank can tell his twin has come to some sort of harm. He wants the details immediately.

"What happened to twin, *man*?" Tank asks, as he *impatiently waits* to hear what has his mother so upset.

Pearl is still crying and trying to tell them what happened. But Jb has the story firsthand, from big mama. And he's *pissed*. He gives the phone back to his mother, gives her a kiss on the cheek and wipes away her tears.

He says, "Calm down, ma. Don't worry about it. She's gonna be alright. We're gonna go get her and we're gonna handle that fool too."

Then he turns to Tank and says, "Come on, bro. We need to holla at crew." They hug their mother and tell her everything will be okay. Then rush out of the house and over to Chill's. They want to catch him before he lays down. Pearl doesn't even try to stop them. This is 1 time she wants them to handle their business, *anyway* they see fit. Meanwhile big mama is still on the phone. Pearl is a little calmer now but she's still crying as she talks.

"Mama let me speak to my baby," she says.

"Pearl, she's sedated," big mama says, "The doctor gave her a sedative and she needs to rest for awhile. You just do what you have to do to get help to her, alright? She's okay, right now. But I want Raymond's ass taken care of. Send those boys on before your daddy finds him *first*."

"Mama when she wakes up, tell her we're coming to get her," Pearl says, "Okay? Tell her that for me. Please tell her I love her and I'm gonna get her home. He won't hurt her, *anymore*. Her brothers are gonna make *sure* of that. Will you tell her as soon as she wakes up?"

She's still sobbing and feeling guilty, as she asks, "She's gonna be okay?"

"Yes, baby. It's gonna be alright," big mama says.

84

She tells Pearl that her father is already out looking for Raymond and so are the police.

Then suddenly the officer, who is assigned to Ebony's room, knocks on the door. Big mama tells him to come in and he does. He informs her that they had just apprehended Raymond White.

"He's in custody, misses Jones," the officer says, "We *got* him."

"Thank you, Lord!" big mama screams, then she relays the news to Pearl, "They arrested him, Pearlie. He's been picked up. He's in jail now. Send those boys on down here to take care of his ass."

She says it in front of the officer, who doesn't respond or seem to care.

"Mama we'll be there on the next flight out of here," Pearl says.

After several more minutes of conversation, Pearl reluctantly hangs up.

Instinctively, she grabs a suitcase and begins packing while dialing her phone. She calls granny and papa to tell them the news and to asks if they'll take Jesse and make sure he goes to school until she returns.

"I'm on my way to get him, right now. Just have his things ready," papa says, "And I want to suggest something about the trip to Houston."

"What is it, papa Jack?" she asks.

"Take Ajay along with you. Or let him go, *for you*. I know this is a trying time but you have many options. This situation *right here,* is one for her brothers, Ajay and her crew to handle. We're gonna make sure Ajay has a ticket because he won't stay behind. I guarantee it. But it's just my opinion. If you're short on tickets. Let them go. Me and Pearline are buying three tickets, so we'll get Tank, Jb and Ajay in the air. I know Chill and Renee are gonna get tickets. Her crew is gonna want to be there to handle that jackass. I want them to be there, for that same reason."

Pearl acknowledges his suggestion but says Ebony would never forgive her if she didn't go. He tells her that he's on his way to get Jesse and to keep thinking about his suggestion. They hang up and she calls John, on his portable phone to tell him the news.

He's livid. He tells her he's going to grab a flight from New Mexico and head to Houston. She tells him what his father suggested. He tells her, his father is right. She should let the guys meet him there to handle this. Ebony will understand. They hang up and Pearl gets dressed. She thinks about Ebony and how much pain she must be in. Not only physically but mentally too. She feels she's to blame for Ebony getting hurt.

If only she had let her see, "Ajay!" she shouts. "I'll make sure he knows he has a ticket and I want him to go with me. That's what I'll do."

She grabs her purse and goes to Chill's house.

When she arrives, they already know the story. Chill and Renee are

85

pacing the floor. Renee is on the phone with the airline. Chill is animated with every word. He paces back and forth, twisting his *Bulgaria* wrist watch with every step.

"Baby get as many tickets as we can. *Fuck it.* Everybody's riding on *this* one! This muthafucka gotta go!" he says to Renee, who's on the cell phone with Southwest Airlines, reserving 9 tickets to go with the 3 granny and papa reserved.

Granny had called her with the confirmation numbers and 3 names; Ajay, Jb and Tank. This gives the crew a total of 12 tickets, thus far. There's 1 for Chill, Renee, Tonya and Jb. Lynn, Tank, Nina and Jan. Bre, Rob, Jr and Ajay have tickets too. Renee and Chill know T-baby, Rich, Rebbie and June have to make this trip with them. Everyone will *want* to go. But someone has to stay and run the club. The females who are pregnant will stay home, as well. Chill says he'll decide who'll go after he alerts Ajay. But they're taking enough crew to handle business.

"Where *is* Ajay?" Pearl asks.

"He stayed at Rob's," Renee says.

"We're not even gonna tell him until it's time to go," Chill says, "He won't get it. He won't ever relax on this shit. Until he can see Ebony's eyes. He loves her *more* than he loves himself. Everyone is about to learn that, very shortly," he says, looking directly at mama Pearl.

He doesn't normally use foul language in the presence of any of their parents. But this isn't a normal situation. He's highly emotional as he apologizes to Pearl, over and over. She says she understands and has used some bad words today too. She tells him John was full of them too. But still she wants to speak with Ajay.

"I need to talk to him," she says as the crew looks stunned.

They aren't aware of the talks they've been having the past few months.

"We're gonna handle it, mama," Jb says but Pearl is out the door. She goes and gets her and Jesse's bags, then puts them on the porch. She gets him up and tells him to get dressed. Within minutes, papa is there.

"I want us to let big Kenny handle this one," papa reiterates, "His crew is just the medicine that bastard needs. I'd kill that son-of-a-bitch myself if I could get my hands on him. Pearl this is one for her *own* crew. We know she's not in any danger and all of her injuries are superficial. They'll all heal in a little while. But I don't want that bastard to sleep another peaceful night. I want him to be scared to close his damn eyes. And when he does, he needs to see Ajay, John Jr and Tank's faces. He needs to feel the wrath of what this family calls justice."

Poppa had called and riled papa up, even more. Pearl tells him she's still
86

thinking about his suggestion and that John and Jb had suggested the same. Papa says he and John had talked and he has talked to her father too. They all agree she should let Ebony's crew handle it. He gets Jesse into the car and heads back to *The Point*. Big mama will be calling granny with an update on Ebony, soon. He doesn't want to miss it.

As soon as they leave, Pearl gets in her car and heads to the U. She's going to get Ajay, herself. The only thing on her mind is her daughter's protection. She knows he'll protect her against anybody.
He even stopped me from hurting her. All I want from you Ajay, is to protect my baby. I know you care for her. I'm so sorry I forced her to stay away from here and you. I thought I was protecting her. I'm so sorry.

She still believes Ebony *has been* raped and her mother is trying to keep her from worrying by not telling her the real truth. She doesn't even know if she could stand to see her child in that condition. She can barely drive now. She's still crying as she thinks about what her husband and father-in-law suggested.

Renee is on the phone to Rob's apartment. She tells him and Jan what has happened to Ebony before Pearl can get there.

"Please don't let her tell Ajay," she says, "We're on our way."
She hangs up. Then her, Chill, Jb and Tank drive to the U. They call the rest of the crew from their cell phone.

Nina, Rebbie, Trisha and June. Rich, Lynn, Bre and Jan, Ajay and Bruce, all still have school. But instead of getting dressed for school, they're packing a bag. All except Ajay. He still doesn't know. He's exempt from his test so he's sleeping in. Tonya, Jr and Bre are going to pick up the rest of the crew. They'll meet at Rob's apartment.

Mama Jo is coming in from picking up Al from work, when they each get the news. They follow them to the U. Al wants to be there for Ajay.

Pearl is the first to arrive. Jan's waiting for her. She opens the door and invites her in.

"Where is Ajay?" Pearl asks.

"He's still asleep, mama P," she says, "We're not gonna say *anything* to him until it's time to leave. He'll go crazy, up in here, over this news. Mama P, he *loves* Ebony and with her being way down there a*nd hurt.* And he *can't* be there to know she's okay. He's gonna hurt somebody. We wanna keep him calm for as long as we can and as much as possible."
Rob gives Pearl a drink to calm her nerves. She takes a few sips of her *Hennessey* and *coke,* then she pours her heart out.
87

"I want Ajay to go and get my baby," she says, "I don't care if they're together. I wish I would've just let him see her. I'll buy another ticket if y'all need it. She's gonna want him to be there and I know she will. Probably more than she'll want me. I just want her to be alright."

She starts to cry again. Jan puts her arm around her and says, "It's okay, mama P. We know you didn't want anything to happen to her. She knows that too," she adds as she hands Pearl a box of Kleenex.

Once she's calmer, Pearl tells them the extent of Ebony's injuries as she knows them. Jan and Rob try to keep her calm and not allow her to go into Ajay's room.

"Mama P, you know we're gonna get that bastard, right?" Rob asks, "His ass is ours. *Period*. I don't know if you need to be there for that." Pearl doesn't bother to comment. She could care less about what happens to Raymond. Her only thoughts are of her daughter.

Chill and the others arrive at the same time and come inside the apartment. Nina and Rebbie are already in tears as they asks Pearl how Ebony's doing. T-baby isn't crying. She wants to fight somebody. June puts his arm around Rebbie. Nina goes to Tank and hugs him. Even though they haven't been getting along. They both love Ebony and she knows he's hurting, a lot. He hugs her and gives her a kiss. T-baby even allows Rich to comfort her. Everyone is there now. Ajay has to be told.

Chill, mama Jo, Al and Pearl go into the room where he's sleeping. Chill goes in, only as a buffer. He doesn't want Ajay to be calm about this one. He wants Raymond's head. Al leans over and shakes Ajay's shoulder.

"Ant. Get up, son," big Al says, "Get up. We need to talk to you."

Ajay turns over, rubbing his eyes and stretching. When he sees his mother, father, Pearl *and Chill* standing over him, he sits up quickly.

"What's up with y'all?" he asks, "What y'all thinking? I'm not up to nothing, if that's what y'all think. I just slept over here, that's all."

He thinks they are there to chastise him.

"We know. That's not why we came," Jo says, "It's Ebony. She's been hurt-"

"Ha? Hurt *how*? What do you mean she's been hurt, ma?" he interrupts and bolts to a sitting position with his feet on the floor.

"She's gonna be okay, Ant. But we want you to go and-"

"Hurt *how*? How did she get hurt?" he interrupts her again. His voice is growing louder, "What happened to her?"

"Let me talk to him, Jo," Pearl says.

"Somebody needs to talk to me. What's going on?"

Jo and Al leave the room. Chill stays by the door. Ajay is way to anxious.

88

"Ajay, I am so sorry I made my child go back down there. I was wrong-" she starts.

"Please mama P. Get to the *point!*" he yells.

He makes eye contact with her. She knows he has no patience for her stalling.

"Raymond beat up baby girl last night," she says in one breath, as the tears come back to her eyes.

Ajay frowns. Then he turns his head to 1 side as if the news has to enter 1 ear and travel around to the other ear. He squints his eyes as if he feels a migraine coming on. Then he jumps to his feet and puts on his shirt.

"Please, Ajay please, honey," Pearls says and cries, "Go and get my baby for me. She needs you. I know she does. Please go and get her."

Pearl pleads with him. Even though she doesn't have too. He's ready to go in an instant. He's dressed in record time as he grabs for his keys. Pearl is still talking as he walks by Chill and out of the room. He notices all of his crew in the front. That's when he knows it's bad. He doesn't say anything.

Chill tries to reassure him, saying, "She's alright," as he comes up behind him and places a hand on his shoulder.

"If she's alright, then why all of y'all here?" he asks, "She's not alright, bro. Don't lie to me. I told you to let me handle that bitch ass nigga, last year. He's gonna go on the run now. I know that already. *Fuck.*"

He plops down in the recliner and attempts to put on his *Timberlands.* But he's struggling. His hands are shaking so badly, he can't do it. He's too nervous. His mind is in Houston, obviously. Jan does the honors of lacing up and tying his boots while he stares at her. Everyone else is staring at him. This is the first time *most* of them have seen him, not in control of his emotions. The first time they've seen him show insecurity or confusion. It's a lot to take in. Big Al has seen it only a few times. He knows exactly where his son is, emotionally. Chill has witnessed it less times then Al. But he knows Ajay is ready to get this feeling over with.

"We're gonna handle this however you want," Chill says.

"Bout time," Ajay says and he's eerily calm all of a sudden. He asks, "When are we leaving?"

Al watches his son and recognizes the look in his eyes. Ajay wants to see Ebony and *make* her okay. It's the same look Al has when he's worried about his wife or his children. Because he has to protect them. Ajay fidgets with his shirt and doesn't make eye contact with anyone in the room. Al walks over and squats down in front of him.

He says, "Show them you're the man, son. You're gonna make everything okay for Ebony. That's what she needs you to do. Go and take care of her. I

89

want you to get her back home safely and you get back here too, alright?"
Ajay looks directly into his fathers eyes. No other words have to be said. Al
knows his point is received and at the same time, Ajay knows his father
knows *exactly* what emotions he's feeling. He knows he isn't going to do
something dumb. That helps them both relax. Al know Ajay isn't going to
go to Houston and make *any move* that's going to put Ebony in more
danger. Nor is he going to do anything that will cause him to lose sight of
her either. Al will explain it to Jo and Pearl later. So they don't worry that
Ajay is going to prison in Texas.

"We have a flight in less than three hours," Renee says.

"*What*!?" Ajay screams.

"That's the earliest one they *got*, Ajay," Renee says, "We got the
first thing out of here. Out of all the airlines."

"I need to go by your crib," he says to Chill, calmly.

"We got you, man," he answers.

"I'm not worried about no clothes," he says, still eerily calm, "I can
get clothes in Houston."

"Like I said. We got you, man," Chill repeats, just as calm.
He has already spoken to Ron. They're going to provide whatever weapons,
vehicles and motel rooms they'll need.

"Ajay, papa Jack got a ticket for you and I reserved tickets too,"
Pearl adds, "We wanted to make sure it was enough for you to get one."
He stares at her for a few seconds, then looks away. He wants to tell her
something to make her feel okay but he can't. His only concern is getting to
Ebony as soon as he possibly can and seeing her eyes. That's the place
where his real solace can be found. Regardless of what anyone says or does.

"We got tickets for everybody to go," Renee says, "Except the
expecting mothers and those who'll run the club. Everyone else is going."

"I don't give a damn *who go*. Let's just get the fuck on!" Ajay says
as he storms out the door and runs to his car, while everyone goes behind
him.

Arthur sees all of the cars at Rob's place. He comes tearing up the
sidewalk to see what's going on, just as everyone is coming out. Chill and Jr
fill him in. Now he wants to go too. But he has to stay and open up *The Chill
Spot*. Chill announces the list of who's going to Houston and who will stay
and run their businesses. Arthur, Kilo and Wayne, Tonya, Bre and Bruce
will stay. And with the help of their Greeks and parents, operate the
businesses until the rest of the crew returns.

Chill, Renee, Ajay and Jr are going to Houston. Rob, Jb, Tank and
June are going too. They're shipping some essentials before the flight to
90

insure they have everything in place. Rich, Jan and Lynn, Nina, Rebbie and T-baby are making the trip to check on Ebony too. She has to have her girls there. Lynn and Jan want to find Sonya and Shuntay, so they can beat their asses. While the guys plan to do harm to Raymond White.

Those who are going have been announced and Pearl hasn't been named. Papa and John had talked to Chill and they told him to have Pearl stay behind and they'll come later. But actually, John is planning to meet them there. He doesn't want Pearl to be there to hold *him* back from his mission with Raymond, about his only daughter.

Chill, Al and Jo pull Pearl to the side. They tell her, they know she's feeling guilty but they don't feel that's a good thing for Ebony, right now. Besides, they want the crew to handle this 1 just as papa and John suggested. And deep down, so does Pearl. They are all angry and sick of Raymond's meddling.

"Mama Pearl, why don't you stay here and let us take care of it," Chill says, "I know you have two tickets. We'll use the twelve we have plus your two and take our crew. Here, take this money. There's extra money to send her flowers, plants and gifts too. Let us use the tickets and you send some gifts to her room. We'll handle the hands on part. O*kay?*"

"No way. I have to be there for my baby," Pearls tries, "She'll never forgive me for not coming to get her."

"She'll forgive you because you're sending us, instead," he says, "Ebony is gonna want someone to come down there and have a show of force. She knows her big brother Chill is gonna do just that. And she knows Ajay *will not rest* until he puts a foot in Raymond's ass. That *right there* is the reason she won't be angry with you, mama P. It'll actually help her to see that you do accept him. Because *you're sending* him. She'll want to see him more than any of us. Because she'll be looking for someone to take Raymond to task for hurting her. She knows Ajay will. She'll be alright with that. Okay? I'll make sure she knows *you* wanted him to come and get her. *Alright*? Big John and papa called me and told me, *not* to let you go down there. I have to listen to my fathers. You *know* that. Please mama P. You know I was raised in this family, so I have my orders."

It takes a lot of reasoning while Ajay is growing more impatient by the minute. Finally he comes over and says, "Mama P, do you remember the talks we've had this year?"

"Yes."

"Do you believe, I mean *really believe,* that Ebony will be mad if you send me and you don't go?" he asks.

"No. I think she'll forgive me if I send you, instead," Pearl says,

91

TIME TO GROW-RELOADED-TIME WILL REVEAL 2

"Because she'll know I approve and that I won't interfere when she tries to see you."

"Then can I go in your place?" he asks.

"Will you call as soon as you talk to her?" Pearl asks as she sobs.

"Yes ma'am. You've got my word."

"Okay. I'll stay here," she says.

Finally, with help from Jo and Al, they convince Pearl to stay in Cleveland.

"Besides Pearl, John will be down there," big Al says, "And he says no sooner than she's released, she'll be flying back."

"John could be more of a problem then a solution," Pearl says as she concedes, "But okay. I'll stay here. I just need to know every change. *Everything.*"

It's settled. The crew get their bags. Pearl, Jo and Al, with the help of Tonya, Bre and Arthur, take them to the airport. They board their flight ahead of schedule and are in route to Houston, in under 2 hours.

Ajay is quiet throughout the flight. He says nothing and wisely, no one says anything to him. He still doesn't know the extent of the injuries Ebony sustained. No one wants to tell him unless he ask. He doesn't ask. As far as he's concerned, Ebony is the *only* person who can tell him how she's doing. His thoughts are jumbled in his head, at this point. He closes his eyes and lays his head back on the head rest.

Just hurry up and get me to my baby, please. I need to see her and know she's okay. Then, God knows, I'm killing Raymond's muthafuckin ass.

Poppa picks John up from the airport and brings him to the hospital. He arrives at 1:00pm. Ebony is still sleeping. Big mama tells him she had only awakened briefly, about an hour ago.

"She was muttering something. I couldn't understand what she was trying to say," she says, "The anesthesia is something she's not use too. She was sailing when she woke up," big mama laughs, "That stuff will have her sleeping for twenty four hours, straight. She's not use to being under."

Initially John can't speak. He looks at his daughter. He's pissed, as any father who loves his daughter, would be. Then he puts his arm under her head, hugs her, holds her head to his chest and cuddles her to him. He starts to cry.

"Why in *hell* would he do this to my baby? Daddy's here, baby girl. I'm here now," he whispers in her ear, "I'm gonna kill his ass. Don't you worry, none. He won't get away with hurting daddy's girl."

He stays with her a long while and calls Pearl to let her know he's there. Big mama goes for a walk, to stretch her legs and get some fresh air. When she
92

returns, the doctor is in the room with the latest news. John is still on the phone with Pearl. According to her medical reports, Ebony is going to be fine. There is no extensive physical damage to her head. She'll have to wear a cast on her wrist for 6 weeks. There aren't any other broken bones and the stitches can come out in 7 days. He prescribes pain medication and antibiotics for her. They had given her a tetanus shot and all of her other test were clear. With Pearl on the phone, John wants to know if she was raped. The doctor assures them both that she wasn't. Then he leaves the room. John gets back to his conversation with Pearl.

"Are the guys on the way?" he asks.

"Yes and the girls too. Fourteen of them left this morning," she says, "They should be there by three. All of the guys came except Bruce. Bre and Tonya stayed because they're pregnant and don't need to be there."

"Good. We'll get some shit done before I leave here," he says.

"John don't do anything foolish," she says.

"I won't baby. He's done that already."

She starts to go on but he isn't in the mood to be talked down. He says, "That's the reason I didn't want you to come, baby. I'm not gonna be calm about this. This bastard tried to rape my daughter. *Our daughter*! Which tells me this is something he was intending to do, all along. For all of this time he's been bothering her, this is what he wanted to do. Now all I wanna do is bash his damn head in. And if I get my hands on him. That's *exactly* what I'm gonna do. You just get things in order, at East General. She's coming home as soon as they release her from here."

She tells him she's already working on getting her records transferred.

"Cool and thank you for listening to your man," he says, "I didn't want you down here trying to talk me out of protecting my baby girl."

"I know, John," she says, "Honey just make sure that you and all of her crew are able to leave there, when she does. I'm calling Wheeler, just in case."

He tells her okay and they hang up. Then him and poppa leave the hospital heading to the jail to see about visiting Raymond.

When they arrive and try to sign in, they're told they can't visit him. No one can visit him except for his immediate family, his attorney and his coach. His coach had hired an attorney for him, nearly as soon as he was brought in. The limited visitation was ordered by the coach as well. John and poppa leave. They're going to visit the coach.

They arrive at his home, get out and are immediately invited in and asked to be seated. Once inside, John makes himself, *very* clear.

93

"Raymond is *going* to pay for what he did to my daughter," he says, "You can try to hide him all you want but he won't get away with hurting my daughter."

"His trial will determine his guilt or innocence," the coach says, "Let's not try *and* convict him before he even has a chance-"

"To what,.. *lie*?" poppa interrupts, "Ebony knows him and so do I. This is not about mistaken identity. I know his ass and you *know* I know him. Because I've been to the school, *many times*, about him bothering her. I've talked to you, *specifically*. You did absolutely nothing. Her blouse, that he tore off of her, was still in his car. There's no innocence for him."

"Teenagers have disagreements-"

"Her name is Ebony," John interrupts, "Say her *damn* name! Don't exclude her name. Because *then* you might not be able to remember that she's human. This wasn't no *damn* disagreement. This was an attack and an attempted rape. And it was on my daughter. My *only* daughter."
The coach listens to John but doesn't offer any comment. He says he refuses to believe his star athlete is capable of such a deed.

"He's capable and you know, for a *fact*, he is," John says, "This ain't the first damn time we've talked on that matter either. He's capable. He's a sorry son-of-a-bitch who tries to take advantage of girls. You know his history, man. Just because the other girls didn't do anything about it, doesn't make it any less rape. He wasn't successful in raping my daughter because she's a warrior. But he tried too. He beat her up. He had a gun and was threatening to kill her if she didn't give in. Still she didn't give in to him. Those are the things he's capable of, sir. Whether you like hearing it or not. You shouldn't condone or try to hide his behavior."

"I don't condone it, mister Brown," he says, "I'd just like to see him have a fair trial and a chance to make it *to* trial."

"I would've liked to have seen my granddaughter attend her going away party and make it back to my home without this bastard trying to take her innocence," poppa says, "But he saw fit to try and change that. And even though he wasn't successful in raping her, he did beat her and put her in the hospital. He's gonna pay his debt. One way or the other, he's gonna be held accountable."

"He most definitely will be," John adds.

"I just don't believe he's capable of what you're saying," the coach reiterates.
Oh really? I know he is and he's gonna find out what the price is, for fucking with my family.

94

"What the *hell* is wrong with you, man!" poppa screams.

John loses it. He can't stay seated anymore. He jumps up and punches the coach, knocking him to the floor. He commences to choking him. He chokes him nearly unconscious, before he lets up. He kicks him while he's sprawled out on his living room floor. Then storms out of his home. He's shouting obscenities and threats as he and poppa drive off, heading back to the hospital. The coach's neighbors stand and watch as they leave.

At 3:45pm, the flight from Cleveland lands. Chill gets the van and the car, Ron had reserved at the rental agency and they head to the hospital. The Houston crew had already arrived at the hospital and they've just finished their visitation when they receive word, Chill and the crew have touched down and are in route to the hospital.

"Well it's time to get things poppin, then," Charles says.

April adds, "True. Cause Ajay don't play when it comes to my girl, Ebony."

"He's coming here, ready to knock him down," Yolanda says.

"No shit," Ron whispers as the crew files down the hall.

The crew arrives and are greeted by April, Yolanda and Carolyn, Ron, Charles and David. Big mama had called to tell April and Yolanda, this afternoon. But Ron had already made them aware. He's pissed off that Raymond did such a dumb ass deed. And even more angry, because he had hung around his *hood* to see when she left. Even after he'd told him to leave.

The staff have to regulate Ebony's visitors to no more than 4, at a time. Her girls don't want to wait another second. Nina, Rebbie, T-baby and Lynn go in. Ajay leans against the wall. Big mama comes over and hugs him. She see that he's disengaged from the others, like he wants privacy.

"She's fine, baby. She'll be so glad to know you're here," she says. He hugs her and hangs on for a minute longer. She can tell he's hurting and he's worried too. Still he says nothing and she knows not to pry.

Inside Ebony's room, her girls begin to cry as soon as they lay eyes on her. She's all bandaged, battered and bruised. They can't handle it and soon have to be brought out. Ajay watches as they come out. The wrinkles in his forehead deepen. Jan, Jb, Tank and Rob go in next. Jb can't stand it and comes back out immediately. He's angry as he heads outside of the hospital. Jr goes in. He comes out with Jan, Tank and Rob. Chill, Renee, June and Rich go in. Chill and Renee talk to her while June and Rich stare at her in shock. Shock which turns to anger, just as it had with the others.

"We're gonna take care of it, Ebony," Chill whispers, "Don't you even sweat it. You know I always had your back any time a nigga try to hurt you and I got it even more now."

95

His eyes well up with tears. Seeing her in a helpless state, reminds him of when she was 6 and he was 13, all over again.

He says, "This shit here wasn't even called for. Not at all."

June and Rich leave the room. Renee leaves with them, going to get Ajay. She tells him, he can go in.

"Nah, that's alright. I'll wait," he says as he turns his stare to Ron and Charles. He asks, "Where's he at?"

"He's still in lock up," David says.

"We're gonna bail him out when they post it," Charles adds.

"And hand deliver him to you," Ron says.

"Uh huh," is Ajay's response.

Then there's silence. The crew are discussing the sleeping arrangements, Ron and Carolyn provided them with. Ron and Carolyn have the same status in Houston that Chill and Renee have in Cleveland. The crew accept their offer with gratitude as they prepare to leave the hospital for the motel. Chill isn't ready to leave, just yet. He won't leave until Ajay goes in with Ebony. He knows Ajay isn't going to share his visit with anyone. He wants to witness him go in, so he can get a gauge on where he is, mentally.

"Ajay, you haven't been in," Chill says, "You have to let her know you're here, man."

"I'm going in by myself," he says, "When everybody leaves."

Chill gives him a hug. Then he turns his attention to the rest of his crew. He doesn't even have to say much. They know Ajay wants privacy. They all head to the cafeteria and take big mama with them, so they can treat her to lunch. They all head down the hall, leaving Ajay alone outside of Ebony's door. He turns to face the room.

A few minutes later, he walks in and closes the door behind him. He stands just inside of it for a few more seconds, looking down at the floor. He's still doing the same thing he's done since learning about her attack. Trying to *imagine* what condition she's in. He finally looks up at her, from across the room. Like a magnet, he's drawn to her. He walks slowly over to her bed, sits down next to her and takes a closer look. His eyes tighten. His lips tremble. He's angrier, instantly, as he stares at her. He touches her lips and her face. He says nothing. He rubs her hair gently, then her face again. He needs to see her eyes and hear her voice. She's only a shell of herself without her beautiful eyes and her sultry voice. He needs a response. He continues touching her face, waiting on a reaction. A reaction he knows will come for him and him only. Because it has too. Ebony knows him better than anyone else knows him. So she knows if she's conscience, that he needs reassurance. He touches her lips. She begins to breathe harder, as her

96

eyelids flutter. She knows he's there. She can feel his presence. He talks to her.

"Are you gonna wake up for me?" he asks, "I really need to know how you're doing. I need that so much, right now. So I can breathe, baby."
She continues breathing heavy. *Heavier*. Her chest rises and falls faster.
He darns a light smile as he leans over and whispers in her ear,
"Ebony wake up. You know who it is. It's your man. Wake up, baby," he whispers desperately and directly into her ear. "Come on. Please baby girl."
She begins to squirm. Her eyelids flutter again. She tries to open them. He smiles. It's working. *He's working*.
"That's it. Wake on up," he says, "I need you to see me."
She opens her eyes, sees his face and starts to cry immediately. He raises her head up and holds it in his arms, close to his heart.
"I'm here, baby girl," he says, "Don't cry. I'm here now. I'm here to take care of you."

"It....was...Ray-," she tries but he interrupts her.

"I know. I already know it was him," he says and she cries harder.
"Ebony I'm gonna kill him. You know that, right?" he says very calmly.
"Yes."

"Listen to me," he whispers, "I don't know what he did and it don't matter to me, alright? I'm killing his ass and that's all it is to it."

"Anthony," she says softly.

"Yea baby."

"He didn't get to do it. I didn't let him," she whispers.

"I don't wanna know, baby," he says again.

"Please listen to me," she says softly, trying to clear her throat.
He holds her head while she speaks slowly. He wants to know she's alright but a part of him is afraid to know the details. Still she clears her throat and gives him a 1st hand account of her attack. Because she knows, he needs to know that she wasn't raped. Whether he admits or not. She *knows* him.

"He tried to get me but... I didn't let him. I fought him. I fought for.... For everything I love. I fought for you and for me. I fought for us..... And our love, Anthony. I wasn't..... I couldn't....... let him hurt.....hurt us. That's why I fought. I fought, *so hard*. He had a gun, Anthony.... he kept pointing it to my head, ...saying he was gonna shoot me if I didn't take my shorts off," she says, getting stronger as she speaks, "But Anthony. I kept telling him to kill me. Kill me. Cause I would rather die," she begins to cry hard again.
He rubs her face and head. He listens. She continues, "I would rather die then to hurt you like that. I would rather die." Her voice fades.
97

"Baby you can't hurt me by something another muafucka did. But I'm glad you fought him. I'm glad you,... he..., *man*," he starts to cry too and says, "Baby you're okay now. Your man is here. You know I'm gonna handle my business. But I'm wondering. Why didn't you have your pistol with you?" he asks.

She tells him she had never carried it because she was afraid of it.

"I remember how I felt when you told me you needed me," she whispers, "That gave me all the protection I needed. I didn't need a pistol to stop a coward like Raymond. I proved that to myself, last night."

"I do need you. That's why I have to take care of you and keep you around. I don't wanna live if you're not in my life. That's how I feel."

"I know," she says, "I feel the same way, Anthony. You know that night before I left. When you told me you had killed somebody before?"

"Uh huh."

"I know I told you that I didn't understand how you could just take somebody's life, like that. Do you remember?" she asks.

"Oh yea," he says, "I remember."

"*I could do it now*," she says and her voice is as clear as a bell.

"I hear you. But you're not gonna have too, baby. I got this one. Believe me," he says as he lifts her head and kisses her swollen lips.

"Ssss oh. That's the first time a kiss ever hurt me," she says.

He laughs and she tries to smile but it hurts, too much.

"Anthony I *wanna* smile for you but I'm all messed up," she says, "I missed you, so much. I hate it took this for you to be able to come back."

"Baby these are scrapes and bruises, *you know*? All of this will heal," he says, "There's nothing that can fuck wit your beauty. Not in my eyes. I know where to look. It's in your heart. I'm here to make *damn sure* it stays there. But don't ever tell anybody else to kill you. Please don't do that again. He's a punk ass bitch, so he wasn't gonna shoot you anyway. He was just trying to scare you into giving up. He ain't got a clue about the fight in, *my girl*. You didn't know it but he had raped Sonya and Shuntay. Ron told Chill about it when he called them to tell them about your attack. Chill told your dad about it and he's pissed off, just like me. Because that news should've been out so everybody would've known what he was capable of doing. Big mama didn't even know. So the way I figure, he was hot for you, from jump. Then after he saw you wasn't interested. He had plans of having you anyway."

She starts to comment but he cuts her off saying, "Don't say anything. You don't have too. Those ho's wasn't raised right and we all knew that shit. They know what he did to them. They didn't report it because he convinced

98

them that it was a mistake. And after knowing what he did to them, they went to him and tried to blame us for what they got *themselves* into. They told him it was us because they wanted him to go at you, the way that he did. I ain't got no love for none of them muthafuckaz and they're gonna meet their maker. Ron's crew is all in," he whispers, "They're gonna deliver this nigga and them ho's, to the crew. *Your crew.* They're all gettin it. You're gonna learn how much I love, need and care for you, behind this bullshit here. If you don't know already. I need you, Ebony. You're the best thing in my life. So don't ever tell anybody they can just *kill* you. Hell no. I don't want nobody to kill you. They would be killing me too. And all my plans for the future. I don't wanna live without you in my life, okay? So don't ever tell anybody that again. Do you hear me?"

"Okay."

"That's my only complaint out of everything you've told me. I'm proud of you and I'm so happy that you're my girl. I'm so glad you fought," he says and smiles, "I'm taking you home with me, okay? Mama P sent me to get you. We're gonna call her right now. So she'll know you're up and you're alright. She didn't even feel like she had to come. She sent me. She wanted me to come and take care of you. Because all she wants is for you to know that she's gonna be there for you. She came and got me and told me about it. She asks me to take care of her daughter and that's exactly what I'm gonna do, from now on. I'm not leaving here without you," he says.

She hugs him as hard as she can. She still cries.

"I'm taking my baby home. I mean that," he says, wrapping her up in his arms as she cries.

He can't hold back his tears. They hold each other and cry together.

99

CHAPTER 15

C-TOWN BOUND!

Ajay stays with Ebony until the late evening. The crew had gone on to the motel, to get settled in. They return to pick him up after Ebony is resting. John and poppa are with the crew when they return. They've been out talking to witnesses, as well as students from Smiley high. Big mama stays with Ebony while they all go to Ron's house. They're anxious to get some news on Raymond's bail hearing which is set for 9:00am, tomorrow morning. Ron gives them information on Raymond's family and where they can be located. Now all they have to do is wait for him to bond out.

Before they left the hospital, poppa gave Chill the use of Ebony's car to drive and suggested they return the rental. They took his advice.

With Ebony's car, the crew come up with a new part to their plan. A lady crew member will drive it and keep April and Yolanda close, at all times. They're hoping to bait Raymond to try and finish the job when he bails out. They want to snuff out Shuntay, Sonya and Tina, in the process. The crew females want to stomp them for setting Ebony up, in the 1st place.

Tonight, Renee drives Ebony's car while April, Yolanda, Lynn and Jan ride with her. They hope to see either or all 3 of the hood rats. But they have no luck tonight.

Chill and Ajay stay at Ron's, most of the night, smoking party flavors and waiting for a call about Raymond's release. The rest of the crew hit the streets. Charles and David ride along and show them the spots to check out. Even though the crew's arrival had been secret, Raymond's clique is ghost. The crew can't find anyone who conspired against *Ajay's girl*. They return to Ron's house around 10:30pm, only to learn that Ajay and Chill still haven't heard any news either. Nina, Rebbie and T-baby go back to the hospital to stay with Ebony, while big mama goes home to rest. The rest of the crew hit the nightspots, all the while searching for new leads. It seems all of Ebony's conspirers are hiding out, so they turn in early. They want to be well rested for tomorrow.

Friday morning they get up at 7am and go back to *Ron's house*. Before leaving the motel, Ajay calls the hospital to check on Ebony. She's in better spirits this morning. He figured she would be, since her girls had spent the night. She feels better but her appetite still hasn't come back. He wants her to eat so she can get her strength back and get released.

"You know you have to eat something, right baby?" he asks.

"I'm just not hungry, right now," she says.

"Okay but you're gonna eat when I come back out there," he says.

"When are you coming back?" she asks.

"I'm not sure. I need to peep things out first," he says, "But I'm gonna be there as soon as I can. Okay?"

"Okay. I'll see you then," she says, content he'll be back soon.

"In a minute, baby," he says and they hang up.

She feels better having her crew here *for her* and her girls here *with her*. She's so happy her mother sent her crew. She never thought Pearl would've put her feelings first. But according to Ajay and her girls, her mother wanted them to come and take care of her and Raymond. Instead of coming down to *baby her*.

Ajay had called her mother to tell her, she was awake and she got to speak to her briefly. She's had many phone calls from all of her family. Her father had been in to check on her throughout the night too. In addition, Tonya and Bre called and talked to her for a long time. She's also gotten calls from granny, all of the mothers in the crew, Coach H, April and Yolanda, which had her on the phone most of the morning. Jan, Renee and Lynn come by to see her after leaving the motel. They have April and Yolanda with them. They're picking up Rebbie, Nina and T-baby so they can meet the guys at Ron's house. Big mama is back to stay with her. Ron and Carolyn leave for the hearing while the crew wait at their house.

At the courthouse, they learn Ray's coach has arranged for him to be released, *only to him* and *only he* is allowed to post bail. During a phone call, Raymond had told his coach he fears for his life. He knows Ebony's crew and he knew they'd come to Houston after finding out what he'd done. He also knows they're tight with Ron and can get the inside scoop on his location, anywhere in the Houston area. Coach arranged to have him go and stay with relatives until his trial. Coach reminds the judge of Raymond's previous assault, earlier in the month, *'by some guys from his neighborhood'* and *'he needs to be protected.'* Coach has no idea the crew are here. Or if he does, Raymond had to have told him. Coach tells the judge about the visit he'd had from John and poppa, 2 days prior. With that alone, the judge permits Raymond to leave until his trial date. Trial is set for 6 months later. Coach leaves the courthouse with Raymond in his *Ford* Pickup. Ron and Carolyn follow them in a borrowed car. They phone the crew after they notice the coach taking the airport exit.

"Y'all need to get out here, man," Ron tells Chill, "It looks like these muafuckaz is heading for *Hobby*."

101

TIME TO GROW-RELOADED-TIME WILL REVEAL 2

The crew load up and hurry to the airport with plans of catching Raymond while he's in pre-boarding. But Coach is still a step ahead of them. He had arranged for 2 officers to escort them into the terminal and to the gate. He knows big John wants blood from Raymond. Especially after he'd spilled his. The cops are going to remain there until Raymond departs safely. Ron and the crew can't risk getting close. They have a hard time keeping Ajay from approaching Raymond at the gate. But eventually, Ajay does make his way around them and blends in with the other passengers. Before Chill can say anything, Ajay is in Raymond's line of sight. He stares him down. After catching 1 glimpse of Ajay, Raymond won't dare return the eye contact. Nor does he alert anyone that he's there. Nervously he waits for his flight to be called. Soon his flight boards and he heads to the tarmac. Ajay can't tell which city he's going too. There are 4 gates in the area, past the security checkpoint where Raymond was seated. He's either going to Spokane, Topeka, Jacksonville or Dallas. There's no way to know, for sure. Just like that, his trail is cold. Ron doesn't have a clue about whom he could be visiting in either of the 4 cities. He can only asks around and see if anyone else knows. Earlier in the courtroom, the judge didn't disclose the destination because the hearing was opened to the public and coach had made his case for disclosure. The crew have no idea where Raymond has gone. They're all upset that he has slipped through their fingers.

Ajay is visibly enraged on the trip back. Instead of going to the hospital, he asks Charles to take him to where the coach lives. He wants to take him out.
He says," I wanna take his head off for helping him, after the shit he did."
Chill agrees with Ajay but tells him they can find out where he lives, for now. But they'd have to come back for him after they've planned their exit.

"Man, *fuck* that! I want this muthafucka *now*, cuz!" Ajay yells.

"Keep your head. We're gonna get him," Chill says calmly.

"Fuck that, *we're gonna get him shit*, man. What's up wit y'all?!" Ajay shouts as he looks around the van at everyone, "I thought we was gonna follow my game plan with this bitch?! Now you *changing* shit? You saw baby girl, *right*?"

"We're gonna get him, man," Chill reiterates, "And you know this. But we have to strike like crew always do. With a plan, *alright*?"
Ajay kicks the seat in front of him, in frustration. Eventually he calms down a bit, as his crew coax him into waiting for the plan.

"Fuck *all* this shit," he says, starting off calm, "Take me to my baby, Junior. Y'all muafuckaz come get me when y'all ready to get down. Y'all *feelin'* me? Ha? This is bullshit. I ain't wit it at all. Fuck this riding
102

around and shit, crew! I didn't come down here to *sightsee*!" he yells.

No one says a word but Charles smiles. He loves Ajay's attitude just as much as he hates Raymond. Chill loves Ajay's passion when it comes to Ebony but he knows Al didn't send his only son down here, for him to allow him to get locked up. Ajay rambles on, all the way to the hospital.

"Let me the fuck outta this van," he says as they pull into the parking lot of the hospital.

Jr drops him off. The rest of them go to the motel to freshen up and hook back up with their girl.

The females are still yearning to catch up with Shuntay and her rats. Yolanda and April tell them about a park where everybody hangs out. They guess the 5 girls or at least, some of them, will be there at some point during their stay. The crew decide they'll go out there later. Folks usually gather in the evening after the sun goes down, is what April tells them. They make plans to hang out at the park.

Chill and Ron get together and organize a hit on the coach. Ron suggest it go down after Chill and his crew are gone. Chill is more in favor of his own crew handling it. But for now, things are too hot. Especially with the coach telling the judge about John and poppa threatening and beating him. Plus he knows Ajay will not wait if he sees the coach either.

"It's gonna go down," Chill says to Ron, "Just let things calm down. I know Ajay's fired up but I can't let that get in the way of his logical thinking. When he settles down, he'll see it like this too. He's a soldier that loves his girl and that's all good. But my brother is going to the NBA. I refuse to allow him to fuck that up. I'll do Raymond's bitch ass in a heart beat, *in front* of the Houston Police station, before I allow any of my crew fuck their lives up."

Ron agrees. He knows how, as a young gangster, 1 is ready to go out there on emotion, before thinking things through carefully.

Ron says, "He's gonna be cool. But I see that *that homeboy* is down for his lady. When you have a lady that's true, *like she is,* you're suppose to be. I'm riding for those two. No doubt."

Chill gives him a pound as Ron says, "You've got a solid crew, brother. We're family now and we're definitely gonna keep this link fed."

"Oh for *damn* sho," Chill agrees, "We're gonna feed the hell out of this link, bro. We're all in now. We got a lot of money to make and we're gonna keep churning this butter like dairy farmers." They laugh.

Ajay is at the hospital by lunchtime. He stays on Ebony's case until she eats at least, a third of her food.

"I was hoping you would eat more than that," Ajay says.

103

"I can't eat anymore right now, baby. Okay?" she pleads.

"Alright that's good for now," he says, "That's better than nothing. Like I heard you did this morning. Baby girl you didn't eat anything, earlier."

He smiles at her as he takes her tray to the nurse, who has come to the door to pick it up.

"Can she keep the apple and the cake in the fridge, for later?" Ajay asks.

"She certainly can. I'll mark it and put it up for her," the nurse says with a smile.

She winks at Ebony as she leaves the room. Signaling to her that she has a good man. Earlier, this same nurse told Ebony that Ajay had called the nurses station and asked for their assistance in making sure she had all of her favorite foods. He said it was because he wanted her to eat good for lunch.

Once the nurse leaves, her doctor comes in. He has great news.

"As long as you continue to improve like you are and regain your strength, you should be able to go home tomorrow morning."

She's excited. She know the sooner she gets out of the hospital, the sooner she can go to Cleveland. Ajay doesn't want her in here, 1 day longer than she needs to be.

"What did I tell you?" he asks, "You've gotta eat to get your strength back, baby," he adds, "Then I can take you home."

She agrees with him. The doctor leaves and they're alone again.

"I'll be back in a few minutes," he says as he leaves the room, heading to the gift shop.

He gets her some more flowers and another teddy bear. She has received many get-well wishes, cards, plants and flowers from everyone. Her room is filled with everything her crew thinks will make her feel better. Ajay brings back a deck of cards too.

"Come on, so I can whoop up on your head in some *spades,* for awhile," he says and they laugh.

He scrambles the deck while displaying his poker face. She giggles. He's great for her recovery. They play cards for most of the afternoon. He calls Chill to check in. After learning they're still planning to lay off of the coach, he tells Chill he's staying at the hospital, "But I need some gear."

Within the half hour, the crew are there to take him to the motel to shower and change clothes. All of the females stay with Ebony while he's gone. They play several games of spades.

Ajay returns by dinner time and has dinner with her. The crew go

104

to the cafeteria. She eats most of her dinner which makes him happy. Everyone leaves, leaving them alone again.

Mama Jo, Al, granny and papa call again. Granny wants to fly down but Ebony convinces her she's alright and she'll see her, real soon. After the call, her and Ajay watch TV and talk. Then he calls Pearl, who's on duty at *her* hospital, to let her know Ebony is still doing fine. Ebony looks on, in shock. She didn't know Ajay and Pearl had formed a trusting relationship since she's been gone. But she will soon. Ajay tells Pearl what the doctor said today. Then he gives Ebony the phone. She takes it and thanks her for wanting Ajay to come and look after her.

"He's trying to make me eat, *too* much, though," she says.
Pearl agrees with Ajay, saying, "You need to eat, baby. So you can get your strength and come on home."

"My doctor said I can go home in the morning, if I'm doing good."

"That's wonderful, baby girl. I want you to come home as soon as you can travel, okay?" Pearl says, fighting back tears.

"Alright," Ebony says, feeling like she'll cry if her mother does.

"I made arrangements for your charts to be sent to East General," Pearl says, "You can have the stitches removed here and the cast too. I took care of that, first thing. I just want you to come home on the first flight out of there. I want you to come home, so I can look after you."

"What about my car?" she asks.

"Daddy worked it out with big Chill, to get your car home. I want you on a plane, baby. Not on the road. Not for *that* long," Pearl says.
Then Ajay tells Ebony that Jr, Rob, Chill and Jb are driving her car back.

"You mean you didn't wanna drive it back, for me?" she asks him.

"I'm going with you, baby," he answers quickly, "I'm not taking my eyes off you, *no more*. Not unless you're in Cleveland, near *my* crew."
Pearl laughs, on the other end of the phone. She likes his answer, a lot.
Then she remembers and says, "Oh yes. Tell daddy to be sure Jb and Lynn get back here in time for graduation night."
Ebony says, "Mama Jo and big Al already told me the same thing."
They exchange phone hugs and kisses before hanging up. That makes them both feel, even better.

The female crew don't run into Shuntay and her rats while at the park. They'll go back tomorrow. Renee bring Ebony's car to Ajay, so he can drive her to big mama's in the morning. Nina, Rebbie and T-baby spend the night at big mama's, to help her pack up Ebony's things. They call and talk to Ebony while they're packing. She tells them what to leave and what to ship. She's leaving her stereo, a gift for her 14th birthday.
105

That's so big mama and poppa knows, she plans to come back and visit. Ajay is planning to come back with her. Before they hang up, she tells her girls they can sign her cast. Ajay had to sign it first and he has. He'd drawn a heart and written, *only his name* in it.

"You didn't write my name," she says after hanging up the phone.

"Because that's my heart," he explains, "If you want your name in a heart. You have to draw it on me, because I have yours." He smiles.

"So I have *your* heart?" she asks, smiling and looking into his eyes.

"You see it, *don't* you?" he asks as they smile at each other.

"You can be so sweet, sometimes. *You know that?*" she asks, looking serious.

"Don't let that get out. Muafuckaz might think I'm soft," he says and they laugh.

"That's just for me to know," she says, still looking into his eyes.

"Exactly. It's bout time you get it," he says, kissing her still, slightly swollen lips.

She's getting tired, so he tells her to lay down and get some sleep. He tucks her covers up tight to her chin and kisses her goodnight. He hasn't told her Raymond got away. He feels the news will depress her. Besides, he doesn't want to talk about Raymond, if she doesn't.

He goes to the nurses station to get some blankets, to make up the sofa bed, for himself. He positions it so it sits between her bed and the door. She watches him as he takes off his shoes and top shirt.

"I'm gonna sleep in everything else," he says with a smile, "I can't get naked up in here and have these nurses trying to get at me."

"No we can't have that," she says as they laugh.

He lays down and covers himself. They watch TV until she falls asleep. He watches her, while thinking of all he's going to do to Raymond for putting her here.

Very early the next morning, the doctor releases Ebony to big mama and poppa. Ajay drives her home. The crew are waiting when she gets there. Her girls had set up her bedroom with the gifts from her hospital room. She feels a bit self conscience about her appearance, so she opts to stay in her room, instead of downstairs with everyone else.

The girls help big mama prepare a large dinner which takes them well into the late afternoon. Ron, his family and crew come over to hang out and have dinner too.

After dinner, they're all going back to the park. Nina, T-baby and Rebbie want Ebony to go with them but she declines.

106

"I'm messed up," she says, "I don't wanna be seen like this."

"Ebony, we know what you look like and so does everybody else," Nina offers.

"We don't want you sitting in this room, worrying about that trick," T-baby says.

"You're our beautiful sister," Rebbie says, "Bruises can't fuck with that."

"Thanks y'all. Really. But I'm just not ready to go out," she says.
They try to change her mind. But after 30 minutes of trying, unsuccessfully, they give up.

Renee has called the airport and updated their tickets to the next morning. Chill's has been refunded and 1 is purchased for Ebony. Jr, Jb and Rob cash their's in. They're going to use the cash for the drive back to Cleveland, in Ebony's car. Ron hooks up a nice package for them as well.

Later, they all go back to the softball and baseball complex. It's the big hang out spot for Houston's youth, which April and Yolanda had shown them. They spot Sonya and Shuntay before they get out of their vehicles. The girls want Ebony to be there when they whoop these rats asses.

"Ajay we should go back and get baby girl," Lynn says, "We want her to be here when we stomp these bitches out."

"Alright, lets go back," he says, "I'll get her to come. But she's not fighting *nobody* today."

"Cool," her girls say, "We got this, *anyway*."

They go back to the house and Ajay goes up to Ebony's room. He convinces her to ride along.

"You don't have to get out, baby," he says, "Your girls about to handle these ho's, *for* you. They just want you to be there and I do too."

"Okay. As long as I don't have to get out."
Even though the temperature has soared to well above 80 degrees, she puts on blue jeans, a button-down oxford shirt and a baseball cap. Lynn puts a little makeup on her face, to hide the bruises, while Ajay gives his input.

"I really don't like makeup on her," he says.
He's willing to accept it for this mission. He adds, "She's pretty without it."
Ebony blushes as Lynn laughs.

"Okay, Ajay," Lynn says, "You do the same thing to mama when she gets dolled up."

"So do pops," he says as he returns the laugh, "We've got some beautiful ladies, who don't need that paint on them to look good."
They all laugh, as Lynn finishes and they head out again.

On the way back, they stop at a mini mall so Ajay can buy Ebony a pair of sunglasses.

"Yea, kid. You're *way* fly now," Jan says with a smile.

Ebony returns the smile as they head back to the park.

They arrive and pull under a huge tree, 30 yards behind the bleachers where the 3 rats are seated. Renee, Jan and Lynn, plus Nina, Rebbie and T-baby get out of the van and walk over and stand behind the bleachers. They reconnect with Carolyn and her Houston crew. They are there to back them up. Ron's going to make sure this doesn't turn into some sort of *coastal* thing. He lets his set know that this beat down is legit and warranted. Shuntay and company still haven't spotted the Cleveland crew. Not until the male crew get out and walk from behind the bleachers and pass their girls. They go around and stand directly in front of the bleachers where the rats are seated. As soon as the rats see the Cleveland guys, they come down. They're pretending to be concerned about Ebony. The female crew are standing with Carolyn's posse, just out of direct view, as the rats start the phony inquiries.

Sonya asks the guys, "How is Ebony doing?"

"Why don't you ask her, yourself," Chill says, "She's in her car."

The 3 rats, who are soon joined by Tammy and Rolanda, the 2 who had instigated the fight at school, walk over to the Accord and their future ass whooping. Ajay and the guys come along. The rats still don't notice the females. Not until they, along with Carolyn's crew, walk up behind them. Other bystanders get word there's about to be a brawl. They join in and follow behind the females. When the rats get to the car, Ajay tells Ebony to get out. She does. Only because she knows the attention won't be on her, for long. And she wants to see this stomping, up close and personal. After she's out, Ajay starts to unleash a verbal assault.

"Y'all muafuckaz set my baby up," he says, "Because she got me and I didn't wanna fuck y'all."

"No we didn't have nothing-" Shuntay starts.

"Shut your *lying* ass up, bitch," Jb breaks in, "I know, already. You fucked up when you decided to fuck with *my* lil sister."

"No shit. That's my twin. Y'all know, from when I lived here, how I hold it down for her," Tank adds, "Y'all muthafuckaz fixing to get it, though. Damn this idol chatter, as *Willie D* would say it."

The guys chuckle. They're calm. They know justice is about to be served. All the crew girls, along with the H-town girls, surround the rats. Along with others who want to see a fight. The rats are trying to talk the ladies into squashing it. They have the nerve to look to Ebony to help them.

108

"Ebony we don't want no problems with your crew," Tina tries, after she notices the obvious, "Tell them we ain't got no beef with you."

"Don't say shit to her," Renee cuts in, "We know you ho's set her up. Y'all had that bitch ass nigga to go and fuck with her because of y'all trifling asses. So you *do* have a problem. A *big* muthafuckin problem."

"Yes they do and we already owe you ho's a stomping, anyway," Lynn says as she squares off, "Which one of y'all ho's fucked my man?"

"I'm getting in all they asses," Jan says, "I'm already knowing the deal."

"Fuck all this talking and shit, *crew*. Lets do this!" T-baby yells and punches Sonya in her face.

Her girls swarm and the fight is on. All the guys stand around them, making sure nobody can get in or out. Ebony wants to join in now.

"I wanna get some too!" she yells.

"No, baby. You stay right here with me," Ajay says as he puts his arms around her, "Let them handle it, this time."

But she can't take watching her crew fight and not join in. Even though her girls are very much in charge.

"I can't just stand here," she says as she pulls away from him.

She turns around and picks up a broken off branch, from under a tree and shouts, "Let me in!"

Ajay doesn't try to stop her. She has only 1 good wrist and arm, so she chokes up on the branch, like a baseball bat. Then she waits for a clear swing. T-baby, who's handling Tina, notices her waiting to get some shine. She shoves Tina toward her. Ebony clocks her as hard as she can, then waits on the next lick. 1 by 1, she gets a chance to hit each of her 5 conspirers, at *least* once. When her girls have all 5 rats on the ground stomping them, she joins in and manages to break a sweat. She gets so involved, Ajay has to pull her back. Once the guys are satisfied, they stop the fight. Onlookers urge them to let the girls continue. April and Yolanda want to fight along with the crew but Renee says no. Only because she doesn't want the conspirers to retaliate on them, after the crew are gone.

Carolyn quickly assures Renee, "That *will not* be happening as long as I'm around and these funky ass bitches, already know. They know I hand out ass whippings for a living."

She's the head female of her crew in South Acres. Most of them are here today. Her crew is rough. They fight for the love of it. It doesn't even have to be a cause. April and Yolanda are a part of them now, so Carolyn tells Renee to rest her mind, "Nobody's gonna fuck with my crew either."

"I hear *that*, sister," Renee says as they hug each other and laugh.

109

Once the fight's over, Chill tells everyone to load up, "Let's roll out."
He turns to Sonya and her whipped posse of rats and says, "Tell your bitch ass nigga, this shit *here,* is nothing compared to what's in store for his coward ass."
The 5 rats, battered and beaten, lay there groaning and wincing. Looking as if their injuries will leave them in far worse shape then Ebony's. Ajay opens the passenger door for Ebony. T-baby, Nina and Rebbie hop in the back seat. The rest of the crew get into the van.

As they leave for the motel, other fights break out with the rats. Other girls who'd been put in similar situations as Ebony, decided to get some justice as well. As the rats continue to get what they deserve, the crew go to the motel to freshen up and cool out for the rest of the evening.
First mission accomplished!

Ron and his crew come to the motel to kick it. They play spades, drink, eat and smoke. They also fill the crew in on the full history of Raymond and the rapes of Shuntay, Sonya and several other girls.

"I didn't know about it until after he tried to hurt Ebony," Yolanda tells the crew.

"My mother told us about it when big mama called," April adds, "She said she wished she had known big mama didn't know about him. Because she would've told her. Plus she knew Ebony wasn't about to go nowhere with him. So she thought she didn't have that to worry about."

"His ass wasn't successful, this time," Jb says, "And if I have my way, he won't live to fuck with nobody else."

"True that," Lynn adds.

"You'll get your way," Ajay adds.
The H-town crew prepare to leave around 1am, so the crew can get some rest for their trip, later this morning. April, Yolanda and Ebony say their goodbyes, as do all of the crew.

"We'll see you in four weeks," April says.

"Not this time, partner," Ebony says, "I'm not coming back for a long time. I'm going home for good, my southern sisters."

"But we're coming for the wedding," Yolanda says.
Carolyn has already told Renee that her and Ron are coming for the wedding ceremony and bringing their crew with them. Ebony's happy that her *true friends* from Houston are finally coming to her city. She wanted them to come this past Christmas. But their families wasn't able to send them. Unfortunately, Shuntay and Sonya had made the trip. That will not happen anymore.
110

TIME TO GROW-RELOADED-TIME WILL REVEAL 2

Once the Houston crew leaves and before the crew turn in for bed, they call big mama and poppa to let them know everyone is staying at the motel. They'll see them by 8am. Their flight leaves at noon. Chill, Rob, Jb and Jr will get on the road at 9am, for the drive to Cleveland.

They all say goodnight to each other and go to their separate rooms. T-baby stayed in the room with Rich during the entire trip. They're slowly getting things back on track. Nina and Tank made up on the plane trip to Houston. Ebony sleeps in the bed with Ajay but they don't have sex. He holds her while she sleeps. He senses her tension, once she *did* manage to fall asleep. But she was very restless, the entire night.

The next morning, they have breakfast at big mama's. Ebony calls Pearl with their flight information while big mama packs a lunch for the guys who are driving back. The driving crew say goodbye and leave for Cleveland. The rest of the crew check in with their families, then say their goodbyes as well.

Their flight leaves on time. They turn their attention back to getting home and handling any *unfinished* business. But Raymond is still at the forefront of all of their minds. In flight, Ebony tries to explain to Ajay about her reluctance to have sex last night.

"Its alright, baby. I understand," he says.
She senses some tense feelings from him. But for now, she isn't going to talk about the incident. She's still not even comfortable thinking about it.

They arrive in Cleveland 2 hours late and tired. Everyone goes home and goes straight to bed. The school crew have 2 and a half days to complete before summer break. Plus they have make-up work.

The next day, Pearl has an errand to run and Ajay shows up to visit Ebony. He's going to do his make-up work while he's there. He heads up to her room as Pearl is leaving. She doesn't object. When he walks into Ebony's room, she's happy to see him. She expects her mother to come in right behind him.

"Hey," she says, when he walks in.
"Hey, baby," he says, "How are you feeling today?"
"Good but I'm hungry. My mama's making lunch?"
"Nah, she had to run some errands," he says, "I told her I'll baby-sit you until she comes back." He chuckles.
"She let you come to my room and she left?"
"Yes."
"Wow. Y'all *are* closer. I can see that now," she says, "She would

111

never have done that before I went to Houston and you know it."

"Yea we are closer," he says, "But so are you and I."

She never thought her mother would allow him to come to her room when she wasn't going to be home but she has. Ebony is slowly starting to see the bond Ajay had made with her mother while she was in Houston.

She tries to help Ajay with his make up work but he doesn't need her too. He's always been good with his books. He finishes his work, on his own, then they make lunch and eat together. They talk and watch TV, afterwards. He stays until she falls asleep and Pearl returns. Before he leaves, Pearl asks if she can talk with him.

"I know it's a school night. But I need to talk to you when you get some time, okay?"

He think she still feels guilty about how she'd acted in the past, about him and Ebony's relationship.

He says, "Yes ma'am. I'll be back right after school, to check on baby girl. We can talk then. Before I go back for after-school practice."

She agrees, they say goodnight and he goes to Chill's house to go to sleep.

Him and Pearl don't talk the next day because she gets called in to the hospital early. He stays with Ebony. Then later after practice, him and the guys go out on the set. They always have profits to collect and more dirt to do. The females convince Ebony to come to Tonya's and help with the wedding plans and arrangements. They finish the ceremony programs and make their appointments to be fitted for their dresses.

Once school is out for the summer, everyone's focus turns to Jb and Lynn's graduation which is this Saturday. They're having a big graduation party at *The Chill Spot,* afterwards.

By Saturday, Ebony's bruises are milder but still visible. She wants to go to Graduation, nonetheless. Lynn does her makeup under mild protest from Ajay, once again. Nina and Tonya do hair for all of the girls in the crew. They're great at cosmetology. So good, in fact, many females in their area make appointments with them to get a fresh do. Nina and Tonya plan to open their own salon at their mini mall property, in the future. Tonya is already taking business and cosmetology classes at CSU. Nina plans to follow in her footsteps after she graduates high school.

Jb and Lynn signed scholarships to *Georgia Tech* in Atlanta. They'll be heading to there in the fall.

The crew and their parents attend graduation 1991, together.

112

After the ceremony, they go to the club for the after party. Lynn and Jb have a motel room, just as they did on prom night. Ebony attends the party but she stays upstairs most of the night. She isn't ready to answer questions about her cast or her bruises. She's ready to leave the party, fairly early, so Ajay takes her home. Tank and Nina are going to use her car while her and Ajay go to Chill's house, where they're all alone.

Ajay starts to do what comes natural to him. When he tries to kiss her, she backs away. Then after realizing she'd done so, she steps forward and gives him a kiss on the lips. She looks away, then into his eyes. He'd noticed her reluctance to be affectionate at the party, in the car and all week since they returned from Houston.

"You're still not ready for this, ha?" he asks as he places his fingertips under her chin and lifts her head.

"I wanna be. But every time I try to get into it. I still see-," she starts before he interrupts her.

"This is me. *Anthony*, alright? The man who looks out for you. I'm not that stupid ass from down the way. I wouldn't hurt you like that."

"Anthony, it's not you. It's me. I just need some more time."

"Alright. Whatever you say. I'm cool," he says as he steps away.

He's obviously disappointed but tries not to let it show. He sits on the couch, grabs the remote control and flicks on the TV. She sits down next to him but neither of them say much. She catches him staring at her but whenever she looks his way, he quickly looks in the other direction. She figures she'll try to strike up a conversation to avoid the silence.

"Was you going back to the party?" she asks.

"I was planning on kicking it with you," he says, "Why? Are you ready to go home or something?"

"Yes. I think I should. Because I'm kind of tired," she says, "And my wrist is itching and irritating me."

"Cool," he says, not trying to convince her to do otherwise.

But he's very disappointed. He can feel how tense her body is, at the moment. He doesn't know how she'll react if he tries to help her unwind, so he gets up and grabs his keys. He turns to her and says, "I'll walk you home."

They walk across the street to her house. He gives her a kiss on the cheek and says, "I'm not gonna try to take it no further. But just so you know. I miss you a lot, baby girl. I just want you to get back right. Okay?"

"Okay," she responds with a slight smile.

"I'll see ya, baby," he says.

"In a minute."

113

She goes inside, closes the door and leans back against it. She has a familiar feeling in her gut but she can't figure out why. She heads on up the stairs. *How can I have dé·jà vu and not know why?*

Anthony walks to his car, gets in and drives away. He's going back to the party. He's thinking as he drives.
That was one of the few times, me and Ebony have been alone together with the opportunity to fuck and we didn't. Will she ever come back to me? Will she ever really come back from this experience? What's it gonna take from me to get her through this? Do I have it in me? Will I wait for her? That's my baby. I have too.

For Ebony, he's going to wait. But for sex? Not Ajay. He's going to get his jimmy waxed tonight. Then tomorrow, he'll talk to mama Pearl about helping Ebony to come around. Not just for him but for all of the crew and her family too. As far as tonight, after the party, he's going to fuck Angel. *Why not? She's more than willing and I haven't had no pussy in weeks. I'm not waiting another day.*

He goes back to the club and hangs out with his crew. Angel and her friends are still there. She's happy to see him come back alone. He thinks about asking Rich to hook it up. But him and T-baby are cool again and Rich isn't even trying to go near Tameka. Tameka is seated with Angel, so Ajay gets Arthur to hook it up for him. He isn't about to approach another female in front of the crew ladies either. They wouldn't be cool with him doing that and neither would Chill, who makes that clear every chance he gets. He doesn't want Ebony to know, by the word of her sisters, that he has cheated on her. And if Ajay was to go inside The Chill Spot to get Angel, Ebony would definitely find out.
"She's gonna know it's true, if one of her girls tell her. It's not like if one of them ho's or somebody else say it. She's gonna take what crew say, to heart."
Chill has said that often and Ajay knows he's right. Besides, he never wants to see that sad look on her face again. The one he'd seen on 4th of July, when she saw him fucking Anita in his room. The same look she had when he was living with Darlene. He doesn't want to see that look, ever again and especially not now. He heads out to his car. He's not going to hang around the club a minute longer than he has too, once Angel comes out. He's not trying to be seen with her at all.
Inside, Arthur handles it like a pro. He tells Angel to meet Ajay

114

outside at his car. She does and they leave immediately. He takes her to Arthur's crib, where they spend the next half hour.

On the surface, Angel seems to be a really sweet girl, in a lot of ways. She doesn't seem like the promiscuous type. He hasn't heard 1 *ho report* on her. But then again, he hasn't asked around. He's been made aware of a few guys she's been with though. But it isn't a priority for him to know her past because she isn't his future. She seems like she might make someone a good woman, one day. But it won't be him. However, she *was* quick to jump on his dick and give him head with no hesitation. So later, on the way to take her home, he questions her about her habits.

"Hey look here," he starts, "I'm not complaining or nothing like that. But I'm just curious. You seem like a good girl and all. So why was you so quick to serve me?"

"Cause I heard that's what you like and I want you to like me, like I like you," she says in one breath, "Like the last time before y'all went down south. That's what you ask me to do. Plus the talk is out there."

"The talk? What talk is that?"

"That *that's* what the niggaz from the crew are into. The bitches who give the best head," she says boldly.

He thinks over her comment for a few seconds, while fighting the urge to laugh. Then he says, "First of all, there are no niggaz in my crew. You understand? There are only men and women in my crew. Make sure you get that tonight and don't ever come at me with that nigga shit again. Now if you wannabe a bitch, you can be a bitch if you like. That's on you. As far as the crew being into getting *head? Y*ea they're right. They're damn sho right," he says as he laughs and drives on. Then he says, "That's all a bitch can do for me and that's for sure."

If she wants to believe it, she can. He knows it isn't true of him and Ebony. But if it gets the *Angel's* of his world on their job, then cool. In Angel's case, it's much better than her conversation anyway. He gets to the parking lot of her mothers building. Still he has a question.

"Are you telling me *you'll* do whatever I want you to do?"

"Uh huh. I'm really feeling you, Anthony-"

"Don't call me, Anthony. Call me, Ajay," he cuts in.

"Sorry. Ajay I always have liked you. I've wanted to be with you since seventh grade. But you was always with girls from high school. So I figured you would think of me as being too young for you. Until I found out about Ebony," she says, "I have liked you since Abe Lincoln middle school."

"I like all ages of women. Anyway, its not the age. It's the attitude," he says, "You do what you suppose to do and I'll fuck you. I'm not gonna
115

say I'm looking for nobody to be up in my face, twenty four seven. I have a girl already and yes, her name is Ebony. Her place is held. It's solid. We can fuck when it's convenient for me, as long as you understand that."

"Alright. I guess that'll have to do, *for now*," she says.

"Forever," he says, "It's not up for compromise. Understand me?" Angel looks as if she doesn't want to believe him. She opens the car door and before getting out, she leans over to kiss him.

"I don't kiss either," he says quickly, "Unless it's Ebony."

She smiles, gets out, closes the door and goes inside. He heads to Chill's house.

Everyone has left the club. Some of the crew have stopped by Chill's. Ajay smokes with them, then goes to bed. Before falling asleep, he thinks about Ebony and how he misses her and being intimate with her too. She's the only girl who turns him on with only the thought of her. He thinks about the past times they've been sexual and his dick gets rock hard. He reminisces about her sex faces and it starts to throb.

"I need to cut this shit out, man," he says aloud, "Damn, I miss my baby. Lord knows."

He realizes he's talking to himself and smiles. He manages to remove the thoughts of sex with Ebony, from his mind. Only to replace them with thoughts of Raymond's demise.

Where you at, muthafucka?

He thinks about Ray's death, more than anything else, these days. He tries to appear calm when he's around Ebony. But the fact is, he's thought about it everyday, all day. He can't think about much else. Especially when he has to try not to think about sex, until Ebony is ready for it. Dreaming of ways to kill Raymond is the only thing that can take his attention away from thoughts of having sex with Ebony. There's no way he's going to let Raymond live his life after what he's done to, *Ajay's girl.*

"Shit. There's no fucking way," he says aloud.

Again he finds himself thinking of how many ways he can punish Raymond White before his certain death. Eventually, he clears his mind and falls asleep. But he tosses and turns, most of the night.

The next day after church, when Ajay and Pearl have their talk, they're joined by his parents. The 4 of them talk for a long while, in Pearl's living room. They get a lot of issues out in the open and resolve most of them. The parents let him know, they know he isn't using Ebony. They believe he genuinely cares for her and she genuinely cares for him too.

116

"I will never interfere with you and baby girl's relationship again," Pearl says, "Not as far as trying to stop it from happening, I won't. *Ever again*. I've learned a lot of things about myself, this past year. I just don't feel good about a lot of it, at the moment." She starts to cry.

"What happened to Ebony is *not* your fault, mama P," Ajay says, "Please don't cry. Don't blame yourself for what that animal did. You and I have talked a lot since she went down there. And I understand why you felt the way you did, when you sent her to Houston. We wasn't doing things the *right* way. She was breaking rules, just to see me. I didn't want her too but I wasn't doing anything to stop her, either. I also understood how much your feelings had changed, when you *sent me* to Houston to bring her back."

"I remember how you looked at me, at that motel, *that* night," Pearl says, "Everything in me told me you loved her. I want you to know that I've never thought you was bad for her. *Never*. It's just that I felt like she wasn't old enough for you, as strange as that sounds."

"Ant it was because you're more experienced than other young men, your age," Jo adds.

"But at the same time, he's more mature than a man his age," Al offers, "And you ladies can thank me, John and all the males in this crew, for that."

"Oh hush up, Allen," Jo says as they all laugh.

"*Seriously*, Joanna," Al says, "I already know my son is gonna be successful. And Ebony is gonna be successful too. They don't have any other choice. He knows if Ebony becomes pregnant, he has to drop out of school and go to work. He wants to play basketball as his career. He don't wanna mess that up. Every since I found out he liked Ebony, back when he was like five or six years old, me and John have been grooming him. He turned out to be *way* more mature than either of us thought. We did a *real* good job. But I *was mildly* surprised when I learned that she liked him already. I wasn't expecting that they was sexual though. That part threw me for a loop and I told him as much, the day after the motel situation. I asked him to back off and let her grow up. Neither of them backed off."

"Yes, she surprised me *too*," Pearl says, "But Ajay, you *are* mature. The way you stepped up to check Ebony when she sassed me back or didn't wanna speak to me. Even though I hit her with my hands. Something I will regret, for life. You still insisted she not hold a grudge against me and she changed. I saw *real* good things while she was in Houston, this time. I know it's because you was telling her to do the right things. Then you came to me, for her sake. I appreciate that and now I know. Even if you wasn't doing the right things, *yourself*. You wouldn't be willing to let harm come to her."

117

Ajay says, "Let me start with my pops, first. I don't ever wanna drop out of school for any reason. I have what it *takes* to make the NBA draft, like a *top* lottery pick. *Top ten.* So I'm not trying to make no babies until we get married. I wanna make a lot of money *for* Ebony," he says as he looks at Pearl, "It's not like she demands it because she doesn't. She would live in a tent with me, if that's all I had. But *I* want to make a lot because *I* wanna give her the world. I love Ebony with all of my heart," he admits, "That's new for me. There are things we still have to work on. I know that and we will. But we're not gonna leave each other alone. We both know that too. So I just think we need to come to some kind of an agreement. Because I can't hide with her. I'm not gonna try to hide, *no more*, either."

"Don't you get *too* cocky, up in here, Ant," Jo warns.

"He's not, Joanna," Al says, "The man is speaking his heart. I did the same thing. *Remember*? So did John. Now we have to trust the way we raised these two and recognize that they're doing what they see us doing. Standing strong for each other *and* for our love. That's what I *see* when I look at them. Even more so than some of the other couples. I don't doubt these two, at all. They know if they mess up, we're gonna be all over them."

"Mama P, she's just like you," Ajay says, "She wants everybody to feel equal. Do you remember when we would be on punishment and mama wouldn't let us have a treat?" he continues as Pearl smiles, "You would wait until she wasn't paying attention and still sneak and give those of us, who had gotten in trouble, a treat."

"And Ant, you was always in that trouble group," Jo says with a laugh.

"He was maturing," Al tries as they all laugh again.

Ajay says, "But for real, mama P would say, '*All of you are good kids and all of you are getting a treat. Just remember whenever someone tries to make you feel like you're bad. You're not.*' And you would smile at us and tell us to keep it a secret."

"I remember that," Pearl says and smiles, "And it's true. You were always a good kid."

"Ebony is the same way. She wants everybody to feel equal. She don't see bad in people. Even when I thought of myself as a bad person. She wouldn't hear it. When I first realized I liked her, I tried to shut it off because of you guys," he says, looking at Jo and Pearl, "But I can't and I won't. I don't even want too. She won't allow it anyway."

"She's stubborn and spoiled," Pearl admits, "When she wants something, she's steadfast."

"I love you and big John, just like my own parents," he says, "And

118

TIME TO GROW-RELOADED-TIME WILL REVEAL 2

I know y'all love me too. I knew it was never about whether I was good enough for her. But whether I would make sure she stayed good and kept her virtue. I wouldn't want her to ever change, any of that. I promise you. *All of you.* I will be more than responsible for her *and* with her. I *love* her and I really need to be able to step things up. Especially, right now. Because she's stuck in this mind frame of fear, almost. Because of what that fool did to her. I have to bring her back for all of us and I'm the only one who can. I need her in my life, to make it whole. I need the confident girl who went down there. Not the insecure one who came back. I have so much anger in my heart, at Raymond, for trying to steal her innocence. I would never want that gone. And I promise you, I'm gonna help her to come back from this and preserve that innocence too. I need her more than she'll ever need me. And it's for that very reason, that I'm sitting here pouring it all out. She's the prize in our relationship. Not me. I know that already. Just give me a chance and have faith in me."

Al smiles proudly and looks at his son. Jo is proud of him too. Pearl gets up to hug and thank him. She's willing to let them date, as long as the 2 of them remain respectful of the rules. The rules that they, as parents, set forth. John had already agreed by phone, before the meeting started. He and Al are more on Ajay's side than they are Jo and Pearl's side. But Jo and Pearl agree now also. They give their approval for him and Ebony to date. After the incident with Raymond and now this talk, they are most convinced Ajay and Ebony have staying power. Both of them still have a lot of growing up to do. But based on the accounts from big mama, poppa and his crew, on his actions following her attack and even his actions which they've witnessed, is enough to convince them that he truly wants to be more than just some fly by night fancy with her. Today, they give him their permission to date her. He thanks them.

After their talk, he goes upstairs to check on Ebony. She's due to have her stitches removed tomorrow. He expects her to be in a good mood. He's exactly right. She's excited about it and she darns a big smile when he mentions it to her.

"You know I'm glad about that, ha?" she says.

"Yea, I knew you'd be in a good mood today," he says as he reaches over and pinches her cheek.

"Ouch! Oh you *wanna be starting something*?" she says as she grabs his arm and tries to twist it behind his back.

"Who you suppose to be? *Michael Jackson*?" he asks jokingly.

"*He-he*," she sings, imitating *Michael Jackson* and being goofy, as they both laugh.

119

She struggles, 1-handed, trying to twist his arm back. He gives her the slightest resistance and proves to be *much* to strong for her. Eventually, she gives up. Something she would never have done before the attack. He tells her about the meeting he just had with their parents. She smiles and says, "Big mama and poppa told me to just hang in there and it'll happen."

"Big mama is my *dog*," he says as they laugh again.

He gloats about his so-called special relationship with her grandmother. She feel he's just laying it on thick, now that their parents have finally given them permission to date. Either way, she feels safe with Ajay. She knows he'll look out for her. They play cards and talk. She lets him look at her journal of poetry and songs. She wrote many of them, to and about him.

He says, "You wrote a lot of stuff down there, ha?"

"I had to do something at night time and on the weekends," she says with a smile, showing signs of the old Ebony today, by relaxing a little. She lets him kiss her, several times. But that's about as far as she'll go. He lets his mind wonder while they kiss. He envisions taking her to Chill's house and being intimate. He can see himself sucking on her neck and her breast. Naturally, he lets his hands roam. Then he takes his lips to her neck. She allows that too. She feels only mildly tense, to him. He goes for her breast and he senses her tense up. He stops.

Then he says, "It's time for me to *really* show you my car."

"It sure is," she says with a smile.

"You wanna go for a ride with me?" he asks as he stands up.

He pulls her up off of the futon and they head for the door.

"Can I drive?" she asks as she smiles.

He chuckles but doesn't offer an answer. She smiles too, as she follows him down the stairs. They asks their parents, who are still sitting in the living room, if he can take her riding in his car. They say it's okay. Him and Ebony head out the door and jump into his convertible. She sits right next to him. He can see their parents watching from Pearl's living room window. He starts up his Impala, backs out and takes her for a ride in his six four with the top down.

She loves riding in his car. She gets even more hyped when he tells her, he'll let her drive it. Though it's only after they get to the park, she still loves it. She parks next to their crew, who are already there. Ajay's car is clean. He had it detailed at their shop. She thinks he looks more like the pimp type with his car all chromed out. It was more obvious when she drove through the park past all the girls to get to the crew. Girls was calling his name, every few yards. He'd simply thrown up 1 finger as she drove past. He wasn't going to disrespect his girl by giving another girl attention.

120

Not to stop and talk to no ho's! Hell nah! I got my baby and she's who I need.

After they join the crew, Ebony hooks up with her girls. The 4 of them sit and talk next to Ajay's car. She declines their offer to go walking around. She doesn't even want to stay long. After only 30 minutes, she tells Ajay she's ready to leave. Her girls notice she's still shy about being outside. What Raymond did to her is affecting her life with everyone. Her girls miss being with her, as do her whole crew. That in itself is the fuel which keeps the fire burning under the pot which contains the crew's potion, for Ray's *definite* demise. They haven't given up on finding him. They're *going* to kill him. It's only a matter of time before he slips up and they find out his whereabouts. Big Chill feels the same as Ajay feels. The only way Ebony will ever relax is if she knows Raymond is forever out of reach of her. The crew are prepared to help her through this ordeal, by any means necessary.

When her and Ajay leave, the crew leaves also. All of the couples get together at Jr's house. Bre and Ajay are the only 2 there without a mate. Everyone knows why Bre is there alone. Stoney had been killed, 6 months prior. But it seems as though Ebony is dead too or still in Houston. She went home after they left the park. Instead of kicking it with her man and her crew. That's something she would never have done before Raymond attacked her. Tonight's move just adds more fuel to the crew's fire and their need to get Raymond White, gone for good.

The next day Pearl takes Ebony to Dr Stansfield to have her stitches removed. She's told her cast can come off in 3 weeks. But Ebony protests that, immediately.

"Oh mama. Does this mean I have to wear this thing while I'm in the wedding?" Ebony asks Pearl, with a sad expression on her face.

"Yes baby. It looks like it. But we can decorate it and make it match your dress. I'm sure aunt Sandy can fix it up."

"I want you to asks the doctor if she can take it off by the twenty eighth," she begs, "Even if it's *on* the twenty eighth. I just don't wanna have to take wedding pictures with it on. Because *every time* I look at the pictures, I'll think about what he did, instead of my families wedding."

"You make a very good point, baby. I'll talk to her and try-..... No, I'll *get* her to do something for you before the wedding, alright?" Pearl says and smiles. "That's not something you need to remember when you're trying to remember a crew wedding. We'll get her to do something."

"Alright. Thanks, ma," she says, returning the smile.

"You're welcome, sweetheart. You're very welcome," Pearl says.

121

She hugs her and gives her a kiss on her forehead. They leave the doctor's office and go to lunch. It's been a long time since they hung out together. They use to be very close. And thanks in large part to Ajay's efforts, they're finally able to work on getting that closeness and friendship back. Ebony's assault, in it's own way, has brought her and her mother back together. But at the same time, it seems to have driven her farther away from her crew, her closeness with her girls and the intimate relationship she shared with the young man that she adores. That's something that will have to change and right now. Her entire crew feels that way too.

During troubled times, you <u>need</u> your friends and family near.
During the good times, you <u>want</u> your friends and family near.
But during hard times, good times or anytime, <u>there is no better friend in the</u>
<u>family or in your life, than your MOTHER.</u>

The next weeks are spent getting ready for the big double wedding. All of the girls have been to their final dress fittings and every cut was perfect. The tuxedo's are picked up on June 27th. The programs are printed, the invitations have long been sent out and the RSVP list is complete. The grandmothers have the food prepared for the rehearsal dinner and the reception. Both are being held at their club, *The Chill Spot.*

Ebony's cast is removed this afternoon, before the final wedding rehearsal. She's given a brace to wear for 2 more weeks. Her doctor tells her, she can remove it during the ceremony and for the pictures. But she should wear it, otherwise. She promises to follow her instructions and she's pleased to finally have it off. Pearl puts it in a plastic bag, at Ebony's request, to preserve Ajay's heart. Otherwise, she would never have wanted to save it. Once home, Pearl stashes it in Ebony's bedroom closet behind Ebony's hope chest of collectibles which she's saving for her future home.

Today is a very hectic day, as wedding eve's tend to be. Poppa, big mama and the Houston crew arrived in the early morning. Poppa will give Renee away and papa will give Tonya away. The 2 brides don't have very close contact with their families. But their crew have all that handled. Their fathers are absent but the crew are going to make their day perfect.

Renee's father was never a part of her life. She doesn't even know where he is or if he's still living. Her mother put her out of her life when she found out she was pregnant with lil Kenny. She'd moved out of state, since then. However, her mother will be attending the ceremony. Renee has 2 sisters, both older and married, who live in Milwaukee and Chicago. Her
122

oldest brother had been killed when Renee was twelve. Her younger brother Wesley is in the military. He has a wife but no kids. Him and Renee are the only family members who keep in touch. Thanks to the crew mothers, all 3 of her siblings and their families will attend the ceremony.

LaTonya's family is attending as well. Her mother lives in Detroit with her new husband and Tonya's younger sister and brother. She had gone to visit them for 4th of July, 2 years ago. Her and her stepfather still didn't get along. Her biological father, who had left her mother when Tonya was 7, is no longer alive. He was killed in a car accident in 1982. Tonya was very close to him. He's the reason she had moved to Cleveland. Her and Renee admire the crew for sticking together, much the same way that Stoney admired them. They have love for all of the families for accepting them and treating them like equal and true family.

The mothers of the crew have decorated the church and the club. The guys will get their tuxedo's, from Belinda, Sandy and Rena, after the tonight's rehearsal dinner. The girls will get their gowns from these same mothers, at the church. The 3 mothers have made a total of 20 gowns and/or dresses. They fitted every female associated with the wedding. The gowns and the dresses are gorgeous.

The rehearsal dinner is at 6:00pm. All 37 members of the wedding party attend. After the rehearsal dinner, the males go to the bachelor party at the Fillmore Hotel. None of the females know where it's being held. Renee and Tonya's bachelorette party was held 4 nights ago, in a hotel somewhere downtown. Chill is staying at Jr's house. Tonya is staying at Renee's house. They won't see their soon-to-be spouses, until they walk down the aisle.

It's the morning of the wedding. The hair salon and barber shop are booked solid. Only the wedding party, their families and special guest of the wedding party are being groomed. But before Chill and Jr can go to the alter, them and the guys go visit Stoney and Chill's parents graves. They have to make them a part of this special day too. Had Stoney not been killed, he would've been Chill's best man. Bruce is standing in, in his place. While there, the photographer Arthur or money shot, takes photos of the grave markers at both grooms request. These will go in their wedding albums as well. With that done, it's time for them to get to their appointments with the barber. The first of the 3rd generation crew weddings, the double wedding, featuring the *dynamic duo,* the nickname for Renee and Tonya in their crew, just like *The Foursome,* is on today!

123

CHAPTER 16

HARD TO SAY GOODBYE

_____

_____

YOU ARE CORDIALLY INVITED

TO ATTEND THE WEDDING CEREMONY

OF

RENEE ANGELISE STEWART

TO

KENNETH RAMON PAYNE, SR.

AND

LATONYA DENISE WALKER

TO

BRADLEY LEE WILSON, JR.

SATURDAY JUNE 28, 1991
AT
4:00PM

FIRST BAPTIST CHURCH OF CLEVELAND, OHIO

WHAT GOD HAS JOINED TOGETHER, LET NO ONE PUT ASUNDER!

TIME TO GROW-RELOADED-TIME WILL REVEAL 2

Prelude...soft music
Lighting of the candles..Host and Hostesses
Entrance of the Grooms...................…..……….Mr. Kenneth Ramon Payne Sr

....Mr. Bradley Lee Wilson Jr

Honorary Best Man..........................Mr. Cheston Wayne Coleman [deceased]
Best Men....…….....……..John Brown Jr......................Bruce Dalvin Wilson
Processional...Wedding Party

The Wedding Party
Bridesmaids.......Escorted by.........Groomsmen

Ebony Eloise Brown..Anthony Devante Jackson
Latrisha Nicole Brown..Richard Trevon Williams Jr
Nina Shalon Jackson...Jeremy Marcus Brown
Rebbie Shantell Wilson...Brian James Jr.
Janice Marie Logan...Robert Leon Jenkins

Maids of Honor....…..Lynora Shontay Jackson.......Breanna Shontia Wilson

Entrance of Junior Groom...................................Kenneth Ramon Payne Jr.
Entrance of Junior Best Man..............................Archie Joseph Wilson Jr.

Junior Bridesmaid.........Escorted by...............Junior Groomsmen
Kimberly Celina Logan...Shannon Tyreek Wilson
Erica Maureen Jackson..Gregory Brown Jr.
Brittany Neon James...Samuel Logan Jr.
Pamela Darius Jackson...Jesse Lee Brown
Ruthie Nakia Williams...Steven Davon Brown

Junior Maid of Honor..Alicia Mallory Wilson
Flower Girls
Chaundra Laurnea Coleman,....................... Charlotte Elaine Coleman

Ring bearer..Brandon Shawn James

Entrance of Junior Bride...Brina Shaunice James

.............................ALL STAND PLEASE...
125

TIME TO GROW-RELOADED-TIME WILL REVEAL 2

......................ENTRANCE OF THE BRIDES......................

......................RENEE ANGELISE STEWART......................
..........................Given by Percy "poppa" Jones......................

.........................LATONYA DENISE WALKER......................
..........................Given by Jackson "papa" Brown Jr......................

Devotion...Pastor Larry Tucker
Prayer.................................Mrs. Eloise Wilkes "big mama" Jones
Duet.....................ALWAYS.............Mr. and Mrs. Allen [Joanna] Jackson
Poem.................................Mrs. Pearline Anderson "granny" Brown

......................Pledging of Vows ....

......................Exchanging of the Rings......................

Lighting of the Unity Candles...Soft Music
Song.................WE'RE GOING ALL THE WAY........Mr. John Brown Sr
Salute to the Brides and Grooms......................................
Prayer...Mr. Charles Leon Wilson
Poem to the Couples...................................Mrs. Annabelle Johnson Wilson
Benediction Song.... JUST AS I AM.. Mr. And Mrs. Joshua [Sally] Logan

......................Recessional......................

Coordinators......................................Mrs. Pearline Jones-Brown
                                                Mrs. Brenda Jones-James
                                            Mrs. Joanna Williams-Jackson
Seamtresses......................................Mrs. Belinda Carter-Logan
                                                Mrs. Sandra Logan-Brown
                                                Mrs. Rena Baker-Wilson
Hostesses......................................Mrs. Debbie Williams-Wilson
                                                Mrs. Anna Wilson-Williams
Host......................................Mr. Bradley Wilson Sr.
                                            Mr. Allen Devante Jackson Jr.
                                                Mr. John Brown Sr
......................Mr. Richard Trevon Williams Sr.

126

TIME TO GROW-RELOADED-TIME WILL REVEAL 2

....Mr. Brian James Sr.
....Mr. Samuel Logan Sr.
....Mr. Gregory Brown Sr.
....Mr. Archie Joseph Wilson Sr.

Ushers......The Ladies & Gentlemen of *Delta Sigma Theta Sorority* and *Omega Psi Phi Fraternity*

Decorations and Floral Accessories........................by the Mothers of the Crew

Catering and Wedding Cakes....................by the Grandmothers of the Crew

Photography..........by Arthur *"money shot"* Owens of Que Psi Phi Pictures

Reception to follow at the crew owned, *"The Chill Spot"* ....
With music and all sounds provided by Lil Rob of Jenkins Jams Company

THANK YOU'S
Thanks to GOD for teaching us patience, endurance and consideration. With him all things are possible.
Thanks to you; OUR CREW, friends, family and relatives for sharing in our special celebration. WE LOVE YOU!

FRIENDS ARE FRIENDS FOREVER, WHEN THE LORD IS LORD OF THEM ALL.

CONGRATULATIONS

MR. AND MRS. KENNETH [RENEE]PAYNE SR.

AND

MR. AND MRS.BRADLEY [LATONYA]WILSON JR.

SATURDAY JUNE 28,1991
FOREVER!

127

The reception is off the hook. All 3 generations attend. And just as they do with anything else, all of the crew families and closest friends are a part of the celebration. All the couples friends and families are here, as well. Arthur takes hundreds of beautiful pictures. The food and the music are wonderful. Everyone has fun dancing, drinking, eating and even singing. The foursome sing but Ebony doesn't dance, except to slow songs with Ajay. Rob and Jb catch the garters which are tossed to them by Jr and Chill, deliberately. Ajay doesn't even line up for the toss. The brides toss their bouquets to Jan and Lynn since *their guys* caught the garters. The newlyweds had planned to do this before the wedding.

4 hours later, the brides change into lovely travel outfits which was given to them by their real mothers. That was a suggestion from the crew mothers. Everyone says farewell and the newlyweds get into their black stretched limo for the ride to the airport. They'll be flying to Miami for the night and staying at the *Hilton Downtown* on Biscayne blvd. Tomorrow, they're taking a 7 day/6 night Caribbean cruise on the *Carnival Destiny*.

After the newlyweds leave, the rest of the wedding party change their clothes. Ebony puts on her wrist brace, reluctantly. But she's ready to leave shortly afterwards. Several guest are asking questions about the brace and why she's wearing it. She lets Ajay know she's feeling uncomfortable and he agrees they should leave. Tank keeps Ebony's car, again tonight. Something he does often. Especially since she usually rides with Ajay. After the reception, the crew and their friends from Houston, go to Jr and Tonya's house with Bre. Arthur follows them and brings some of the Omega's and Delta's, for the after party.

There's 1 Omega named Cedric Hamilton from New York city and he's interested in Bre. She explains to him that she isn't ready for a relationship. Besides, she's carrying Stoney's child and it's too soon after loosing him to have another guy in her presence. Cedric knows about her pregnancy and tells her how much he really likes her. He says he's liked her since meeting her at Tank's party in January. He also tells her, he isn't going to give up. He's willing to give her all of the time she needs. She goes to bed and leaves the crew in charge of him and the rest of the guest.

Ajay invites Ebony to go to Chill's house with him and she accepts. He has the house to himself, for the week. Lil Kenny is staying at Jo's house, in Ajay's room. Tank and Nina, Rich, T-baby, June and Rebbie come to Chill's house with them. April, David, Yolanda and Charles want to go but Ron says they can't. He knows Chill wouldn't mind but Ron would rather them not party there without Chill being home. Jan, Rob, Lynn and Jb stay at Jr's with the H-town crew and others while Bre sleeps.

128

Once at Chill's house, Tank turns on 1 of Rob's *mixtapes* and the 8 of them have their own party. Nina, T-baby and Rebbie start dancing, immediately. Ebony opens up, a bit, only after sipping on some Hennessey mixed with coca-cola. She even takes a few hits off of a blunt when Tank passes it to her. They laugh and talk for another hour or so. It's getting late and they start to wind down. Rich and T-baby say goodbye, then head out to their private spot in Mentor. June and Rebbie go up to lil Kenny's room. Nina and Tank are staying downstairs on the couch. Ajay is in the mood for romance. He asks Ebony to go upstairs with him and she does.

As soon as they get inside of the room, he starts kissing on her. She kisses him back, this time with no hesitation. He thinks maybe she's opening up and coming back to him.

"Mmm, I miss this," he whispers and she says nothing.

"Let's lay on the bed," he suggests and again, she says nothing.

He takes her hand. She follows him over and sits down on his bed. He begins kissing her as he normally would. On her neck and face, as his hands slowly explore her hair, face, neck and her breast. She becomes tense.

"Wait. Wait a minute, Anthony. I- I don't want too," she says.

"Why not?" he whispers, disappointed but still trying to kiss her.

"I'm still not comfortable," she says.

"Just lay back and I'll do the rest. Okay?" he tries.

She lays back on the bed. He begins again. Kissing on her neck and lips. As soon as he starts to unbutton her blouse, he can feel her tense up again. He can tell that she isn't thinking of this moment. He continues, only slower.

"I can't, baby," she says and sits up, "Not right now. I can't get myself *right*," she says, pulling her blouse together with both hands.

"Come on, Ebony. When are you gonna come back to me?" he whispers as he's losing patience now.

"I'm just not there," she says as she fumbles with her buttons.

"Let me see you. Please," he pleads, "I'm your man, right?"

"Yea. Yes. Yes, you are but I can't-"

"Come here," he whispers, "Yes you can. If you try to put that other shit out of your mind and think about me and you, for a change. I'm trying to be here for you. But you're shutting me all the way out, like I'm the one that hurt you. I'm not trying to hurt you, baby. I'm trying to love you and make you feel good."

He eases her back down on the bed and starts kissing her on her chest again. She lays there staring at the ceiling while he sucks on her nipples. All she can see is the inside roof of Raymond's Benz 190. She trembles and tells herself this is Ajay, as he continues. She can't tolerate it anymore.
129

"*Stop*. Just *stop*. I can't do this," she says, struggling to get up.
He holds her there, initially. Until she starts to panic. She screams out and he lets her go. That freaks him out, *so badly*. All he can do is stare at her. Her eyes are distant. Her breathing, rapid. If he knew what to look for, he'd know she has actually gone back to that night in Raymond's car. He watches as she tugs at her *own* clothes to keep them closed. She trembles. He doesn't realize she's gone back to that night. He doesn't know what to think of it all. She jumps up and starts fastening her buttons in a panic. He's frustrated because he wants things to be back like they use to be. His emotions and impatience get the best of him.
Suddenly, he says, "*Damn*. The way you're acting, you make me think that nigga *took* my pussy."
Seeing the look on her face, he wishes he could take it back immediately. She reacts very negatively, as one would expect. She storms out the room, runs down the stairs and out the front door. She runs home, crying.

He gets dressed and comes downstairs. Tank and Nina are off the couch now. Nina is in the doorway calling Ebony's name. They both inquire of Ajay, about why she'd run out so fast. Ajay tells them what he said. But he tells them he'd said it out of anguish.

"She's not over it yet, Ajay," Nina says, after closing the front door, "You have to be patient with her. You should never have said that."

"Yea man. It's gonna take some time," June says.
He has come downstairs with Rebbie. They heard the commotion too.

"How much time? I've been waiting for months," he says.

"*One* month, Ajay," Nina reminds him, "It's only been a month."

"I don't know how much time," Tank says, "But I know she's been out of it, *since* that shit. I've noticed it too."

"I'm gonna have to kill that fool before she gets back right. I'm telling you," Ajay says, "I'm tired of her jumping and flinching every time I touch her. Like I'm *that* muthafucka."

"He can run but he can't hide," June adds, "Not for long."

"I wanna be there when *he* go out," Rebbie says.

"You're gonna be there," Nina and Ajay say simultaneously.

"If things go like I planned it. Everybody will get a piece of his ass," Ajay says as he goes into a ghostly stare. Then he says, "Everybody."
Nina and Rebbie leave to go check on Ebony. Ajay goes back to his room to lay down. He figures he's done enough and should just let them handle Ebony until she's had time to calm down. He thinks about going back to Jr's and kicking it with the crew and the crew from Houston. They're staying for 2 more weeks to spend time with the newlyweds, when they
130

return. Instead, he decides to stay in bed. He *could* fuck. But tonight, he only wants Ebony and she isn't down for it. He lays in bed thinking about sexing her. He masturbates for the 1st time since being at State school. He gets off on his spread. He laughs to himself. He's feeling silly for jacking off, instead of getting 1 of his ho's to do him. He could've done that but the only pussy he wants, had just left. He misses making love to Ebony, so much. But he doesn't really know how to tell her. He definitely doesn't want her to feel pressured. But he wants to fuck her like he did in Houston, during spring break and the times before. He knows he'll have to get her to relax all over again. He wonders if he's even capable of doing so. But at the same time, he knows he had better be. Their parents have given their blessings. He has to get her passed this tragedy.

"How in the *hell* am I suppose to do that though? I'm gonna have to kill that nigga. Maybe then baby girl can get over that bullshit," he whispers to himself until he eventually falls asleep.

The honeymooners return on 4th of July weekend to an all inclusive party. Jb's 18th birthday, Chill's 22nd birthday and June's 16th birthday are included in the celebration. They all spend more time with the crew from Houston and have a huge barbeque at the park, on Saturday. The party will be at their club, Saturday night and it's sure to be banging.

Ebony catches up on old times with April and Yolanda. She manages to laugh some, just to make them feel comfortable. But she's still not really ready to remember Houston. Ajay watches her all day. But he doesn't say much to her. He isn't sure if she's ready to talk to him. He talks to Chill, who tells him to take his time with her and,

"Do whatever she wants to do, until she's ready."

Ajay *says* okay. But he still can't help but wonder just how long he'll have to wait to hold her.

Tonight, Ebony's driving her own car. She says goodnight, early and is preparing to pull away when Ajay approaches her car.

"I need to talk to you," he says as he leans into the window.

"I'm going home," she says and drops her head.

"That's okay. I'll catch up with you later, alright?" he says as he lifts her chin.

"Alright," she says.

He kisses her on the cheek and smiles. She smiles too. Then she backs out and drives away. She doesn't go home. She goes to granny's house, to stay. So she can spend time with big mama and poppa before they leave out tomorrow. Ajay is disappointed to get back to Shaker Heights and her not

131

be at home. He considers going to papa Brown's house but opts not too.

The next evening, everyone meets up in *The Point* to take big mama and poppa to the airport. When their flight leaves, Ajay tries talking to Ebony again. She leaves and goes home. This time he goes straight to her house, where John and Pearl answer the door.

"Hey mama P, big John. Is Ebony here?" he asks.

"Yea, son. She's up in her room. Hang on a minute," John says as he goes upstairs to get Ebony.

She comes down to the living room and sits on the couch. Ajay sits next to her. Pearl and John go into the kitchen to give them some privacy. Ajay looks at Ebony as he begins to talk.

"You don't wanna see me anymore, baby?" he asks as he looks sad.

"I do but what you said was *so* mean and hurtful," she says.

"I know and I was wrong," he says, "I was *dead* wrong. I just miss you and I don't know how to handle it. I need you to know this is rough for me too. I'm so use to being able to be up front with you. Be open. Say and do whatever's on my mind."

"I want it to be like that too. But every time I try, I start thinking about it. It messes up everything. I don't know how, *not* to think about it."

"I can't say I'm gonna say all the right stuff. Or that I'm not gonna try to be with you. I know I'm gonna keep trying to be with you, baby. Because I'm addicted to you." She looks at him as he continues, "Just give me something to go on. If you're worried about him hurting you again. Baby, it won't happen."

"I'm not worried. Not *now*. Not since I'm at home. It's just that until that happened, no one else had ever touched me or saw any of my private parts. Except you. I wanted it to stay like that because I was raised knowing only one man is suppose to see me undressed. And that man is to be my husband. But he saw my breast. Now I can't go back to that," she says as her eyes well up with tears. She continues, "When he was touching me, it just made me feel so nasty. I don't wanna feel like this."
She breaks down. He puts his arms around her shoulders and leans her against him.

"There's no way you can ever be nasty," he says, "You're the purest person I know. But I need to ask you something and this is the only time I'm gonna ask. I want you to tell me the truth, okay? Did Raymond rape you?" he asks and she tells him no. He asks, "And you're sure?"

"Yes I'm sure." she says looking into his eyes, "I told you at the hospital. I fought him. I kneed him in his nuts and I got away. Anthony, I
132

promise you, if he had raped me. I wouldn't be alive. Can't you see how *hard* it is to live, just knowing he put his mouth and hands on me? If he had raped me," she says as she flails her arms, shakes her head and her tears flow freely. She looks into his eyes and says, "I would've killed myself if he had raped me, baby. I had already decided I was gonna die in that car. Because I was never gonna let him ruin what I was born to do. I was never gonna let him have me," she says as she cries and his eyes well up too.

"Baby there could *never* be anything dirty or nasty about you. I told you. You're the purest girl I know and I would still want you, even if he had. That wouldn't changed how *I* feel for you and about you," he says, "I need you in my life, so much. I can't even put it into words. We can get through this, baby girl. I love you. We can get through anything. Just please. Don't shut me out. Talk about it so we can get past it."

"I would never hurt you and I would've never let him hurt you, like that," she says, "I was gonna make him shoot me before I thought about that tape from health class. I remembered the tape that the girls had to watch in seventh grade. Then I just calmed down and started thinking of ways to make him trust me, so I could fool him into believing I was gonna give up. When he put that gun down, *that's* when I knew I was gonna get away. I felt energy. I felt you. I could see your face. I could hear you saying, *be strong for me. Keep it tight for me and only me.* I knew then that either I was gonna knee him. Or I was gonna beat him to that gun."
She's crying now. So is he.

"Can I have a hug?" he asks, taking her away from the horror.

"Please hold me," she whispers.
He does and she cries on his shoulder. He holds her as they both cry. He fights the urge to cry harder but it takes him over.

Pearl and John spy on them from the kitchen. Pearl is crying. John's eyes well up but still, he comforts Pearl. They knew their daughter's attack will be hard for her to handle. But watching how Ajay is trying his hardest to make it go away, really touches them both. They're impressed by how much he wants her to be okay.

"Oh John, I think it's beautiful," Pearl whispers through tears.

"It is. Ajay *is* sincere, baby," he whispers, "That's why Al and I, we wanted you and Jo to give them a chance. We feel what they have, is the real thing. Besides, we know we raised them right. He'll be good to her."

"Of course it is and yes he will," she says, "Look at what they see from us. It's real, for sure. I know that now. Oh yes."
John and Pearl continue to witness the conversation between Ebony and Ajay, as they hold each other. Ebony continues to cry as Ajay still holds her
133

tight and dries her tears. His have subsided. He comforts her and he lets his mind wonder. He settles on an idea and shares it with her, as her parents still listen. For his 17th birthday, he wants to take her somewhere, out of town, away from Cleveland and away from everything and everyone familiar. This is something he had thought of, after talking to Chill about their honeymoon. Chill had told him how relaxing it was to be away, in a strange place, none of them knew and just relying on each other to get from 1 point to the other. Chill had told him it was so peaceful and they had formed an even tighter bond, that they'll share forever.

"One day," Chill had said, *"The whole crew needs to go."*

Ajay knows they can't go on a cruise. But at least they can go to another city. He thinks of the places that are recruiting him for college. Somewhere he's interested in playing ball and somewhere he can take her. After several minutes, he comes up with Cincinnati. They're already recruiting both of them to play basketball. It's only 4 hours away. They can go down there, spend a few days and talk about whatever she wants to discuss. And see if she'll relax and come back to him. Then he can fix the rest.

"Baby," he says, lifting her chin up, "Do you wanna go to Cincinnati with me for my birthday?"

"Why are you going to Natty? What about your party?" she asks.

"What about it? It's not gonna be about nothing if you're not over this situation," he says, "As far as a party, I can wait and celebrate with T-baby in two weeks. Like June and Chill just did. You know we've been saying we're gonna start doubling up anyway. It'll be my official visit too, so what do you say? Do you wanna go?"

"What are we gonna do there?" she asks.

"Whatever you wanna do. Like getting to know a city, we *might* end up going to college in and just learn our way around. See the sights and all that," he says as he smiles, "See if you'll come back to me."

"I want too," she says with a smile, as she looks into his eyes, "I really want too. I really do miss you, baby. I miss us."

He wipes away her tears and admires her smile. That's something else he's been missing.

"I'm gonna make it happen, alright?" he says.

"Okay."

"I need a kiss. Then I'm gonna let you rest," he says.

She kisses him, long and passionate. Her parents see this too. They still don't interfere. They've seen the real compassion in the 2 of them and tonight's display was enough to make them reminisce back to 1970 and see themselves. Ajay and Ebony talk, even more.

134

"I'm gonna talk to our folks about it and see what they say. If they don't agree, we're going anyway," he says as he chuckles, "Because you've already told me you wanna go. And the way you smiled at me, I know I have to make it happen."

"That's the Anthony, I know and love," she says as she laughs.

"And that's one thing about you that I miss," he says, admiring her beautiful smile. They kiss again, then say goodnight.

"I'll call you when I get out of the tub," she says.

"Do that, baby. Please do that," he says, "I'll see ya, girl."

"In a minute, baby," she says with a smile and he likes that a lot.

He goes to Chill's house to wait for her call, while she goes to take her bath.

Pearl and John overheard their discussion about Cincinnati. John gives Pearl his permission to allow them to go, right away. He wants Ajay to bring his daughter back. And he knows Ajay is the only 1 who can do that. John will be in Cincinnati. He's going back on the road in the morning, before Ajay will come back by to ask them. He'll be able to check them into their hotel. He's going to link up with them and take them out for Ajay's birthday.

"But make him sweat, first," John says with a smile, "We don't want them to get to over confident with our approval of their relationship."

"Oh for sure. Or they might turn into us," Pearl says and laughs.

"*They're* us, already," John says as they laugh too. Then he says, "Put them in the *Clarion*. Nothing but the best for crew."

They kiss as they can hear Ebony skipping up the stairs. That's a welcomed sound. Much better than the moping she's been doing since her return.

On Tuesday afternoon when Ajay talks to Pearl, John has already left. Ajay thinks it's easier to convince Pearl, then let her pass it by John. He'll find out later, John is an easier sale than Pearl. Because John understands the plight of a young man in this family. Ajay tells Pearl about his birthday plan. She acts as if she's against it, as John had instructed her to do. Ajay keeps talking. He reminds her that she must have felt more comfortable about his feelings for Ebony and his intentions. Because she was the one who'd brought them back together. And after the talk they had 2 days ago, she said she knew he was sincere.

"All I'm trying to do is to get her back to being herself again," he says, "Because she's not back, mama P. She don't hardly talk to her girls or come around her crew. That's not Ebony. I'm glad she's back tight with you, though. But I miss her too. I can't lie."

Pearl admits she's worried about how withdrawn Ebony has been since

135

returning home. She says, "But I'm not sure if giving you permission to go off, for days, is the answer either."

"Give me an idea of what *you* think I can do. Or if you can come up with something else," he says, "Please just think about it, okay? I told her I'd make this happen and she smiled. That's what I miss. I just want her to get back to being herself and stop dragging around like she don't have any friends. We all love Ebony. She's special to a lot of people."

Pearl finally lets him off the hook and agrees to think about it. She says she's going to run it by John, this evening on the phone. Then talk to Jo and Al, as well.

"Cool. Just please can you let me know something by tomorrow night? I wanna take her car to the detail shop to get it serviced. Then leave early Thursday morning. You know, Friday's my birthday," he says with a smile, "We'll come back Sunday before dark."

"You'll be seventeen," she says and smiles, "Time really flies."

After some fast talking, he feels he has Pearl on his side. Now all that remains, in his opinion, are the words from John and his parents.

After their talk, he heads to Chill's house to put on his basketball gear. He's taking Ebony to the courts with him. He wants her to work on getting the strength back in her wrist so she can get the spin back on the ball, when she shoots a jump shot. Plus he wants her to get out of the house.

The next 2 afternoons leading up to his birthday, he spends a lot of time with Ebony at the basketball courts. The crew go, as well. On Tuesday, he challenges anybody to play them, 2 on 2. Even if it's 2 guys, they play them. And though Ebony is favoring her wrist, she plays well.

"It needs to get strong, baby," Ajay says, "The only way to do it and not throw your shot off, is to play. Your left hand is what helps you to guide the ball, so you need to play it back into shape. Let's take these fools to school, baby girl."

They beat all of the couples they play. Including the couples from their crew. Ajay talks trash for Ebony, telling her female opponents before the game even starts, "You're about to go to a clinic, alright? She's cold as ice." She backs it up too. Ajay brags on *her game* and he's a superstar. Which gives Ebony, even more confidence, just to hear that he has so much faith in her ability. She's just as much a superstar, in his eyes. They play against 2 Cleveland court legends and beat them, twice.

"Y'all ain't ready," he says, "She's unconscious, man. Cool as a cucumber. And you already know these are *my* courts. I christened them at age six, players," he talks trash with the best of them.

136

TIME TO GROW-RELOADED-TIME WILL REVEAL 2

Ebony had gotten *quite* good in her game while she was in Houston. Even Ron, who is still up visiting, talks trash about her game too.

"I've been watching her play for two years," he says, "My money's on baby girl too."

They play until the late evening. Ajay has onlookers placing bets on them to win. They bet and he gets part of each pay off, as he says,

"The house always get a cut."

He's a true hustler who has the game down to a science. All the while, he's doing sideline sales with his steady customers between games.

By Wednesday evening when they return from the courts, Pearl and Jo are waiting to talk to them. Renee is there, as well. Their mothers tell them they've all agreed to let them go to Cincinnati. They're getting Renee to book the room where they'll stay and John will be there, through Friday. They'll have to get in touch with him as soon as they arrive. They agree to contact John, then Renee reserves the room at the *Clarion hotel*, where John will be staying. It's all set. Ebony is so excited but Ajay is more than excited. He's beside himself, knowing both of their parents have that much trust and faith in them to allow them to go on this trip.

Before first light the next morning, Ajay and Al take Ebony's Honda Accord to the detail shop to be serviced for the trip. As they sit in the diner, down the strip, Al talks with Ajay about his responsibilities, once more. He tells him how proud he is of how he's handling the Raymond White situation.

"I am so proud of the way you're looking out for your girl, son," Al says and they both laugh initially.

Al continues, "I'm serious, though. You have shown a lot of maturity. I'm *proud* of that. That's why we agreed to let y'all take this trip. A few years ago, I wouldn't have believed you'd be able to show this level of devotion to one lady, this soon in your life. What you're doing *now* is how it *was* before your lifetime. This is how we did it. Folks would be married for a couple of years by the time they reached your age. Our crew's traditions come from the old school, as y'all call it. You're already there. That's huge, son."

"Earth Wind n Fire say, we *need devotion*," Ajay sings and laughs.

"I know you still have other girls out there," Al says, "But at least now you're showing *me* you can adapt to tough situations. I use to sit and wonder where in the hell you got all that pimp attitude-"

"It's Mack," Ajay interrupts.

"Pimp, Mack. Whatever y'all say now. Six of one. Half dozen of the other. It's the same game," Al says, "Anyway, Joanna called me out one
137

night. I was saying I didn't know where you got that shit from. You know, trying to sound like a responsible adult and all."

"Called you *out*?" Ajay asks, "What you mean, she *called you out*?"

"I use to be *hell*. *What*? You think *you* started it?" Al asks, as he smiles and reminisces about the days before mama Jo settled him down.

"I had a couple of girls selling their bodies and I didn't even tell them too. I was crucial."

Al laughs but Ajay looks angry. He isn't finding this amusing, in the least. Al catches his son's expression and realizes he's thinking the worst. Al quickly explains himself, as he says, "Oh no, son. Jo was never going out like that. She's all mine. *Do you hear me*? I've told you that *many* times. She was all mine, *then*. Still is now and always will be, a*ll mine*. Me and me only. *Forever*," Al clarifies.

Ajay was thinking Al was implying that his mother had compromised herself. Al explains further, "Jo is *my* lady, son. No other motherfucker has touched Joanna but me. For life. That's *my* girl. The only girl I ever devoted myself too. Before Joanna, I never allowed a girl to kiss me in the mouth or meet my family. Some of them knew Jessica, from college. That as far as that went. But Joanna met my parents within a week of me knowing her. *And* I gave Joanna my last. Including my last name. That's how you treat your *main* girl. I taught *you* that. When she's a good woman, you keep her satisfied at all cost. Never leave her feeling like she has to go looking for satisfaction. It's lots of dogs in this world, son. Don't ever think you're the biggest dog."

"I'm the *best* dog, according to Ebony. I'm gonna stay on the porch too. She's *way* too bad to let her off the chain," Ajay says with a devilish grin and they laugh.

"I had ho's selling ass and bringing me money. *Knowing* I was giving it to Joanna," Al adds, "Sometimes Joanna would go and get the money, *herself*. She'd be out there chastising *my* ho's."

They both laugh hard. Ajay really think that's hilarious.

"Pops that something Ebony would've done before this attack. She's like mama. She don't play me slacking off. Not my court game, my responsibilities to her or at mama's house. Anything that's for my own good or the good of our relationship, she stays on me. Insisting I give it a hundred percent. She's got fire in her. Don't be fooled. She's getting grown. She's all mine and it's gonna stay that way too. She won't tolerate me playing her weak either. She knows I'm the man. But like.., okay. Let me tell you like this," he tries to think of a scenario. Then he says, "Remember Fourth of July, a couple of years ago, when she was upset and left our house crying?"

138

"Yea son. When you had that floozy in your room? That was a nasty tramp. She couldn't hide that. It was in her walk."

Al and Ajay had since discussed what had really happened. He told his father the truth about a week after him and Ebony got caught at the motel. He still doesn't like to think about that incident with Anita Davis.

"Yea that bitch," Ajay says as him and Al chuckle, "Well anyway. I bought Ebony a gift and had Tank to give it to her. But she took it back to the store, got the refund and told Tank to give me the money back. She told him to tell me to think of another way to fix it. I knew then I had to come *absolutely* correct. That made me respect her, *so* much more. But *then* you said I couldn't date her, so that was kind of rough on both of us."

Al is cracking his side laughing. Then he says, "That was really to keep your mama and Pearl off of me and *John's* ass. They was on me and him, to make y'all wait until she turned eighteen. But it was no way to stop it. But I always knew Ebony wasn't the type who could be bought or bribed. Who does that sound like?"

"Mama."

"Damn right," Al says, "She did me the same way and I didn't even get caught in the act, like you did. Deb, Rena and Pearl told her they saw me with a girl. But she *still* made me beg, for *days*."

"Them ho's is trouble, man," Ajay says, laughing too, "Any ho I mess with already knows Ebony is my woman. But it shocks me how they'll still put it down, just to be with me. I let them do whatever they want too. I know those girls would sell ass, just for my attention. But the only woman *I want and need*, is Ebony. None of them ho's will do. I want my girl," he says as he looks at his father with pride and confidence, "That's what this trip is all about. I need her to be alright so I can be alright, pops. I won't be okay until she is. True story."

"Then you're doing what you need to do. John and I, we want you to keep doing it. We're proud of you. All the men are. Especially me."

Then he gets back to the whores, "But son, you got that pimp shit in your blood. You come from a long line of pimp ass brothers."

They laugh loud again before Ajay starts to tell him how good Ebony has gotten on the basketball court.

"She's got ice water in her veins," he says, "She knows no pressure. I guess playing away from home really made her tougher."

"Poppa told me she's all American status, already," Al says, "She's gonna get a scholarship, just like you are."

"Most definitely," he says, "She's gonna come to school with me, wherever I decide to go. She already told me she's signing wherever I sign.

139

I'm leaning toward *Cincinnati, Ohio State* or them *Tar Heels*. Each of them have high powered men and women's teams and great business programs."

"Y'all are gonna make some superstar babies, one day," Al says and they both laugh, "But you'll really be doing something special if you can make more than one *male* child. I kept trying and I got only you."

"I know," he says, "All the way down the line, of all of the Jackson men and Williams on mama side, there's only one male per family."

"You and Ebony will shatter that mold. I'll bet you," Al says, "John and I discussed that already too. The two of you are perfectly suited for each other. We think y'all will change a lot of shit in the crew. Just try to keep most of our *good male* traditions, son. Don't let her break you *all the way* down." They laugh.

"We're gonna do our best," Ajay says, "I want five kids, just like you and mama. But it may be more, because Ebony wants two sons."
They laugh again as they talk more on basketball and where he's been thinking of going to college. They're sitting in the coffee shop. Al is having coffee and Ajay is having orange juice, when they see Brian Sr drive Ebony's Accord out of the service bay. It's ready for the road. They finish up and go get her car so Ajay and Ebony can hit the road.

On the way home, they compare notes on the pimp game then versus the Mack game now. Ajay says, "Like you said, one in the same."
This is the 1st time they've talked this open since Al found out Ajay was seeing Ebony. Al always knew his son had the potential to run game on any lady, if her mind was weak. Or if she hadn't been taught morals. But Ebony doesn't fit that mold *and* she's family, so her morality was never a question. Al has felt the need to protect Ebony since way back, a few years after Chill's mother, Willamena had passed away. He had taken Ebony under his wing and took on the father role when John had asked him too. Because John's job keeps him on the road. Al wants to make sure Ajay does the honorable thing with Ebony. Al and Ajay feel good about their situation then and now. They was always more like brothers, than father and son. They had this type of relationship long before Ajay had gotten into the crew. During their drive back to Shaker Heights, Al mentions Raymond just to get a gauge on where his son's head is, 6 weeks after the attack.

"I'm also sure I know what your plans are for that sorry ass bastard," Al says suddenly, "Without even asking you."

"Good," Ajay says, "I'll keep it quiet. I won't shame the family."
They pull into the double driveway they share with John and Pearl's property. There's no need to speak on Raymond White anymore.

It's still early morning when Ajay and Ebony leave for Cincinnati.
140

TIME TO GROW-RELOADED-TIME WILL REVEAL 2

Ebony drives as far as Columbus. They have very stimulating conversation along the way. They make a stop there and call Chaundra and Charlotte. Mama Jackie meets them and they follow her home, where she makes lunch for them. Ebony calls Pearl and to tell her they stopped to visit Stoney's family. Pearl is pleased she called and says,

"Call me when you get to *Cincy*. I'll be at work, so charge it to the house."

Ebony agrees to call. Her and Ajay eat lunch and soon, they're back on the road. He drives on to Cincinnati.

They arrive at the hotel in the early afternoon. She calls her mom first, then her dad. Renee booked them into *The Clarion Riverfront*. John is there. He's going to take them to dinner this evening. Ebony unpacks their things. Ajay calls the coaching staff at Cincinnati to tell them he has arrived. Then he calls his house. Jo and Al are gone to work but Nina answers and tell them she'll let the crew know they arrived safely.

"And y'all better bring me something back," Nina demands.

"We will, kid. We're gonna bring everybody a lil something," Ebony says before they hang up.

Her and Ajay go visit the Cincinnati campus. John meets them there. They tour the campus and meet the *Bearcats* coaching staff, then have an early dinner. After dinner, John shows them around town. He leaves them on their own and lets them know he's going back to the hotel to get some sleep tonight, because he's treating them to an *elegant* dinner tomorrow, before he has to pull out at midnight.

After John retires to his hotel room, Ebony and Ajay find a mall and go shopping. They go to the movies to see *Terminator 2: judgment day*. They go sightseeing also. They get lost several times but manage to find their way back to the hotel. They rent *Predator*, get some snacks then go back to their room to relax.

"It's an *Arnold Schwarzenegger* kind of night," he says as they both laugh and put the movie in the VCR for later.

"And you're right. The *Terminator* with him on the evil side *was* better than part two," she says.

Ebony gets out her big t-shirt, 1 of the t-shirts he'd gotten with their names on it. She goes to take her bath.

Ajay is in a contemplative mood as he lays across the bed waiting on her to finish. He's thinking of what he should do next to help her relax. He says, "Oh yea," as he springs off the bed and goes to the bathroom door. When he turns the knob, the door is locked. He goes back and lays across the bed but he isn't planning to lay there for long. After only a few seconds on the bed, he goes back to the door and this time he knocks.

141

"Ha?" Ebony replies as she turns down the radio.

"Open the door," Ajay says.

She sits quietly in the tub for a few seconds, before asking, "What's the matter?"

"Nothing, baby. I just wanna come in," he says with his voice low.

She gets up slowly, wraps herself in a towel and opens the door.

"Let me come in and wash your back," he says, smiling as he enters.

"I can do it. My wrist is alright now," she tries.

"It has nothing to do with your wrist, baby," he says, "That's not why I wanna bathe you. I wanna wash your front too." He chuckles.

She stands there wrapped in her towel, dripping water on the floor.

"You think you're slick, Anthony," she says with a slight grin.

He laughs and says, "I had to figure out *some kind* of way to see you."

She still stands there cooling off. Her lips begin to quiver.

"Go on and get back in the tub where it's warm," he says, "It's okay. You know me."

She goes back over to the tub, drops the towel and jumps in quickly. Submerging herself into the bubbles, up to her neck. He laughs as he sits on the edge of the tub.

"What's so funny?" she asks as she smiles shyly.

"You," he says, "You act like I've never seen you *naked* before."

"I know you have," she says, "But not while I'm taking a bath."

"It's a first time for everything," he says, "I wanna see how you look in these bubbles anyway. Why do you think I bought 'em?"

"Because you think you're slick," she says with a smile.

He says nothing this time, as he puts his hand into the water to search for the washcloth. His hand grazes her leg. She lays very still. He lets his hand wonder across her thighs intentionally. In his search, his fingers brush across her pubic hairs. Still she doesn't move. She looks up at him and finds him staring back at her.

"It's okay," he whispers as he finds the washcloth.

He's already a master of seduction at nearly 17 years old.

"Get up on your knees so I can bathe you," he says, his voice almost demanding while his eyes are still and piercing.

She does as she's told while making sure the suds fully cover her privates. He sees this as only a minor obstacle. He washes the bubbles from her back. She realizes where this is going, now that her backfield is exposed. He wets the towel again and squeezes water over her left shoulder. It washes down her chest and removes the thick bubbles which covered her left breast. She lets out a little sigh of embarrassment. His face is chiseled stone. Focused.

142

He wets the towel again and does the same thing over her right shoulder, exposing her right breast.

Then he says, "Stand up," and his voice is deep and penetrating.

Again she does as she's told. He wets the towel again. He has the disposition of a surgeon. As if this bath is a tedious run of the mill event or something which requires little to no thought or concentration. He glares at her body, now only half covered with bubbles. His eyes say everything but tedious. He tries to appear unaffected but it isn't working.

His eyes can't lie at all. I see why he doesn't try to lie to me.

He washes away the remaining bubbles, then soaps up the towel. He stands and says, "Face me."

He's deliberately trying to take her focus off of being naked and more on getting her bath completed. She turns to him, exposing her full nude front. He begins to bathe her. He starts with her neck as he looks directly into her eyes. She looks away, shyly.

"This is the dope move, right?" he asks, breaking the silence.

"It feels strange," she replies shyly as she's still not able to look into his eyes. Not while he's bathing her.

He says, "No baby. This is the *shit*. I want you to bathe me, next."

She just smiles. Too shy to talk while her naked body is fully exposed to him. But again, he requests for her to bathe him and this time she answers.

"Okay. If you want me too," she says.

"Hell *yea* I want you too," he says rather loudly, as he continues washing her breast, arms and stomach.

She's still shy and innocent. He likes that she hasn't lost that.

She's still my innocent baby girl.

He skips down to her thighs and legs before moving back up to her kitten.

"Open your legs for me," he whispers, looking into her eyes.

She does. He washes her pussy for what seems like forever. He kisses her gently as he moves to her bottom and washes it thoroughly. She feels more relaxed and now that he's done, she sees this whole bath episode as truly romantic. She understands why he did it and she's glad he did. It helped her open up to the idea of being touched in her most private areas again. This reminds her of 4 years ago, when she had first allowed him touch her.

"You can sit down," he says, "I'm just getting you ready for a lifetime with me, Ebony. That's all. Big John told me, Jb and Tank about this move. Mama P said he still bathes her."

"He does," she says as she smiles and sits down quickly.

143

He washes her back, thoroughly. Then he rinses the soap from her body, washes her face, her ears and finally, her feet. At the end of her bath, he gives her a kiss on the nose and says, "You're all done. That wasn't so bad. Was it?" he asks as he unplugs the drain.

"No. It wasn't so bad. It wasn't bad at all," she answers as she stands up quickly and steps out of the tub.

She reaches for her bath towel but he gets to it first.

"I bathed you. I get to dry you off too," he says quickly, "This is my chance to touch you and I'm going to finish it. I have to touch your body as much as I can, *while* I can."

She giggles as he's drying her off. He rinses the tub and draws water for his bubble bath.

"Stay here. You have to bathe me," he says as he disrobes in seconds.

He stands naked in front of her. She stands wrapped in only her towel. He gets into the tub and asks her to hand him a washcloth. She does. He puts it in the tub. When his tub is filled with water and bubbles, he turns the faucet off, lays back and puts his hands behind his head. Then with a blank stare, he says, "Alright. I'm ready."

"Don't you wanna soak for a little while?" she asks.

"No. Not unless you're getting back in here," he says with a smile.

She shakes her head and smiles as she searches for the washcloth. She can't find it until he points it out.

He says, "There it is," gesturing toward his pelvic area, where he had deliberately placed it directly on top of his penis. She retrieves it quickly. He moans, just to tease her. It makes her feel a little embarrassed but more so, *turned on*. She hadn't heard that sound from him since his spring break.

"You have to do me good, like I did you," he says with a sly grin "So don't half step on my bath, alright? I feel *real* dirty," he says adding a chuckle.

"Whatever, goofy," she says and smiles as she puts soap on his washcloth.

He doesn't even realize it yet. But she's already in the mood. She knows he planned this trip so they could get back to the lovemaking. She wasn't sure how she would feel about having sex once they got here. But it was just something about the way he looked into her eyes while he washed her pussy that certainly heated the bathroom up for her. She would be willing to fuck him right here, if he was to make an advance.

All he would have to do is make a move like he did after the wedding and insist on it. But he won't. He's gonna slowly seduce me. I know this. He always takes his time with me and I really love that too. Tonight is gonna be no different. I love him for having patience with me. I miss him, so much.

144

She needs to see if he'll get hard when she touches him. She's so ready now. "Stand up," she instructs, trying to sound like he did when he was bathing her.

"Yes ma'am," he answers in a silly tone, as he stands.

She begins to wash him. He guides her shy hands as she washes his penis, making certain she's thorough. She's enjoying it. Before allowing her to move the towel, he makes eye contact and kisses her on the lips. He moans which makes her nipples hard. He sits down. He's playing this seduction scene up to the best of his ability. She's relaxed a lot more now, so it's obviously working. She rinses him well. Then she dries him off. She takes extra time drying his penis while he tongue kisses her with fervor. She's way more relaxed then she was before he came into the bathroom. And that's exactly what he'd hoped would happen.

"That's it, baby. You got the hang of it," he say as he laughs.

They're both thoroughly clean and wearing only towels. They brush their teeth, then exit the bathroom.

"Get your hair brush and come sit down," he says as he stands next to the chair in front of the mirror.

She brings the brush to him and sits down. He brushes her hair just as gently as he had done it at granny's, before she'd moved to Houston, 2 years ago. The night he climbed through her bedroom window.

When he's finishes, she goes and sits on the bed. She's hoping he's in the mood. She certainly is. He puts the brush on the nightstand, then he comes over to the bed. He lays down with his head on her lap.

Softly, he says, "I feel like I have to start all over with you."

He's trying to find a way to explain that he wants to be closer without asking her to submit to him.

"I notice you're doing the things you use to do when we first started going together. It's working. It's really nice," she says, "I'm glad we was able to come here. Real glad. Baby you're really good to me and I wanted to just say, thank you. I know I'm a very lucky girl to have a man who goes all out for me. I love you, *so* much."

"You're welcome and I'm glad too, baby," he says, "I wanna do this everyday. And I will, if that's what it takes to help you to be alright. I just want you back. I want you to be yourself again. You *feel* me?"

"Yes I do. I am relaxing too. Okay?" she says.

"Alright. That's all I ask," he says.

He gets up and grabs something from the side pocket of his bag. He gets *Predator* ready to play, then he lays back down. This time he lays across the bed where he can see the TV. He invites her to lay down next to him. She
145

accepts. Then he pulls something from behind his back and presents it to her. Then he smiles and says, "I saw this yesterday and I had to get it for you," and while still smiling he hands her the *Mariah Carey* album on cd.

"Oh wow! I *wanted* this cd, baby. I wanted it, *so bad*," she says as she kisses him on the lips. Then she says, "My tape is wound up so tight, it's about to pop. I'm gonna let T-baby keep the tape, now that I have the cd. Thanks, baby."

"You're welcome, baby girl. Mariah has another cd coming out next month called *Emotions*. I'm getting that one for you too."

"I know she does and I can't wait to hear the whole thing," she says and laughs, "Good thing I have a cd player in my car."
He bought her the cd player from a street vendor *or crack addict* who sold it to him *for a steal*.
"I left my stereo with the cd player, in my room in Houston. Poppa and big mama got it for my fourteenth birthday. It bumps but not like my car."

"I'm gonna buy cd's, for you, from now on," he says, "Any tapes that you wanna replace or any music you want, just let me know. I got a Prince cd that I want you to here too. Renee use to play it, all the time."
She blushes as he says, "You can start our music collection. Make sure you keep them in good shape and in the cases. They'll be on display in our home, one day," he say, smiling and kissing her gently on her back.
He's massaging her shoulders and neck as she lay very still on her stomach and feeling very aroused. He kisses her down her spine and though the towel is still present, her insides tingle with excitement. He slides onto her back and plants sweet kisses on her bare shoulders. She feels that familiar grind of his, as he rubs his hands through her hair. He takes his hands and turns her head to the side as he looks into her eyes. His stare goes to her lips. He wants a kiss. *A real kiss.* She senses this from his stare. A stare which seems to penetrate her heart. The look in his eyes is a lonely one and she wants to take him out of his misery. She kisses him, very aggressively. She feels his penis become thick and hard. He's still laying on her back. It's obvious he enjoyed the kiss because his dick becomes hard as a brick.
"That was so sweet, baby," he whispers.
He seems deflated. Like he's all out of ideas and *a bit* confused. She gets it now. He's bothered. Sexually bothered. That's very new. He's in the mood but he isn't sure if she's ready to open up to him. He can't read her, at the moment and he doesn't want to upset her. His eyes have a lonesome look as he plants sweet kisses on her face, over and over. He lifts up off of her, rolls her over onto her back and lays back on top of her. The towels barely remain. He kisses her aggressively, again and again. First on her lips, then
146

on her neck and finally, her shoulders. He's working his way to her chest.

"I wanna move these towels out of the way, baby," he whispers, "But I don't wanna make you pull away from me. Are you gonna be okay if I move them?"

"Yes," she whispers as her eyes search for his, "You can."

He removes her towel. Then his. They are finally, completely nude. He's still laying on top of her. He thinks she's ready but he still can't be sure if he's getting the correct read on her.

"Are you okay?" he asks again softly.

He's always concerned about her comfort level. He wants to be sure she's not *uncomfortable*. That didn't just start tonight either.

"I'm okay," she whispers.

She wants to tell him to go ahead and do it. But she remembers he wants her to let him lead when it comes to sex. So she remains quiet. He begins sucking on her neck. He moves to her nipples and suckles them, very gently. This feels good to her and familiar too. She puts her arms around him and begins to grind against him. He really likes this. He moans to the response he's receiving. She's ready for him to really hold her. She doesn't want him to worry any longer, about whether or not she's willing. She has to let him off the hook.

"Anthony," she whispers.

He stops suddenly and asks, "Ha? What's wrong, baby?" as he expects her to panic, "Are you okay, baby?" His voice is dejected.

"Yes baby. But I wanna make love," she says.

Without hesitation, he parts her legs and enters her. He's ready too. He's *been* ready.

"Oooo," she moans, at the suddenness of his penetration, as her body starts to immediately react as if it's getting the fix it's been deprived of, for so long.

He moans in response to her body talk as he grinds slowly. He whispers in her ear during this reunion session. Making sure she knows just how much he's missed her. And that he never wants to be without her loving again.

"I missed you too, baby," she whispers, so he knows she's missed him too.

He wants to make the most of this moment as he holds her close to him and very tight, while kissing her over and over.

"Come here. Show me how much you missed me, baby," he says.

Tonight's session is more passionate then any session, *ever* was before. This isn't some re-familiarization of old lovers. But more like the 1st feast for a fasting couple. Their bodies are in automatic as they unconsciously do, just what the other desires. She feels like if she doesn't come soon, she's going

147

to explode. She grinds against him with everything she has. His request for the wettest action he's ever had the pleasure of bringing out of her, is about to be granted. He knows she's almost there. Her body is trembling.

"Give it to me, baby," he whispers, still holding her tight.

He's kissing her neck, mouth and breast wildly. Like a man who had been starved for weeks and is now allowed to feast. There isn't 1 inch of her body he hasn't touched, caressed and/or kissed. She feels *extra* liberated. As free as a bird. She's feeling like their lovemaking has gone to another level tonight. A damn good level, as she lets her sweet juices escape.

"I love you, Anthony! Oh God! I love you! Mmm, I love you! Yes!"

She feels his thrust become harder and harder still, as he heads for the zone. He's whispering *and saying aloud,* everything that's on his mind. All of the things he's held inside for weeks, he lets go of tonight. He even wants her to testify as to how good she feels and not to be shy.

"I missed you, Ebony," he says, "Oh baby. I missed holding you."

She grinds against him as she holds him tight and returns the wet kisses he's sending. He's more vocal than ever.

"Baby this is the pussy, right here," he whispers as he pants for breath. He can feel his nut coming, "Tell me who makes you cum, baby?"

"You do, Anthony," she moans.

"This is my pussy, baby," he whispers, "All mine. I missed it, so much. I missed you, baby. *All* of you."

She erupts. "Yes! It's yours, Anthony! It's yours, baby!" she screams, holding onto him while he churns into her flesh.

He *cums* violently. All of the pinned up aggression from waiting for her, for weeks, comes out of him in 1 orgasm. She holds him as tight as he holds her. At this point, each of them are heavily emotional as the tears flow from both of them. They're relieved and satisfied that she was able to shake the horror known as Raymond White and get back to making love to him. Raymond was gone from her mind long enough for her to bond with the man she loves. The man who loves her. Anthony loves her for everything good that she brings to his life. They hold each other and as light tears still escape from both of their eyes, they slowly and steadily catch up to their breath.

"I feel safe with you, Anthony," she cries, "I know you love me."

"You *are* safe with me, baby," he say as the tears stream, "And I *do* love you." Most of his tears drip onto her shoulder. He says, "I love you more than life. I didn't really know how to say that before. But on the flight to Houston, I promised myself and God, that I would start telling you how I feel about you and telling you what you mean to me. I'm gonna do that more. I feel like the luckiest man alive."

148

She smiles and gives him another sweet kiss. It's *so* obvious to him that she has missed him too. She's holding him so tight, air can't even seep between them. He's hot but he doesn't want her to loosen her grip. Not in the least. It's been so long since they've marinated together and he's in no hurry for it to end. Their breathing starts to stabilize.

****

Meanwhile, back in Cleveland, T-baby is on the phone with Rich. He's trying to convince her to sneak out with him and go to their private spot in Mentor. A spot all their own. No one else from their crew hangs out there. People party all night and they don't care if you break the rules. The grown ups seem to be relaxed about everything. Even about who spends the night. T-baby doesn't know how Rich knows them but she figures they must be his customers. When they stayed there, the night of the wedding, her and Rich had the master suite. It's a large mansion with lots of antiques and sports memorabilia. She had asked him who lived there. He said someone from the Cleveland Indians. She isn't familiar with baseball so she can't be sure if it's a player, the owner or whom. But it was like their own house, when they was there. No one bothered them or asks them any questions. Rich is there again tonight. He has 1 of the fancy cars which belongs to the owner of the mansion. He wants her to join him. She wants to go but she has to stay home with her younger brothers, Greg Jr and Steven.

"Do you think I should come over to your house, then?" he asks.

"I don't know, baby. You sound *real* drunk," she says, "We might get caught."

"Why do you think we're gonna get caught?" he asks, talking very loud, slurring his speech and sounding highly intoxicated already.

"Because you're already loud *now*," she says as she laughs, "I can hear you without pressing the phone to my ear."

"Sneak out with me," he says, almost demanding.

"I can't. My uncle Sam is coming by to check on us," she says, "And Jan told me he was already out riding around. He could come at anytime. Or just sit outside watching the house until my mama and daddy get back from their date."

"Well fuck it then. I'll *holla*," he says and hangs up without another word which leaves her dumbfounded.

Why would he hang up on me? He needs to stop drinking if he's gonna act like that.

149

TIME TO GROW-RELOADED-TIME WILL REVEAL 2

Ajay and Ebony are both exhausted after round 1, as they lay in each others arms. It's been 10 minutes since the reunion session ended and they're still sweating and panting for air. Neither has let go of the other though. Nor have they taken their eyes off of each other. They rest a little more, while they smoke a blunt. Then they make love again. It's slightly past midnight by the end of round 2. They had celebrated 2 first, today. Their 1st trip out of town together and the 1st time they had bathed each other. She loves keeping up with their milestones. It feels late, so she grabs his watch off the nightstand. That's when she realizes her man had reach another milestone, minutes ago.

"Happy seventeenth birthday, baby," she says with a smile.

"Yes it is, baby," he whispers in her ear, "It's been a happy birthday already. And it started off *perfect*."

He gives her a long kiss and she's ready to go to sleep. She scoots down under him and snuggles up close to his chest, where she sleeps all night, secure in his arms. He's content that she's sleeping peacefully and not fidgeting and jumping as she had done the first 3 weeks after the attack. He's glad to have her back in his arms and in his bed. Sleeping much more peacefully then the last time he watched her. This helps him sleep as well.

It's early afternoon when Ajay wakes up to the phone ringing. He looks at Ebony, first thing. She's still sleeping safely, right next to him. He reaches over to the nightstand and grabs the phone.

"Hello," he answers, still groggy.

"Happy birthday, bro," Renee says.

"Thank you, sis. What's up?" he asks.

"Obviously, not you. Y'all still sleep?" she asks.

"Hell yea. What time is it?" he asks.

"Man, its one thirty," she says as she laughs, "Y'all better get cracking."

He nudges Ebony slightly to wake her.

"Huh," she grunts as she wipes her face and stretches her body.

"Renee's on the phone," he says as she sits up and reaches for his watch, "She said it's one thirty and we should be up."

"It's one thirty, already?" she asks in disbelief.

"That's what Renee said but we're an hour behind, down here," he says and Ebony sets his watch to central standard time.

"It's twelve thirty here," she says with a smile as she snuggles back up under him, "What's the crew talking about?"

"What y'all doing?" Ajay asks Renee.

150

"We're gonna go to the park, for a minute. The usual."

"Getting paid, ha?" he says and chuckles.

"You know it."

Some of the crew are at Renee's house and they're already in party mode. They speak to Ajay and Ebony, then hang up soon after.

Ajay and Ebony cuddle a little while longer, before they slide out of bed and go take a shower. They make love again and as the water beads down their bodies, she notes another first.

This is the first time we did it in the shower. I love this man.

They get out, towel dry each other and get dressed. Then they go riding around the city. They decide to park and take the *Queen city tour*, John had suggested. Afterwards, they go back to the mall, then out to *Kings Island amusement park.*

Ajay becomes very animated at the park. He loves rollercoaster's and any other scary ride. But Ebony doesn't. In the parking lot, they begin the back and forth about what rides they're going on. Of course they end up riding anything that looks daring. She's hesitant but he convinces her to ride the biggest rollercoaster. She pushes for the slower, more romantic type rides. They experience both. They ride through the tunnel of love and the haunted castle. She doesn't care for the castle as much as she likes the tunnel. But of course, Ajay favored the castle. That is until she starts to kiss on his neck while they're riding through the tunnel.

He says, "Baby we need to ride this again so you can finish that," as the tunnel of love car slows down, then stops at the platform.

"Oh, *now* you like the tunnel of *love?*" she asks as she laughs.

They climb out and begin their walk around the park while he plans their return to the tunnel. They find the basketball shoot-out. He has to stop and try his luck. He wins a large teddy bear for her. She shoots next and wins 1 for him. He trades it for the Lion. She continues shooting because *he says* she's on a roll. She even shoots for other couples and bystanders. He starts to place side bets with some guys from the University, who had stopped to watch. They know of him, about their recruitment of him and his national ranking. He introduce them to Ebony and lets them know she'll be ranked this year. He doesn't fail to tell them that she's *his* girl also. Then he bets 1 of the football players that Ebony can make 10 shots in a row. She makes 15 before she misses. He manages to get the money up to $500, by getting others in on the bets. He's a natural hustler.

"Alright baby. Can we go eat now?" he asks as she's gearing up to shoot again.

151

"Okay," she says as she laughs, "My baby's hungry."
She loves the way he supports her game. It makes her want to show off, at times. He gives her the $500. They ride the tunnel again, then go to the car. They have to shop for evening attire. Big John had given her a credit card, last night and told them to get some dress clothes for the evening. They go pick up some great gear, then go back to the hotel and get clean.

They look very elegant and handsome in their evening clothes, as they head out to meet John at a very exclusive and fine dining restaurant which has valet parking. He treats them to a fancy dinner for Ajay's birthday. Immediately he comments on how exquisite they both look. He can't believe how grown up his daughter looks when she's dressed up. He knows it's only a matter of time before she'll be grown up and out on her own. He also knows Ajay is going to be the 1 to take her off of his hands. Because he wants to be in her life for the long haul. He figures it's time for him and Ajay to talk with Ebony present. He starts that talk over dinner. He tells Ajay, he's willing to give them his blessing and it's okay with him if they date.

"This is my only daughter, so I'm only gonna say this one time," John says as Ajay listens intensely, "Don't asks me for her hand and take her out of my house unless you're planning on keeping her and taking good care of her. One other thing. Make her a wife before you make her a mother. Alright?"

"Okay," Ajay answers, as Ebony frowns in embarrassment.
Ajay smiles at her as if he has been anticipating this conversation, as he says, "I know how special she is. She's special to me too. She always has been. Every since we use to shoot basketball together on our driveways. When she didn't even like me. I use to tell big mama about it and I asks her to help me out. She helped me out a lot. Ebony *knows* I love her now."
Ebony looks amazed. She can't believe her father and her boyfriend are talking like this. Of course, they've always been cool with each other. But she thought her and Ajay's relationship had put a strain on theirs. It doesn't seem so, tonight. Still she feels awkward during this conversation.

"Should I go to the bathroom or somewhere so y'all can talk in private?" she asks, "Y'all seem to be the only two people here. I can give y'all some space, if you need me too."
She smiles but she's feeling a little left out of the loop. She's always the spoiled baby girl who wants all of their attention on her. These are the 2 men in this whole world that she knows will give her, *her* way. But now that they're all here, they seem more interested in talking *about her,* then *too her.* And though it's good, she has to try to change it immediately.
152

"Why do you wanna leave?" Ajay asks.

"Y'all talking about me like I'm not even *here*," she says.

"We know you're here, baby girl," her father says, "We're just trying to get some things out into the open, that's all. These are the things the two of us are gonna *have to* discuss, sooner or later, you know."

"Yea. I thought you *wanted* us to talk," Ajay offers.

"I do but y'all act like we're fixing to get married or something," she says, "*God*. Please stop it. Just chill out."

"You're planning to marry him, one day, right?" John asks.

"I don't know," she says, rather embarrassed.

"You're not planning to marry me, Ebony?" Ajay probs.

"You'd better be. Since I gave you *my* permission to go on an overnight trip with him," John says with a smile.

"Yes, one day. But talk about something else," she tries.

"We talking about our favorite subject," her father adds, "*You*."

"We've got your daddy, right here. You know how you always felt like they didn't understand us trying to be together?" Ajay asks.

"Uh huh," she answers as she pouts.

"He's just trying to see what my plans are, that's all," Ajay says.
She gives him a look which convinces him to tread lightly through the rest of this conversation. "What's wrong, now?" Ajay asks.

"I can't talk about this. Not with my daddy here," she says with hesitance.

"You're just like your mother when you get cornered, baby girl. You just want it over," John says while chuckling, "You should be happy we're talking marriage. Who do you think is gonna give you away?"

"But not *today*," she says as she uses her best daddy's girl voice.
John decides to give her a break.

"Alright, baby girl but I want you to promise me you won't get married or run off without letting me be apart of it, okay?" John says.

"She won't," Ajay assures him, "I promise. We're going all the way traditional. Just like the crew's before us."

"Okay. I promise. Now change the subject. Please?" she begs.
With that, they finish dinner with some lighter conversation.

Later, they say goodbye to John as he pulls out of the restaurant parking lot, heading for Memphis. She turns her sights on Ajay and vows to get even.

"I'm gonna get you," she says, "Putting me on the spot, like that. Come here."
153

She chases him around the parking lot while they wait for valet to bring the car. He lets her catch him as the car pulls up in front.

"You already got me," he says with a kiss, "Now let's go."
He opens the passenger door and waits for her to get in. Then he goes around and gets into the drivers seat. She kisses him, this time. He starts up the Accord and they ride around before going back to the hotel.

After talking, making love, watching movies, smoking weed and sipping the wine John had given them, they're so tired they pass out.

Saturday is much like the day before. Except they go to the mall and buy gifts for everyone in their family and crew. She uses the $500 from the day before, to get them more matching shirts. She gets matching shirts for her and her girls, in their favorite colors. John had given Ajay 2 tickets for the *Budweiser Superfest* at *River front stadium*. They go and enjoy the concert. She likes *Jodeci* the best. They go to the hotel after the show and she packs up their things. He puts them in the car for the trip home, in the morning. They spend the rest of the night talking and indulging in each other. They had a lot of time to make up for and they make sure to get it in.

The next day, they return to Cleveland in time to see the Houston crew before their flight home. April and Yolanda brag about the great time they had with her crew and her girls too. They had really gotten closer to Nina, Rebbie and T-baby while Ebony was in Cincinnati. She really loves that all 5 of her girls are familiar with each other.

"We're gonna be the *sensational six* now," Nina says and smiles.

"Sounds like a winner to me," Yolanda adds as they all laugh.
It's now time for them to board their flight. They do and the crew remain their until their plane is out of sight. After seeing Ron and his crew off, the crew get together at Jr's. Ebony gives all of them their souvenirs. Most of them go to the park while the foursome take souvenirs to the rest of the family, then they hook back up with their crew at the park.

When the foursome arrive, they're discussing plans for Ajay, T-baby and Rebbie's birthday party. It's set for the 26th of July. They spread the word throughout the evening, with others who was already anticipating a crew party in the making. Ebony and Ajay are still tired from their trip. After they leave the park, the foursome go to T-baby's house for the night. Ajay goes to bed early, at his mother's house.

It's early August. T-baby and Rebbie are 15 years-old now. Ajay remembers being released from state school, a year ago. Tonya and Bre are anticipating the births of their babies. The foursome look forward to their
154

sophomore year and all of them being back in school together again. Ajay and Jan will be seniors. Tank, June, Rich and Bre will be juniors. Lynn and Jb have gone away to college at Georgia Tech in Atlanta.

Tonight the foursome spend the night at Jo's house. Ajay comes home to leave his laundry for his sisters to do. Ebony offers to do it.

He says, "Okay. You may as well get use to it, ha?"

He smiles at her. He leaves and she starts his clothes. She washes and dries them all. Then puts them away in his room as he'd instructed. He still keeps clothes at home because he still sleeps there, from time to time. When Ebony opens his underwear drawer, she sees something that gets her attention. There are 2 pairs of panties in there. She smiles as she calls her girls in to witness. She yells, "Nina! Y'all come here!"

The 3 girls rush into Ajay's bedroom and she shows them the panties.

"Better not be for him," Rebbie says and they crack up laughing.

While laughing, Ebony says, "No girl. He still has my panties. These right here are from the first night at the motel, when we got busted and Tank went to jail. These are from the night at granny's. Before I left the first time," she whispers as she smiles.

"That's pitiful, Ebony," Nina says as she laughs.

"Fuck you," she whispers and they all snicker. "And he doesn't have anybody else's either," she adds.

"I guess that's a good sign, ha cuz?" T-baby asks.

"For *Ajay?* Hell yea," Nina says as they laugh and leave his room.

Later in the week, as the crew are hanging at Jr's house, a show called *Crime Stoppers* debuts on the local TV station. The host discusses unsolved murders in the Cleveland area. Among the 38 unsolved cases mentioned, Ebony realizes the crew are linked to 15 of them. Among those listed are Stoney, Eddie, Danny, Jake, Greg and those 6 busters from the Grove who had tried to set up shop at the crew warehouses, over 2 years ago. The host talks about Stoney's murder, which the police still hadn't bothered to solve. But as far as the crew are concerned, it's solved. They're not about to offer any information on his case. Nor any of the others, for that matter. Jr changes the channel.

The August party on the 16th is for Jr, who turns 20 and Jan, who's 17 years-old now. It doubles as a going away party for Jb and Lynn as well. Although they had already left for Atlanta, 3 weeks ago. The crew included them in T-baby, Ajay and Rebbie's party. They miss them already and just wanted to hang their banners again.

155

The next few weeks bring significant change to the crew's lives. Jb and Lynn are away at college. Ajay and Jan are seniors. Bre, Tank, June and Rich are juniors while the foursome are in 10th grade. The most exciting change is the birth of Bradley Lee Wilson III to Jr and Tonya. He was born on September 1, 1991. *Labor day.* Add in the fact, *the Chill Spot, Crew Details* and the Dee-jaying venture, which Rob runs firsthand, have all taken off. Renee begins her senior year at CSU. With all the great things happening, it's still not the *best* news. The hottest news comes via a phone call Chill gets from the crew in Houston.

After school today, Ron calls to tell Chill that Raymond White is back on the map. Though the news reports said he wasn't going to college, he *had* accepted his scholarship and is already attending school at Ann Arbor State. It was kept intentionally secret, with no big media blowout. Ron had found out today, after some of his henchmen returned from a road trip where they saw him on the campus. Ron also tells Chill that Raymond will be returning to Houston in October for his arraignment.

"Good looking out, fam," Chill says with a smile.

"My pleasure," Ron says, "Now, what do you say we go on and handle that *other* problem for you?" Ron asks, "Since I'm back in H town."
Chill says, "Alright. You handle that, bro. But we want the main prize, so hold your killers back. My brother needs to calm his nerves."
Chill knows Ajay, very well. He also knows how much he has needed and wanted to know Raymond's whereabouts.

"Consider it done," Ron says and he assures Chill that his Houston family is going to take care of the coach, before they hang up the phone.

When Chill relays this news to his crew, Ajay becomes very animated and jolly. He's so hype, the crew have to calm him down long enough to discuss a plan.

"We're not waiting for no trial," Ajay demands with confidence.

"No bro," Chill answers quickly, "Definitely not."
They're going to get Raymond while he's in Michigan. It's closer for them and the entire crew still wants to ride on this one. All 18 of them plus Arthur and a few of the Omega's. Raymond wants to pledge Omega but Jr and Arthur make contact with their frat brothers and get him blackballed.

"He's not Omega material," they told their frats.
They make plans to go to Michigan the weekend of September 20th. That's when Jb and Lynn will be home. But they have no idea that they are about to lose another member of their beloved crew.

On September 15, Pearline Anderson "granny" Brown, Pearl's

156

namesake, John and Greg's mother and big mama's best friend, dies suddenly due to complications that caused her heart to fail. She suffers a massive heart attack. The crew are devastated. Ebony and T-baby take the lost hard. T-baby has to go under a doctor's care. Big mama and poppa come from Houston the same night and the Houston crew come back with them. Jb and Lynn fly in from Atlanta. John gets a flight in from Arizona to bury his mother.

The funeral is September 22nd. There isn't a dry eye in the Church, during her service. Granny was dear to everyone who had the pleasure of knowing her. She was active in her community and everybody spoke very highly of her. She'll be missed more than words can say.

The crew rally around papa so he won't be lonely. Him and granny had been together for over 40 years and married for 37 years. John and Greg take the lose of their mother, very hard. They don't communicate with anyone for several days. Except each other and papa Jackson Brown.

"I'm just happy that she knew our oldest children had already selected their husbands and wives," John says, "She was in complete agreement with the paths they're on."
Other then that, he doesn't say much else. Greg Sr doesn't say that much. Pearl and Sandy wonder if their husbands will be able to bounce back.

Tonight after the service, the crew get together at Jr and Tonya's house. Ajay comforts Ebony throughout the evening, as he has done all week. She's having a hard time dealing with the lose of her grandmother. They go up to Bre's room to be alone and talk. They talk about the dinner they had, at granny's house, before Ebony moved to Houston. They're both happy knowing they have her blessings on their relationship. For the 1st time ever, Ajay talks to her about the way he felt when he lost both sets of his grandparents.

"I never knew mama's daddy. He was killed nine years before I was born," he says, "Her mama died when I was two and a half. But I can still remember her. Mama looks just like her. Daddy's mama died when I was six. His daddy passed in eighty three. You remember that?"

"Yes," she says "I do. I remember how much Lynn and Nina was crying. I understand how much they was hurting now too."
The tears come back to her eyes as she says, "I can't deal with this."

"It's hard to accept when you lose somebody that's real good in your life, like a grandparent. Even though it's been years since I lost mine. It's still hard to say goodbye to them," he says, "It's even harder when you lose the ones you chose to take their place, in your life. Like granny was for us. For me and my sisters, we're losing our third grandmother."
157

He has always seen Ebony's grandparents as his own, once his were gone. All of the crew share each others grandparents and parents. They're 1 family. Everyone in this crew has a prominent role in each other's lives. Tank, Ebony, T-baby and Jb go and stay with papa for a few nights. They don't want him to be alone. Big mama and poppa leave on the 28th with the crew from Houston.

After Jb and Lynn go back to school, Ebony, Tank and T-baby go stay with papa to keep him company. When they go, Nina, Ajay, Rich, June and Rebbie aren't far behind.

It's October and the crew are getting back settled into their schools and jobs. Ebony, T-baby and Jan are playing basketball. Nina and Rebbie are cheering. Ajay, Tank, Rich and June are on the basketball team but Rich and June are also in the middle of football season. Football is their best sport. Bre won't be joining the girl's team until after the birth of her baby. She already know she's having a little girl. Still she goes to every practice with her crew. They're all looking forward to basketball season.

On October 11, she gives birth to Chastity Jacquel Coleman. Grandma Jackie is there for the birth of her new grandbaby. She helps Bre to give Chastity, Stoney's last name. Jackie stays in town for a week, along with Chaundra and Charlotte. They all help out with Chastity. CJ, as they would later call her, is a beautiful and healthy baby girl. The Omega, Cedric Hamilton, is at the hospital for the birth also. He has become a familiar face around the crew. He still wants to date Bre.

Life is complicated. Sometimes you can lose so much. And just when it seems like you're at the end of your rope, life gives you a win. Less than a year ago, the crew lost Stoney. Then 6 weeks ago, Brad III was born. 2 weeks later, they lost Granny. Now they have CJ, a part of Stoney, back with them again.

Life lessons keep coming for the crew. They continually face each test with courage and love for each other. With the commitment they've been shown all of their lives. Love *unconditionally* will pull you through the hard times and make the good times plentiful.

PEARLINE ANDERSON *"GRANNY"* BROWN
MAY 9, 1936-------SEPTEMBER 15, 1991
You will live on, through your crew, forever!
We Love you, Eternal!
Rest In Peace, Granny,
-Your Crew

CHAPTER 17

SO MUCH TO BE THANKFUL FOR

Richie Rich's birthday party is held on October 20th which was Stoney's *birth date*, instead of the *first of the month*. It was postponed due to the birth of Stoney's daughter, lil CJ. Rich has been in a great mood, these days. At his party tonight, him and T-baby are *inseparable*. By now, all of the crew have been to see *Boyz n the Hood*, with *Ice Cube*, at least 3 times each. They haven't stopped raving about it and comparing it to their own lives. This is the same reaction they had when *New Jack City* was out.

At Rich's party tonight, they honor Stoney's birthday too. They realize he would've been 22 years-old, if he was still living. They're having a great time but a crew party couldn't be complete without some drama.

Tameka, Michelle and Angel are in attendance. The old punching bags; Anita, Angie, Alana, Darlene and Nicole decide to show up too. *What's been up with these skeezers?*

Anita has hooked up with a small time pimp from the Westside. Child Protective Services has taken 1 of her 2 children, while the other child is with it's father in Gary, Indiana. Anita has always been quick to fuck. But now rumor has it, she has a crack habit to support. For that reason, she has started to sell her body as a means of supporting her drug addiction.

Angie and Nicole are still up to the same game of sleeping with any members of the crew they can get with. Ajay had pushed them all the way off since the attack on Ebony. Still to date, they've had sex with every guy in the active crew including Bruce. The night the guys turned Bruce onto his 1st sexual experience, which was New Years night 1990, it was a tag team with Angie and Nicole. Ajay had called Houston and told Tank about it but Ebony never knew of it and she still doesn't. Jr, Rob, Stoney and Chill had set it up and was in attendance for the early part of the evening. Nicole and Angie had their hands, mouths and everything else full of the 5 of them, the entire evening. The 2 girls just seem to like tag teaming. They're best friends and do everything and everyone, together. For Bruce, it had been a hell of good way to celebrate turning 12 years-old.

Alana is trying to play the good mother role these days. Tank had learned not to mess with her but that didn't stop Rich, Ajay and June from gangbanging her last April, at her aunt Darlene's apartment. Darlene was at work when they all hooked up, after a Smith High school track meet.

TIME TO GROW-RELOADED-TIME WILL REVEAL 2

Darlene is 27 and still longing for 17 year old Ajay. He can fuck her anytime he wants but he would only let her give him head for her money, if he was to even go near her. Since Ebony's been back home, he hasn't been interested in Darlene at all. He doesn't want to give her any reason to try and confront Ebony about him. He knows she'd try too and he'd have to get rid of her. His focus is on getting to Raymond now. He doesn't want to get sidetracked by any bullshit which would surely come from Darlene.

Tameka and Rich have been messing around since the fall school session started. Tameka's learned to play the role of the other woman. T-baby knows nothing of their reconfirming. At least, not yet. But it's only a matter of time before the lid blows again.

Michelle use to be on a Queue-dog binge. She wanted a Queue-dog as her boyfriend. But she hasn't been chosen by one yet. She likes Cedric Hamilton but he isn't interested because he wanted and still wants Bre. Lately, Michelle has cooled out on all the Omega binging and set her sights on Arthur aka *money shot*. She volunteers her time helping him to get his photography and video business off the ground. She doesn't hang out with Alana too much anymore. She's slowly weaning herself away from both Tameka and Angel too. That's mostly due to the fact that Arthur is loyal to the crew and she really wants him. Plus the crew are his *major* investors. They're helping Arthur to fund and break his business. He has applied for a suite in their strip mall and he isn't willing to risk the business or personal relationship he has with his crew.

Angel had a chance to fuck Ajay in August. He had only spent time with her once during the summer. It was the night Arthur had sent her out to his car. Prior to that, the only time he'd been with her was the night Raymond attacked Ebony. On that night, she only had time to suck his dick. He hasn't said a word to her since then. The hook up in August included Rich and Tameka. The girls had gotten a double room at the motel. Rich and Ajay tried to get them to switch up but they wouldn't. It'll only be a matter of time before they do. Because if they don't, Ajay won't mess with either of them anymore. He's only interested in 1-on-1 sex with Ebony. She's the only girl that he insist has to be monogamous. The rest, he shares.

Later into the evening, Tameka steps to Ajay and inquires about Rich. Ajay isn't paying her any attention. She tries to be persistent by holding his arm and playfully yanking on him. But he jerks away from her, very rudely which gets Ebony's attention. She's on the dance floor with Chill at the time it happens and becomes instantly irritated when she sees it. Chill keeps her calm as long as they're dancing. But as soon as they leave the floor, Ebony goes directly to Ajay. She's a little perturbed.
160

"Hey baby," she says, "Are you ready to dance with me?"

"Yea, come on," he says, "Let me see what you're working with."
They walk away, leaving Tameka standing alone. She folds her arms in disgust which gets T-baby's attention. Ajay goes to Rob and asks for a special request. Then he takes Ebony to the center of the floor. They slow dance to *Jodeci's, Stay* and *R. Kelly's, Honey Love.*

Ajay is unpredictable like that. In his own way, he's showing his devotion to Ebony and at the same time, avoiding being approached by any of the hopefuls who showed up thinking they'd have a chance to be with him. His expression is all too clear as he holds Ebony close. He wants everyone to see that she's his girl and he isn't interested in getting with any other girl in attendance. After their dance, Ebony and the foursome take to the floor for some group dancing. Of course Chill joins them. The foursome had gotten back to singing and dancing together, in September. They're planning to enter talent shows this school year.

Bruce is an official member of the crew now. He's interested in Kim, who is Jan's only sister. Chill tells him the rules and regulations he must abide by if he's going to date any girl from their crew. He has to wait until after her 13th birthday before they can have a date. Kim has to be 13 before she can come out with them. She's still twelve. For now, all they can do is talk on the phone, which they do every night.

"I wanna get with her but she's not old enough to come out with the crew yet," Bruce tells Chill, "All we can do, right now, *is* talk on the phone."

"Jan told me you two are always on mama Belinda's phone," Chill says, "But she won't party with us until May. If you're still digging her then, get it *poppin* cousin. But you'd better be up on your crew codes."
Bruce understands this is the way it was for Chill and most of the crew. They couldn't attend crew parties before the age of 13. With the exception of Jb, Ajay, T-baby and Rebbie, who had gotten to go early. In the girls case, they're a unit with Ebony and Nina. As far as Jb and Ajay, they was rebellious and went anyway. Bruce is willing to wait for Kim's coming out party. He gives Chill a pound, then heads off to get a female to dance with him.

"The crew is gonna go on forever, dog," Jr says, after hearing his younger brother express interest in a female from their crew family.

"It don't stop, cuz!" Chill yells.

It's Halloween afternoon when big mama and poppa call Pearl's house. They went to Raymond's arraignment with Ebony's attorney and
161

they want to give them the latest news, as big mama had promised to do. Ebony answers the phone, "Hello."

"Hi baby. How are you?" big mama asks.

"I'm kind of nervous," she says, "I've been nervous all day, thinking about having to come back down there and see his face."

"Well that won't be for awhile," big mama says.

"Why not, big mama? What happened?"

"His lawyer asks for a continuance and the judge granted it," she says, "No matter how much our lawyer objected, the judge gave it to him."

"*How* big mama? Are they gonna let him get away with what he did to me?"

"No baby," big mama says, "They'll have to kill me, Percy and most of this family, if they don't convict him. But there's no telling how long his lawyer will drag it out. He can try to hold off until that jackass finishes college."

"Oh no. No way! I can't deal with this for *four* more years! No way!" she says, as she becomes angry. "When is the new court date suppose to be, mama?" she asks, on the verge of tears.

"May, first," big mama says in a disappointed tone.

"Another six *months*!? No way! No way!" Ebony shouts.

Big mama talks her down and they hang up shortly afterwards.

Ebony sits in her room thinking of the whole incident. She replays it over and over in her mind. She remembers how she felt at the time. How it seemed like she had been there before. That night during the attack, she remembers flashing back to a similar incident or similar feelings. She can't remember anything that terrible ever happening to her.
Why does this feel like déjà vu?

"Maybe I'm losing my mind," she says aloud, "But something about that night is familiar to me. I can't remember why."

She dismisses the thought, for now. She's still very angry and ultimately, still afraid of seeing Raymond White in person. Ajay is still at after-school basketball practice with Tank, Rich and June. They'll be home soon. She's very anxious to tell them the latest news.

Later that evening while Ajay is telling the crew about Raymond's new situation, Chill gets a call from Ron. He further enlightens Chill on why the request for a continuance had been granted.

"It appears dude's life is in *danger* or something," Ron says, "His coach and the coaches whole family was killed a week or so ago. Then just
162

recently, some of Raymond's family members was found dead while they was on some trip or something. So the judge felt like the same ones who got them, might get him too," Ron says, "Crazy *right*?"

He's telling Chill as if he knows nothing about the tragedy. Chill plays along. He know Ron's crew did the deed because he'd issued the hit. Ron had assured him it would be done. Last month Ron had confirmed that the hit on the coach and his family would be carried out when he called with Raymond's whereabouts. Him and his crew had beaten the coach before killing him and his family. There's no need to discuss it further. Since then, Ron's crew has taken out several members of Raymond's immediate family as a bonus. That's because Raymond had left Houston owing Ron money. Poppa has even been questioned once and John has been called as well. But details aren't going to be discussed any further. Before Ron ends the call with Chill, he tells him he'll be up to visit soon. They hang up.

Chill tells the crew about his conversation with Ron. Now they feel certain the justice system isn't going to handle Raymond the right way. The crew wants him dealt with before he's another year older. So they set their own Ann Arbor plan in motion. It angers them more to see the way Raymond is sliding through the system.

"I'm going to Ann Arbor and get that bitch, *myself*," Ajay says.

"Hell yea because them muafuckaz gonna fuck around and let his ass walk!" Tank adds.

"That muafucka walking straight up in that muthafuckin chamber, homie. That's my word," Ajay states, "And he might not be able to walk."

"Let's work crew," Chill says and they begin, right then and there, planning their strategy.

Their plan has to be precise and thorough. They're going to use their many connections to get to Raymond White. His coach had out witted them in Houston. But no one is going to out smart the crew this time. They can't allow that to ever happen again.

After an hour of discussion, they have a sure fire plan. Jr will use Raymond's fascination with being an Omega man as their way to trap him. Their plan will launch during the Thanksgiving Holidays, when most of the students are away from campus and the crew are home from college. The Ann Arbor basketball team will be on campus for practice. With the season opener being just 2 days after the holiday, the team will be there for sure. The crew are going to have a few Omega's set up a fake meeting for Raymond's pledge request and let him accept it. This way, they'll know for sure he'll be there. When he shows up to what *he thinks* is an interview to be a potential pledge, the crew will be there waiting for him.

163

"Alright, it's all set," Chill says, "We're gonna leave here on the Friday after Thanksgiving. Go over there, get his ass, bring him on back to the chamber and string him up, as low key as ever."

"I need to torture that bitch for awhile, before I kill him," Ajay says, "You've got to give me that. He's got to feel how bad he fucked up when he hurt *my* girl. Do y'all understand me? So the next nigga will know not to fuck with Ebony Brown. She's spoken for and she's got a man who'll open a niggaz head and chest up, in broad day light if necessary."

Ajay's demeanor is cold and calculating as he talks about Raymond's demise. For the 1st time, his crew can see just how much he has agonized over getting to Raymond. Even more so, Ebony realizes how much he was hurt over not being there to protect her.

"That bitch ass nigga can beg all he wants. He's gonna die real slow, for what he did to my baby."

By now, tears have formed in his eyes. He looks at Ebony and puts his arms around her, then kisses her on her cheek.

"He won't hurt you anymore, baby girl," he says, "I told you."

"I know, Anthony," she says as she lays her head on his shoulder, "I have no doubts about that."

The rest of the crew are silent. They all agree, Raymond White must die. Though Raymond's announcement of what college he would attend had been downplayed and got no media coverage for *safety* reasons. The streets had gotten the word on him. The streets is the still the best network, too date. One would be wise to be good to the streets if they have intentions of moving around in them. Because street justice is a lot more brutal and deliberate then any court in the land. *Any land.*

Chill, Ajay, Jr, Tank and Jb will make the trip to Michigan. Some of the crew thinks Ajay should wait in Cleveland so Raymond is alive to make it back. But he shuns that away and looks at them with a death eye. The guys laugh. Ajay will be in that number. The rest of the crew are to wait until they return. These November days can't pass fast enough for Ajay and the Cleveland crew.

By the end of the first week, Pearl gets a call from George Wheeler. The Cleveland police, on behalf of the Houston police department, want to speak with John about the deaths of the coach, the coaches family and Raymond's family members. They have questioned poppa twice and are bringing him in a 3rd time. They haven't been able to pin anything on either of them but they're going to question them as much as the law will allow. Hoping one of them will crack. John has to leave the road, meet Wheeler in Houston and go to the police station for questioning.

164

TIME TO GROW-RELOADED-TIME WILL REVEAL 2

No matter how much questioning they do, neither poppa or John are able to tell them what happened to the deceased because they don't know. And even if they did, they wouldn't tell them. Neither of them give a damn about the coach, his family members or Raymond's family members either. They didn't give a damn about the safety of Ebony or any other young girl that Raymond White had taken advantage of. If they'd cared, they would've warned people about the animal that Raymond White is.

It's now well into November. The end of football season is near. Basketball season is about to start. The crew are anticipating the season. But not as much as they're anticipating Thanksgiving weekend.

During Thanksgiving week, big mama and poppa arrive along with the Houston crew. Ron and his crew look out on big mama and poppa, back at home. They're family with Chill and the crew, who had asks them to keep an eye out and make certain poppa and big mama get whatever they needed done. Ron's crew know how protective the Cleveland crew are of big mama and poppa Jones. Even more so, after losing granny so suddenly.

Jb has a last minute practice on Wednesday evening. Then him and Lynn catch a flight from Atlanta to make it home for Thanksgiving dinner, which is being served at papa's house.

John Sr isn't able to make it for Thanksgiving dinner. Him and Wheeler are still in Houston for yet another questioning session. They're staying at poppa and big mama's home. He calls his father's home just as the families are gathering to have dinner. He talks to everyone before dinner is served. But then Pearl and John are on the phone for so long, big mama has to remind her that dinner is on the table.

At dinner, Papa blesses the meal with a special prayer. It includes a moment of silence for his late wife granny Pearline and Stoney. He has a reminder for all of the family as well.

"Though we've all had our share of trials and tribulations. We still have so much to be thankful for," he says, "We've come along way as a family and still got a ways to go. We have offspring who have captured our entrepreneurial spirit and are capitalizing on the dream we all started out with. Though we was sidelined by bigots who wasn't disrobed when the civil rights laws was recorded. We never gave up the dream. We just had to preplan and reorganize. Our children's research found the way to get the ball rolling. Their children are bringing it to fruition. To the crew! May we always stay loyal, stand strong and make change!"

Mama Jackie, Chaundra, Charlotte and Jackie's husband Jason attend. The crew's families have taken Jackie under their wing since losing Stoney.
165

BLACK COFFEE   TIME TO GROW-RELOADED-TIME WILL REVEAL 2

They want to make sure *she knows* their definition of what true family means. And they also want to have very close ties with Stoney's little sisters, Chaundra and Charlotte.

After dinner papa and poppa play some of the records they made when they had their band. Big mama sings but she becomes very emotional when she hears the records with granny Pearline on them. The whole crew sing with her. She tells the foursome to imagine if 1 of them was dead.

"How would the rest of you feel?" she asks.

"I can't even imagine it," Nina says.

"It would be worse than anything I could imagine," Ebony says. T-baby and Rebbie agree with them.

"I would lose my mind," T-baby says.

"I would go crazy too," Rebbie adds.

"That's how lost I feel without Pearline," big mama says, "We still have Sally and Joshua, Annabelle and Charles Leon, Jackson, Percy and myself. But big mama Jo, Allen Saul, Bertha, big Allen senior and now Pearline are all gone from our crew," she says, "Jeb junior and Jessie Mae, Ree Ree's grandparents, are still exiled in London. They won't even come back to the states. Their marriage was threatened just because they was of different races. Big Paul and Shirley, Chill's grandparents, was a part of our crew as well."

"The original crew!" grandma Annabelle yells, "We had a lot of good times. But when we was the street crew, we had racial things to deal with on a daily basis. Racism was a lot different and more deliberate when we was young kids. Jeb Junior marrying a black woman led his own race to wanna harm *not only her* but him too. Even the laws on the books was unjust. Our children did the integrating in the sixties and seventies. *Eighties* in some places. Which was a bad chapter in itself. But when they was old enough to work, they could go to work in stores or established businesses. But not us. We had to start our own stores. Or sew for the community. Do the washing and all. That's where we learned to be entrepreneurs. We kept to ourselves, spent our monies with our own businesses and raised our own food too. If we wanted to work outside of our own businesses, we had to work for white people. In their homes or on their land. Sometimes you didn't have a choice about working for them. They'd force you too, one way or the other. But you would not work in their companies. That was unheard of in our youth."

"It wasn't the usual thing when we was young," papa says, "In this family, it was uncommon. Not until John got on with mister Baker. Allen Saul had worked for the *Colonial Bread* company down in Tennessee. That
166

was the only out-sourced job from our generation. But we still sent all of our children to college. We worked our fingers to the bone to make sure they benefited from *all* the hard work we did. Even with getting things integrated. For whatever good *that* did."

"That land where the car shop and club is," grandpa Charles Leon says, "That was Allen senior and Paul senior's land. It was taken away by some bigots up here. That's the true story of how it got lost in the first place. We had *many* stores over there. But the bigots took the whole thing because we was independent blacks and they didn't like that. Then they lost it. We kept up with it and our children got it back and then some."

"We wouldn't tell your parents it was taken by racist folks, when they was younger," grandpa Joshua says, "Because they would've gone out there with guns blazing. We waited until they was parents before letting them know. We knew they'd be more responsible. But they got it back in their own way and the truth stayed a secret until now."

"I vote for the guns blazing," Tank says as everyone laughs.
Grandpa Joshua chuckles and continues his story, "I know your generation would've rather died then work it out. If you had known what we went through just to keep up with how the hands were changing over there. Still, being up here was better than what we'd come from. Down south, it wasn't but a horseshoe throw away from slavery. I took many beatings for things I never even knew anything about. Not until they was beating me. And they would've killed me if I'd said I didn't do it. But I hadn't done a damn thing but be born with my beautiful black skin."

"As children we would get beat for trying to learn. Just for going to school," grandpa Charles says, "We dealt with injustice all the time. In every case. But laws supported it. It was a cast system."

"Every one of these grandfathers in here, had to quit school to work in the fields," poppa adds, "We come from the south. Texas. Mississippi. Louisiana. Alabama and Tennessee. We migrated to Ohio. Some of us with our parents, looking for a better life. But Sally and Joshua was run off from Mississippi in nineteen fifty. It took them nearly fifteen years to get here and settle down."

"I wasn't but fourteen and she was twelve," grandpa Joshua says, "The *klan* burned down our lil community, one night in Philadelphia, Mississippi. They killed all the folks who hadn't escaped Neshoba county already. Just because they was mad at the attention the blacks was getting from the government. *The national government.* My daddy, granddaddy and two uncles had been killed long before that. My mama escaped to Maryland and lived there until she died. But Sally's family wasn't so lucky
167

that night. Wasn't lucky at all. That was way before voting was passed."

"Bigotry was truly protected by laws then. They're right," big mama says, "Texas wasn't any better. The south had the reputation of Jim Crow and it upheld it proudly. Still does. Only not so obvious as then. But you'll get folks now who say they don't support it and didn't agree with those times. Yet and still they do nothing to uncover the truth. Half of them will make jokes about it and expect you to laugh at shit that's not funny. But rather offensive to you and me. They'll say others might be offended or something of that nature, if they made a fuss. What they really mean is they don't care to confront it and they would rather not be apart of telling the truth. Jeb Baker and his family was nothing like that. Thank God."

"But the bigots, they still want access to our way of living," grandma Sally says, "As long as they don't have to blend it with theirs or let others see that they're interested in our culture."

"From Arizona to Virginia and as far north as the Mason-Dixon line, the laws that allowed it to happen stayed in affect," big mama says, "And that was long after the *so called* legislation. The south was and in some places still is, Jim Crow. When they yell states rights, that's a shield."

"We marched with *Dr Martin Luther King Jr*," grandma Sally adds, "*Reverend Abernathy* and *Reverend Jesse Jackson junior, Andre Young*. They all started out real young and so did we," she chuckles, "But where y'all ride around looking for things to get into, we didn't have that option."

"We broke laws too, is what the ladies are saying," papa clarifies, "But we did it by going into diners and demanding to be served, and the like. Back then the laws *were* unjust. The things we marched against was the unequal treatment. It was just like the Boston harbor and the tea party. When you're a taxpayer in your community, town or city and you don't have any representation, then that's *taxation without representation*. We had to pay the same taxes and prices for goods and services that the others did. Sometimes we paid more if that was what they demanded from us. Because we needed the supplies to maintain. We had no voice in government until *Dr King*, *Fannie Lou Hamer* and *Malcolm X* showed us the way to reach the world. So we need for y'all to know we aren't gonna tolerate any jail time for foolishness. If you go to jail, it'd better be for standing up for something meaningful. And yes, your parents broke laws too and not necessarily *unjust* ones." Everybody laughs and he continues, "They were more rebellious in their time. They had the Vietnam conflict to protest. Us parents ran our businesses. Don't let nobody tell you conflict is war either. Congress declares war. Not the president. Remember that. But still with all of the protesting of war which brought out all races, they still had some
168

racial prejudices to overcome. And its the same as it is for your generation of crew, Kenny."

"Yes sir," Chill says.

"You all, *no matter what,* have to succeed," papa says, "There's no other option. You will not allow the bigots and their *controlled organize slavery* to take over your lives. I don't care what else you do, as long as you do it with the reputation of this family in mind."

"The youth movement is what brought on the real change," grandpa Charles starts again, "This is what we need for *all of you* to understand. You come from a legacy. No matter what kind of cultural things get popularized in your day and age. You have a family legacy to uphold and you *damn well* better respect it. Is that clear?"

"*Yes sir!*" They all reply.

"Now who was that said they can out sing Jackson-Jones Revue?" poppa asks and they all laugh again.

Before the jam session starts, Chill adds that he already knows the feeling of losing special folks and a special friend.

"Stoney was our original crew and after losing my mama, daddy and my grandparents at a young age, this is my family," he says, "These are the only parents and grandparents I have. Granny is missed sorely, right now. My son called her granny and really felt like she was. She even included him in their portraits. I pledge my life and loyalty to upholding the name and struggle that all of you went through for us."

His whole crew cosigns him. They was here for him when big Paul was killed. They remember how much pain he was in and how much damage he had done.

"I know loss too," Brenda says, "I lost my twin brother when we was seven. He drowned on a vacation bible school trip. Me and Brendan was closer than any two people can be. Pearl use to keep us in line. She was our big sister. She took up for us and kept us out of trouble."

"Yes indeed," big mama says, "Losing a child is the hardest thing in the world."

"Amen," Jackie says, "Lord knows it is."

"It's why we won't allow y'all to make drugs your future," poppa says, "There's no future in it. Except death or prison. Basic slavery."

With that said, the family jam session gets under way and last for more than 3 hours.

Later Chill and Jr catch Rebbie's younger brother Shannon and June's younger sister Brittany, kissing on the back porch. Chill tell their parents immediately. They stop and talk to them both, right away.

169

Afterwards, 12 year-old Shannon, best known as Reaper, doesn't understand what made Chill tell on him. He asks him about it in private.

"Chill why you snitch on me, man?" Reaper asks.

"Young brother *didn't* you just hear what all of our forefathers and mothers *just* got through telling us? We have a legacy *and* rules, which keeps that legacy solid. These rules have been in place for like a hundred years, homie. Things have to go a certain way. She's not at the age where they'll agree for her to be kissing. But they need to know y'all like each other," he explains, "It's *my* crews job to let them know what we see from the crew behind us. That way, they can keep an eye on you and make sure y'all come up right, in code and respectable."

"I have to be thirteen, don't I?" Reaper asks.

"Yes and so does she. Chill out. It'll be here before you know it," Chill says with a smile.

He finishes with a pound and Reaper asks no other questions. Soon after, the crew leave for the club.

Ajay and Ebony go to *The Spot* but they don't stay long. They want privacy. Of course they discuss tomorrow's trip once they get to Chill's house. Tank and Nina go to Rob's apartment for some private time. Rebbie and June are spending the night at Jr's. T-baby and Rich are staying at Arthur's. None of the crew hang out for long, tonight. They have a mission of justice of their own to carry out. It's street justice and Raymond is the target. They're anticipating the upcoming weekend and the trip to Ann Arbor, to bring him in.

John calls Pearl and lets her know his 3rd questioning went fine. But he was at the Houston police department until after midnight.

"They tried their damn *best* to pin that assholes murder on me," he says, "But I got log sheets. They couldn't get around those."

"Oh baby. I'm just glad to hear from you," she says, "I worried the whole time we was at your daddy's house and he was too. He wasn't worried about them keeping you for murder. He was worried about your temper and so was I."

"Oh I told them if I could get my hands on him, I'd beat him like he beat my daughter."

"*John.*"

"I mean it, Pearlie," he says, "It's not an ounce of sympathy in my heart for that coach nor Raymond."

"I know it's not," she says and changes the subject, "Daddy said for me to make sure you and George are staying at their house while you
170

have to be in Houston. And mama said she left full meals for two, in her freezer."

"Tell him we're here already and everything is secure," John says, "We're full of good food and I'm missing my wife, even more. Since I'm in your parents home."

"I miss you, baby," Pearl says, "I can't wait until you're home."

"We're turning into Ajay and Ebony," he says and they laugh. Then talk until 3am before they hang up.

It's finally Friday morning. Ajay, Chill, Tank, Jb and Jr leave for Michigan in Wayne's van. Wayne, who's family lives just outside of Ann Arbor, makes this trip numerous times on weekends. It isn't unusual for him to go. Especially with this being the holiday season, which is why the crew chose him to drive them.

When they arrive, Jr calls his frat house. He speaks with his brother Aaron who assures him everything's in order and the meeting is set. Only 2 other frats remain in the house besides Aaron. They're in on the plan as well. The meeting will take place after dark. The crew have an alibi for the house too. After they have Raymond, Aaron will call Raymond's dorm room, ask for him and say he never showed up for the meeting.

By 6:30pm, Ajay is so hyped up, he can't stay seated. The crew are at the frat house and Raymond has just called to say he's on his way. Aaron took the call. Him and the 2 frats are at the house for the holidays. They're down for helping out Jr's crew because they donate and fund them.

When Raymond arrives and Aaron lets him in the house, the crew are outside waiting in the double garage, next to the van. They're going to run in, in ski mask and pretend to be robbing the place so the frats won't be implicated if something goes wrong and Raymond gets away. It's taking everything they have to keep Ajay calm, at this point.

Raymond comes in and takes the seat pointed out to him by Rashon Dunning, 1 of the 3 Omega's in the house. Raymond is excited about having the opportunity to be an Omega man. At least, that's what he thinks he's doing there. Two minutes later, the crew storm the room. Before Raymond can see him or even blink, Ajay attacks him. He hits him in the back of his head with his blackjack and knocks him unconscious. They drag him into the garage, put a sack over his head and tie a rope around his neck to keep it in place. They hog tie his wrist and ankles. Within minutes, they are headed back to Cleveland.

Raymond regains consciousness due to Ajay hitting and kicking him, during the trip. The others remind him to save it for the chamber but
171

Ajay is in the zone. He has dreamed of *this* day for *far* too long to relax.

"Bitch ass, do you know how *long* I've waited for this?" Ajay asks Raymond.

Ajay is extra emotional, which is *very* unlike him. But still, he isn't yelling. Him being emotional is what alerts the others and lets them know just how pivotal this moment is for him. This was a test Ajay had to pass and the relief he had to give Ebony in order to forgive himself for ever allowing it to happen in the first place. He feels like Raymond attacking his girl was a test of his manhood. Now that he has Raymond in his hands, he's not going to let up. He hits him again and yells, "I need this muthafucka to see me!"

Chill says, "No. We're leaving him covered up like we planned. It'll keep, cuz. It'll keep."

Again Ajay kicks and hits him relentlessly. Finally, Chill has to put him in the front seat to keep him from beating Raymond to death before they can even get him to the chamber and get a piece of him too.

The foursome met up at Jr's house this morning, while the guys went Michigan to get Raymond. Ebony is very nervous and overly excited. She's nervous about being in the presence of Raymond White again. But she's excited that her man and crew will have control of the situation, this time. She's angry at the stress this ordeal has caused to her and her crew. The foursome ride with Tonya and Renee to the airport to pick up Ron and Carolyn. They want a piece of Raymond's ass for the money he owes them. Ron has already started the cover story for why Raymond had disappeared from college. Him and Chill will discuss it later.

Alas, the guys arrive in Cleveland and take Raymond straight to the chamber. They hang him up on the chains, leave his face covered with the sack, then wait for the rest of the crew to arrive.

Before the crew gets there, Ajay has beaten Raymond severely. He has to be restrained by his own crew. They restrain him with cuffs for the time being.

"This is some bullshit and y'all know it!" Ajay yells in protest, "Y'all owe me him! This nigga owe me his life! I never said I was gonna take it easy on that bitch and y'all know it!"

As hard as it is not to give in, Chill and the others won't let him get loose again until later, after the entire crew are there and there's more help with keeping him off of Raymond. And not until he's calm enough that he won't kill him on impulse and blow their entire plan.

The first night, all of the crew are present. The foursome watch as the others take turns beating Raymond. Nina, T-baby and Rebbie join in.

172

Ebony doesn't. She stands in the background watching and trembling at the mere thought of being near Raymond again. She's nervous already and she hasn't even seen his face. Chill steps away from the beating and orders everyone else to stop. They do. Ray is still alive and begging for his life. He still has no idea who snatched him. He thinks it has something to do with his coach and his families murder's. Which he has to know was ultimately about him or something he's done. He has fucked over so many people in his life, he can only ask over and over, "What did I do? Who are y'all, man? Tell me your name, please. I didn't do nothing!"

Chill says to Ebony, "Come stand in front of him."

She can't do it. Not on her own. Ajay brings her closer. She has that feeling of dé·jà vu, once again and still can't figure out why. Chill removes the sack from Raymond's head. When he sees Ebony's face, he freaks out.

"Oh God! I'm so sorry! I promise I wasn't gonna hurt you!"

Ajay hits him in the face with his club and says, "Nah bitch. Later for that shit. You did hurt her, muthafucka. That's where you fucked up. I told you not to fuck wit her. Tank told you. Her daddy told you. Everybody told your bitch ass to leave her the *fuck* alone but you couldn't, could you?"

"Didn't I tell you not to fuck with my sister, nigga?!" Tank yells, "But you waited until I moved back home and fucked wit her anyway. You can save that noise, bitch. You're dying in this muthafucka."

Ajay continues talking to him in a chillingly calm tone. He hits him again and again. Tank and Jb join in. Then Lynn. Then Nina and soon, the rest of the crew are on him again. Chill has to stop them all again.

"Baby girl what do you wanna do with him?" Chill asks.

Again she feels Dé·jà vu. It seems she's heard Chill ask her this before. *But where? When? Why?*

She doesn't say anything when he asks again, so Ajay jumps in and says, "We're gonna kill his ass, that's what! Make no mistake about it, nigga. You will not leave here alive."

"Its up to you, Ebony," Chill says.

"I don't want him to be able to hurt me again," she says slowly.

"Then let me kill his ass, baby and its over," Ajay urges.

"No. Hold on Ajay. Not until she's ready," Chill says with a look of Dé·jà vu on his face also.

Ebony looks at Chill. He looks back at her. The others offer solutions.

"We need to torture his ass for a few more days," Tank says.

"I'm wit that shit," Bre agrees.

"I got the gasoline, homie," Rob adds, "We can slow cook his ass

173

until she's ready. It ain't shit. It's never been a problem to cook out."

Then turning his attention away from Ebony, Chill says, "Alright! We're gonna do this a lil bit every day until this bitch is done."

They decide to end the torture for tonight and start back tomorrow. Jr and Chill are staying at the chamber to guard Raymond. Ajay insist on staying too. Everybody agrees he shouldn't and even though he's protesting their decision, it changes nothing.

"You have to go with baby girl," Chill whispers to Ajay, "Get her mind right for this mission. She's gonna be the one who's gonna shoot this nigga, if he don't bleed out first. So the next time she thinks she's in danger, she'll carry her piece."

"Let me do this nigga, man," Ajay tries, "What the fuck we waiting around for?"

"She can do it," he says, "Don't ever underestimate her."

Reluctantly, Ajay finally agrees to leave as the others prepare to go.

"Let me give his bitch ass some water," Renee says.

"Yea so he don't go dying on us before we can kill him," Tonya say as she laughs.

Ajay hits him once more, for good measure. Before his crew drags him out to his vehicle and makes him get in and leave. The rest of the crew leave too. Jr and Chill are left alone to guard Raymond. They think of other ways to drive their point home.

During the night, they talk to him about his mistakes and torture him more by pouring salt in his wounds. He screams. They douse him with cold water to prevent him from going into shock. Keeping him healthy until time for his murder is torture in itself. They even feed him and give him more water to drink throughout the night.

Before daybreak, Chill calls on Arthur and tells him to bring those do-do chasers from the Grove by the chamber. *Do-do chaser is a term they use to describe homosexual males*. Since Raymond tried to rape Ebony, they want him to experience firsthand, what would've happened if he had gone to prison. Or they make Raymond think that's what's going to happen. Chill tells Arthur to bring the 2 chasers who owe the crew money. Lastly, he says, "Make sure they know the special instructions."

Soon after, Arthur arrives with the chasers.

"Raymond," Jr starts, "You know we're saving you from being somebody's bitch, right? If your monkey ass was gonna be around to do time, this is the shit they do to rapist in the penitentiary."

Jr, Chill and Arthur lower his knees to the floor then step outside, leaving him alone with the chasers. He doesn't know it but Chill gave Arthur

174

specific instructions. The guys are not to have sex with Raymond. Chill would never go for anything like that, even though he hates Raymond. He gave instructions that they are to just scare him by feeling on him and making him believe they're going to rape him. They leave the door open so the chasers think they're watching. Though they aren't. From outside they can hear Raymond scream and struggle. They hear the taunting and wolfing from the chasers. After 15 minutes, Chill bangs on the door signaling to the chasers their time is up. Him, Arthur and Jr go back inside. Immediately, Jr pulls his 9mm, cocks it back and kills the chasers instantly.

"They thought they was gonna live to tell about this shit?" Chill ask and laughs, "They fell for that *we're gonna excuse your debt,* story?" Arthur is laughing as he says, "They really believed you would forget the four grand if they did this and followed instructions. Stupid motherfuckaz. Like I said, nobody saw them come by and get in the ride, so fuck it."

"Muafuckaz *know* the crew ain't down with no play like that," Jr adds, "Not on no *collaborating* type shit. Hell no."

"Hey Ray. You're going to the grave knowing the crew ain't about no rape or no other punk shit either. Yo ho's lied, as you can see," Chill says, "Crew didn't assault them bitches. They was trying to fuck all of us." They hoist him back into the air, then hide the chasers bodies until they're ready to dispose of Raymond. They'll bury the 3 of them together and let law enforcement try to figure it out. The first night of torture is done.

Ajay arrives first, with Ebony by his side on Saturday morning. He's extra animated today. It's obvious he was anticipating coming back. He starts off with a swift blow to Raymond's body with his blackjack.

"I dreamed about you, last night," he says to Raymond with a smile, while he's stretching and flexing his muscles. The rest of the crew aren't far behind them. Today they allow Kilo, an Omega from New Orleans whom Jr met at CSU, to come along. Ron and Carolyn come too. The money Raymond still owed Ron when he disappeared, is the motivation which brings him to want to see his demise. Not only that but he tested Ron's power with the meddling of Ebony. Even after several warnings and whippings by Ron and his crew. Ron has a vested interest in seeing him executed. Rob walks in with a can of gasoline.

"Let's get the charcoal going," he says as he pours a little gasoline over Raymond's chest and lets it seep into his shirt. The females flick cigarette lighters to his chest and watch as his minimal chest hairs burn away, one at a time. This was Kilo's suggestion. He's been putting in work for years with his clique in New Orleans. He just loves to see and do dirt. Ajay finally convinces Ebony to take part in the torture.

175

She takes a cigarette from him and puts it out in Raymond's mouth. The rest of the crew do similar torture for hours. Ajay takes part in all of it and doesn't have to be convinced. Even when the others take a break, he doesn't. He wants to see Raymond squirm. He also wants to see his girl get angry enough to return the harm to him that he'd done to her. He needs Raymond to help him take Ebony back to that night. He figures the only way to do that is to have Raymond talk about it. He insist Raymond tell him, in his own words, exactly what he'd done to Ebony. It takes Raymond a few minutes but after a few brutal whacks from Ajay's blackjack, he slowly begins to recount his version of his assault on *Ajay's girl*.

The crew stand and listen and become even more angry after hearing him speak on it. He reveals detail after detail of the incident. Ebony cringes as she hears him admit he'd been following her the whole week, just waiting to catch her alone. Waiting for an opportunity to steal her virtue. Chill takes a *throw away* .357 magnum from Ajay, who's getting antsy and ready to shoot. He fixes it in Ebony's hands. He remembers now why he has déjà vu. At this moment, he recalls it. He makes eye contact with Ebony which gives her the strength she needs to do this. She's poised, standing directly in front of Raymond. Ajay is coaching while Raymond gives vivid details of how he'd attempted to rape Ebony. He has to assure Ajay, he didn't succeed because Ajay has to hear it from him. Raymond tells how he forced Ebony into his backseat then ripped her shirt and bra off. Hearing him say it is what helps Ebony find her strength. She unleashes.

"Tell them how you beat me with your gun, you piece o' *shit!*" she yells while still standing directly in front of him.
That's a phrase she had gotten directly from big mama. She screams other facts at him, as tears come. She tells him how much he'd terrified her. How hard it was for her to trust anybody after what he'd done. The crew stand and watch in amazement, as she confronts her attacker. She's insisting he finish the whole story. She screams her accounts of it each time he stumbles over a fact. Even Ajay is stunned now at how in charge his girl is. When Raymond talks about how he was trying to suck on her breast, she starts to tremble as if she's reliving it all over again. She points the gun toward him as she trembles violently. Ajay looks at her. His expression is one of doubt and impatience. He doesn't think she can do it. Chill looks at her. His expression is one of familiarity. He knows she'll shoot to protect herself and her crew. Ray is revealing the part where he was trying to get her out of her shorts. But she kneed him and got away. And how he quickly recovered and went after her. She's heard all she needs to hear. She's done all the *reliving the moment* she needs too. In her mind, it's May 28, 1991.
176

TIME TO GROW-RELOADED-TIME WILL REVEAL 2

She can see herself struggling to get him off of her. She can see herself begging him not to hurt her or please don't hit her anymore. Or just kill her and get this whole nightmare over with. She's begging him to leave her alone but he won't stop.

He's punching me and beating me. He's gonna rape me. He's gonna ruin me and Anthony's love.

Bang! Bang! Bang! Bang! Bang! Bang!

She unloads the revolver into Raymond's body. He dies instantly. His body swings back and forth, hanging from the chains in front of her and her crew. Some of them are shocked and staring at her. Ajay is 1 of the shocked. He didn't think she could do it but she has. Then the reality of the moment hits her like a ton of bricks falling out of the sky.

"Ah! Oh God!" she screams and drops the gun on the floor.
Her knees go weak and Ajay grabs her before she can collapse. She has fainted. Ajay takes her from the room as Jb grabs the gun from the floor.

"No traces," Chill says and the guys move with precision while the girls stand out of the way.
Rob, Tank and June take Raymond down and puts him in the cast iron tub in the back room. They even take time to dig the spent bullets out of his body or those they can get too. They do the same with the chasers.

"No traces," June says, repeating Chill's words.
Rob pours gasoline all over Raymond's body and Rich sets him on fire. They all watch as he burns rapidly.

"Now that's what I call a controlled burn," Rob says with a grin.
The crew still hits Raymond with sticks and bats as his body burns. One at a time, they toss the chasers in with him and let them burn to bones.

Ebony was in no condition to stick around for the cleaning. Ajay left with her immediately, going to the motel and to room 111. He wants to calm her down and be certain she's able to handle what has just happened before she can go back to Shaker Heights.

At the chamber, the crew clean and clear out all clues and evidence. They wrap Raymond and the chasers remains in plastic and cloth. Then they clean the tub and the chains thoroughly. After the chamber is cleaned, Chill, Ron, Kilo and Rich, along with June and Rob, drive back across the state line and to some undeveloped acres of land somewhere in Michigan. They bury what's left of the 3 bodies.

"Let's see them explain how he ended up dead with two fags," Kilo says as they drive back to Cleveland and put the matter of Raymond to rest
177

and vow that he'll no longer be an issue for the crew or Ebony, ever again.

After hours of talking and trying to get Ebony to relax, Ajay finally manages to calm her down and she takes a nap. Later, they talk.

"I feel like I'm reliving a nightmare," she whispers as she lays in Ajay's arms in room 111.

"It's alright now baby. I got you," he says.

Later, Tank brings her girls by the motel to be with her.

By late evening, she's calm enough to go home. Ajay drives her back. They go to *the Chill Spot* with the rest of the crew, where they all kick it together. She's settled as long as she's close to them. She thinks and speaks about the murder she committed, several times throughout the night. But only to her crew. As the evening goes on, she manages to put it in the back of her mind and though she still feels like she's been here before, she can't figure out why. But as far as today's incident is concerned, she knows she'll never forget it.

Once their back in school, she finds it easier to live with the ordeal. She has her girls and her man by her side. They're at school with her. Ajay keeps a close eye on her, daily. Though this is her only memory of killing someone, she feels strangely familiar with the whole cover up part of it. She knows now that she can handle it and if necessary for the safety of her, her family and crew, she can do it again.

Just before Christmas break, Ajay puts her car in their detail shop. His gift to her this year, is going on her car.

Christmas break comes and goes. Ebony and Nina turn sweet 16. Nina gives Tank a herringbone. He gives her a diamond and gold bracelet. Ajay puts expensive rims and a kit on Ebony's car for her birthday and Christmas presents. She gives him starter jersey's and caps from the *Cleveland Indians, Browns and Cavaliers.* Plus his favorite basketball team the *Chicago Bulls.* She also gives him the latest version of *Air Jordan's.* He has both styles now. Her Honda Accord is tight with accessories just like her man's six four. Plus he gives her the same bracelet Nina has. Chill and Renee get a 1992 Blazer. Chill keeps the 1989 as his vehicle. They call them *his and hers* Blazers. Jr and Tonya give the Sentra to Bruce and buy a 1992 Bonneville. Rebbie gives June a pair of Air Jordan's and a *Cross Colors* outfit. T-baby gives Rich the same. The tight-as-they-come foursome, all got diamond and gold bracelets from their guys.

After New Years, Bre returns to the basketball team. Bruce celebrated his birthday with a crew party. He's 14 now and heavy in the
178

the crew life. He has also developed into an excellent football player. So good, in fact, he's moving up to play with June and Rich next fall.

The start of the spring semester finds Ebony doing a student job in the main office as an assistant. She's able to give her crew hall passes which keep them from being marked tardy. She can get them out of class from time to time too. Miss Whitman, a young teacher, had recommended her for the position and she assists her with helping her crew. Ebony thinks it's because she likes her and she's a *down ass* teacher. But Miss Whitman has her own agenda. She's always buying gifts for Ebony, who figures it's because she's nice. She never speaks about Miss Whitman to Ajay. But her girls know about the gifts and the favors. It isn't until Miss Whitman gives her a make-up kit and shows her how to fix her face up, that Ajay gets involved. Ebony doesn't usually wear make-up but she does wear it to school the next day, as a gesture of her appreciation to Miss Whitman for buying it. As soon as Ajay sees her, he insist she go wash it off. She tries to explain to him that Miss Whitman had given it to her as a gift and she feels it might seem unappreciative if she didn't at least wear some from time to time. He still insist she go to the girls bathroom and wash it off.

"You don't need that on your face," he says, "I don't care who gave it to you. She needs it. You don't."

"Can I just wear it until after second hour?" she tries, "Until I'm done in the office? Then I'll go and wash it off."

"No," he says, "Ebony you don't need that mess on your face. You look so much better without it. Wash it off now," he insists, "I'll handle her if she have anything to say."

Ebony goes into the bathroom to wash her face then she goes straight to the office afterwards. Just as she'd guessed, Miss Wittman asks her why she isn't wearing the make-up.

"My boyfriend don't like it on me and I really don't like to wear it either. I just washed it off," she says, giving her a slight smile.

"Oh *really*?" Miss Whitman replies, "It's probably because he knows I gave it to you."

Ebony thinks about Miss Whitman's comment for a moment. Then she dismisses it saying, "Anthony don't like a whole lot of people. He most likely don't think I should be that chummy with a teacher either. He *has* had his share of trouble with y'all since he's been here."

"I wonder if that's it," Whitman says, smiling as she walks away.

"Whatever," Ebony says as she attends to her filing duties.

179

It's nearly the end of March. It's closing in on spring break and the crew are still doing what crew do. Rich is sneaking around with Tameka again. Ajay has seen Angel again as well. The shit is surely about to hit the fan.

During spring break the foursome are in a talent show at the spot. They win hands down and of course, the crew celebrate. Later that evening after taking the foursome home, Rich, Ajay, June and Tank hook up with Tameka, Angel, Nicole, Angie and Alana.
What the hell is on their minds?

They have an orgy at the motel which was the only way Ajay would go. Before Spring Break ends, the word gets back to the foursome. The same day the girls hear the rumor, all hell breaks loose at the park. They show up and confront their guys. The girls are understandably furious and the guys have no explanation. June, Tank and Rich try to lie about it but Ajay tells Ebony the truth about his part. It hurts and frustrates her, even more. T-baby is especially upset and isn't even willing to hear Rich's explanation. She tells him it's over. Then she demands Ebony take her home, "Now!" Ajay won't let go of Ebony's arm. She can't go to her car. That's when T-baby snatches the keys from Ebony and gets into the driver's seat. Rich tries to stop her and she curses him out. Without thinking, he punches her in her face. The others try to stop him but he grabs her and pulls her through the window, then he begins to choke her. She tries to fight him off but she can't handle him. Not on her own. Eventually the guys do get him off of her but then the foursome attack him. Chill and Jr arrive as it's happening and they run over to break it up, along with Renee and Tonya. Chill assesses the situation immediately. Him and Jr agree that Rich is going into circle tonight. He has no argument.

Later the same night, in Chill's backyard, him, Jr, Rob and Ajay, along with Tank, June and Bruce, beat Rich's ass for putting his hands on his girl. After he suffers the circle, Rich is banished from the crew for a week. Not only can he not come around but he can't be out anywhere. Not even with Tameka. He has a week to think about his wrongs and try to make good on them. He's only allowed to go to school and to school functions. Immediately Rich Sr enrolls him into an anger management class. A group he had been a member of, not so long ago. T-baby is through talking to him forever, as she said, which leaves him unable to make up with her. After his banishment is up, he's cool for awhile. But soon he feels free to see Tameka or whomever else he wants to see. For the foursome, things just keep getting worse with their guys.
180

April brings on an incident which will be a turning point in Ebony and Ajay's relationship. She finds out why Miss Whitman was so certain Ajay would have a problem with the 2 of them having contact. The weekend of April 3rd is when it all goes down. Lynn and Jb are home for spring break and Ebony is discussing the make-up kit incident with Lynn.

"Anthony was upset when he saw me with it on," she tells Lynn, "But it seems like he got more pissed off when I told him she gave it to me. I guess he didn't like me being that close to a teacher or something."

"No, it's more than that, baby girl," Lynn says, "That bitch *there*, done had every guy in the crew including Jb."

"*What*!?" Ebony yells in disbelief.

"Hell yea! She done fucked every one of them from Chill on down. Renee knows about it."

"I'm not even believing this," Ebony says, " Damn! Is it *anybody* Anthony hasn't fucked with?!"

"Huh," Lynn mutters as she continues unpacking her suitcase.
Ebony doesn't wait for her to reply. She's already out the door. She gets into her car and goes to Rebbie's house to meet up with her girls.

After telling them about her conversation with Lynn, the foursome are determined to confront Miss Whitman. And they aren't willing to wait until Monday at school. They're going to her apartment. They get into Ebony's car and she drives to Miss Whitman's apartment in Central City.

When they turn into the parking lot, Ebony spots Ajay's six four parked in front of Debra Whitman's building. He's parked right next to her Nissan Maxima, the car she drives to school everyday. Without hesitation, Ebony and her girls get out, go up to the apartment and knock on the door.

After more than 5 minutes, Whitman opens the door. She fakes 1 of those embarrassing smiles with that *what-did-I-tell-you* expression on her face. She's draped in only a robe. The foursome barge in and all at once, they're flinging question's at her through heated tempers and lots of profanity. T-baby is ready to fight her. Miss Whitman tries to stall the girls by asking them to "have a seat."

"Nah bitch! We don't wanna sit down in your funky ass place," Nina shouts, "We wanna know if my brother is here and why have you been fucking our men?!"

As Miss Whitman stutters for an answer, Ajay emerges from the bedroom fully dressed. Ebony goes into a silent rage but her girls are very vocal. Ajay says nothing. He puts on his shoes and glides out of the front door of the apartment, gets into his car and leaves. Ebony is in shock as her and her girls make their way back out to her car. She's in no mood to drive, so
181

T-baby takes the wheel. They're going to see Renee and Tonya, right now.

Lynn had finished unpacking and made her way to Renee's house. Tonya is there also. When the foursome asks, Renee and Tonya validate what Lynn had told Ebony earlier, with even more details.

"I'm breaking up with him," Ebony says suddenly as she cries, "My heart can't take this kind of shit no more!"

"It's time we all take a break from their asses," Rebbie adds.

"True that!" Nina agrees and so does T-baby as she has already broken up with Rich.

It's declared right then and there that the foursome are officially single. Lynn, Tonya and Renee express their doubts. They've been here before, in their own relationships. They all certainly hate Debra Wittman equally and with a lot of passion. Not just the foursome but every female in their crew who's man attended MLK in the past decade.

Saturday night at *The Spot,* as Lynn celebrates her 19th birthday, tensions are high. The crew are split right down the middle by gender. Even Chill hasn't been spared from this one. Ajay getting caught with Debra Whitman the day before, had rehashed some old feelings in Renee and the older girls. They couldn't help but recall when their man had been seen or was rumored to have been intimate with Debra Whitman. The party is ruined. They shut down early and the ladies go their separate ways.

At school the next week, the news about the break-ups travels fast amongst the students. The girls who want to get with the crew men are happy to hear it and they're not the only ones. *Billy Joe Johnson,* better known as *BJ,* a senior football star who has admired Ebony from afar, see this as an opportunity to approach her and ask her to the prom. He's very handsome and seems to be a decent guy. He asks her after her 1st period class. She doesn't answer him right away. But she does take his number and tell him she'll let him know by Friday.

By Wednesday, the news of BJ's invite gets back to Ajay. He's noticeably angry but he decides he isn't going to go to Ebony. He figures that's exactly what she wants him to do but he couldn't be more wrong. Before the end of the school day, Ebony tells BJ she will go to the prom. When that news reaches Ajay, the bell has rung to dismiss school and Ebony has gone to her car. Her and her girls go to Rebbie's house after school, so they can rehearse for an upcoming talent show at the civic center.

When Ebony gets home, Ajay is at her house in Tank's room. She

182

goes to her room without a word. To her surprise, Ajay doesn't say anything to her. She takes her bath and decides to call BJ. During their conversation, someone picks up another extension and never puts it down. She knows it's Ajay. She tells BJ she'll talk to him at school tomorrow. They hang up. It *had* been Ajay on the other phone. Now he knows per her words that she's going to prom with BJ. She expects him to barge into her room any second and demand that she call it all off. He never does.

At school the following week, Ajay treats her very cold. He acts unaffected by her accepting a date with BJ. Like he's someone totally different. She sees him talking with Angel and her crew. And even though this really hurts her to see him with other girls, she holds her ground. She figures they must be the one's occupying his days and nights lately. Because he hasn't been to see her nor has he called. She quit her job in the office. She can't stand the sight of Miss Whitman anymore. She decides if this is the way Ajay wants things, then this is the way things will be. She distances herself from him completely. She hangs with her girls, all week. She thinks about the time when she lived in Houston and how she would cry for a chance to be at home. The chance to go to school with her man and her crew. Now she's at home and it seems that all of the real love, loyalty and understanding she had with Ajay has vanished. Ajay acts like someone else, most days. Not like the guy who rescued her from her fears of Raymond White.

Did he lose himself after Raymond's death? Did he forget what he was born to do?

The distancing was fine and well for a few days. By Friday, Ajay can't resist anymore. He wants Ebony. He had sent messages all day and night on Thursday. She hadn't responded. He'd sent them via everyone. He wants her to meet him behind the gym during 4th lunch break. He waits and she never shows up. After lunch, she goes into the gym for 5th period to work on her shots. This is her free hour now that the season's over. The girls and boys teams had both won state titles. She spends 5th hour in the gym everyday because she knows no one will be in there. Most of her girls team had gotten into a study hall. Or in Jan and Bre's case, found something less productive to do. They goof off either getting high in 1 of the crews notorious hiding spots around campus or visiting other classes. They always end up back in the gym with Ebony before the bell rings for 6th period.

Ebony goes into the locker room to change. As she removes her

183

shoes, she hears a noise which startles her. She turns around and sees Ajay. He had come into the gym to wait for her, since she didn't show up outside. He knows she comes in here and she's usually alone.

"Did you get my messages?" he asks in a soft voice.

"Yes."

"How come you didn't show?"

"I didn't wanna talk."

"Really?" he asks being somewhat sarcastic.

"Uh uh," she says, keeping her answers short.

"Guess we're gonna talk now," he says as he steps closer to her.

"I don't see what we have to talk about, Anthony."

"We have a lot to talk about," he says, getting even closer.

"Like what?" she asks as she's very nervous now.

He can hear her trembling which only turns him on.

"Oh just things, you know," he answers with and grin as he tries to put his arms around her.

"Uh uh. That's not cool," she says as she tries shoving him away.

He holds her tight, lifts her chin up and puts his lips to hers. She squirms to get free but he isn't letting go. He sticks his tongue in her mouth and she snatches her head away. He retrieves her lips and holds her chin forcefully. He snaps, "Give me a muafuckin kiss, *girl*."

She gives him a kiss thinking that'll calm him down and make him feel like he's won. She soon learns different. She learns that he's not willing to stop with just a kiss. He becomes more aggressive. He pulls her shirt up quickly and unsnaps her bra. It seems to be all in one motion.

"Tell me you miss me," he demands, sounding almost desperate.

She says nothing. Though she has missed him, she refuses to say so.

Again, he demands she tell him but she still won't.

"You don't miss me, Ebony?" he asks somberly.

"What difference does it make," she asks.

"A lot," he says, "Do you?"

"Yes I do," she whispers.

Suddenly his mouth is on her nipples. He opens her pants and has them halfway down in seconds. She pulls away from him. This makes him more determined that he'll have her. He jerks her foot free from her jeans and rips her panties completely off. He undoes his pants quickly with 1 hand while pulling her free leg around him with the other. He stabs his fingers inside of her pussy and shoves his tongue into her mouth, over and over.

Who is this guy? God, what is wrong with Anthony? This isn't him. This is the guy from his fifteenth birthday! This is Ajay!

184

"Anthony why are you doing this?" she asks as her voice trembles.

"Because it's mine," he whispers, pausing to look into her eyes.

"Why do you keep messing over me, if you want me so much?"

"Do you love me or not?" he asks.

"Yes."

"Do you want me, Ebony?"

"Do you want me?" she asks.

He doesn't answer. In an instant, he's inside of her.

"Oh God! What is wrong with you?" she asks as she pushes against his chest but not really trying to push him away.

"Ain't shit wrong with me," he answers with a muffled voice.

His mouth is around her breast. He's *too* familiar with what to do with it.

"Why do you act like this when I get tired of you messing-"

"Do you *think* I'm gonna let that nigga have my pussy, baby girl?! Ha?!" he erupts, "You must be loosing your muthafuckin mind! I told you a long time ago. This is mine! I'm not gonna share it! I'm not sharing your time with him, *either*."

She tries to reason but soon gives up. There's no stopping his actions until he's done. He wants her and he wants her now.

Nothing or nobody will ever stop me from wanting you or having you.

He's always said he would never be denied when it comes to her. That's what he's always said. She wants him too. But on her terms. She wants him to stop cheating and having gangbang sessions with the guys in their crew. He said he'll stop but she doesn't believe him. She feel he's only saying it because he wants her to cancel her agreement to go to prom with BJ. Her accepting the invitation from BJ or the fact that they've barely spoken this week, *aren't* exceptions. He's going to have her regardless. Rather it's willingly or forcefully. That in his mind, is up to her. He's always going to fuck her. His heart tells him she loves him and only him. She belongs to him and only him. He's going to keep it that way. At the start, he thinks he's forcing her. But there's nothing she'd rather do then to lean back on the counter and let him finish. She can feel that familiar pain. She knows he's really frustrated with the whole BJ/*Whitman*/*Angel* situation. He has always shown aggression during sex. But unlike Rich, he'd never hit her. He's not that kind of young man. Besides, his father would kill him before hers could. That familiar pain is now turning to pleasure. He's doing what feels natural, which is pleasing her. He can't hold back his natural instinct. To give her pleasure is what's natural for him. No matter what his emotion. He wants to make her feel loved and satisfied as a woman on every encounter.

185

Even though she's in his crew and says her love for him is what keeps her faithful. He knows it's a fact that giving her an orgasm, every single time they make love, keeps her planted as well. If that's not it now, when love is new. It certainly will be in years to come. Their love sessions have been out of this world. Today is no different and she can't hold back. She tries to pull away before giving him the pleasure of pleasing her. But as always, he knows she's there and that's exactly where he wants her to be. In ecstasy. With him and him only.

"You know this is mine, baby. How that nigga gonna touch you like I do?" he whispers.

He becomes louder and more aggressive as she tries to reason again.

"I don't want him to touch me like this, Anthony," she confesses, "I don't want nobody to touch me but you. But you keep hurting me."

"I'm done with that, Ebony," he whispers, "I promise."

He barely gets his words out before her body takes it's natural course. She can't stop herself from being satisfied. Her body won't allow her not to be. "Come for me. Give me *mine*," he says in a seemingly loud voice.

She doesn't know whether it's the fact that they're at school or that she hasn't had any loving in a long time. But at this moment, she's more turned on then she's ever been. What started out as an aggressive encounter, has turned into 1 of the best lovemaking sessions they've ever had. She *cums* loud and violent as she clutches to him with every ounce of energy she has. Her head dangles.

He whispers, "You miss this baby? Huh? I do. I miss this, so much. Can you feel that?"

She can't answer. She's in ecstasy. He knows it and he watches her cum.

Dear God! Is this the way he pleads his case to me? How can I ever resist him? I can't even stop him from fucking me when we're suppose to be broken up! I don't even want him to stop. This is so good! Oh God!

A few minutes later, he reaches his climax. Her tear soaked face assures him that, even though he had given her pleasure, he had still put the hammer down enough to get his point across. When he's done, he pulls her to her feet and leans her against the wall. He fastens his pants. Then he gets her spare underwear from her locker and puts them on her.

He knows every damn thing about me.

She looks at him through half closed lids as her limp body leans against the wall, next to the counter, he'd just taken her on. He redresses her, brushes her hair, then puts her ponytail holder back just as it had been before he'd
186

gotten into her hair. Before he leaves, he takes her face in both hands and kisses her passionately.

Then he whispers, "You can call us broke up or whatever you wanna call it. But nothing will stop me from being with you. Nothing will ever stop me from wanting you. Do you understand?"

Before she can answer, he kisses her on the cheek, then whispers in her ear, "I do love you and I'm not gonna share you."

He leaves her alone in the dressing room. She can hear Jan and Bre come into the gym as he's leaving. She can hear them showing each other love as they usually do. Like there's nothing different. Actually, seeing him leaving the gym from her workout sessions is normal. Before the infamous spring break fiasco, he was always in there shooting with her. Jan and Bre come on into the dressing room as she's washing her face. They ask her if she's alright.

"Yes," she says quickly, "I have to be."

They shoot ball for the rest of the hour. Ebony seems dazed but she continues to say she's fine. When the bell rings, they go to 6th hour classes.

Kim celebrates her 13th birthday and becomes a full member of the crew. Her and Bruce are finally able to date each other, *officially*.

By his trial date, Raymond has been listed as missing nationwide. With no body or suspect, they have to continue the court date again. And once again, big mama calls Cleveland, *disgusted*.

The foursome lose the talent show. Ebony had been noticeably distracted for weeks prior to the event. Her girls mentioned this to her several times but she was never ready to talk about it. In the talent show, they faced Cleveland's Finest, *Bone Enterprise* and they wasn't nearly prepared to compete. These guys will later hook up with non-other then *Easy-E* and become known to the world as *Bone Thugs-N-Harmony*. And put Cleveland on the *HipHop* map. They're great and destined for fame and fortune. All of the folks and true thugs in Cleveland, know it. After losing the talent show, Ebony let's BJ know she can't have contact with him nor can she go with him to prom. Her heart belongs to Ajay. She isn't going to play the, *dating someone to make him mad*, game. The prom is May 23rd. The same day Renee graduates from CSU and receives her 4 year degree in *Business Administration*. It was through much pressure from Ajay and all of her crew that Ebony had to tell BJ she couldn't go to prom with him. He didn't seem surprised at all. He had heard she was going to cancel, long

187

before she actually did. Though her and Ajay are allegedly broken up, BJ had gotten the word from Ajay, firsthand. Ajay had met with BJ through a meeting which was arranged by June and Rich. They're on the football team together. He agreed to meet with Ajay and the meeting didn't last long. Each of them spoke only once.

Ajay had said, "I will never let her go out with you or no other nigga."

And BJ's answer to that was, "I was expecting to hear this from you, a lot sooner."

After that exchange, they went on about their day.

Ebony is attending Renee's Graduation with the rest of the crew and their families. Ajay insisted she ride with him and Rich. She does but T-baby doesn't. She rides with Chill, Renee and lil Kenny, instead.

Ajay and Ebony are together at Rob's, afterwards. He tells her he's moving into his own apartment, at the U after his graduation. One week from tonight. He signed a full scholarship with *The University of Cincinnati,* last month. He'll be leaving for college in August. He also tells her *she'll* be spending a lot of time at the apartment. Their crew will maintain it for him while he's away. He expects her to be in charge of it and keep it nice for them, for when he comes home to visit.

The next few days are filled with Ajay doing things to keep Ebony's attention on their relationship. He plays a lot of Prince and Mariah songs, along with Mary J. and Jodeci. Ebony finds herself in the position of trying to keep her time with Ajay from being known by her girls, because her girls relationships aren't doing well. Ajay isn't concerned with anybody else's situation but his and Ebony's. Still she tries to get him to convince Tank, Rich and June to make up with Nina, T-baby and Rebbie.

He says, "That's not my job. My job is to keep you with me. And that's where I'm focusing my energy. Baby girl I have to leave this fall. I want our shit flowing smooth when I leave and while I'm away. Tank and them will have to get their own shit right. I didn't fuck theirs up. At the same time, they can't tell me what to do when it comes to you. Do you understand?"

"I guess so," she answers, "I just wanna see all the crew couples fill their destiny. We was all born to be together, Anthony."

"Then I suggest they get about the business of keeping their own shit tight," he says, "My concern is us. You feel me?"

"Yes."

He closes the subject and plans to leave it closed. But a situation will occur in the coming weeks which will lead him to having that talk with his boys.

188

CHAPTER 18

THE FOURSOME AND THEIR *4 ADMIRERS*!

A week later, the crew and their families attend MLK high school's graduation. Jan and Ajay graduate on May 30, 1992. Both with full athletic scholarships. Jan has a scholarship offer for academics as well. But she accepts a softball scholarship to the University of Cincinnati. Her getting a full scholarship for softball is no surprise to anyone. She has been fast pitch champ since she was in little league. Every team she was a member of, won the championship, 12 out of the 12 years she's been affiliated. She also graduates Valedictorian with a perfect 4.0 GPA. At their graduation party, Sam Sr and Belinda present her with a one hundred and fifteen thousand dollar certificate of deposit which had been put up for her by Belinda's now deceased parents, when Jan was born. Jan plans to use the money for medical school. Her goal is to become a pediatrician and have an office at their *CrewLand* strip mall, in the future.

Ajay has a full scholarship to Cincinnati, for basketball. Ability wise, no one is shocked. But his quick temper and lack of patience kept his family and his recruiters on guard. He had been highly sought after, for his skills, since his freshman year. He finishes high school with an academic 3.4 GPA. Athletically he averaged per game; 30 points, 10 rebounds, 8 assists, 4 steals and 3 block shots. He's ranked number 1 in the state of Ohio and number 3 in the nation. Him and Raymond White were both, great athletes. Raymond was ranked in the top 50 poll his last 2 years in high school. Ajay had been ranked in that poll since 8th grade. When Ajay learned that a ball player was sweet on Ebony, initially he had looked forward to competing against him on the collegiate level. But that was before Raymond started harassing, then subsequently attempting to rape his young love. On the hardwood, they was already going to be adversaries. Raymond had known Ajay was receiving higher accolades then him, in the polls. Ajay felt that was ultimately the reason Raymond wanted *his* girl for a trophy. Something he could say he'd beaten Ajay Jackson at, for once. And they hadn't even met at any of the basketball camps over the years. Ajay hasn't attended a basketball camp since he was fifteen. Raymond became aware of Ajay through rankings and national polls. Ajay was ranked 25 on the high school top 50 poll as an 8th grader. Raymond didn't surface until he was a junior in high school. Ajay and Raymond never played a game against each other. But their history of competition is 1 that will forever be apart of Ajay's life.

TIME TO GROW-RELOADED-TIME WILL REVEAL 2

The week after graduation, Ajay, with help from Arthur, Jr, Rob and the Cincinnati alumni, gets a lease at the U. Him, Tank, Rich and June furnish the place modestly. Ebony already knows she'll be spending a lot of time there because she wants too. Ajay had already made it clear that he plans to spend this summer with her, before he leaves for college. She's definitely okay with his plans, wishes and demands too. Tank, June and Rich also plan to spend a lot of time there. But Nina, Rebbie and T-baby have no plans of even seeing the inside of the place. Their breakups had been honored by their guys, where Ebony's hadn't been. Now Ebony gets pressure from both sides. From Ajay, who still considers their relationship unchanged and unaffected by anything that's going on with his outside interest or their crew. From her girls, who want her to be loyal to them and honor their 4-way split with Tank, Ajay, June and Rich. She's never been pulled like this before and she doesn't like the jousting at all.

A few days after getting the lease, Tank asks Ebony if her and her girls will go shop for Ajay and decorate the apartment.

"Why *should* we?" Ebony snaps, "So y'all can have them tramps up in there? Let them ho's shop for you."

"Twin we're not *stud'n* no ho's," he tries, "Just do it for me alright? I'll break you off something."
She tells him she'll think about it, as Pearl overhears their conversation and lights in on Tank immediately. She reminds him that he hasn't graduated high school yet and he won't be moving out there.

"You still have a year left," Pearl says, "So don't even think about moving nor staying out there when school starts back. Forget about it."

"Ma I just wanna stay out there some during the summer," Tank pleads, "While Jb and Ajay at home. Just so we can all kick it together before they leave for college. Like we did for Jb, out by Arthur's crib."
Pearl is already done talking to him and is now focused on Ebony.

"Miss lady you won't be moving over there either. Do you hear me?" she asks with her eyes peering at Ebony.
Ebony is fully dressed and on her way to get up with her girls when she answers with, "I know, ma," she says quickly as she runs down the stairs and out the door heading to Jo's house.
She's never actually heard her mother fuss at Tank about staying out *all night* until today. She feel it's because the news of the orgy and subsequent breakups had touch something in the mothers, from their families as well. Whatever it is, Ebony likes that her mother said it. Maybe now with the help of the mothers, their guys won't be accessible to the ho's like they had
190

TIME TO GROW-RELOADED-TIME WILL REVEAL 2

been before. The guys are able to be out all night. While the foursome had to be home before curfew. And that is when *their* guys do the biggest of their fucking up.

Ebony goes inside mama Jo's house. She has to tell her girls about what Tank had been bold enough to ask them to do.

"Nina are you ready?!" she yells from the bottom of the stairs.

"Yes kid! Here I come!" she yells back as she descends the stairs.

"I just got off the phone with Tee and Ree Ree. They're ready and waiting."

"Good. Lets be out," Ebony says as they head out to her car.

Tank is headed to Chill's as they're leaving. He looks disappointed that Ebony never answered him. And even more sad because Nina didn't speak to him. Technically the foursome couples have been broken up for more than 8 weeks. Only Ajay and Ebony aren't apart of it, by word of Ajay.

Back at home, Pearl is in their utility shed preparing to do laundry when she discovers $3700 in the pocket of Ebony's blue jean shorts. Curious about the money, she decides she'll put it in Ebony's night stand drawer, then ask her about it's origins as soon as she returns. She heads back inside and up to Ebony's room. When she opens the nightstand drawer to put the money in it, she spots birth control pills.

"I don't know what's going on with my *own* children," she says. She takes the pills and the money into her own room and puts them on her nightstand.

"She'll have to see me about all of it," she say as she heads back to the laundry shed to continue her duties.

Ajay, Rich and June are at Chill's house to get Tank. They're going shopping to find some things for the apartment. They gather in the living room as Tank tells them the girls refused to shop for the apartment.

"Y'all have to shop for yourselves, ha?" Renee asks as she teases them. She adds, "Y'all better learn. My lil sisters ain't having that mess y'all been pulling."

The 4 guys look at her impatiently. It still bothers them to hear about their wrongs. When Chill agrees with Renee, it doesn't help matters any.

"Y'all act like y'all think baby girl and them don't have a mind of their own," he says, "I don't care who you are. If you keep dogging your woman out, no matter how good she is, she'll leave your ass."

"True that," Renee says before heading into the kitchen.

"You got married and whooped," Ajay says and they all laugh.

They head out to the mall as they continue to discuss and weigh their relationships. Ajay tell them he's not broken up with Ebony. Rich, June and Tank have been going through the motions and taking T-baby, Rebbie
191

and Nina for granted. When it comes claiming they honor their breakups, that is. When in fact, they don't. Ajay's not playing that game at all. He's not broken up with Ebony, even if she had said say they was and she hasn't. "Ebony is still my woman and I'm her man," he says, "We still do the same shit we always have. I ain't broke up and neither is she."
The other 3 guys really aren't either. What they're doing is using this as their chance to fuck around with any girl they want. While at the same time, hoping their girl will wait on them to find the right way to apologize. They don't even anticipate what's in store, once they arrive at the mall.

      The foursome arrive at the mall, enter through the food court and take a booth. They're going to grab a snack before they cruise the stores. Immediately after sitting down, they notice 4 guys watching them.
      "Those guys are just *staring* at us," Rebbie says as they sit.
      "They *sure are*," T-baby says, looking back and smiling at them.
      "Stop flirting with them, Tee," Ebony says.
But it's too late. The 4 guys are already walking toward them.
      "In case you don't remember, we're *all* suppose to be single ladies," Nina says, with a slight grin.
      "I'm not single-" Ebony starts.
Before she can finish, the 4 admirers have made their way to their booth.
      "Do you mind if we join you?" 1 of the 4 guys asks as he looks directly at Ebony.
      "No, we was talking-" Ebony starts.
      "-Not at all," T-baby interrupts her, "You can sit right *here*."
She's patting the seat next to herself.
      "Oh girl, we're terrible," Nina mumbles as she giggles.
Two of the guys crowd into the booth while the other 2 go get chairs to sit on either side, next to Rebbie and Nina. The 8 of them are cozy or their seating arrangements, say as much. Justin is seated in a chair next to Rebbie, on 1 end of the booth. On the other side of Rebbie is Craig. He's sitting in the exact spot T-baby had pointed out to him, next to her. Ebony is on the other side of T-baby. Tim squeezed in next to her. Nina is on the other side of Tim at the end of the u-shaped booth. Roger, seated in a chair next to her, is already trying to get a hug. The guys seem really nice but Ebony wonders where they came from all of sudden. It's like they'd come into the food court especially to talk to them. The guys will be sophomores at Cleveland State, this fall. They *are* handsome. T-baby exchange digits with Craig. The other girls are hesitant but Nina eventually take numbers from the other 3 guys for herself, Ebony and Rebbie. They're all enjoying
192

pleasant conversation. Laughing loudly and joking, when all of a sudden, "So is this why y'all couldn't shop for us," Tank asks angrily.

He's walking straight toward them, followed by June, Rich, Chill and Ajay. Ebony panics. The look on her face represents much more than what's actually going on. She looks guilty as sin when all she's doing is talking to some guys they've just met. But she knows with Ajay, that's more than enough to constitute a sin. Ajay doesn't say anything. His eyes glare at her with a blank stare. As if he doesn't even see Tim seated next to her. Chill speaks to the foursome as he usually would, then he prepares to leave the food court and go shopping. June has other plans.

"Come here for a minute," he says to Rebbie, who starts to get up.

Chill says, "Nah, let's go man. Let these ladies finish their talk. Y'all can catch up with us in the mall, alright?" Chill says to the foursome.

He feels like these guys are trouble, just by the way they looked at him and the guys when they entered the food court. They had a look of familiarity. Like they know who he and his crew guys are. And if they know them, then they know these girls and who they belong too, as well. Apart of Chill feel like they aren't even after the girls but a much bigger catch. He dismisses it as protective paranoia and walks off. His guys are reluctant to leave.

"Alright," T-baby says to Chill's salutation.

She smiles and looks goofy because she thinks they're leaving. Rich gives her an evil look which she quickly returns. Ajay isn't so diplomatic.

"Catch up with me now," he says to Ebony.

She gets up. But Chill comes back and tells her to stay seated and finish her lunch. Then he insist that the guys come on and go shop. He wants to see just what move the 4 admirers are going to make. Instead of Tank and the guys leaving the food court, they choose to take a booth directly across from the foursome and order burgers and fries. Chill laughs at them as he sits down and gives them the *I-told-you-so* look.

Needless to say, the foursome break up their little chat with their new found friends. Or at least they try too. That's only because Ebony and Rebbie insist they leave the food court and walk the mall to keep their guys from blowing up the spot. The 4 admirers prove to be not-so-easily bullied, as they walk around the mall with them. Even though Ebony and Rebbie *keep telling* them it isn't a good idea.

"Y'all shouldn't be doing this. It's only gonna piss off our crew," Rebbie says.

"We wanna be friends," Tim says, "We're not doing nothing but walking in the mall and talking. That's it. What's wrong with that?"

"A lot," Ebony says as they continue to walk on.

193

Tim seems to like *her*. That *bothers* her. He's over 6 feet tall with light skin, very muscular and very handsome. But he's not the man she wants. That's the end of it. Though she shows no interest, other than being cordial, he's still very persistent.

"I'm a tight end," he says.

"Amen," T-baby says as her and Nina laugh, then they all laugh.

All 4 admirers are on the football team at CSU. Tim has curly hair and gray eyes. Ebony wonders about his race, so she asks, "How are you classified?"

"I'm a sophomore," he answers, thinking she means in college.

"I mean your race. If that's not too personal," Ebony clarifies.

"No it's not. My pops is Black, Cherokee and Asian. My mom is Italian American," he says.

"Are you guys from here?" Ebony asks, getting as much info about them as she can for Ajay's inquiries which she knows will come later.

"Cincinnati," Tim says while the others don't offer an answer.

"We have Native American in our families too," T-baby says.

"Cherokee and Choctaw," Nina offers.

"And Black," Ebony says.

"And White," Rebbie adds as they all laugh again.

"See, we already have a lot in common," Justin says.

The foursome prepare to leave but before they do, the guys asks them to go to a movie later that evening. Nina and T-baby accept for all 4 of them. Again before Ebony or Rebbie can protest.

"I'll call you later with details," Craig says to T-baby before kissing her on her cheek.

As the 4 guys walk away, T-baby looks right into Rich's face. She has a guilty look on her face. Rich walks away. Ajay didn't like that at all. He notices Ebony stayed *way* away from the guys. But his sister didn't. That's really pissing him off more, so he sounds off.

"I guess y'all done lost your damn minds, ha?" he asks Nina.

"Oh and *y'all haven't*?" she asks as he turns his attention back to Ebony, where his eyes had never left.

"Come by the apartment when you get through fucking off with your hardheaded ass girls, alright?" he says but she doesn't say anything.

"Bring your girl with you," June adds.

"All of em," Tank adds as they walk away, behind the admirers.

The foursome are left standing and wondering what in the world just happened and feeling like this whole incident might blow up, momentarily. Is this their 1st step to becoming independent from their guy in the crew? Are they ready to seek independence from the family and their legacy?

194

TIME TO GROW-RELOADED-TIME WILL REVEAL 2

Or are they just playing the game? As always, *Time Will Reveal* this too. Ebony doesn't believe her girls *really* want to leave their guys. She feels they're just playing the game. The same game she'd played on Ajay when she wrote him that letter from Houston, just to get his attention. She can understand her girls desperation. At the same time, she hasn't forgotten how angry *the game* made Ajay.
Oh brother! I'm not going there again. He's gonna get his shit together so I don't have to play games.

Something has to shake, pretty damn soon. For Ebony, she's too afraid to face Ajay, right now. A part of her feels ashamed. Guilty even. Just because she was talking to another guy and he saw her.
What will he say? Worse than that, what will he do?

Instead of returning home, Ebony and her girls go to T-baby's house to kick back and discuss today's events.

"So are y'all gonna go to the movies or what? Because it's all or none," Nina says to Ebony and Rebbie.

"I'm wit it," T-baby says quickly.

"I don't know," Rebbie says.

Ebony doesn't respond. She's still trying to take in the fact that Ajay had seen her with another guy and he didn't rip her head off.

"We've got to do something to shake their asses up, Ebony," Nina says, "They've been fucking over us anytime and anyway they want too. Rich had the nerve to hit T-baby because she didn't want to deal with it."

"Twice! How long do y'all think it's gonna be before they all try that shit?" T-baby asks.

"Anthony would never hit me," Ebony says, "I know that. Big Al would fuck him up before my daddy could even get to him."

"Brian better not try that either," Rebbie says, "But I know what you mean, T-baby. Remember the ho's from Houston, Ebony?"

"And the Cleveland ho's too. We can't just be leaving all them ho's out of this shit," T-baby adds.

"And that bitch Debra Whitman, to add to all of the bullshit," Nina says, "Ebony you said you was pissed off about that and you was gonna stand your ground. So *now* what?"

Ebony knows her girls want her solidarity. They need her to shake Ajay because he has more leverage over Tank, June and Rich than anyone else. If he doesn't want to do something, like mess around with other girls, then they're less likely to do it. She knows why her girls need her participation.
195

But they're asking her to do something which could damage *her own* relationship.

"Damn Nina. This *is* your brother we're talking about," she tries.

"Hell yea and yours! And my cousin and your cousin! So what of it?" Nina snaps.

"What about your cousin, Ebony? *Me*?" T-baby asks, pouring on the guilt, "I'm your cousin and we're all like sisters in this. If we don't do something now, they're gonna forever dog our asses out."

"Y'all don't understand what I have to deal with when Anthony gets pissed," she says.

"It can't be worse than me. Is he kicking your ass?" T-baby asks.

"Worse," she says.

"What's worse than *that*?" Rebbie asks.

"He finds a way," she says, still not wanting to admit to them that she's still having sex with him. But her girls catch on quickly.

"Ebony y'all *are* broke up," Nina says, "You need to stop sleeping with him so maybe he'll know that too."

"I tried too," she lies.

"Girl, just say *no*," T-baby says, "Stop being so weak for him."

"I do and it don't work," she says, "Or maybe, secretly I want it."

"Ebony if you tell him you don't wanna fuck, he can't just take it," Nina says.

"Oh really? Well maybe you should tell him that!" she screams as all of her girls go silent.

"That's rape," Nina says.

"That's worse," Rebbie adds.

"Word that," T-baby says.

"It's not exactly rape when I don't say no," she says, "What I was telling y'all since spring break is, he won't take no for an answer. You know what he did in the gym, right?"

"Yes," they whisper.

"Well it was like that everyday for awhile. Because I was trying to go with the code *we* set up. But that shit is hard for me y'all. Because I want him too. He's not broke up with me either. He's not fighting it. What am I suppose to do? I love him and I want it too."

"Stay away from where he is," Nina selfishly insists.

"That's our crew. How do she do that?" Rebbie asks.

"Tell Chill about it. He'll know what to do," T-baby suggests.

They offer suggestions as to how she can stay away from her man when that's not what she wants to do. She has to come clean and she does.

196

"I don't wanna avoid him, Nina. And really I don't wanna say no," she admits, "I just want him to treat me right and stop fucking around on me. That's what my game is and that's what y'all want too. So y'all should just *say that*. I don't wanna be broken up with Anthony. I know there's no other girl that's gonna take my spot. I believe that with all of my heart. So I never *really* say no. I just try to get him to talk to me first. Sometimes he does. But once he touch me, that's all she wrote. I'm all in. He ain't taking shit. I'm giving it to him freely. And I *know* the difference."

Mama Sandy comes in from work. She talks to them while she takes out dinner preparations. "Are y'all staying here tonight?" she asks.

"If we can," Ebony says.

"You know you can. But call your moms and get permission first. You know the rules," she says before going into her bedroom. "Where's lil Greg and baby boy at?" she asks before turning on her bath water.

"They're at papa's with lil man and all the little boys. They're suppose to spend the night," T-baby says, "Papa said he was gonna call and check with you and daddy."

"It's fine with me," Sandy giggles, "Greg and I can find something to do with ourselves on a Friday night, baby. You know?"

"No and I don't wanna know either," T-baby says as they laugh.

Sandy didn't hear her smart comment. She had already closed the door to her bathroom and started her water. The phone rings and T-baby answers.

It's Craig, calling to make arrangements for the evening. The foursome are going. Though Ebony and Rebbie are apprehensive about it, they're going to go too. T-baby and Nina assure them this isn't something they're doing out of spite. Nor does it mean they never want to be with Rich or Tank anymore. Because the fact is, they do want to be with their only loves. They just want the same thing Ebony and Rebbie want. They want their guys to act like they care about the break up and be persistent like Ajay and June are. They want Tank and Rich to know, as long as they keep disrespecting them, they aren't going to be together. Ebony and Rebbie agree with them on that point, as Ebony thinks.

They're just playing the game. Just like I thought. Oh brother! Here we go again!

Pearl is still doing laundry when Tank returns. She has started lunch and dinner also. Ajay, Rich and June are at Chill's house waiting for Tank to bring word on where the foursome are.

"Ma, *Ebony been here*?" Tank asks.

"No but I do need to talk to her," Pearl says, "Have you seen her?"

197

"I saw her at the mall," Tank says.

"When you see her, tell her I need to talk to her about a couple of things," Pearl says as she goes back into the kitchen.

Tank goes back to Chill's house to tell the guys that the foursome didn't even come by Pearl's since leaving the mall and Ajay is annoyed instantly.

Ajay says, "I told her, *plain as day,* to come by the U. This shit will not work."

"They all done flipped there fucking lids, *cuz,*" June says in anger.

"Trisha ain't fixing to forgive me anyway. I may as well not even stress over this," Rich says.

"Crew y'all full of shit," Chill says, "Y'all been stressing over this shit, the *whole* time. That's why it's in conversation."

They all laugh. All except Ajay. He's already in a foul mood.

"Cousin dial T-baby's number for me," he says to Rich.

"You think they over there?" Tank asks.

"Your sister better be or I'm fucking her up," he answers.

Once again they all laugh and he doesn't. Rich dials T-baby's number and Ajay takes the phone.

"Hello," T-baby answers.

"Tee let me speak to baby girl," Ajay says, "I know she's there."

"Hold on," T-baby says. "*It's Ajay,*" she whispers as she hands the phone to Ebony.

"Hello," Ebony says.

"You didn't come to the U. Why is that?" he asks.

"We came over here, instead," Ebony says.

"I told you to come to my apartment. What's the deal with you?"

"It's not a deal. We just stopped here first."

"Meet me at my apartment in twenty minutes."

"I'll see about that, Anthony," she says, "But I'm not sure how soon because everybody made plans."

Nina and T-baby listen in surprise. They're amazed to see her standing up for *their* plan. They didn't think she would. But what they don't realize is *their way* isn't the healthiest way to reach their guys and Ebony's way is.

"I got some plans of my own," Ajay says calmly.

"I'm going with them," she says, against her better judgment.

"Going where, Ebony?" he asks.

"Somewhere. I'm not sure where but I'm driving so I'll know something before I move an inch," she says, feeling more confident the longer she talks without interruption.

"You're meeting that nigga, baby girl?" he asks.

198

"I doubt it," she tries.

"You know I'm not going for no shit, right?" he asks calmly.

"Me either," she states and with that, he hangs up the phone and so does she.

The girls keep their movie date with the 4 admirers from CSU. After they see *Batman Returns,* they all go for pizza. Then the foursome thank the guys for a nice time, though the girls had paid their *own* bill the entire evening. After T-baby agrees she'll call Craig later, the guys leave, discussing how different it was not paying for the girls.

The females in this family are taught, at a young age, never to except money or gifts from any man. Not unless they're willing to return a gift of that man's choosing.

The foursome had honored that the entire date. When they return to T-baby's house, Greg Sr and Sandy are on the living room sofa kissing. They break it up when the foursome barge in.

"Oh y'all *ought a* know better," T-baby says in embarrassment.

"Don't hate," her mother says as her and Greg Sr giggle.

Nina, Rebbie and Ebony smile. They think it's romantic and say as much.

"Yea right. That's because it's not *y'all* folks," T-baby says.

"Not tonight," Ebony adds as they go into T-baby's room.

"Everyone of your mother's have called me!" Sandy yells from the living room, "W*hat's going on?"* she yells as her and Greg Sr remain on the couch.

Nina and Rebbie call home. Their message to Ebony is the same.

"Mama P is looking for you," they both say.

"Ebony what have you done?" T-baby asks as she laughs.

"Nothing. But there's no telling," she answers, "I wouldn't be surprised if Anthony haven't already told her about today."

"That's the bad part about all our families being close," Nina says.

"If our parents know we went to the movies with guys we just met today, they're all gonna be mad," Ebony says, "Especially after what I went through with Raymond. Because we *know* better. I'll bet that's it. Anthony told my mama about it and Tank was probably *right by his side.* Mad because you didn't drop everything to talk to him. Mama won't tell on y'all. Not until she hear *my* side. Anthony told her. Not just because I was out with a boy but because he really cares about my safety. He's even more nervous since the attack. He told mama *and Tank* backed him up."

"Jeremy is sulking because I'm not a *damn* fool," Nina says as she giggles, "But I'm glad he's worried. He'd better be *if* that's the deal."

"Dang that's messed up if they ratted us out," Rebbie says, "I

199

thought crew was suppose to hold each other down, no matter what."
T-baby says, "That crew code shit goes out the window when Ajay thinks a
man is pushing up on Ebony. The crew code has to take a backseat, as far as
Ajay is concerned. They all should be that way."
They laugh but they also agree.
Then Ebony says, "Come and go home with me to see what's up. We'll
come back over here when she's done with her sermon. Unless we *can't*."
They giggle as they follow T-baby out of her room. They tell Greg Sr and
Sandy where they're going, then hurry out the door. They had disturbed
them again. Greg Sr locks the door behind the girls, switches off the lights
and returns to the couch with Sandy.

Ebony arrives home with her girls. Pearl is calm as she goes
upstairs, gets the money and the pills, then she returns to the living room
where the foursome are waiting. Ebony chose to discuss it with her girls
present. So Pearl puts the pills and money on the coffee table, then looks
Ebony in the face. Ebony looks stunned and gets defensive immediately.
"Why are you going through my stuff?" she asks quickly.
Pearl shoots it down, by asking, "Where did you get *this* money?"
"From Anthony, *ma*," she answers.
"Nearly four thousand *dollars*?" Pearl asks.
"Yes. He asked me to put it up for him," she answers.
Ebony keeps Ajay's money. This is the money from his sales and alumni
from this weekend, alone. It's obvious Ebony had left it in her jeans pocket.
She has much more stashed in her room. Ajay always gives her large sums
of money to hold. Pearl insists she give him the money back. She says she
will, just to calm mother's worries but she won't give it to Ajay until he
asks for it. He prefers she keep his large sums of money in case he's
harassed by cops or wannabe *jackers*. For the crew, harassment from police
is common. She's been in the car with him when he's gotten pulled over and
jacked up. The cops would usually search him and/or his car but never her.
About the birth control pills, Ebony tells the truth about those as well.
"Big mama and poppa put me on birth control as soon as I got to Houston,
because they knew about me and Anthony in the motel," she says, "They
wanted to make sure I don't get pregnant, if we did that again. They talked
about it with granny and papa."
"*If y'all* do that again or *so y'all can* do that again, is more like it,"
Pearl says and her response appears to be shock.
Shock turns to a look of betrayal and eventually, straight up anger. Ebony
gets a certain joy out of seeing her mother dealing with the possibility of
questioning *her own* parents judgment. She wonders how she'll handle it.
200

Surely she isn't gonna go off on big mama. Or get all gangster about her own father's decision.

Ebony has underestimated her mother. After all, she had to have gotten her spunk from somewhere. But right now Pearl is wondering what her parents motives were.

How did they get the pills for her? What did they say, exactly? Do they think we can't handle our daughter? Why wasn't John and I consulted?

She questions Ebony on all the facts before she makes the call to Houston.

"I'm gonna call mama and daddy, right now," she says, grabbing the pills and money and before she heads upstairs to her room, she says to Ebony, "You wait here until I'm done with this call, miss lady."

"Yes ma'am," Ebony says with a bit of sarcasm in her tone.

She's thrilled by the fact that her mother has to call her *own parents* about a situation concerning her.

"I wouldn't miss this for the world," she whispers to her girls.

Suddenly Tank storms through the side door and says, "All of y'all need to come outside for a minute."

"*Oh drama*," Ebony sings while rolling her eyes to the ceiling and smiling.

"*Please*?" Rebbie says sarcastically as she giggles.

"Damn. Come on twin and stop bullshitting! Come on!" he yells.

"*Alright down there!*" Pearl yells from her room.

"My bad, ma!" he yells back. Then turning to Ebony, he whispers, "See there. Now want you come on."

He isn't about to say anything to Nina. Not until they're outside. The girls follow him out the side door where June, Rich and Ajay are waiting.

"Come here," Ajay says as soon as he sees Ebony in the doorway.

June and Rich have a more relaxed disposition when they approach Rebbie and T-baby. While Tank and Nina are already disagreeing loudly as they make their way to mama Jo's front porch. Rebbie and June sit on Pearl's front porch and talk. Rich and T-baby sit on the trunk of Ebony's car. They aren't saying much of anything. Ajay walks Ebony to the double shed.

"Come in here," he says as he opens up the door to his family's side of the utility shed.

She goes in, though she doesn't feel at ease being alone with him. She hasn't learned to tell him *no* and be affective. He releases the tailgate on Al's truck and sits down.

201

"Come over here and sit down," he says calmly and she does.

He's quiet initially as if he's trying to sort things out before he speaks. She looks around at the truck as she sits. It's the 1967 Chevy, her and all of her crew use to beg for rides on the back of when they was little. Tank loved it and would be happy if he knew big Al was restoring it.

"I didn't know your daddy still had this truck," she says trying to break the silence.

He looks down at his hands as he frowns, then he looks into her eyes.

He asks, "I'm gonna asks you one time, so listen good. Where you been?"

"To the movies and to eat pizza."

"With?"

"My girls," she answers

There's awkward silence before he asks, "Did anybody else go with y'all?"

She hesitates. He looks down at his hands again as they rest on his lap. She wonders if he already knows the truth.

Did he see us go into the movies or come out? Does he know we met at Pizza hut? Does he know anything or is he trying to intimidate me? Maybe he doesn't know and is trying to trick me into telling him.

"No," she says.

Only her girls rode *with* her. She figures he'll reveal it now if he knows their admirers was there too. But he doesn't. He's very calm.

Thank God! He doesn't know.

"Ebony are you ready to get back together, all the way. Or do you wanna end this now?" he asks.

"I want you to respect me," she says.

"So you do or you don't? That's all I asked you."

"If you're ready to be with me and treat me right, then I-"

"Just answer me about what you wanna do. That's all," he insists.

"You don't act like you want me, baby," she says, "I want us to be together *forever*. We can be if you just stop messing around on me."

"Let's go to the U," he starts, "We can talk there. I think we all need to talk things out."

"I can't leave. Not until mama gets off the phone with big mama."

"What's up with that?"

"She found your money. *My bad.* Plus she found my pills too. She's tripping about it."

"She's talking to big mama about getting the pills or is she sending you back?" he asks with a sly chuckle.

202

"You know it's not that. She's talking to them about getting me the pills in the first place," she says.

"Cool. So when she finish talking to you, meet me at Chill's," he says, "Unless you're gonna come up with another excuse."

"Ajay-"

"Baby you don't call me *Ajay*," he corrects her.

"Anthony I'm not trying to come up with excuses," she says, "I'm trying to tell you the truth."

"About everything, right? *Right*," he says, answering himself as he gets up and kisses her forehead.

"Let's go. We can talk about all that truth and shit, later."

She hurries to get out of the shed and doesn't hear him mumble, "and lies and consequences."

She's already left, feeling as though she has dodged another encounter with, *The Ajay*.

Her girls leave going to Chill's house with their guys while Ebony goes back inside to finish the talk with her mother.

Pearl gives her the money back with instructions to give it back to Ajay immediately. She says she will but instead she'll hide it in her room. Pearl doesn't give her the half used pack of pills back. Ebony isn't worried about the remainder of that pack. She has a supply that will last until next November, 1 month before she turns 18. After that, at 18 she can get them herself. Her mother offers to have a discussion with John on whether or not she'll get birth control pills. Even though her mother has to know she has multiple packs, she never ask her to fork over the rest of them. Ebony feels like that's her mothers way of saving face. Of course she doesn't volunteer to hand over the others either. She's still good on pills until she can sign for them. She isn't going to push the issue any further. After their talk is done, she heads to Chill's house to meet up with Ajay.

The other 3 couples are still there. T-baby and Nina are playing cards with Chill and Renee. Ajay is in the kitchen talking to Rich and Tank. She passed Rebbie and June on the front porch. They seem to be getting along well. She's happy to see 1 of her girls making an approach at staying *solid*. Nina and T-baby are both stubborn, as are Tank and Rich. She knows they'll need more time to gel. As far as her and Ajay, he's never going to acknowledge any so-called break-up where their relationship is concerned. Neither will she.

But is he ready to give up his cheating? Is he ready for that? God I hope so.

She wants him to be faithful and she hopes he's ready to be. Because she's
203

here. He had asked her to go to his apartment. He wants to talk to her alone which means they have to leave Chill's house. If they're going to his new apartment, surely talking isn't *all* he's going to want to do. She knows she won't resist. She can't. She asks him to stay outside and talk in his car. But he insists they go to his place. He puts her on a guilt trip by saying, "You haven't even been over there."

With that, she agrees to go. For her to say she doesn't want to go after he's invited her, wouldn't look good. And knowing Ajay like she does, she figures he would've driven her there regardless.

The ride to the U is no different than any other time she rides with him. He plays his stereo loudly. He has a banging system, so talking now is out of the question. The sound from his speakers are very clear. So clear in fact, it seems as if *En Vogue* are in the backseat singing. Instead of coming from the CD. *Giving him something he can feel* oozes out. *En Vogue* added a little pop to this *Aretha Franklin* classic soul tune that their parents play all the time.

This is definitely a song for a well kept lady. Big mama told me that.

That thought makes her smile. She begins to wiggle her hips and sway her body while in her seat. She imagines herself singing this to any of the ho's and hopefuls who want her space and wonders how she's able to keep it. She feels this may be the reason he's playing it at this moment. Knowing him, it is. He's always on point. He has mastered the art of making up, as well. He's very smooth. She never knows which angle he's going to come from but whichever angle he chooses for whatever situation, it's ultimately to get back to their intimacy. Something that's very important to his idea of a healthy relationship. She doesn't have a problem with that because their intimacy is very important to her also. She smiles to herself. As she does, she glances over and finds him staring at her while she still sways and wiggles. He's always her captive audience anytime she moves her body. The traffic light turns green and they roll on. He turns into the parking lot, drives under his carport, lets up the soft top on his Chevy and tells her to stay seated. He gets out, comes around and opens her door. She gets out and thanks him with a smile. She has been to these University apartments many times with her crew. But never to her *own* man's place. She has *major* butterflies. They're use to going to Arthur or Rob's place to kick it after they'd left the rest of the crew at *The Spot* or doing likewise. But this time, they're going to Ajay's apartment. He promised her he would get his own place every since *the Darlene situation*. He has. His apartment is 2 stories with a patio and a 2nd floor balcony in the front and back.

204

He stands just inside of the door and says, "Come on in."
She walks in and sits in the recliner near the door. She admires the apartment. It's the largest of the 3 bedroom floor plans. He goes into his kitchen and returns with 2 glasses of ice, a bottle of Hennessy and a coke for her mixer. He makes a drink for both of them and hands her, her glass.

"Thanks."

"You're welcome. Come sit on the couch by me," he says.
She smiles and moves over next to him. He lights up a blunt.

"I like how it looks in here," she says with a smile as he looks at her, "But it still needs my touch."

"So do I," he whispers, sending chills through her body.
He's definitely a master at making up. She doesn't respond to what he says. He blows her a charge, then puts the blunt in the ashtray and sits his drink on the coffee table. He puts 1 arm around her and the hand from the other arm, he puts on her thigh and pulls her closer. He takes her chin in 1 hand, a fist full of her hair in the other and kisses her passionately.
I haven't even seen the whole apartment. At Chill's house and in the shed, he was ready to talk about our relationship. But not anymore. Talking isn't on his mind. Fucking is. He should've just said this is what was on his mind and not lie to me by saying he wants to talk.

She pulls away from his kiss, feeling she needs to make her case. She looks into his eyes and says, "I thought we needed to talk *more*."

"You already know what I'm gonna say," he whispers smoothly.
She loses patience, thinking he just wants sex and to stake his claim on her.
Maybe because he doesn't want to admit that he's still messing around. I see why my girls are angry. They just keep messing up and nobody ever talks. He's gonna talk to me.

"You said we was gonna talk things *out*," she reiterates.

"Okay, let's talk," he's says, agitated and with a look of impatience. He has been at this juncture with her. When she wants to discuss things without really discussing them. She wants to control the situation, instead of going with the flow. Like allowing him to calm his nerves before delving into the events of the evening. But she's impatient. She wants to talk now.

"Alright, let's talk," she says softly, trying to keep him patient.
The feelings he had after seeing her with another guy are still at the very forefront of his mind. He tries to avoid those thoughts but she's persistent.
I was trying to get into her and play off of her body chemistry. But no! She wants to talk. She's already started off by stalling and lying. Fuck!
205

"Okay. Tell me why you feel like you need to lie to me again? Let's talk about that shit," he says, sounding frustrated, intentionally.

His voice is more stern but not yelling. She feels a little nervous about what her next words should be. But still she's procrastinating with the points.

"Why don't you tell me-"

"Don't bullshit around, baby girl," he says suddenly, "I know where you've been. I know about the movies. The pizza. The whole nine. So spit it on out so we can get to the business. You don't wanna talk to me. You wanna fix it up in a neat little *bow*. There ain't shit cute about you telling me you was out with another muthafuckah. I'm just letting you know that, from jump. So since you wanna talk, so *bad*. Let's start with that shit."

His voice is impatient. He seldom yells. But his voice is *really* impatient. Its to the point where she call already tell, he doesn't want to bullshit or play around with the truth. He wants it, point blank. She know she has no other choice but to tell him. So she does. Carefully she starts with the mall. Then the phone call to T-baby's house and then the movie. He stops her for every detail as he rifles off question after question.

"Who was the call for? Who talked? Who agreed to do the date? Who did you sit next too at the movies and at *Pizza Hut.* Because I saw the seating arrangements at the food court," he snaps.

She tells him T-baby talked on the phone and made the arrangements. Nina agreed to go on the date.

"We met at the movies and walked in together. But we paid our own way and bought our own snacks," she says in 1 breath.

"Go on," he says.

"Then we went inside the movie and sat down," she says, "They wanted us to sit like couples. But we told them we was gonna sit together, Or at least, two and two. Tim tried-"

"Who is Tim?" he asks.

"One of them guys-"

"That's the nigga that wanna fuck you?" he asks.

"No," she answers quickly.

"Bullshit."

"Anthony there was no talk like that, at all," she says quickly.

"Oh no. Of course not," he says sarcastically, "First you say they wasn't even there. Now they *was* there but nobody said shit. Get your lies straight, Ebony."

"I don't even know what the movie was about because I spent more time in the game room and the bathroom, then anywhere else," she says, "I was busy looking for you, Anthony. Because I thought you-"

206

"You should've been here, like I asked you too," he says bluntly.

"You didn't ask me. You told me-"

"So *fucking* what?!" he yells, startling her. He says, "I told you and you didn't come! On top of all that, you tell me a muthafuckin lie! So you can go out with somebody you *just met!* A nigga *at that!* What do you think I'm suppose to do!? How do you think I'm suppose to act right now!?"

He's furious. She's only heard him yell at her twice. Now and Christmas 1990. When he read the letter that toyed with his emotions and ultimately, led to her to seeing his reaction when he's hurt, for the first time. That was caused by her lying to him. The thing he's angry about now and was angry about then, was the fact that she lied. He knows she's not going to cheat. But he has to break her from lying. For him, that's the ultimate betrayal. Cheating isn't. *Lying is.* Now she knows why he was so quiet in the shed and in the car on the ride over. It was the calm before the storm.

I should've just fucked as soon as we sat down. Oh sure, he would've been aggressive. But he wouldn't have had this little extra to add on to it.

He's going to punish her and she knows it. She can see it in his eyes. But he's hurt too. She can see that as well. It's because of her actions, all day today. She realizes now that she has the power to change how his day goes. Just as he does with her. Because he does worry. He worries about her. He's usually calm and calculating. But not tonight. Tonight he looks vulnerable and seems unsure of himself. He's not the *confident in his position* Ajay that he usually is with her. She can sense that and she feels horrible that she has wounded him again. He's her man. And his 1 and only vulnerability is her. She'd learned that since the letter. As they grow into young adults, she's going to see that he's not trying to push for some *double standard* as she'd thought before. It's just that his 1st priority is her safety. He doesn't want her to end up in another Raymond White situation. It's something about the way those 4 guys was smirking that seriously rubbed him the wrong way. He's worried for her and her girls.

"I don't trust them niggaz, Ebony," he says, "They're up to something. They're pushy. They just met y'all today and wanted y'all to go out with them *tonight*? Hell no! You're *my* girlfriend and those muthafuckaz was looking at me like I had no business stepping to you. Like I was intruding. You are my business and my personal and I'm the same to for."

"I didn't know they did that because I was looking at you," she says, "I was so scared when I saw you."

"You should've got up and left with me," he says, "Ebony that's not even you. That's the part that makes me the most upset."

207

"I know," she says, "I get pulled from both sides though. My girls don't wanna be hurt no more. Neither do I. Can you talk to Tank and them?"

"Yea I can," he says, "But first things first. I need to handle my own girl and my business with you before I go trying to tell another man something. This shit is bugging me, Ebony. Don't you ever go off like that no more."

"Okay," she says, "It was wrong and no matter what they wanna do, I'm not ever gonna go out with other guys again. To tell you the truth, I didn't feel good about it. Me and Ree Ree was trying to change all of their minds. Even before y'all came up. We was telling them they shouldn't be sitting with us."

"Yea but you didn't stick to that," he says, "You went and met them. And none of y'all know them. You gave all of them my time. I don't have control over what Nee and them do. But you? You're my girl, Ebony."

No matter how she tries to soothe his wounds, he's determined to put it in her face. He's got to save face too. So the punishment is imminent. For one, she went out with another guy. Two, for not meeting him as he'd told her too. And three, for lying about the whole date. He doesn't want to talk anymore. She knows not too. His facial expression switches from 1 of anger to contemplative. He needs to see and feel her body. He needs to reassure himself that this is the girl he's willing to die or kill for. That girl would never go out with another man because she only has eyes for him.

He removes both of their clothes and surveys her body, as if he's looking for signs that she's been tampered with. After he's satisfied she's free of any evidence, he takes her right there on the sofa. Twice. Then again on the floor in front of the sofa. Even later, in the bedroom. The 5th time as she was trying to wash up to get ready and go home, he gives her more of his maximum force, in the bathroom. He's still upset, hours later.

"You know better than to lie to me," he whispers, "I know you do."

She apologizes repeatedly. She even cries, at times. But he doesn't let up. Not even when she begs him too. His mentality is this. He know she's playing it up for sympathy because she knows what she did was wrong.

"You're gonna learn the rules. One way or the other. I don't share you. I don't lie to you and I don't play games," he whispers while drilling into her. They finish session 6 at 4am. His climax sounds loud and violent. She needs to go home before John pulls in, if he hasn't already. She asks Ajay to drive her to Shaker Heights.

"I'll take the heat from your folks and mine too, if necessary. Just like always," he says, "But you're not leaving me. Not right now."
208

"I can't stay all night," she says, "Mama just told me and Tank that today before I went to the mall."

"Does mama P know you went out with a boy you don't know?" he asks suddenly, "Do any of y'all parents know that?"

"No."

"That tells me everything I need to know," he says, "You argued with your mother to see me. Yet you don't even *tell* her about that fool? You knew better all the way around. Just lay down, baby girl. I'll take the heat if there is any. I'm gonna tell big John why I was mad and why I wouldn't bring you home too."

She lays down and as they cuddle, she thinks over the last 24 hours. If she could take it all back, she would. She has decided to never 2nd guess herself again. Not even for her girls. If she doesn't want to do something. She isn't going to do it. No matter who asks. As he holds her close, she can feel the sting of her vagina and the many passion marks that cover her. Her body is very sore from all of the aggressive episodes with him. The more she had fought, screamed and begged, the harder he had drilled into her. Now he wants her to wake up in his arms for another round, no doubt.

Rebbie and June made up shortly after Ajay and Ebony left. They made out often in Ajay's old room, at Chill's house. As it nears dawn, June is still very apologetic about his cheating ways. He promises Rebbie he'll be faithful to her if she gives him another chance. She agrees to give him the chance to prove himself. Now they have to get home. Tank is suppose to drive the foursome back to T-baby's house in Ebony's car. That's where they was suppose to sleep last night. But Ebony hasn't come back from Ajay's apartment. Tank knows she isn't coming back before dawn so he takes her girls to T-baby's, then comes back to Chill's and goes to sleep.

The sunlight session is much more passionate but her pussy is so sore it seems to have closed up. However Ajay manages to find his way in and bring her to another climax, just as he had done in the earlier, more aggressive sessions. He always said he would make her come every time he fucked her. No matter what the circumstance. As he lay in bed trying to catch his breath, his phone rings. It's his mother with Pearl on 3-way.

Nina and her girls are at Sandy's and they're looking for Ebony. He tells them they'll be there soon. Ebony starts to get up but he tells her to lay back down. He gets up, goes to the bathroom and draws her a bubble bath. Then he returns to the side of the bed.

"I wanna bathe you," he whispers in her ear.

"I can do it," she says, feeling he may become aroused and want sex

209

in the bathroom again. She's too sore for any more sessions with her man.

"No doubt you can," he says, "But I want too. It's just the bath, alright? I'm not trying to fuck. Well not this morning. But I'll see you tonight. You wanted all of my time. You got it. And you're gonna have to deal with me on every level. Even my sexual appetite too. Because from now on, I'm fucking you and you only. I'm done fucking around."

She gets up and goes into the bathroom. She sleeps naked when she sleeps with him, so she gets right into the tub. He bathes her without incident. She puts on his *Jerry Rice* football jersey, her blue jean shorts and her sandals. He takes her home.

At her house, he comes inside with her. To both their surprise, no one is waiting to talk to them. He hugs her while kissing her repeatedly. She can feel her eyes well up with tears. She has hurt him again.

"I will never be able to handle seeing you with another guy, baby girl. So don't do it. Not if you wanna love me. Okay?" he whispers as he holds her tight, "I'm changing what I've been doing and I'll talk to crew."

"Okay," is all she has the strength to say.

She's beat and all she wants is sleep. He kisses her again before going to his mother's house. She goes upstairs to her room and goes to sleep.

During the next few weeks, the crew celebrate a year of marriage for Chill and Renee and Jr and Tonya. June had his 17th birthday. But the highlights are Jb turning 19 and getting engaged to Lynn at the 4th of July celebration. And Lynn winning the chance to compete in the National NCAA track and field competition and World Championships. Plus Ajay turns 18 and registers to vote while T-baby turns sixteen.

Ajay had looked forward to the day he registered to vote, as he'd been taught too. He's proud to be a registered voter and he struts around showing off his card.

"My grandfather, who I never got to meet, gave his life for me to have this," he says, showing his card to everyone.

This whole family participates heavily in the democratic process. The elders work the polls on voting days. Every member of the crew are registered voters and they all vote. They would be ousted from the family if they didn't participate. The voter's rights movement was a huge part of what brought their grandparents and great grandparents together as a crew. Everyone else is just following suit, as they was raised to do.

The crew open up *Crew Cuts & Styles,* their 3rd business venture. It's a hair salon and barbershop located right next door to *The Chill Spot,* in their strip mall. Nina will do shampoos and have regular employment.

210

She will also be part owner when she receives her cosmetology license and business degree. For now, Tonya is the only licensed stylist but Nina will still style her regular customers. Ebony, Rebbie and T-baby help out however they're needed.

August rolls in and Rebbie turns sixteen. The next week Jr turns twenty one. Him and Tonya start their senior year at CSU. Jan will turn 18 in Cincinnati, in a few weeks. The crew are gearing up for the grand opening celebration of the salon plus the *going-away-to-school* party for their 6 college bound crew members. Jr, Tonya, Jb, Lynn, Ajay and Jan are the college crew this fall. They make it a point to be on their best behavior at the celebration. This will be their last Saturday night together for a long while. They have a great time. All of the parents make appearances early in the night to show support for the new business venture and their college bound, as well. Afterwards, the parents go home and the crew are left to finish the night. Chill, Renee, Jr and Tonya have a great time with Jb, Lynn, Ajay and Ebony. Rob, Jan, Tank and Nina are there to party with Rich, T-baby, June and Rebbie. Bruce and Bre celebrate with their mates, Kim and Cedric, who are the newest crew members. Bre hasn't committed to Cedric sexually but she's found his company comforting and more tolerable these days. The immediate crew of 20 strong plus Arthur, Kilo, Wayne and their friend girls are present and they celebrate for hours. Rob and Jan, as well as Ajay and Ebony, go to the U to be alone. Ajay and Jan will be Cincinnati bound on Monday morning. The thought of Tim and how he may try to make a move on Ebony while he's away, weighs heavy on Ajay's mind. But Ebony has told him the mistake she made in June isn't going to happen anymore.

FALL 1992

This fall Tank, June, Rich and Bre are high school seniors. June and Rich are captains of the football team. The foursome are juniors and very active in school, sports and the community. Rena, Debbie and Belinda expand their catering business to include meals-on-wheels for the elderly citizens of Cleveland. Mrs. Green is the 1st name on their list. The girls deliver her breakfast before going to school each morning. They take dinner to her when they leave after-school practice. The catering service was already profiting. Now they have a legitimate charity which qualifies them for federal funding. Things can only get better from here.

After school and cheering practice, Nina goes to work at the salon. While Ebony, T-baby and Rebbie deliver dinners. This promises to be a
211

busier year than the last one for the crew and they're ready for it.

Down in Cincinnati, Ajay is just glad to know Ebony has lots of activities to keep her busy. Which doesn't leave her any free time to have dates with Tim, if he does try again.

Jr and Tonya's baby, lil Brad, celebrates his 1st birthday with a party at the salon. The foursome and Kim volunteer by sweeping up hair, booking appointments and even babysitting for the clients who're being groomed on normal days. Renee and Tonya come up with the idea to open a daycare in the salon but that will come later. The salon already shows profits, thanks to Tonya and Nina. They had a total of 50 clients, prior to the opening. The salon is another successful business venture for the crew. They have plans to open a restaurant on the other side of their club, after New Year's. They have the blessings of their parents and grandparents. Plus they'll need their help to run and maintain the many businesses. Actually the crew want them to manage the restaurant completely. Their parents love the idea. Especially Rena, Belinda and Debbie. They see this as a way to further expand their already successful catering business. The mothers can work there fulltime and run it, while the grandparents do the menu, recipes and run the kitchen. This will be an opportunity for all 3 generations to work together. This is the dream the 1st generation raised them on. Chill's crew is making good on that entrepreneurial dream and plan, just as the elders envisioned it. The older generations are even more impressed because they not only have fulltime career opportunities within the businesses but they'll be self employed as well.

Roll on crew!

Ebony and Ajay are in touch regularly. The crew are doing well. Bruce is in the 9th grade but he's playing football and now basketball, with the senior high school teams. Kim plays basketball for 8th grade this year.

Just when the crew are settling in and focusing on their dreams, school work and businesses, Alana Casey transfers to MLK, the Friday before Shannon "Da Reaper" Wilson's 13th birthday. Rebbie's brother is now full fledged crew. His coming out party on Saturday is filled with talk of a bomb rush on Alana. The foursome are hyped over the opportunity for Nina to beat her ass. They're planning their attack strategically, the way the crew do things. Alana already knowing Angel and Tameka, ally with the 2 of them on her 1st day at MLK. This makes the foursome even more furious and more determined they'll whoop all 3 of them. They see her transfer as a plot to get closer to their boyfriends. In reality, Alana's parents had sent her and her daughter to live with her aunt Darlene Casey because they couldn't handle her anymore.

212

Michelle had graduated with Ajay and Jan. Tameka didn't have enough hours to graduate. Alana and Angel are both Juniors but Alana is a year behind.

On October 11, the day of Bre and Stoney's daughter lil CJ's 1st birthday, Nina confronts Alana during lunch because she's still been up to her old tricks. She's still calling Tank's house and hanging up when Ebony answers the phone. She's still sneaking around to be with him every chance she gets. Tank isn't doing a whole lot to help her situation but he isn't hindering it either. Nina and Alana start to fight in the courtyard outside of the cafeteria while her girls keep everyone else at bay. Nina beats Alana convincingly and viciously, sending her to the hospital. The foursome get suspended for 2 weeks and aren't allowed to practice with their squads.

Ebony and T-baby even miss out on the practice where *coach Pat "Head" Summit* from Tennessee is suppose to scout them. They do speak with her on the phone and she expresses her disappointment in not being able to see them perform. She warns them that any athlete who comes to play for her program has to have a good attitude. *Period*! She said she would be in touch to see how they're coming along and if things go alright she can arrange a trip for them to tour the campus in the spring. T-baby and Ebony are disappointed they didn't get to meet Summit but they aren't remorseful about Alana getting her ass beat. Furthermore, Ebony already knows she's going to Cincinnati where her man attends. T-baby will too if Rich signs there this winter. He has already said he'll commit to UC.

The foursome return to school after their 2 week suspension and resume their activities. There are rumors of an all out brawl against Alana, Angel and Tameka. The showdown brawl is being largely instigated by the student body. Some of them who dislike the foursome's opponents equally or they dislike the foursome. There are still others who just want to see another beat down and who'll win it this time.

Early in the 1st week, after she's back in school, Ebony has words with Miss Whitman. Whitman tries to have her removed from the team and expelled for the school year, which is absurd. The Faculty won't support her recommendation. However this action by Whitman angers the mothers in the crew. Pearl, Debbie and Jo have had enough of Whitman and decide to take the lead. It's time for them to have their say in the matter. They inform the faculty of Miss Whitman's sex offenses with their sons while they were attending school there. As well as with the ones who are there presently. Their sons submit letters and nude photos Whitman had given to them to back their mother's claims. Each 1 of the guys had at least one. Attorney George Wheeler takes it from there. The principal agrees that

213

Whitman's recommendations for Ebony are too severe. He gives Ebony 1 day of in-school suspension then fires Whitman and brings charges. She's brought up on sex offender charges, among others. The crew really likes how their mothers flexed their crew muscles.

MLK opens their basketball season, November 10th. T-baby and Ebony start as shooting guard and small forward respectively. Bre is the starting senior point guard. Both the girls and boys teams win their openers. The 4 admirers attend the 1st game and the next 4 games leading into the holiday. By Thanksgiving break, both teams boast 5-0 records.

The college crew come home for Thanksgiving but Ajay and Jb have to return to school for Friday evening practice. Tech and Cincinnati season openers are on the Saturday following Thanksgiving. But on the eve of Thanksgiving, Ajay expresses his displeasure with Tim and his crew being at Ebony's games.

"Big John asked me who was the guy who kept yelling your name last night," he tells her as they head to Jo's so she can help prep the meal.

"Anthony please tell me you didn't tell him about the movie," she pleads, "I promised you I wouldn't say another word to him and I haven't. You promised you wouldn't tell my daddy unless I did."

"I haven't told him about the date," he says, "But I told him he's stalking you."

They laugh and she says, "Good. I feel like he is and it wasn't a date."

"Since you accepted his date, he feels like he has ownership."

"No he don't and it wasn't a *date*," she says, "And I had nothing to do with him being there. I haven't talk to him since *Pizza hut*. I wouldn't invite him to anything. I know you're at school and worried. I'm a loyal girl and you know it."

"I haven't told him anything," he says, "But if he pressures me for it, I'll have too." He doesn't say much more. But he makes her aware of his feelings when he says, "Just because I'm not here in Cleveland it don't mean I'm not still checking for you."

"I know you're checking for me," she says, "You'd better be."

"Me and big John did talk though. And my pops too," he says, "They reminded me to be careful and don't get caught up on this age thing."

He tells her about the statutory age law and the fact that he's 18 and she's 16. "That's statutory rape in a lot of places in this country," he says, "Did you know that?"

"No and I don't care."

She dismisses the thought of Tim and the age thing and tells him the only
214

thing she's thinking about is him and she's already anticipating his next trip home.

"I know you don't care but we have to be careful until Christmas."

Jb and Lynn fly out early the next morning for Atlanta. Ajay leaves at 10am driving back to Cincinnati. Rob will bring Jan back on Sunday. Ebony wants to go with Ajay and ride back home with Rob. She ask her parents and tell them she can return with Rob on Sunday night. But Pearl says she can't go and John agrees. Ebony is thinking about being defiant and leaving anyway. Ajay reminds her of the age factor and how that could bring trouble for both of them. Especially him. Plus he says he won't be apart of her disobeying her parents, ever again, in order to see him anywhere at anytime. Ebony pouts.
Darn him! Why is he trying to be so responsible now?

It's into December where going to basketball games are the biggest highlight of the crew evenings. They run their club, their other businesses and they still party every chance they get. By now T-baby and her *admirer* Craig seem to be getting closer. This leaves Rich out in the cold. Rebbie and June are talking a lot more. While Nina and Tank are more distant than ever. Roger still tries to see Nina. He goes with Craig and T-baby on their dates. Nina agrees to go because T-baby isn't going to go alone. However Tim and Justin don't push the issue with Ebony and Rebbie. Nina only likes Roger as a friend and not nearly enough to have real contact with him. But she does accept his invitation to be her date at her and Ebony's 17th birthday party. That's something Ajay isn't going to fancy in the least. Nina and T-baby are still playing the game. After learning of the invite, Tank ask Rhonda Cook, a cheerleader from Smith High, to be his date just to be spiteful. He knows that will make Nina angry but Nina had turned him down when he'd asked to be her date.
She had told him, "I already have a date for my party."
She's still playing the game. That foolish and very dangerous game of one *upmanship*. The 1 Ebony has decided she isn't going to play ever again.

It's party night and things are tense between Nina and Tank. They hardly speak to each other. Ebony know that makes them both sad. No matter how much they try and play the game, she's not fooled. They didn't even get each other gifts for Christmas which was uncalled for. Neither did T-baby and Rich. However, Rebbie and June did. Her and Ajay did too. But because of the tension between their friends, they didn't exchange much else. At least not at the party. T-baby is there with Craig. Rich is there with
215

Selina Pharr, a friend of Tank's date. Roger is Nina's date. *Very strange.*

Ebony and Ajay give their opinions and disapprovals on the way their girls or boys are acting. Ajay and Nina get into a huge argument where they're joined on either side by Ebony and Tank. The rest of the crew are determined they won't let it ruin their party. This is Christmas and they will have to get through it. Chill and Renee decide to stay out of it, this time. They know their crew needs to try and work this out for themselves. But Chill does remind them that they're family and business partners. Regardless of what they do in their personal lives. He's confident they'll work it out soon. As couples, they need to either be together or split for good and stop doing things just to annoy the other. Chill and Renee warn them that someone is going to get hurt if they don't stop. Nothing is settled tonight or the week following. Ebony and Nina are 17, *finally.*

The crew celebrate New Year's and Bruce's 15th birthday. The new year comes in with Tank and Nina, still kicking it with Rhonda and Roger. Rich and T-baby are still dating Selina and Craig. If matters aren't already fucked up enough, Tank and Rich add insult to injury when they show up at the club with Alana and Tameka. Nina and T-baby consider them over, *for good*! Playing the game has gone to an all new low.

Bruce asks mama Belinda and big Sam if he and Kim can go to the movies for his birthday. They say it's okay. But Jan know they aren't going to the movies but to the motel instead. Jr and Tonya have already arranged everything. Jan had found out in a letter she received from Kim while at UC, that Kim is sexually active. Kim had told Jan she was ready to give Bruce her virginity and Jan had helped her only sister get birth control pills. That was during the Thanksgiving break. Belinda and Sam know of the pills. They have been educating Kim on sex since she was 10 years old.

Jesse, who no longer wants to be called lil man, just turned 12 and is already trying to coax Tank into taking him out. Tank lets him smoke a little weed with him, sometimes. But he can't allow him to go to the parties or hang out with them. Not until he turns thirteen.

Tank makes 18 and has a slamming party. Nina and T-baby reminisce on his 16th birthday party when all of this trouble seems to have started. Tonight Alana comes to the party and so does Rhonda. Tank is going back and forth between the 2 of them. Not only at his party but also most days. But everyone knows he's longing to be with Nina. Even Nina knows it. But by now, neither of them want to admit fault and their brash stubbornness is driving them farther apart.

When Ajay comes home for Valentines, he finds out Nina and Tank

216

are officially over. He doesn't like hearing this from either of them. To make matters worse, there are rumors all over the set about 1 of their foursome girls not being sexually exclusive to her foursome guy.

On Sunday night, Ajay hears that T-baby and Craig are an official couple. If he didn't believe it when Wayne first said it. Then he's convinced later when he sees her coming out of Craig's apartment at the U, at 3am. Nina and Rebbie are with her. Ebony is with him when he sees this. He won't even allow her to go over and speak to her girls. He acts annoyed. But Ebony knows it's more to it than just anger. He questions her immediately.

"Did you know she was over there?" he asks as they're getting into his car.

"Yes."

"She's fucking him *now*?"

"I don't know."

She knows T-baby isn't having sex with Craig but she isn't going to give Rich the satisfaction of *knowing* she isn't. Ajay will tell Rich, for sure. He's going to tell him he saw her. That's going to work out just as T-baby wants it too. She wanted Ajay to see her so he could tell Rich that he did. Ebony doesn't really care if he tells Rich or not. She'd rather not be apart of it. She just wishes they would all stop playing this stupid game.

"You're lying," Ajay says of her saying she doesn't know, "Y'all know everything the other one does. Don't give me that."

"She said she wanted to do it tonight," she says, lying per her girls plan and still hating it. "That's what she told us," she embellishes, "But I don't think she did."

She's trying to do her girls bidding and at the same time, foil their plan to make Rich and Tank angry.

"I don't care," Ajay says and he's lying too. He adds, "I don't want you around her and that kind of shit. Do you hear me?"

"Ajay that's-"

"Stop calling me, *Ajay*," he snaps, "I keep telling you that."

"Anthony that's my blood and-"

"I don't give a damn if she is. I don't want you around none of them niggaz and since she's fucking one of them-"

"You don't know that," she says, figuring this would happen.

"I *see* her. You're not gonna be around her," he says sternly.

"You be with Rich and Tank. They're fucking around-"

"Watch your mouth, baby girl," he snaps again.

"Rich and Tank are always messing around and you be with them. What's the difference?" she asks softly.

217

"You're not me."

"So you can be with *your* friends and family, no matter what. But I can't be with *mine*? Is that what you're saying?"

"If that's how you hear it then yea, that's what I'm saying."

"What happened too *ride for your crew*, no matter what?" she asks, quoting what he said after he'd helped to kill Stoney's murderers. This time he just looks directly at her but he doesn't speak. She's upset at this double standard. He's just waiting for her to come with another smart remark so he can really fly off the handle. But she just buckles her safety belt and looks out of her window. He starts up his car and drives through the parking lot, approaching the street. What pisses her off most is that this game is causing waves in her and Ajay's relationship. That shit isn't going to continue. Big mama would strangle her if she knew she was jeopardizing her own relationship for some foolishness.

Her girls notice his car and wave. They know she's in there. They can't see her through Ajay's tint but they know she sees them. T-baby know Ajay sees her too. She has nothing to hide. She had a nice evening with Craig and even though they didn't have sex. She knows Rich will find out she's been to his place and think that she did. For T-baby that's payback enough. Let him worry about where she is and what she's doing, for a change. See if he can handle being treated this way. This sighting, this morning, will change T-baby and Ajay's relationship for months to come. It will be only a matter of time before he tells Rich he'd seen her at the apartments. Her and Rich's relationship is beyond repair or at least, that's how Ebony sees it. Especially if T-baby had gone all the way with Craig. But Ebony knows in her heart, she hasn't had sex with a new guy. Not without all of them being there. No way! She still wants all of her crew to be couples. Still she knows her cousin deserves a life without black eyes and busted lips. Or constantly being cheated on and dragged into fights and fits of jealous rage. Plus phone calls from Rich's ho's all times of the night and just the day to day down spiraling of her self esteem. She knows T-baby hadn't slept with Craig. But now that Ajay knows about her seeing him and her intentions, the shit is sure to hit the proverbial fan.

Ajay is quiet and creeping along the highway as if he's in thought. Ebony know he's upset but he's more so hurt and for the same reason she is. Because his cousin has fucked up the relationship with the only girl he's ever loved. However Ebony doesn't know just *how sad* this makes Ajay. Ajay will never let her know he's sad about it. He'll only show his masculine side. He's always been that way. Still she knows her cousin and her girls. No sex happened. She knows it and that's her final comment and answer.

218

As soon as he gets her home safely, he's heading back to Cincinnati. He's going to call Rich from his cell phone and she knows that too. She can't help but think of how he seems to be ignoring all of the events leading up to this point. Including his *own* indiscretions. Now that he's in college, their troubles with the outside women have tapered off. But she still has her doubts. More so, she's always supported her girls in everything they've done and voiced her displeasures to them only. She won't stop now.

Just as T-baby suspected, Rich knows about her trip to the U. He confronts her at school this morning. She doesn't confirm or deny it as Rich goes on about how he knows she was a the U until nearly daybreak. He believes she had sex and she lets him think the worse.

"I guess you're gonna be with that nigga then ha?" he asks, trying to appear unconcern.

"Yes I am," she answers, doing the same.

He walks away and so does she.

But on their way to 1st period, T-baby tells Ebony she hadn't gone all the way. In fact, they kissed a couple of times with no tongue. But she wants Rich to feel the same hurt she's been feeling for the past 2 years.

"I knew that already," Ebony says, "Don't forget what happened to me when I wrote that lying letter. You're going too far, cousin."

"Oh God. Okay. I remember," T-baby says as they head to class. Her girls support her but still they remind her of the consequences this lie can bring.

During the next month, nothing changes with the crew except the days. T-baby is still accepting dates from Craig. Nina is still seeing Roger, occasionally. Tank and Rich are still masquerading between their other 2 females. Bre and Cedric are more intimate but are yet to take the sexual plunge.

Ajay is still checking in with Ebony, every morning and evening. On his next trip home, he will get the news that there's going to be a new addition to the crew. One of the ladies in his crew is pregnant and due in October. The 1993 year is already bringing new additions and more of the same problems. The problems and the time wasted fixing those problems are when the crew are at their weakest. Surely it will take another loss or the threat of a loss, to wake them from their non-crew like activity.

219

CHAPTER 19

GROWING PAINS AND SORROWS

Big Chill and Renee are expecting their 2nd child and their entire crew are excited about it. They're already making plans for the arrival of lil Kenny's sister or brother. They all hope for a girl because that's what Renee and Chill are hoping for.

Despite all of the turbulence within the crew, MLK manages to win the boys and girls state titles again this year. They were state champs for Football again also.

Ajay calls to congratulate Ebony, Bre, T-baby and the guys too. Ajay and his *Bearcats* advanced to the Elite 8 of the NCAA tournament. Before losing to *North Carolina*, who went on to win the 1993 title.

Next the crew open up their restaurant, next door to *The Chill Spot.* Appropriately they *n*ame it, *The Crews House of Soul Food.* Rena, Debbie and Belinda are at the helm. This is the 4th business venture. The grand opening celebration is set for the end of March. However the 1st celebration for March is Brittany's 12th birthday on March 10th. Reaper is excited that she has only a year left before she can attend their parties.

This weekend is also the start of college spring break. Most of the crew and Greeks are going back to Atlanta with Jb and Lynn for what's known as *FreakNik 1993.* Ebony wants to go but she knows with the name alone, her parents are sure to say no. Ajay doesn't want her to go, that's for sure. She's very upset with him because he's going and so are her brothers. And neither of the want her to go.

"*Niggaz* and ho's be buck wild, down there," Ajay says and he can't stop laughing which upsets her even more.

The foursome nor Kim can go. The others leave Sunday night while Ebony sits in her room thoroughly pissed off. Tank, Rich, June and Bre plus Bruce and Reaper are allowed to skip school to go. All of their fathers, who are mostly *Omega Psi Phi*, go along as *so-called* chaperones.

"Who's going to chaperone *their* asses?" mama Rena asks.
The mothers, who are ladies of *Delta Sigma Theta* themselves, agree with Rena. They're upset that any of the youth can skip school to go. The fathers insist they need to experience it and promise they'll be there to watch them. But at the same time, they were unable to shield their own eagerness about going. This is suspected to be the *real* reason the mother's are upset.

The entire crew are Greek affiliated. All of the men and women who had gone to college and pledged, are Omega and Delta. The mothers would never have been allowed to go and can't believe Brad Sr and Sam Sr allowed Jan and Bre to go. But Lynn goes to school down there and those are her best friends.

"They had to go," was the excuse the men gave.

FreakNik is wild, just as they'd expected. Jb and Lynn have *mad props* in Atlanta. The crew are ready to have a wonderful time.

Big Mama calls on Saturday to talk to Ebony and Pearl about the disappearance of Raymond. She's still insisting his family is hiding him to avoid prosecution. She has nearly started her own task force, in Houston. She has Ron on speed dial. While him and Carolyn act as if they're working as hard as she is to find out where Raymond White is *hiding out*.

"It's hard to believe that bastard just fell off the face of the earth," big mama says to Ebony, "I *still* say his folks know where he is. Some of his folks got killed, awhile back. I told you all about that. And that coach and his family too. I'll bet you it was somebody looking for him."
Ebony plays along but she doesn't like this game either. She doesn't know exactly *where* Raymond is either. After hearing all she can take of his name, she gives the phone to Pearl. She hasn't thought about Raymond for several months. She doesn't care too think about him now either.
"The rest of his family is steady on the news making public plea's for his safe return. And anyone who knows his whereabouts and all, to please contact them or Houston Police. I think it's all bullshit," big mama says while talking to Pearl.

"I saw it a couple of times on our TV," Pearl says, "It's like a nationwide hunt for him since his coach and all of them turned up dead."
Ebony listens to her mother's end of the conversation. She's trying to hear if the police have any leads. From her mother end, no one knows anything. She goes on upstairs to get dressed and hook up with her girls. She know Raymond isn't coming back. Not alive anyway.

When John returns from *FreakNik* on Sunday, Pearl is still upset about him going. They're so busy arguing, they pay no attention to Ebony and Ajay's request for her to go to Cincinnati the following week, for her spring break. Pearl is bothered by John attending FreakNik. Ebony had packed her bags days in advance. Her and Ajay had discussed her going to visit during her spring break. She leaves with him and Jan that evening.
221

When they arrive at UC, Ajay and Jan are so tired from their week at FreakNik, they go right to bed. Ajay isn't too tired for a lovemaking episode before falling asleep though.

The next morning he has to have her again before taking her to breakfast on campus. She attends classes with him to get the full college experience. He introduces her to all of his teammates, the women's team and his partners too. They already know of her from pictures and from his discussions. It's all good and makes her feel good to know that he's talked about her so much.

She meets the women's basketball coach. Cincinnati is already recruiting her, so she's pleased to meet coach Sanders and the team. They all hang out at the condo where Ajay and Jan live while attending college. It's provided by alumni. Though that part isn't public knowledge.

Ebony spends the next day at the condo while Ajay goes to class. She cleans and organizes his room and doesn't find anything incriminating. After class, he takes her shopping. While at the jewelry store, he buys a ring for her without her knowledge. He has the sales clerk to wrap it up so he can surprise her with it later. Then they ride around Cincinnati to the spots they visited on his 17th birthday trip.

Tuesday night, she goes to his game, then they hang out on campus. Ebony loves it. She's already looking forward to college life. Ajay is treated like a celebrity. He has many fans and a fat townhouse to share with Jan, who's a celebrity as well.

Wednesday night she sees pictures from the Atlanta trip which 1 of the Omega's brought over. On some of the pictures, she see Angel, Alana and Michelle. Also Tameka, Darlene and their Cleveland whore buddies. 1 picture is of Ajay and Angel, solo. And although he isn't posing, he's in the picture with Angel looking caught off guard. Ebony takes *that* photo and goes into his room. She doesn't return.

Later he comes to check on her and finds her in bed crying.

"What's wrong with my girl?" he ask and she shows him the photo.

"Ah they was down there too," he answers.

"Did you hook up with her, baby?" she asks.

"I fucked her, Ebony," he admits softly with regret in his voice.

"So that's why I needed to stay home?"

"No. It wasn't planned," he offers.

"Anthony why do you have to keep fucking with her?"

"Watch your mouth."

"I meant it just like that, Anthony. *Why?*"

"You don't talk to me like that. I don't care what the fuck I did."

222

"I know you don't care. I might as well not care either," she says, "Because while I'm sitting at home waiting like a fool. You're screwing anybody you-"

"I don't wanna talk about that. That was some bullshit anyway. Stop taking that type shit to heart, baby."

He grabs her and holds her in his arms. She struggles to get loose but he's too strong. He tries to explain how the chance meeting took place and that it meant nothing. She's upset, nonetheless. But she's in his territory. Even if she wanted to leave, she doesn't know where she'd go. Nor how she would get there. He isn't letting her out of his sight. Not when she's angry.

"Why do you have to be with her, Anthony?"

"I don't have to be with her or no other female except you, Ebony. She was just there and I hit it. I regret it too."

"You said you wasn't gonna mess around anymore."

"I wasn't planning too," he says, not wanting to admit that their fathers was apart of it too, "And I regret it. But it wasn't no solo shit."

"Were you with her the whole week?" she asks, her eyes welling up with tears.

"Hell no! We did the same shit we usually do to girls like them. All of us. We hit them a couple of times on the first night. Then we didn't fuck with them or nobody else for the rest of the time we was there. We just partied and bullshit," he offers, "And kicked it with Jb and Lynn's folks, down there. Ron and his crew was there too."

She's still crying. He says, "Baby don't cry. I promise you she don't mean *nothing* to me. Nothing at all," he says as he wipes the tears from her face and adds, "You're the only one I *need* to be with baby. That's my word."

"I know when I get back to school, that's all I'm gonna hear around campus. Is how she was with you in the *A-T-L*," she cries.

"Baby you've got my heart. She never had it and never will. That's for you and you only."

She cries even more. He looks at her. He can't stand to see her cry. He wants to stop her tears. He has to do something right now to make her believe he wants to commit to her.

The ring he had bought when they were shopping yesterday is only a promise ring. He had only paid $700 for it but it's a promise of his intent to stay with her. He was planning to give it to her on Sunday before they leave for home. But he's thinking now would be a better time to give it to her. He gets the box from his drawer and walks back over to his bed. He lays across the bed, facing her and hands the little black box to her.

"Open it," he says as she sits up and wipes her face.

223

Before taking the box, she looks at him. "Open it up," he says again and she does as she looks back at him.

"It's beautiful," she says while staring at it.

"Just like you," he says, "I'm sorry for messing with ho's."

That brings a smile to her face.

He says, "When them ho's come at you with that bullshit. Just let them see my ring."

He takes it out and says, "This is my promise to always be with you. No matter what or who." He slips it on her finger and says, "Wear it for me until I can get the real thing. Okay?"

He seals it with a gentle kiss and a smile. He asks her if she'll wear it as a symbol of her commitment to him. He promises to make a real effort to change his ways, this time. She accepts the ring. *Keep it real.* She's upset that Angel saw him in Atlanta. But she isn't about to let it spoil her chance to get the last laugh and all the props too, when she returns to school next week. Surely the pictures and stories about how Angel had spent spring break with her man *again* will be circulating. But she'll counter with her promise of eternity from him. She know he loves her and only her. Every part of her wants to believe he can be faithful too. But she still has many doubts. She isn't about to leave him, by any means. She knows that in her mind, body and soul. However, she does give him an ultimatum.

"I'll wear your ring and accept your promise. Because I do love you with all my heart. And I know deep in your heart, *somewhere,*" they laugh and she continues, "you love me too. But no more Angel. I mean it. No more. Or I'm gonna kill that girl. I don't trust her. Promise me."

"Okay. I promise. Now come here," he whispers and he seals it with a passionate kiss.

"I hate to think about your lips kissing her," she says.

"I don't kiss nobody but you, baby girl," he says, "My lips don't touch no other girl. You *have* to believe that. I keep telling you but you don't believe me. My lips don't touch nobody but you. I tell them ho's that."

"Nothing else better not be touching them either," she demands.

She puts her arms under his and pulls him closer. She's in the mood for loving. She's not going to let a 1 night stand with Angel ruin her spring break, in Cincinnati. She'll deal with Angel later, if necessary.

"Yes ma'am," he says jokingly. Then more seriously, he says, "I'm sorry," as he lays her straight back on his bed and looks into her eyes. "You're the only woman I cannot do without. I'm gonna show you that, one of these days, baby girl," he says, "I'm still growing but I'll get there. I have to start thinking with my heart. Then I won't mess up."

224

She pulls on him to scoot up next to her. He does and she unbuttons his pants. That's a sign to him that she's in the mood. He begins kissing her and removing her clothes. They spend the rest of the night reconfirming their commitment to 1 another. They go to sleep in each other's arms. Something no other woman or man has done with either of them. Nor will they ever.

The next morning before he leaves for class, he destroys the picture she had shown him. He rips it into tiny pieces then sprinkles the pieces all over her as she sleeps. This wakes her, for sure.

"What are you doing, baby?" she asks.

"That's that picture. You won't see that muafucka *no* more. I didn't even know he took it," he says.

"Alright," she says as she smiles, "You're leaving for class ha?" she asks with her eyes saying she wants him to hold her again.

"Not yet," he says as he lays down and pulls the covers over them. They have a morning session and he still apologizes for his chance meeting with Angel.

They get up later and make breakfast. Jan joins them. She's excited about the visitor who's coming today as she says, "Rob's coming down to spend the rest of the week and I can't wait."
After breakfast, Ebony drives the 2 of them to class in the six four.

"When I get out of class, I'm taking you to lunch," Ajay says as he kisses her then goes on to class.

She drives Jan to class. On the way, Jan tells her about the Atlanta trip. She's pleased Ebony already knows. She verifies the hooking up with Angel had only been on Monday then no more. Ebony is happy to know Ajay had been honest with her. But he usually is. No matter how brutal it is.

After class he takes her to lunch at a nice restaurant. After lunch, they go back to the condo and begin what will become known in their relationship, as *Naptime.*

"Ebony only you can make me go to bed in the middle of the damn day. If that's not commitment. I don't know what is," he says, pulling her closer to him.
They make love and a lot of noise along with it, as they take advantage of no one else being in the condo but them.
Afterwards while trying to catch his breath, he says, "If I'd known naptime was this dope. I would've participated when I was in Kindergarten."
They laugh.

"It wasn't gonna be like *this* though," she says as she smiles, "You are so crazy, baby."

"So I didn't miss shit, ha?" he ask as he holds her close to his chest.
225

"I love this ring," she says, "It means a lot to me, Anthony."

"Good because I sure as hell want you to be with me," he says, "I need you in my life. I never fronted about that."

"I'm *gonna* be in your life. That's automatic."

"I mean not just because we're crew. Even if we wasn't. I still need you *for me*. You're good for me. I always knew that too," he says.

They hold each other and take a nap until the early evening.

Pearl and John made up long before today. But now he has to go back out on the road. She always hates when he leaves. Even though he has been driving long distance for over 20 years. The day he leaves is still the hardest for her. They talk with Ebony, down in Cincinnati. She apologizes for leaving without their permission. John tells her he'll be gone when she gets back home. But to never do that again. She says she won't.

Rob drives to Cincinnati to spend the rest of the week with Jan. She's happy to see him. He asks where Ajay and Ebony are. She points to Ajay's room. Not to be denied, Rob decides he's going to get them up.

"Wake your asses up in there!" he yells though the door as he laughs.

"What up, dog!" Ajay yells back, getting up and putting on shorts.

"Obviously not y'all two," he says, "I see some things don't change, no matter what fucking zip code *you're in,* homie," he yells as Ajay opens the bedroom door.

"What's up, dog?" Ajay asks as him and Rob shake hands and hug each other.

"What's up, baby girl?" Rob asks Ebony as she pulls the covers up to her nose.

"Hey, big brother. What's going on?" she asks with a giggle.

"Hey man. Don't be talking to my woman while she's in the bed. I'm the only man who can do that," Ajay says as he laughs.

Him and Rob retreat to the living room to smoke weed and drink Hennessy while Ebony goes to take a shower. Then her and Jan cook dinner. They hang out together throughout the weekend.

When Ebony returns to Cleveland with Rob, she shows her mother her promise ring, 1st thing. Pearl is happy to see her so excited about her relationship with Ajay. She hopes this excitement will last forever but knowing these 2 like she does, she knows it won't. Not this early.

May is graduation time for 6 of the crew. Jr and Tonya graduate

226

from CSU. Tank, June, Rich and Bre graduate from MLK. Tank, June and Rich are going to UC with Ajay and Jan. Tank is going on a track scholarship. June and Rich have 1 for football. Bre receives a basketball scholarship to Tech in Atlanta, where Jb and Lynn will be juniors.

Summer 1993 is bound to be a hot one. The crew are busy handling their businesses and *bidness*. The detail shop, the club, the salon and the new restaurant are all showing big profits. The crews from Houston and Columbus come for 4th of July. Ebony shows big mama and poppa her ring. Big mama likes that move and tells them so. Then later, she has a serious talk with the foursome and their guys about commitment. She tells Nina, T-baby, Tank and Rich that she's disappointed to know that they're not keeping their crew relationships on the right track. Tonight is the 1st time in over a year that the 4 of them have spent any quality time together. They go with big mama and poppa to papa's house for dinner and they talk for hours. Before leaving to join the rest of the crew at The Chill Spot, they sit and talk as couples. The 4 of them decide to work towards respecting the other ones feelings and getting along. Then they meet their crew at the club to have some fun.

When the 4 of them walk in together, their crew cheers. They have a wonderful 4th of July celebrating Jb's 20th birthday plus 2 years of marriage for Chill and Renee and Jr and Tonya. Their hearty entrepreneurial efforts are paying off which is good for all involved. Unfortunately this makes all of them bigger targets for the envious, more police harassment and the competition. Since Stoney's death over 2 and a half years ago, there's been rumors of plots to try and make another move on the crew. But nothing has come of it, thus far. The crew still move, in at least pairs, for safety reasons. It's a fact that the larger they get the more allies they make. But there are some who come to the club or frequent their mall, who aren't happy to see them progress. The crew take it in stride.

Renee and Chill have a prenatal visit with Dr. Gladys Weston, the following day. They're having their 1st ultrasound.

"Good morning, mister and misses Payne. How are we feeling today?" Dr Weston asks as smiles.

"I'm pregnant," Renee says and laughs, "I don't know about y'all." Chill and Dr. Weston laugh as Chill rubs Renee's shoulders.
They do the ultrasound. It reveals that she's carrying a girl. They're happy with the news and can't wait to share it with their crew. But first Renee has
227

to shop. She's been waiting to know the sex of the baby so she can finish changing the décor of the spare room into a nursery. They leave the doctor and go straight to the mall. They're going to get baby clothes and pick out patterns. They grab everything they'll need to decorate. Once they finish shopping, they head for their 1992 Blazer in the parking lot.

"You know I'm gonna spoil the hell out of this little girl, don't you?" Chill asks her as he rubs her belly, "I'm happy I've got a little girl coming. I always wanted a sister and never had one. My son's got one."

"I know that, *proud* poppa," she says, "You finally got you a baby girl. Now you can stop sweating me."
They share a good laugh as they head to the Blazer.

All of a sudden from out of no where, a Regal comes speeding through. It squeals to a stop and dozens of shots are fired directly at them. Then the Regal is gone just as quickly as it had appeared.

There are many witnesses who rush over to help. Chill and Renee are lying on the ground in pools of their own blood. The witnesses are already discussing what they saw but Chill and Renee saw nothing. The bullets had hit both of them. Chill is hit 5 times. Once in his right leg. Twice in his right arm. 1 bullet went into his side and 1 went into his back. He lays slumped over Renee, who was hit twice. Once in her arm and the other 1 in her abdomen. She's still visibly alive and screaming for someone to help her husband. He isn't breathing. A witness dials 911 from his cell phone. Several of them know the crew and recognize Chill and Renee. They know they're friends with Arthur, Kilo and that All-Star basketball player who signed at Cincinnati. 1 of them calls Arthur immediately. Soon Renee can hear sirens approaching as she starts to feel panic. Chill isn't breathing.

Arthur gets the news and runs to Ajay's apartment where some of the crew had gathered waiting for news about the ultrasound. He tells them about the ambush at the mall.

"They're headed to the hospital," he says, barely able to speak.
Within minutes, every member of the crew have been notified and are en route to Chill and Renee's side. Nina calls her parents from Tank's cell phone. They leave work immediately. Rushing, as they head to the hospital. Jo is hysterical as she screams, "Oh Lord! My child! Please spare my babies!"
Al drives excessive speeds and they make it to the hospital after the crew and the EMS unit arrived which had brought Renee and Chill together. They're in the ER when Jo gets inside. Renee is awake and terrified for Chill, who still isn't responding. Arthur had sent Wayne and Kilo to secure the 1992 blazer while he went with the crew to the hospital.
228

Wayne and Kilo get the Blazer from the mall parking lot and take it home. They check it out for anything incriminating. Then they meet the crew at the hospital. Chill is smarter then that but they had to be sure nothing had been planted in it either.

When the paramedics took Chill from the back of the unit, he wasn't moving. The crew remember Stoney.

Once they all get to the emergency room waiting area, they have the place packed. When they roll Chill down the hall, he looks stiff.
Ebony screams, "Is he dead, Anthony?!" and faints in the waiting room.
Ajay sits on the floor holding her and crying. He never takes his eyes off of the door where the staff had just taken Chill and Renee.
How can our leader be gone? My big brother can't be dead.

To have the leader of his crew killed off says to Ajay, their crew is weak. He isn't handling that at all. Al helps him and Ebony get to their feet. The staff say Chill still has a weak pulse and he's going to need surgery, right away. But it's not looking good for him. The doctors promise Jo and the crew, they'll do all they can. They roll Chill to surgery and tell the family it's going to be a lengthy procedure. The crew set in for the long haul.

Chill is losing a lot of blood and he dies twice while on the operating table. They revive him, each time. Renee is in danger of losing their little girl, only 6 months in her womb. She has to go to surgery. The baby isn't due until October. They have to determine the damage to her uterus and if she'll be able to carry to term. They discover the baby is still alive and unharmed, to everyone's amazement. The doctors remove the bullet from Renee's arm. The bullet that hit her in the abdomen had come out of her side. She has lost a lot of blood plus the fluid sack is ruptured. Dr. Weston is on the scene. She determines Renee cannot carry her to term. After talking with Jo, Weston delivers the little girl by emergency Cesarean Section and places her in an incubator. There are so many tubes connected to her little body, you can barely see her.

Chill is still in surgery. He's in critical condition. He has been unconscious since the bullets entered his body and he hasn't come around. The crew are praying for all 3 but the chances for 2 of them are slim.

Renee is in recovery and doing well. Baby girl Payne is alive and getting stronger. Living seems to be her destiny as she makes gains in record time. After finding out Renee and the baby are out of the woods, the crew turn their prayers to Chill. He's in the worst shape. The doctors haven't given him much chance to survive the surgery. Ajay is beside himself. Ebony is afraid for him if Chill dies. She know he's going to go on
229

a rampage and do whatever it takes to get revenge. She'll willing to join him.

After 11½ hours in surgery to remove all 5 bullets, Chill is taken to ICU. The doctors tell the crew he's on his own. They've done all they can. He's heavily guarded and so are Renee and the baby.

"He's a fighter, man. He'll make it," Jr says, not willing to believe anything else.

He holds Tonya while she cries. They breathe a sigh of relief that all 3 are still alive.

Later, Renee awakes screaming. The staff and crew rush to her side. She has awakened, realized she's no longer pregnant and thinks she lost the baby. Not seeing Chill by her side causes a panic. They manage to calm her down and tell her all 3 of them had survived.

"Where is lil Kenny?" she asks, concerned for her 1st born.

Pearl brings him to her immediately. He gets up on the bed, kisses his mother and tells her he has seen his daddy and baby sister and they're alive. Renee cries and hugs him. She asks to see Chill and the baby. Her nurse and Lynn help her into a wheelchair and they go visit Chill. She holds his hand and talks to him but he isn't responding. She kisses him and sits with him for awhile. Then she goes to see her daughter, whom she isn't going to name until Chill wakes up. They'll decide on her name together.

In the meantime, all the men in the family meet briefly in the private waiting room. They send the ladies with Renee. Poppa tells Jr and Rob, who are the next in rank, he wants them to take charge. Their 1st plan of action is to comb the streets and get a report on who had sent the hit, as soon as possible. Rob, Arthur, Kilo and Wayne are going to work the streets today and see what leads they can find. Jr, Jb, June and Tank are in charge of security for Chill and the family. This leaves Ajay, Rich, Cedric and Bruce to handle the street business and to employ the females as needed. Ajay takes the lead with honor. He's looked forward to this day, for his whole life.

By Friday Renee is doing well enough to be discharged but she refuses to go home without her husband and daughter. Dr. Weston keeps her with instructions that she'll be discharged with her family members.

On July 11, Ajay's 19th birthday, there's no party planned. He doesn't want to celebrate without Chill and Renee being able to be there. Neither does any of the rest of the crew. His plans for his birthday are to spend it like he had spent the last 6 days. At the hospital with his crew and 230 working the leads they have. The crew and family go to church but Ajay and Ebony go to the hospital and bring lil Kenny with them. They go to Chill's room and find Renee next to his bed, talking to him.

After a half hour with Chill, Ebony wants to see the baby. Her and Renee go to the nursery. Baby girl Payne is getting stronger everyday. She's truly a miracle baby who suddenly begins to cry. Renee smiles because it's the 1st time she's heard her voice. The nurse tells Renee to try her with a bottle and see if she'll take one. She tries but the baby girl won't eat. She just continues to cry. Her pediatrician say she's going to take her off the machine to see if she can function on her own and allow Renee to hold and bond with her. They unplug all of the tubes and she breathes independent of the respirator. Renee is overjoyed. This is also the 1st time she's held her.

"She looks fine but we want to keep her in the premature ward for a few more weeks," the head pediatrician, Dr Susan Mahoney, says.

"Would it be okay if I take her to visit her father?" Renee asks.
Dr. Mahoney says it will be okay and she sends a pediatric assistant with them for precaution. Ebony, Renee, baby girl Payne and the nurse, go visit Chill. The baby is still crying. Nothing Renee, Ebony, Ajay or the nurse tries will calm her down. They assume she just needs to cry.

"I think somebody is just testing out her little lungs," the nurse says, "She hasn't cried since her birthday."
They all laugh. They're so concerned with the baby girl that they aren't paying any attention to Chill.

"Is that my baby girl crying like that?" he asks, his voice is barely audible.
Renee goes to him. She kisses his lips as if she hasn't seen him in years. She asks if he's okay, over and over. She gives him her special smile for the 1st time since walking with him to their Blazer on that near fatal day.

"No baby. I've been shot up," he says as he tries to smile back.
She cries happy tears. Her husband is awake and with his sense of humor.

"Man you had us scared to death," Ajay says, standing on Chill's right side.

"I can't leave right now. I've got too many things to do," Chill says, still trying to be humorous.

"I love you, bro," Ajay says effortlessly, "Just in case something else happens. I wanna be sure and get that in there."

"Good you do, homie. Because I know my breath is *cuttin'* up," he jokes and they all laugh at him.

"Kenny we're not worried about your breath," Renee says as she gives him kiss after kiss.
231

"I am," Ajay says and they all laugh.

"See bro. Now this is love," Chill says, "When your woman kiss you in the mouth and give you the tongue. And you know your breath smells like something done died in your *throat*. That's real love."

They all laugh again as Renee gets his toothbrush ready. Chill is back and with his good humor. He's going to make sure his woman and his crew know that he's not going anywhere.

"*I would die for you,* baby," Renee says as she brushes his teeth.

"Y'all can tell we grew up on *Prince* and that *Purple Rain* album," he says as he continues to crack jokes.

He's happier than anyone else to be awake and in his right mind. He looks at Ajay. They're both already thinking about retaliation while Ebony and Renee smile at each other.

"Baby it's time for you to meet your little girl," Renee says as she puts his crying daughter to his left side.

"I have to give her a kiss," Chill says.

"Don't man," Ajay says, "That killer breath might be a bit much for her. She's small still," he laughs saying, "One brushing ain't enough."

"Then you come here, homie. Somebody is gonna have to kiss me up in this mother," he whispers and they all laugh again.

Renee gives him a long kiss, once again. Ajay cracks up laughing as Ebony leans in and gives him a kiss on the cheek. Then she calls the church and lets all of the members know the good news.

"Chill is awake and the baby is out of the incubator," she says.

The pastor, the crew and other members are coming to visit after service.

"Kenny we still have to name her," Renee says, "I've been waiting for you to wake up."

"I say we name her Destiny. Because she was destined to be here and early too," he says, "Plus that was the name of our cruise line."

"Perfect. That's her first name," Renee says, "And we can keep the other two names we picked on our honeymoon."

"Yea when I was trying to make her," Chill says as he chuckles.

Destiny Jalene Shante' Payne
[premature] July 5, 1993
Named July 11, 1993. Ajay's 19th birthday

The Payne's are released on T-baby's 17th birthday, under heavy security. There had been an officer at their doors while they were in the hospital. Chill insists they not continue their surveillance at his home. Him

232

and his crew can handle it and they look forward to it. He lets the police know he has control of his life and there is no need for anyone to protect or fear him. Unless they wish him harm. His advice to them,
"Protect those who did this to my family. They're the one's who need you."

His message is all too clear to his crew, as they escort him and Renee out of the hospital and to the car. The staff and officers are in awe at how many people showed up to stand with this brother and his family. Their vehicle motorcade leaves the hospital parking lot and parades to Chill house.

"The hood! Damn it sure feels good to be back in this muthafucka! Now business *first*. How are things going men?" Chill asks as he sits in his recliner and his crew gathers around him.

"Everything's straight," Ajay says, "Cash, loot, buildings, lots, blocks, employees. Everything and everybody counted and added up. You better know your crew got your back in every muthafuckin way," he says calmly as he sparks up a cigar, "Now what are we gonna do about the new situation?"
He had almost single handedly taken over the street aspect of the business while Chill was laid up. Which left the others free to run the legitimate businesses, investigations and security. He also made a major deal with the help of Ron, who is in town with his crew. They came back to check on their Cleveland family. Chill is more than pleased with Ajay and the guys. He gives them the reigns to handle crew trades until he's back to full strength.

As of August 1993, Ajay is the man. This makes Ebony nervous. She doesn't hesitate to tell him every chance she gets. But at the same time, she leaves no doubt in his mind that she's down to ride, no matter what and she loves him unconditionally. She's still afraid for him. Especially after what had happened to Chill and Renee.

"Yea that's right," he says, "I know I'm in danger and so are you. We already was. So you can't expect me to ever lay down and die."
He dismisses the thought and tells her they both have to be careful. She sees something in him that she's never noticed before. He fears nothing or no one but God. He's a confident man with unshakeable love for those that love and care for him. His only vulnerability is her. The shooting of Chill and Renee only brings out the very best in him and eventually, her too.

Chill regains strength quickly. Or more like in record time, once he's home. He's up and walking around within the 1st week. Some think
233

it's too soon. He gets back to his business by the time the crew gear up for the fall semester of high school and college. Still Rob and Bruce move in and stay with them during the post recovery. Jr and Tonya are there so much, it's like they live there also. The guys are quick to point out how this attempt on their leaders happened after most of them *had* to be away.

Jb and Lynn start their junior year at Tech with Breanna, a freshman, on a basketball scholarship. The foursome start their senior year at MLK. Bruce is a sophomore. He's no longer playing basketball but *he is* Mr. Football at MLK. Kim is a football cheerleader for 9th grade. She no longer wants to play basketball. She wants to be near Bruce. Da Reaper or Shannon is in 8th grade and getting heavy into music. He has a friend who raps. He goes by the name, *Mic Checkz*. He's from Miami but visits his grandparents during the summer and the major holidays. They live next door to Rena and big Archie. Him and Reaper are great friends and both aspire to be rappers. Erica, Jesse, Brittany, Sam Jr and Greg Jr are collectively known as *the 99 crew*. They're in 7th grade. Pam and Ruthie are 6 graders. Steven and Ally are in 5th grade. Lil Kenny starts 4th grade while Archie is in 2nd grade. The James twins, Brina and Brandon are in 1st grade. Brad III is almost 2 years old. Lil CJ, who will be 2 in October, stays in Columbus with her grandma Jackie, aunts Chaundra and Charlotte and poppa Jason while Bre attends college. Grandma Debbie works at the new restaurant. Chaundra is in the 5th grade and Charlotte is in 4th grade, down in Columbus.

In late October while Greg Jr is crewed up or initiated, the crew get a thorough description of the car that did the drive by on Chill and Renee. It was a baby blue and white 1987 Regal. They have no idea who it belongs too but they aren't going to rest until they find out.

Another occurrence in October is the missing persons case on Raymond White. It's been updated to presumed dead. The case is colder than ever. The police in Houston and Ann Arbor still have very few leads and nothing to lead them to the crew or Ebony. Ron and several of his crew have been questioned and at times, they were under surveillance. But the police haven't been able to pin anything on either of them. Nothing for Raymond, his coach and family. Nor Raymond's family either. The police have also questioned poppa and big John, several more times. They're still listed as *likely suspects* because they had threatened to kill him before the assault happened and many times since. Ebony still gets major butterflies whenever she hears anything about Raymond White.

She's in constant contact with Ajay at UC. Now with Tank, June and Rich there, her and her girls plus Rob alternate phone calls to their

234

TIME TO GROW-RELOADED-TIME WILL REVEAL 2

mates. They all talk on each call, no matter who makes or receives it. Ajay promises Ebony a cell phone for Christmas. He has already given her a beeper but for him that just isn't enough. He has to be able to contact her at anytime. He wants her to have the freedom to call him anytime as well. He's more paranoid after hearing that Craig is still trying to pursue his relationship with T-baby. She still accepts dates to the movies with him and they still talk on the phone. But to her, Craig seems more interested in the crews business than he is in her. She would never volunteer any info to him. She knows the code. It states, *"no outsiders in the mix."* She just pretends she doesn't know anything when he asks.

On this particular date they're going to a movie, then by his apartment. Nina and Rebbie are with them. Justin and Roger don't come because Nina and Rebbie told them not too. After the movie, they pull into the parking lot of the U. Nina and Rebbie go to Kilo's apartment while T-baby sits in the car. Nina and Rebbie watch from the balcony. T-baby sits in his car listening to *R. Kelly's, 12 PLAY*. He asks her if she's ever planning to sleep with him. She says she doesn't know and she doesn't really believe he likes her. He tells her that's not true. Then he asks her for a kiss. She lets him kiss her without tongue. One kiss leads to another and another. Before she knows it, he has his face in her crouch. She has never experienced oral sex. Her and Rich have talked about it but have never actually done it. One thing is for sure, she isn't about to give any other type of sex to Craig. Tonight or any other night. However she's willing to let him serve her. He undoes her Cross Colors jeans and begins to eat her pussy.
It's great. Damn! What do I do with my hands?

Eventually she grabs his head to keep it in place. She's watching her girls who are standing outside of Kilo's apartment waiting for her and Craig to get out. She knows they're wondering what happened to his head. She thinks of calling them from her cell and having them walk up to the car and see if they'd even know what he's doing. But she gets sidetracked as he licks her to the point of ecstasy. She comes on the seat of his car. He tries to kiss her but she won't allow him too. That doesn't seem right.
You eat pussy. Not me, fool!

She giggles at herself. After knowing he eats pussy, she knows she'll never tongue kiss him. She figures if he ate her pussy so well and so suddenly, then surely he has eaten another. He tells her he wants to go inside. She's thinking about going all the way is what she tells him. But she wants him to take a shower first. She needs to get in there and check things out. She'll
235

make a break for it before he gets out of the shower. She's very suspicious of him nowadays. She wants to see if she's right to feel like he's more interested in her crew than he is her. They go inside while her girls wait on the balcony. He goes to take a shower, leaving her alone in the living room. Her girls have to go home. She says okay as she goes into spy mode.
Now what would crew want me to look for if they suspect him of being foul?

Realizing she has to hurry, she finds a photo album and sits down to look in it. She comes across several pictures of Craig, his boys and friends. On all of the pictures, they're throwing up gang signs. The ones they're throwing down are the same ones friends of the crew, like Ron's family, throw up. More than that, the last 2 photos she see really lets her know *Craig is the ENEMY!*

"Oh my God. This nigga is foul," she says aloud, "I knew it."
She has found what she needs. She leaves and hurries to Kilo's apartment and catch her girls out front. She asks Kilo to drive them all home and he does.

As soon as she gets home, her and her girls hook up on the 4-way with Ebony. She tells them what she discovered while at Craig's.

"I can't believe I let him lick me then I find out he's the enemy."

"Now we know why they always wanted to know about the crew," Rebbie says.

"I knew they wasn't for us. I knew it and I kept telling y'all that," Ebony says, "They affiliated with Jake and Danny Washington and they was using us to try to get info on our crew."

"Muthafuckaz trying to infiltrate," Nina says, shaking her head.

"That wasn't gonna happen," Rebbie adds, "We know the code."

"We don't even really trip about no gang signs but crew got family that's gee's. There was a couple more pictures that *really* disturbed me," T-baby says.

"More than seeing that *gang sign* shit?" Nina asks, "And knowing they was down with the niggas who killed Stoney?"

"Yes."

"Like what?" Rebbie asks.

"I saw two pictures of a light blue and white Regal. I don't know the guy behind the wheel but I bet Craig do," T-baby says, "He looks like Craig too."

"They're related. Bet," Nina says, "Trying to take out our crew."

"Oh my God," Ebony says, "I felt this was wrong. We have to tell Chill and we need to tell him now. We need to know what it is he wants to
236

do about them. I'll bet this whole courtship shit was false. Tell Chill now."

"I am girl," T-baby says and they call Renee and inform her.

She tell them how they are to behave. Of course any further relationship with Craig or any of his crew is out of the question. It was anyway. She doesn't have to say it. The foursome know that already. Renee tells Chill about T-baby's discovery and he sets a plan in motion immediately. Ebony is overjoyed that this turned up. She didn't want her girls seeing the other guys anyway. Ajay was pressuring her way to much about hanging out with family. But she didn't want T-baby and Nina to accompany them to the movies even. She wants them to be with *their* crew.

When Ajay and the college crew hear the news, they're anxious to get home and handle business. But with both football and basketball seasons under way, it'll be difficult to pull off a caper without drawing attention to themselves. It's already mid-November so Chill decides the crew will lay low until Thanksgiving. Then they'll launch the plan for the fools who plotted the infiltration and annihilation of the crew. They agree the quickest way to get to these guys is through the foursome. Ajay disagrees wholeheartedly but that's the plan, nonetheless. He know the game won't wait for his personal opinions.

T-baby is the glue. She's already in, some what. So she's the 1 to keep the ball rolling. She'll continue to accept Craig's phone calls but no dates. Unless it's all 4 of them which is the part Ajay wants removed. Also sex isn't an option in any form. Rich stresses that point, very aggressively. T-baby tells him there isn't a chance she'll go there again.

Rich is still enrolled in anger management and doing well. He's learned to write down whatever situation he's dealing with that makes him feel violent. Then he has too read it back to himself and his fellow classmates. It helps tremendously. He has calmed down so much that T-baby is willing to accept him into her life again. He's broken off things with both Tameka and Selina, for her. She's the 1 he loves. He's her 1st and still only, in all matters that matter. So they get back together in every way. Every since he found out about Craig plus with a lot of pressure from Ajay, Rich had demanded him and T-baby end their split. She was ready to end the break up too. They're an official couple again by mid-month and they soon renew their sexual adventures too. Both seem to have found a way to make each meeting count for something.

During the renewal of their sexual relationship, Rich felt compelled to show T-baby his own tongue skills. In her opinion he's much better than Craig. But he's the man she loves and she had only wanted him to commit to her, which he says he's willing to do now. A lack of real commitment is

237

how Craig came into the picture in the 1st place. Only because Rich was messing around. Now with his anger management classes, he's back to being the guy she learned to love. The 2 of them have been meeting in Columbus along with the other 4 couples. She makes the trip each time her girls and Rob go. They're all in school full time and the Cincinnati crew can't always get to Cleveland. Nor can the Cleveland crew manage to sneak away to Cincinnati and not get caught. They meet up in Columbus whenever possible, since it's only a 2 hour drive for all involved.

As far as getting their revenge on Craig's crew, they're bidding their time. The crew will try to stretch the plan out until the summer. That's when they'll all be home and their alibi's will be solid. For now, it's up to the foursome to slowly spin Craig, Justin, Roger and Tim into their web.

Ebony is nervous about the whole process. She's very vocal about her unwillingness to participate. There's definitely enough resistance from Ajay to warrant her being so. To add more pressure on her, he deliberately has her to undress with the lights on. *He says* so he can fully inspect her body. *He says* he's checking for fingerprints. He smiles each time but she knows he's checking for something. That something is to make certain that she's still as uncomfortable with the plan as he is and to *keep her extra* uncomfortable with it. She knows he isn't okay with their plan and really, he's just keeping her on her toes. Fact is, he isn't going to underestimate Tim's lust for her. He feels like Tim may try to take advantage of her during the running of their scheme. Something like Raymond had done. He'll become to aggressive with her. Or worse. Just not take no for an answer like Raymond hadn't. Ajay is just a natural protector and he still doesn't recognize her strength. He may never because *he is* her protector. He doesn't expect her to have to watch out for danger. He's got that. Furthermore since she had accepted a date with Tim, last summer and actually went. She knows that makes him insecure with her even being in Tim's presence. She wants to assure him that he has nothing to worry about. She loves him and only him. She's only doing this plan because her crew needs her too. Otherwise, she wouldn't dare.

It's the early Monday morning of Thanksgiving week when papa calls Ebony and T-baby and wakes them up before they leave for school. He has very good news.

"I'm proud to say my two granddaughters are ranked in the top twenty in the State and the National Basketball polls," he says proudly.

"What is that, papa?" Ebony asks, "Like the ones Anthony's in?"

238

"Yes cousin," T-baby chimes in, "It's where you get ranked based on your stats, just like Ajay. Girl you should know that. I knew you would make it. I didn't think I would though."

"Well you both did," he says, "Ebony is number two in the state. Trisha you're six. In the nation, Ebony is nine and Trisha is fifteen."

"Where is Anthony ranked now?" Ebony says, knowing he was #1 in the state, last season.

"In college polls he's number four on *Dick Vitale's damper dandies*," papa says as he chuckles and the girls giggle with excitement.

When they get to school there are congratulation banners already hanging everywhere and for Ajay too, though he's a sophomore in college.

"Ebony this is the bomb," T-baby says.

"Y'all deserve it, kid," Nina and Rebbie say, over and over as they walk to their first period classes amidst many *congratulations and way-to-go's!*

"It's alright," Ebony says, "But all I wanna do is win state and sign my scholarship to UC, so I can be with my baby."

"Me too," T-baby agrees.

"Us too," Rebbie and Nina agree.

T-baby has to stop at the bathroom before going on to class. She spends half of 1st period, over the toilet vomiting. The foursome talk her into going to visit the school nurse and they go with her.

She goes to the nurses office at school complaining of an upset stomach. She's given a full examination including a pregnancy test. After her exam, she joins her girls in the lobby to wait for the results. They laugh and talk while they wait.

"Any excuse to get us out of class is cool," Rebbie says and laughs.

"Y'all, I got something. I know I do," T-baby says.

"Don't jump to conclusions," Rebbie says.

"What could you have that makes you throw up?" Ebony asks in her usually naive way.

"A baby! *Hello*?!" Nina says as she laughs.

"What?! Nah!" T-baby shouts.

The receptionist motions for them to quiet down. The nurse comes out with her test results. She's 4 weeks pregnant. The 1st words out of her mouth are, "I have to tell my mama."

Her and Sandy are close and they talk about most everything. T-baby even has a prescription for birth control pills. And though Sandy had stayed on her about taking them daily, she hadn't. Neither of them are taking their pills properly except Ebony. And she's on her last pack. The
239

prescription she got in Houston was enough to last her until the end of this month. T-baby hasn't had a period since the week before Halloween. She gets a due date of July 31st or August 1st.

"Y'all this means I got pregnant when we went to Columbus on the fifth," she says as she recalls her romantic rekindling weekend with Rich.

After school they hook up with Renee and Tonya. They're going to baby sit Destiny and lil Brad while the couples go to dinner. Bruce and Kim are going to dinner with them. Lil Kenny is spending the night with Steven so Renee and Chill can go out. He'll catch the bus from Sandy's house tomorrow. Rob has to go to Cincinnati alone because the girls have babysitting duty. They settle in with the kids and begin to talk.

"This has been a long Monday," T-baby say as they laugh.

Her girls are excited. She's the 1st one of the foursome to have a child and that's special for them. She finally calls Rich with the news. He's nervous but he's very excited. He loves her and he wants her to be his wife and children's mother, so it's all good with him. He calls his parents and tells them. Rich Sr and Anna are back together and have been since after Ebony went back to Houston. They insist they take half of the expenses and Rich has to marry her in the *very* near future. The sooner the better, Anna strongly insist. Sandy and Greg Sr never doubted Anna and Rich Sr would help out. As for the wedding talk, Sandy wants a chance to plan a grand one. T-baby is her only daughter and that's her only condition.

Once she resigns her position from the active team, news about T-baby's pregnancy spreads quickly throughout school. She stays on as a manager and by mid-December, the pregnancy is old news. But that's when the jealousy and bullshit starts. Tameka has already tried to pick arguments with her and the foursome are ready for war. Angel and Alana are still allied with Tameka. They think Michelle is too. Only Michelle isn't in school anymore. The students at MLK know it's only a matter of time before the lid blows completely off.

The crew from UC come home Wednesday. Ajay has to return to school Friday. He seems distracted the entire time he's home and he won't say why. Though Ebony questions him about it, he keeps telling her he's okay and he's just focused on his upcoming game. She knows it's more. Bruce has been spending a lot of time at Ajay's apartment. Mostly with Kim. Ajay only warns him about not sleeping in his bed and to use 1 of the spare rooms. Still Ebony knows that's not what has him so detached.

Friday is a half day of school for the crew and they're out for

240

Christmas break. The foursome are heading to the student parking lot when they're confronted by several members of their football team. These players are all hyped and angry about a rumor they've heard and want to hip the crew to it. They tell the foursome that while hanging out at the CSU campus they heard a rumor that 1 of the football players at CSU is the father of T-baby and Rich's baby. The MLK players are ready to confront the college players on Rich's behalf. They're loyal to Rich, June and the crew because Rich and June had been their captains for the last 2 seasons when they had won state titles. They admire and look up to them like big brothers. Hearing this rumor has really upset them and they want blood.

The foursome become furious after they hear it too. They're going to confront the 4 admirers from CSU, turned infiltrators, themselves. It seems Craig has lied about the extent of his intimacy with T-baby. He's saying he'd gone all the way with her. The girls hurry to Tonya's house to talk to the crew and tell them about the rumor.

T-baby and her girls make Rich aware of the rumor and he calls his former teammates for further details. After hearing them, he starts to feel as if he has been lied too. Those insecurities he had before, resurface. But T-baby swears she never slept with Craig. Rich is enraged and he wants to *go straighten that nigga.*

Suddenly Ajay asks, "Did you sleep with the muthafucka or not?"

The room goes silent for what seems like forever, before T-baby explodes.

"Oh your ass didn't hear *what the fuck* I just said to him *today*! And every other muthafuckin day since I been knowing-"

"-Bitch don't be getting up in my muafuckin face like you tough. I don't play that shit," Ajay says in a firm, yet chillingly calm voice.

"Why in the *fuck* would you ask me some shit like that?!" T-baby yells, "I'm not Ebony. I guess you think I'm not gonna go back at you."

"I wanna know if you fucked him. I know you ain't Ebony," he says calmly with a smile.

The smile is what angers her even more. She's arguing with him and Rich, at the same time now. Ebony steps in.

"Anthony don't talk to her like that," she tries.

"Fuck her," he says, smiling and steadily pissing T-baby off more.

"Fuck You!" T-baby shouts.

"Never that," he says, "That's your problem now. Fucking with them nasty ass niggaz."

"Anthony!" Ebony shouts.

"What?!" he shouts back.

"Come on y'all," T-baby screams as she heads toward Chill's front

241

door, "Lets get the fuck outta here. They on my last *muthafuckin* nerve."

"You're not going, baby girl," Ajay says.

"We're going to straighten this shit out," Nina offers.

"I don't give a fuck what *y'all do*," he says, "Ebony is not going to them niggas and she's not going nowhere to talk about them muafuckaz either. That's *that*."

Ebony is not pleased with him at this point. She storms out of the house behind her girls. Chill asks Ajay to let it go and not heat things up anymore than they already are.

The foursome go to Pearl's house. T-baby calls her mother to come and pick her up. Sandy comes to get her and her girls go home with her. Ebony wants to help her to calm down.

Ajay is furious with Ebony for leaving. He's planning to go and pick her up. But once again, Chill manages to change his mind.

The foursome talk at T-baby's and Ebony takes this time to inform her girls of what she's learned about the consequences of lying.

"Y'all may not wanna hear it but here it is," she says, "Lying about *being* with Craig and letting Rich *think* you was. Is why this rumor breathes. That's why it's happening. Remember when y'all told me not to write that letter cause it was gonna backfire? So I know y'all know the consequences of lying. I wrote it anyway. It backfired. Anthony referred to that letter when he first brought up the day at the mall, when we met these guys and went to the movies. I told y'all it felt wrong from day one. Yes I was angry with Anthony for fucking around but I wasn't gonna put myself in a position of being worse off when it was all said and done. If you'd never went on another date or to that apartment, we wouldn't be here, Tee."

"I know that Ebony," T-baby says, "But Ajay called me a bitch."

"I didn't like what he said and you know it," she says, "But Rich is doubting you now *too* cousin. That's the *real* issue because *he's* your man. Not Anthony. They're *thinking* you slept with him because *you lied and said you did*. Just to make Rich jealous. *This* situation came from *that* lie. Now Anthony saw you there, just like you planned it. You wanted me to accept my consequences. I did that the same night I flew home. I hurt him with that lie which left me hurting worse. What I learned from that was to tell the truth rather I'm hurting or not. I'm not gonna let it turn into something worse than what I'm willing to live with. You and Nina didn't think about *that* part. Ree and me, *we did*. *That's* why we didn't wanna go. It wasn't because we was dumb for Anthony or June. It was because we didn't wanna put ourselves in a predicament we couldn't live with or get out of."

No one else says another word after that truth. They just sit in thought.
242

The phone rings and T-baby grabs it. It's Renee and Tonya. They assure them that everything will work out. Tonya turns them onto a plan to get the truth out of Craig, once and for all. They're going to use it.

T-baby turns on the answering machine and switches it to record. Then she dials Craig and pretends she hasn't heard the rumor. As they're talking, she gets him to speak on the night he had done oral sex on her. He admits how much he enjoyed it and that he wanted to go all the way.

"I just don't know why you never let me hit it," he says, "You never did let me get to the good part but I still want to though."
This is all she needs for Rich to hear. Then he'll have no reason to doubt the paternity or her. Neither will Ajay. But she isn't done.
She asks, "Why are you saying you're the father of my baby?"

"Tameka and her friends *told me* they heard *your* crew saying that shit," he tells her, "I never said that. Not even once. On the real, I was hoping you hadn't gave in to your homeboy and was saving it for me. But I never claimed to be your baby daddy."

"My crew ain't said no shit like that. That bitch wanna lie on my child *and my crew*?!" she says, "Just to try to get with Richard."

"I don't know about all that," he says, "I'm just telling you what they told us. I was playing along, at first. I won't even lie. I was playing along until they said you was pregnant."
He confesses that he lied about saying they had gone all the way. But that was just to save face with his boys. Once he learned of her circumstances, he told his boys the truth. He swears he never claimed to have gotten her pregnant. He adds, "On the real, what nigga *would* say that?"

"Alright Craig," T-baby says. She has to figure out a way to keep him open to talking to her, so she tells him, "I'll take your word for it. I wanna believe you. I really do."
She has to stick to the plan. She doesn't want Craig to think it isn't cool to call her. He isn't even the aggressive type. He's a lot like Rich. He'll go along to get along. She calls the shots. She has been alone with Craig a few times and he hadn't tried to do anymore than she'd allowed him to do. She didn't think he *would* salt up her name but she had to be sure.

"So can I still talk to you later on?" he asks.

"Yes. You'd *better* call me," she says and fakes a girlish giggle.
He says he will and they hang up. The girls have the whole conversation on tape. But now they're really angry with Tameka and her posse. They're ready to confront them again. They know all 4 of them will be at *The Spot*, later tonight. It's *definitely* on.

When they get to the club, their crew are already there. But the

243

bitches they're waiting to confront haven't shown up yet. Ajay spots Ebony and comes directly to her. He takes her into the office to talk about her actions earlier. They're soon joined by Rich and T-baby.

"Why did you call Tee *a bitch*, Anthony?" Ebony asks, "You know we don't wear names like that in this family."

"Because that's what she's acting like," he answers, "Fucking around with more than one man. That's what bitches and ho's do."

"So you just call her a bitch because she doesn't wanna be used by Rich? Because you know she's not one."

"You heard me, baby girl. I didn't stutter," he says.

"Don't call me a bitch. I am not a bitch and neither is my cousin," she says boldly.

"You wouldn't give me the reason to-"

Rich cuts in and says, "Look y'all. I need to talk to Trisha, in private."

Ajay and Ebony leave the office. Rich has a letter for T-baby. One he had comprised as a result of his anger management class. She sits down with him to read it. It isn't a good letter at all. He'd written a poem after hearing the rumor about Craig fathering her embryo. The poem expresses his anger and hurt. It actually describes how he feels about the entire situation. Writing is part of his therapy. He has to put his emotions into words, instead of using his hands. He uses them to write out how he's feeling. He wants her to read it aloud and she does. She reads this poem which refers to her as *'Probably just like the others, fuckin around undercover'* and also *'hanging out with your fo some [foursome], I bet all of y'all ho, some.'* Her feelings are hurt. Stubbornly she decides she isn't going to tell him about the taped conversation which proves she hadn't had sex with Craig. She's back to not giving a damn what he thinks. She's deeply hurt. She goes to get Chill and Renee to ask them to read the poem.

Before the crew can discuss anything, in comes Tameka and her posse. The foursome confront them immediately. Tameka swings on T-baby and they begin to fight. Rich grabs Tameka and throws her to the floor and says, "Get the fuck outta here."

Suddenly he has no interest in seeing her. The crew try to intervene but T-baby can't be stopped. Soon the fight is 4 on 4. Ebony has Angel. Nina has Alana and Rebbie confronts Michelle who isn't willing to fight her. The crew finally manage to bring the mayhem to order. The foursome has won hands down. But now, T-baby is in terrible pain.

She clutches her abdomen, screams and leans against the wall. The crew get her to a car and rush her to ER. Rich calls both their parents while Ajay drives him to meet T-baby at East General.

244

"We're on our way, son," Anna says as her, Rich Sr, Sandy and big Greg head to the hospital together.

When they arrive, it's too late. T-baby miscarried shortly after her arrival. She's crying hysterically as are her girls. They're all saddened as once again, they sit thinking about the consequences of a less then smart action.

Renee, Tonya, Bre and Jan leave. They're going to find the 4 girls and add more to the whooping the foursome had already started.

They do find them and beat them until they get tired. Then they head back to T-baby's side.

When Chill gets the news of the beat down, he's pleased they'd gotten some justice for the loss of their unborn crew. But he wishes the whole incident had never happened.

Rich cries as he tries to comfort T-baby. Ebony notice Ajay is crying too. Rich is still upset with him for what he'd said to T-baby at Chill's house. But he'll never be bold enough to say it to him directly. T-baby has to stay in the hospital overnight. Nina, Rebbie and Ebony stay with her as do Rich, Ajay, Tank and June.

After losing the baby, T-baby is less open to talking to Rich. Three days pass before she speaks to him. When she *does say* he can come over, he comes immediately. The 1st thing she do is play the tape for him. After hearing it, he lays his head on her lap and cries. Now he knows she hadn't had intercourse with Craig and that she *had* been honest. The baby she lost on December 16 was his, no doubt. He cries as he apologizes for everything he's ever done wrong to her. Including the poem. She feels like he really means it. They're finally able to bond. They become closer than ever and vow from this day forward, never to break up again. No matter what. They have to learn to talk things out. The miscarriage of their child brings things into perspective for the 2 of them and it's a bond they'll share forever.

In the Aftermath, Sandy and Anna bring assault charges against Tameka the next business day. Her punch was the fatal one. No one had struck T-baby except Tameka. *Her only* punch caused the miscarriage.

[*Tameka will receive a sentence of 18 months to 5 years for involuntary manslaughter and will be held without bond. She'll be sentenced at the end of May of 1994.*]

But Wheeler tells them she'll have to serve 30 months in a minimum security facility and can be released in November of 1996. The foursome vow revenge upon her release.

Time Will Reveal!

245

By Nina and Ebony's eighteenth birthday party, all of the crew couples are finally back together. They talk about how long it's been since every couple was cool at Christmas time.

"Christmas nineteen ninety," Chill says with a somber look on his face, "When we lost Stoney. It's been three *fucking* years."

"That party at Stoney's crib," Jb remembers, shaking his head, "Tank's sixteenth birthday party when the wolves was howling."

"No shit," Ajay adds, "*Everything's* been fucked up since then."

"We've had rough roads since Stoney passed away," Renee says.

"I think that fucked all of us up at the same time," Rich offers, "It was like everybody started experiencing some different type shit."

"We didn't know how to deal with grief as a crew," Ebony offers.

"I agree with Ebony. I think we was all just trying to deal with loosing Stoney," Bre says, "I still miss him a whole lot."
Cedric is present. He's been inducted into the crew. Him and Bre are an official couple but it'll be awhile before their relationship becomes sexual.

"Then we lost granny," Ebony says, "Chill and Renee got shot and Destiny came early. But Destiny was the good news in all of it. T-baby and Rich lost their baby." She looks to T-baby for assistance.

"And that Raymond shit too," T-baby says, "That was damn near tragic."

"But he's done," Tank adds, "That muthafucka is fried, dyed and laid to the side."
They laugh and are done with that discussion.

On Christmas day, Tank gets a Jeep with the help of papa, poppa and grandpa Joshua. He gets a 1993 Tracker. He's wanted one since he saw it in the movie, *New Jack City*. Ajay gets Ebony a cell phone, more gold earrings and 4 complete outfits with matching accessories. She gives him the newest Jordan's, another gold watch, a pair of small gold hoop earrings and a complete outfit with accessories. She's 18 now and he asks her to spend Christmas night at his apartment. She tells him she can't.

"You're eighteen now, baby," he says, "Big John and mama P said once you turned eighteen, they expect you to move out." They laugh.
Then he says, "Seriously though. You mean to tell me you don't wanna spend Christmas night, *your birthday night*, with your man? You're eighteenth birthday, baby girl. That's special. I was gonna bump that *H-Town* CD and we can be *Knockin' tha Boots*." They laugh.

"I want too," she says, "But I can't because I have a visitor. Aunt flow?"
246

Her period started today, on her 18th birthday. She recalls how Tank and Jb use to act when they shared a bathroom. But Ajay insist she spend the night anyway. He doesn't see the big deal and he makes that point clear.

"If you feel like you can't spend the night unless we can have sex," he says, "*Then you must be the one* who thinks that's all it is to our relationship." She has no response. "Is that how it is for you?" he asks.

"I just didn't think you would wanna be around me," she says, "Not with it on. Jb and Tank hated for me to be in their bathroom with my products and all. I just figured you would be the same way."

"You figured wrong, baby girl," he says, "You said you're gonna be my wife, right?"

"I am," she answers with a smile.

"You're still gonna have it then," he says confidently, "So what are you gonna do? Stay somewhere else when it starts? I don't think so."

"I know but-"

"No butts. Anyway I grew up in the house with four sisters and a mama. I handled theirs and I can handle yours too."

"Alright. I'll stay, Anthony."

"That's what I need to hear you say every time," he says, "When it comes to spending the night with me, that is. You're not suppose to find reasons *not* to stay."

"Okay baby," she says, "You're right. Now play me that *Knockin' Tha Boots*. Even though we can't knock any." They smile at each other.

Her and Nina are 18 now and they are finally able to stay out *all night* without consequence. They were doing it before eighteen. Their parents had all but given in. Knowing they was determined to be with Ajay and Tank.

Nina and Tank stay over also. They have plenty of sex, often throughout the night. Ajay and Ebony can hear them and they think it's funny.

"I wonder if we sound like that?" Ebony asks as she giggles.

"Nah we don't," he says, "You sound sexy when we're fucking, baby. You don't make all of those *weird* ass noises, Nee making. No way. That's irritable."

They both laugh as he grabs the remote and turns his stereo up louder so *Dino*, *G.I.* and *Shazam* can serenade her with that Houston flavor.

"This song still bumps, don't it baby?" he asks.

"Yes it does. I remember when you first played it for me. When you came home from college the first time," she says, "It's made for loving."

"Well we'll play it anyway," he says, "I can't get no loving tonight. But I'm loving being with my baby. So it's cool."

247

Bre and CJ spent last night, Christmas Eve, at Cedric's apartment. It was the first time. Today at Christmas dinner, Cedric asked Big Brad for Bre's hand in marriage and received his blessing. Cedric had talked it over with the guys in the crew, months ago, while Bre was away at college. The crew are in support of them having a relationship. As long as Cedric know he has to marry her. He will propose to her on New Year's Eve. She'll have her engagement ring on her finger when she returns to Georgia Tech. They're going to be married in a triple ceremony with Jb and Lynn plus Rob and Jan, on June 24th of 1995.

It's 1994. Jesse finally turns 13 and gets crewed up at the birthday party he has with Tank and Bruce. Once the crew are back in school, they receive more baby news.

The morning of Tank's 19th birthday, he gets a call from Nina. She's staying home with morning sickness.

"That's a hell of a birthday present, baby," he says, "I'm gonna be a daddy?!"

He yells so loud, all in the condo hears him. He's excited and nervous.

At the same time in Cleveland, Tonya shows up at mama Jo's house with a pregnancy test. Tank talks to her on the phone while Nina goes into the bathroom to do the test. It's positive. Immediately Tank stresses that she be careful.

"I mean it, baby. Don't get into no fights and don't be jumping around on the sidelines," he orders, "I mean it, Nina boo. Don't even look at them ho's who get you pissed off. I don't want nothing to happen to my baby. I've been waiting on this day for all of my life. The day you tell me you're pregnant. We're getting married. You just be careful."

"I'll be careful, baby. I promise," she tells him.

After 2 hours, they finally hang up. Tank goes to class. Tonya goes to the salon to open up for 9 o'clock. The rest of the foursome are at school. Nina calls Ebony's cell phone with the news and she shares it with T-baby and Rebbie. The foursome are very excited.

"I'll bet you nobody is gonna fuck with this one," T-baby says.

She had just gone for her 6 week checkup, the previous Friday. Her and Rich still want a baby, so badly. After hearing of Nina and Tank's pregnancy, it's going to make it that much harder to overcome their miscarriage.

This afternoon when big Al and mama Jo get home, Nina tells them the news. Mama Jo says, "I'm surprise it hadn't happened before now. You couldn't have been taking those pills."

248

She's happy for Nina and Tank but disappointed they hadn't waited until after she finished high school, which was her only stipulation to her daughters.

"I'll graduate before the baby comes, ma," she tries, "I'm vying for Valedictorian plus I got my academic scholarship to UC. I own shares in five profiting businesses and you know Jeremy is gonna marry me."
Her and her mother laugh.

"Yes I know all of that. Still you're both going to wish you had waited," Jo says, "Especially with both of y'all going to college. Let's go ahead and call and get you in to see Gladys as soon as possible. I wanna be sure everything is okay. We can't bare to loose another child."
Jo takes her to Dr. Weston's, this afternoon. She's due September 17th.

By February, after T-baby and now Nina, John and Pearl decide to make sure Ebony gets back on the pill. Though she's old enough to get them herself, she still hasn't done so. Pearl makes her an appointment. The earliest well patient appointment which accommodates Pearl's schedule is late March. They give Ebony temporary packs to sustain her until then. While Pearl stresses the importance of being careful.

"Ebony you need to take these," she says, handing her the pills. She asks, "Are you and Ajay using condoms?"

"Ma that's personal," she says as she giggles, "I'm eighteen. I'm old enough to get my own *and now* you wanna get me the pill?"
Her and her mother laugh. Ebony is laughing because she is still very embarrassed to discuss her sexual activity with her mother. She still finds it hard to talk to Pearl about sex.

"I know you're eighteen and I know it's personal," her mother says, "So *are* you?"

"No ma'am but I still had the pills big mama got me," she answers.

"How many more packs do you have left?"

"None. I finished the last one in November," she says, "I was suppose to renew at my last checkup in December. But I wasn't eighteen yet. They wouldn't let me have them without my parents permission."

"Well I made you an appointment. It's not until next month and we're wanna go with you all. Take the temporary ones, *please*. Rena, Sandy and I are taking you, Trisha and Rebbie," she says, "But you all should use condoms too. Until you can get the pills into your system, alright?"

"Alright," Ebony says, knowing Ajay won't use a rubber with her. *He's said it too many times. I'm gonna suggest it. I miss my baby so much. Mama's ready to get those pills now, since my girls got pregnant. I've been asking. Hello?*
249

Ajay doesn't get home for Valentine's day or the weekend before. His team is finishing their conference finals. They are definitely going to make the NCAA tournament for his sophomore year. The crew are so proud of him and nobody is prouder than Ebony. MLK won 1st place in their conference. They're going to the state tournament in Columbus, again this season. The boys and girls teams have #1 seeds. Jb's Georgia Tech team got a bid to the NCAA tournament just as Ajay and his UC team did. Ajay and UC are destined to finish first in their conference.

Ebony and T-baby leads MLK to a state Championship by mid-February. Then later in February, the entire crew go to UC to watch Ajay play Dayton as they continue to play well for a high seed in the 1st round of the NCAA tournament. They win tonight and their next game will be at UAB. Ebony and Ajay spend that weekend together at the crew's new Cincinnati house which they had moved into last week. The large house is really nice but the alum have already promised them an even larger 1 for the fall, when the foursome come. The alumni supply Ajay with whatever *he says* he needs to feel the comforts of home. Tonight after him and Ebony are alone, she suggest using a condom. She expects him to reject the idea.

"Why? You don't take pills no more?" he asks.

"I got temporary ones but they're not the ones I was taking for four years," she says, "Mama's taking me to the women's clinic on the twenty fifth to get some. She said we need to be careful and use condoms." She watches his expression, "It's her idea, not mine. So if you're gonna fuss. Then fuss at her. Not me."

"I ain't gonna trip," he says, "We'll check it out. I use to use them with every other girl. Just never with you."
He goes to take a shower. She joins him on her own. He's pleased with her taking the chance and initiating sex but not without a jeer.

"You *would* wanna come and get it when I have to wear a jimmy," he say and they laugh. They have sex in the shower without a condom but he pulls out and says, "Let's go in the room."

In his room he gets a condom from his nightstand drawer and puts it on as he says, "No baby girl. Don't ask me *why* I have rubbers in my drawer. I'm a safety guy."
She's about to mention it anyway but before she can, he enters her.

"Uh Anthony," she whispers.
It feels way different to her instantly. It doesn't feel like it usually does which makes her uncomfortable. He isn't enjoying it either.

"Don't feel right, do it?" he asks, sensing her discomfort.

250

"No."

"That's how it is with a condom, baby," he says as he tries to find his groove.

He becomes more aggressive while trying to get to the familiar. She doesn't like it at all. She's about to suggest they stop. But suddenly he finds the right spot. A spot that feels damn good to her.

"Mmm shit," he whispers.

"What baby?" she asks.

"It broke."

"Ah man. What now?"

"Do you want me to stop?" he whispers while kissing on her ears and neck.

He's breathing heavily and has already started to sweat. He doesn't really want to stop.

"I don't want you to stop. Just stop before you cum," she suggests.

"Yea right," he says and snickers.

"Come on baby. At least try too," she says.

"Baby girl it's not a man in this world who can hold back a nut when it wants to go," he says as he laughs, "Nuts come when they want."

"Just try alright Anthony. Just try baby."

"Alright," he says as he pulls out and discards the broken condom into the trash can next to his bed.

They kiss with passion. She's kissing him just as hard as he's kissing her. Both of them are breathing and moaning heavily.

"Put it in," he instructs and she does as she's told. "Mmm yea. Ssss," he moans.

"Mmm ummm. This is good, Anthony."

It isn't long before he takes her to that familiar place known as ecstasy and it feels better than ever. It feels extra. *Damn* good. She can't even form words and something in her hips is exercising a mind of it's own. She can barely control herself as she gives him plenty of conversation and much action from her hips. He holds her tight and smothers her mouth with wet kisses. She feels so experienced. She holds on as tight as she can while he thrusts his dick in and out of her steamy wet pussy until he can't hold it anymore. He warns her he's about to cum. She's pulling him to her, holding him tight and moaning pleasantly. There's no way he can pull out.

"Uh baby. I can't stop. Ssss. Here I cum," he warns.

"Take it out!" she tries.

"Uh uh. Take it baby," he says, cuming harder than he ever has. He leaves it all in her and talks trash as he does. "Damn I missed you, baby.

251

Mmm," he moans as he sucks on her neck. He continues to thrust into her harder and harder as he releases every drop and yells, "Baby it feels so good to me!"

"Anthony you're suppose to take it out," she says, gasping for air.

"I told you I wasn't gonna be able too," he says while still laying on top of her and still gasping for breath. Still slowly grinding. Slowing to a slow stir and eventually dead still, as he says, "Baby girl I can't move."

"I have to stand up baby," she says, thinking of how funny it is that they've never worried about making a baby before.
Not until her mother mentioned it and warned them to be careful.

"What is standing *up* gonna do?" he whispers exhaustedly.
He's thinking of how undeniably weak his body is at the moment. He's drained. He's been tired after sex before but nothing like this. His body feels like dead weight and to go along with that, he suffers from a weak stomach. Something he's never experienced either.

"Let me get up. I can try to let it run back out," she says, pushing against him.

"I gotta lay here for a minute," he says.

"Alright. Don't say nothing if I get pregnant," she tries.

"Uh huh," he manages as he's drifting into a relaxing sleep.

"Anthony you have to let me go take a bath," she tries again.

"Baby let me lay here and marinate," he says, "Just chill out, okay?"

"Are you gonna chill out if I get pregnant?" she asks, looking into his nearly closed eyes.

"I got you regardless, baby. Know that," he says as he lays his head on her breast and closes his eyes. He says, "I just sent one anyway. It's too late to jump up now."
He rolls his tongue around her nipples and suckles them.

"Ajay don't say that."

"Don't call me Ajay, baby girl," he whispers, "You've been around Nina and your girls too long."

"Do you want a baby?" she asks.

"You said you wanted five kids, baby," he says and smiles, "If you get pregnant now, I wouldn't care. Now or later. You're gonna be my baby mama anyway, right?" he tries as he chuckles.

"I'm gonna be your *wife*," she says with confidence.

"Then what are you sweating me for, ha?" he ask and kisses her.
Afterwards they both lay motionless in each others arms. Before he falls asleep, he thinks about big John's request.
252

"Make her a wife before you make her a mother."

He feels like he has just, most probably gone back on his word. He falls asleep.

He continues to feel drained, even in the game at DePaul. But UC manages to win at DePaul and they beat them again when DePaul comes to UC, a week later, for conference play. Their 2nd conference game is against Marquette and Ebony will definitely be there with the rest of the crew.

After the Marquette win, they beat Memphis to win their conference and advance to the National Tournament where they will face Wisconsin in the 1st round.

As spring nears, Tank is already thinking about getting through track season which is what he'll have to do before the semester ends and he can go home and be with Nina.

Jesse turned 13 in January. Erica made it in February, as Brittany does this March. The crew thought Jesse and Erica would date each other because their older siblings date. But they're surprised to find out that Erica likes Greg Jr and Jesse likes Ruthie. Ruthie doesn't turn 13 until December. Sam Jr is 13 and he has his eye on Pam, Ajay's youngest sister. She isn't even 12 yet but somehow she's still able to come to the crew parties. She's Al and Jo's baby. Everybody says they're even softer on her than they had been on Ajay.

Chill's crew is growing up and the next generation of crew are in effect already! June's sister Brittany has her coming out party and crew induction in March, as well. Shannon, who has waited patiently for her, is in attendance. He makes his affection for her publicly known with a rap song he'd written to a track produced by Rob. The songs title is, *My girl*.

CHAPTER 20

THE COST OF INFILTRATION

As Ajay and the UC team head into the NCAA tournament, the crew connect the 4 admirers to the blue and white Regal which did the drive by on Chill and Renee. It belongs to Craig's cousin Carl. Craig is from the Cleveland area. The foursome assumed all 4 guys were from Cincinnati but as it turns out, only Tim is an out-of-towner. The others are from the Cleveland area. Just not Shaker Heights.

Ajay is the one who broke that bit of information. He had taken the liberty of researching Tim while at UC. He knows where his family lives and the mother of his child too. The mother of his daughter goes by the name of Roc. Her government name is Raquel Perez. After meeting Ajay, she was curious about how he knew Tim. Ajay didn't hesitate to tell her Tim tried to talk to his girl but it wasn't going to happen. Roc was interested in hooking up with Ajay before knowing of Tim's interest in Ebony. That's how they had come to meet. Ajay had invited her to come to the crew house if she wanted him.

"I'll ride you if you're wit it. I'll damn sho' hit it," he had said.

The encounter is yet to happen. Yet and still some of Tim's boys relayed the info back to Tim about Roc being on the campus talking to a ball player named Ajay. Tim now feels he has legitimate beef with Ajay. While Ajay wonders what took him so long to get in the damn game. He's *been* wanting to whoop his ass. Or worse.

Ajay calls Ebony the night before her appointment and a week after they lost their 1ˢᵗ round game to Wisconsin. He still hasn't been feeling well since she last visited him. His coaching staff had him to see several doctors but none of the doctors found anything wrong.

"What do you think it could be, baby?" she asks.

"I think it's that food I was eating on the road," he says, "Something is not agreeing with my system."

"Are you still having diarrhea and nausea?"

"Just the nausea now," he says, "But my joints ache."

"And they didn't find *anything* wrong?"

"Nothing," he says.

"We'll have our spring breaks for me to get you well," she says, "I want you to feel better, baby. I don't like that I'm not with you."

They talk for over a hour until he tells her he needs to take some *Pepto-Bismol* and go to bed. She gives him love and they hang up.

Friday March 25 is Ebony, T-baby and Rebbie's appointment day at the Medical complex. The MLK basketball season is over and so is Ajay's season at UC. Ebony is looking forward to spring break in 2 weeks, while keeping up with Ajay and how he's feeling. It's unlike him to be sick. They head to the clinic with their mothers to have their physicals.

Ebony is anemic which she already knows. Rebbie and T-baby get birth control pills. Ebony gets pre-natal vitamins. *She's pregnant.*

"Ebony I *told* you y'all needed to be careful," Pearl says.

To Ebony's amazement, her mother doesn't seem very upset or surprised.

"Mama are you mad at me?" she asks.

"No. I'm disappointed but I'm not mad or surprised," she says, "Mama told me she dreamed about fish. We had a feeling it was you."

"I'm sorry," Ebony says.

"Don't be sorry, baby girl. I don't want you to be sad about it. Because my grandchild will sense that. We'll be okay. Jo and I will be grandmothers twice this year."

"I knew I was getting tired real easily," she says, "And smelling certain things made me feel queasy too. Anthony has had a weak stomach for a month and his body aches for no reason."

"All of those are symptoms of pregnancy for the expecting parents," Pearl says, "Yesterday, Jo said she thought you were pregnant."

"She told me my face looked fatter in those pictures me and my girls took at the spot, last week."

"She told me about it yesterday," Pearl says.

Ebony and Ajay's baby is due in November. She thought her period was due last week. Now she knows for sure it was due the week before.

Rebbie and T-baby get birth control pills and vow to take them properly. Though T-baby knows she won't. Rebbie tells Ebony she wants a baby too. Now that all of them have been pregnant.

"I always got to be the last one to do everything," she says with a smile, "Except to get a boyfriend."

T-baby hasn't gotten over her miscarriage. Her and Rich still want a baby.

The 3 girls head to mama Jo's house and Ebony shares her news with Nina.

"Our babies will be two months apart," Nina says, "They'll be best friends, just like us."

Ebony says, "They'll be first cousins on both sides and won't be able to date."

"No they won't," Nina agrees, "Our fourth generation will be blood relatives."

255

"Except for Chill and Renee's kids," T-baby says, "Right?"

"Jan and Rob's kids won't be related to me and Anthony's," Ebony says, "Who else?"

"They won't be related to me and Brian's either," Rebbie says.

"Me and Richard's kids will be related to everybody's kids," T-baby says, "Except Chill and Renee's."

"But Chill and Renee are *more* than blood to us," Ebony says, "I know them, Tonya and Junior want their kids to be together."

"Brad the third can date Destiny," Nina says, "Stoney, Chill and Rob always said they're kids are gonna marry a crew child."
Ebony asks, "But who all kids can marry in the crew?"

"For Rob and Jan, any kids except mine or my brothers," T-baby says, "We're the only blood relatives to Jan. But Stoney has two sisters."

"That's right and I heard lil Kenny likes one of them already," Nina says before changing the subject, "I just keep thinking about my stomach and how big it'll be. I don't want stretch marks. Granny Sally and Annabelle already have me using *cocoa butter* and *mother's friend*."
Nina hasn't begun to show. Ebony is both scared and excited. She knows Ajay will be okay with it but she doesn't want to tell her father. She's about to call Ajay but decides she wants to tell him face to face. She tells the crew. Then she asks them not to tell Ajay. She's going to tell him herself. Chill tells her Ajay isn't going to like not knowing *ASAP*. But she says she wants to see his expression.

"I don't care how much this crew promise you," Chill says, "I'll bet you somebody is gonna tell him before two weeks."
She knows he's right but she's going to risk it. Her and Nina will spend even more time together now that they're pregnant. Ebony is going to wait and tell Ajay when she sees him. John will be home the week of Ajay's spring break. Together, her and Ajay will tell him. Pearl has agreed not to tell John and says she'll try to keep her word.

"You've got to tell him as soon as he comes home or I will," Pearl says, "I won't say anything before then."

UC season ended early this year. Unlike Ajay's freshman season where they went to the elite 8. By now the news of Ebony's pregnancy has gotten to Ajay. He calls her cell phone immediately. He's angry. It's been nearly a week and she hadn't told him.
He says, "You've talked to me every day and didn't say a word. What's up with *that*?"

"I wanted to tell you face to face, so I could see your expression."

"Then you should've asked me to come home the same day."

256

"But baby I didn't want you to worry about not being here-"

"Fuck that. You was suppose to tell me the minute you knew."

"I'm sorry. Okay?"

He's calmer as he demands to be told the details, just as she has them.

"So give me the rundown," he insists.

"November eighteenth is my due date," she says, "And nobody else knows that but us. I wanted you to know first."

"That's *our* due date," he corrects her, "This is my baby too."

"Are you gonna have this baby?" she asks as she giggles.

"Why are you playing?" he asks very seriously, "I'm not Tank."

"Baby lighten up. I'm sorry. I was gonna surprise you," she says.

"I don't like surprises. You know that better than anybody else."

"Yea I know but this is different," she tries.

"It sure is and you should've told me on the twenty fifth when you found out," he reiterates, "Not four days later."

"I already apologized for that, baby," she says very sincerely.

"I'm cool," he says, "I'm gonna see you next Friday. Our spring break starts then. We're coming home but Tank has to come for track."

"Okay. I can't wait," she says, "I miss you so much. I'm glad we know why you was having those symptoms and body aches too."

"Me too and I miss you too," he says, "Let your girls know we're all coming." Then he says, "I can't believe you're finally having my baby." She can tell by his tone that he's smiling.

"I told you it was gonna happen sooner or later," she says.

"We have to get married, baby girl," he says suddenly.

"No we don't," she says.

"Big John made me promise on my seventeenth birthday."

"I don't wanna get married until I finish high school and college."

"Too bad," he says, "Cause we are."

"We're gonna marry each other anyway, Anthony," she says, "We can talk to my dad about it. But for me, I don't wanna get married just because we have a baby coming. Big mama calls that *a shotgun wedding*." They laugh.

"It might be one for real if big John gets mad," he says as he chuckles, "If he say we have too. Then we have too."

The case is closed. They make plans to shop for the baby when he gets home. And him possibly entering the NBA draft early. They talk for hours. After talking to Ajay, she feels more excited about being pregnant. She can't wait to see their child.

The next week is filled with morning sickness for Ebony while Nina

257

is nearly over hers. Still they both manage to get to school everyday, despite feeling bad.

It's Friday, the 8th day of April. The foursome are excited to see their guys come in from Cincinnati. Ajay, June, Tank and Rich arrive in the six four as the girls watch from the doorway of Jo's house. John is home too. Ajay has already asked him for a meeting and he has agreed to it. Ajay and Ebony in John's living room waiting for their talk.

Tank's jeep is already in Cleveland. He leaves it with Nina so she can get wherever she needs to go without incident. Her appointment today is at 4:00p.m. Tank made it home in time to go with her.

Ebony and Ajay are waiting to talk with big John. Rich, T-baby, June and Rebbie go to the U to Ajay's apartment to wait while Ebony and Ajay have their talk with John. Tank and Nina will meet them at the U after their visit to the doctor. Bruce and Kim, Reaper and Brittany, Greg and Erica plus Jesse and Sam are already out at Ajay's apartment. They was waiting for them to get home from Natty. John comes into the living room where Ajay and Ebony are waiting to talk with him.

"I know this is serious because you called me on my cell phone while I was out on the road," John says to Ajay, "That's something you haven't done since you was seven years old. When Ebony accused you of breaking her bicycle. So let's get to it because I know it's not a bicycle involved this go round. Go on."

Ajay tells him about the pregnancy immediately. Ebony senses that her father already knows. He doesn't seem upset. Nor is he acting surprised.

"I wanna marry Ebony," Ajay says, "I'll do the right thing. She'll still have her scholarship so she'll be in the house in Natty with me."

John doesn't say anything right away. He just listens. He's pleased that Ajay has tried to convince Ebony to get married and he's leaving that decision up to Ajay and Ajay alone. He wants him to make that call.

Immediately Ajay says, "We're getting married at the Jay Pee before my baby is born. I wanted you to be okay with it and know what my plans are."

"I don't want a shotgun wedding," Ebony tries.

"I'll leave my shotgun here," John says as him and Ajay chuckle.

"That's not funny," Ebony says, "Why can't we wait until I finish college?"

"Because *we* didn't wait to make this baby," Ajay tells her, "I don't wanna be one of *very few men* in this family, who wasn't married when his first born came into the world. Okay?"

With that explanation, Ebony says, "Okay. I get it. But I want a wedding later. Not while I'm pregnant."

258

"Just tell me when and I'll be there," Ajay says.

"So will I," her father says before turning to Ajay and saying, "Thanks son for standing up. I knew you would. I'm proud to have you marry my only daughter. I wish y'all would've waited but you didn't. So baby girl it's time to get your wedding shoes on, okay?"

"Yes sir," she says.

"Thanks, big John. This is gonna be an NBA kid," Ajay says with a smile, "I designed our house when I was in second and third grade. I'm gonna take good care of my baby and yours. I promise you that."

"*Hello*?!" she says, "I'm still *here*."

"We know," Ajay says as he smiles and kisses her on the cheek.

John kisses her other cheek then he excuses them and tells them their talk is done. He hugs them both as they prepare to leave. He has plans for him and Pearl.

Ajay and Ebony head out, get in his car and drive to the U. They talk about their future parenthood while he drives to his apartment.

When they arrive and Ajay gets out of his car, he can hear a female calling his name. It's Roc. She's come to Cleveland and brought her daughter to visit her father Tim. Ajay waves at her then he puts his arm around Ebony's shoulders and brings her with him to meet Roc. Before Ebony can asks him *"who is this?"* he's already introducing her.

"So this is your girlfriend?" Roc asks, "I've heard so much about you, Ebony."

"Yea this is my lady," Ajay says to Roc, "This is Ebony Brown. Soon to be Jackson. We're having one of those in November."

He says it proudly as he points to the baby Roc is holding in her arms. Ebony smiles as Roc extends her hand and says, "Nice to meet you. And yes I believe Tim tried to hit on you. You're very pretty."

"Thank you. So are you," Ebony says, "It's nice to meet you too. This is a beautiful little girl. She's so precious. She's just smiling at me."

"That's because you're carrying lil Ajay," Ajay says and smiles.

"Yea probably so," Roc says, "Thank you. She's seven months, almost eight. But she was premature. That's why she's so small."

Roc is Puerto Rican, built like a black woman and has a very thick accent.

"Our niece Destiny was premature. Your little girl is beautiful," Ebony says, "I can't say that enough."

"Thanks. You're really sweet," Roc says in a *Rosie Perez* accent.

It's obvious she'd grown up in an urban area. She uses the same slang as the crew. She'd grown up in a mixed hood, at least. Her thick accent and street lingo are on point. She's pretty. Ebony's 1st thought is Ajay and Roc

259

have probably messed around. But neither of them are giving her that impression, so she shrugs it off.

Suddenly Tim comes out of him and Craig's apartment and spots Raquel talking to Ajay.

"Bitch! Bring your ass here!" he yells, "Did I tell your muthafuckin ass you could leave out of the house?!"

Ebony is shocked. She's never even heard Tim raise his voice. Let alone use foul language. Roc goes to him immediately. He slaps her in her face while she's still holding their daughter. She manages to hold onto the baby but not much else. She catches her balance like she's use to that maneuver or accustomed to it. Tim takes the baby and slaps her again.

"Get your ass inside, bitch! Before I fuck you up out here!" he yells at her then he grins, as if he's doing it for show.

He does this while the crew, who have come out to meet Ajay and his own posse watch. His boys laugh about it. The crew think it's rather sad.

"I'm glad I got that shit out of my system," Rich comments.

"You and me both," T-baby agrees.

They all head inside Ajay's apartment. Ebony still can't believe that was the same guy she'd met at the mall. But she's grown up enough now to know some people are phony.

Later when Tank and Nina pull up, Tim and his crew are still outside drinking, partying and talking loud. Tank tells Nina to hurry and go inside before they try and start something while she's out there. They get to Ajay's apartment door, as Tank reaches for the knob and opens the door, Tim yells something out. Tank can't decipher what he said and wasn't trying to hear him. But Tim wants to be heard so he yells again.

"Hey tell Ajay to let me fuck his bitch and I'll let him fuck mine!" His crew erupts with laughter. Ajay overhears him. He grabs 1 of his 9mm pistols, tucks it into the back of his waistband and walks outside. Immediately Ebony protests. Ajay tells her to stay inside. He's been waiting on this since he saw Tim sitting with her at the mall. He wanted to fuck him up just for being near her. Let alone trying to make advances toward her. June, Rich, Tank and all the guys get strapped and go out the door with Ajay. This won't end well or peacefully. Ebony knows that already.

"Anthony," Ebony tries again.

Again he tells her to stay inside. Nina calls Chill while Rebbie, T-baby and Kim run to the next building to get Rob, Jan, Arthur, Wayne and Kilo. They tell them something is about to go down. Before they can get outside, Ajay has already hit Tim and knocked him to the ground. Tim is no match for him as Ajay punches him repeatedly while talking shit to him at the
260

same time. The crew stand ready for the others if they want to react. Wisely, Tim's posse stays put.

Inside the apartment, Ebony can't wait any longer. She's worried about her man. Everything in her says she has to be there for him. Her, Nina, Brittany and Erica run outside. So does Ruthie and Pam. Both crews are allowing Ajay and Tim to fight to the finish but Ajay is way too much for Tim. The crew aren't allowing anyone from Tim's crew to join in. Not without certain consequence. It would be a massacre. Tim's posse is outnumbered nearly 3 to 1.

Chill and Jr come tearing into the parking lot. Jr lets his tires squeal to a halt. They jump out and quickly assess the situation. The 2 of them have the foresight to know this will turn into a gun battle before it's done. Chill would rather Ajay not fought Tim at all but he also realizes it's personal for him. Ajay had taken Tim's advances toward Ebony as an insult to his manhood. He wants war. The crew are down for battle. They know it's not going to stop at Ajay just beating Tim's ass too. It will most likely take 1 of their deaths to end it for good. Chill plays the odds, figuring if Ajay beats Tim decisively then they'll take their lumps and regroup. But he'll be wrong today. And he'll be the 1 on the offensive when the gun shots start to ring out. For now, he stands with his crew in support of Ajay.

"Get in his ass, bro," he yells while Ajay gets the better of Tim.

Ajay is talking plenty of trash as he hits him. Tim can't get a grip on any part of Ajay. Ajay just unloads on him, again and again. Tim trying to date Ebony isn't Ajay's *only* gripe. He know Tim knows who shot up his crew. He doesn't hesitate to let him know.

"Who shot my brother, muafucka?" he growls, "That's what this ass *whoopin's* for nigga. You can't get near my woman like you want too. I'll never sweat that."

Ebony is outside now and she's even more nervous. Her *instincts* tell her this isn't going to end without casualties. She can't just stand there and do nothing. She's going to make sure her man doesn't perish as a result of this revenge.

I'll ride or die for Anthony. I'm not gonna let him get hurt! Our baby needs his daddy.

She runs inside and grabs his .357magnum. from his bedroom and returns. Kilo spots her coming back with the gun. Instinctively he grabs her and wrestles the gun from her hands.

"You're pregnant, baby girl," he says, "Ajay don't want you in this shit. I can't let you get hurt. Stay back and let him handle it. He's got this."

261

"Let go of me!" she screams.

Ajay can hear her screaming. He tries to see where she is in the crowd as he continues to punch Tim. T-baby grabs the pistol from Kilo and leaves him to struggle with Ebony. He almost gets her calm enough to let her go.

All of a sudden, along comes the infamous blue and white Regal. Chill notices it and lets shots ring out instantly. He recognizes it. It's the car which the shooter was perched on the passenger side window seal of when it drove through and shot him, Renee and their unborn daughter. After seeing Chill let off shots, the rest of the crew begin shooting too. Ajay retreats to his crew and drags Tim along in front of him as a shield. Tim's posse starts shooting back. Everybody is ducking for cover. It sounds like a war zone as bullets bounce and ricochet off of the asphalt. Bystanders crouch behind cars or whatever they can to find cover. Suddenly Craig starts firing toward Rich and T-baby. That's where Ebony is crouching down next to Kilo. In his retreat, Ajay can see bullets ricocheting off the pavement near his girl. He's struggling to get to her. He manages to get there and jump in front to protect her but he's hit *twice*. Once in the leg and once in his back. He falls on top of Ebony. The gunfire ceases and is replaced by approaching sirens. The assigned crew scramble to take their weapons and hide them while Ebony screams more. She knows something is wrong because Ajay's body has gone limp on top of her. T-baby notices it too. That's when she unloads the pistol she has in Craig's direction. She saw him shoot Ajay. She hits Craig in the head and strikes Roger several times. Ajay isn't moving while Ebony is screaming. Nor does he saying anything. Ebony pushes against him. Still he doesn't move. She realizes he isn't going to move.
Anthony's been shot! He can't move!

"Anthony! Baby! Baby get up! Oh my God! He's shot! Anthony got shot!" she screams.

Ajay isn't breathing. She can't bulge him. She calls for help and the crew run over.

"Oh God! Please don't let him die! Please God please! Don't let him die! Anthony! Oh God! Please! Somebody help me!"

She screams and panics as she struggles to lift his dead weight. She tries to calm herself as her crew helps to lift him off of her. She tries talking in a calmer voice, saying, "It's alright baby. Okay? It's alright. It's over."

She's trying to be calm but not working either. Her crew get Ajay in the car before the police arrive. Ebony clings to him, talks to him. Jr speeds out of the parking lot and through red lights with much more of the crew close behind. They have other wounded members in other cars as well. None of
262

their wounds are as serious as Ajay's. They're headed to the hospital, yet again, as Ebony continues to talk to Ajay.

"I need you, baby. Me and the baby. We need you. I can't live without you, baby. I need you to be okay. Please don't go. Please! No! Oh God! No baby! Wake up Anthony!" she screams as he slips further into unconsciousness.

She can't hear him nor can she feel him breathing. She feels he has died in her arms and she isn't able to contain herself any longer. She continues to beg God for his life.

As Jr arrives at the hospital, his 1st cousin is bleeding to death in his backseat. Renee and Tonya are already there when they speed into the emergency room lane. They're all panicking and praying. They've heard the diagnosis and it isn't good. Ajay isn't going to make it. They see Pearl. She tells them she's already notified Jo and Brenda. They're on the way to the hospital. Pearl has to try and hold Ebony out of the way so the staff can get Ajay out of the car and onto a stretcher. But Ebony is holding on to him for dear life. She's still holding onto to him as Pearl takes his vitals.

"Mama please don't let him die. Please," she begs and cries.

"Ebony let us take care of him, baby. Alright?" Pearl says with tears streaming down her face as she whispers to her only daughter.

"He's gonna be alright. It's gonna be alright, baby girl."

Pearl, Renee and Tonya finally get Ebony to let go. But only after the staff convince her that Ajay is alive and they'll take good care of him. The staff roll him into emergency. Ebony begins vomiting uncontrollably. Pearl orders the staff to get her to emergency too.

Pearl says, "And get an I-V in her now! Remember she's pregnant! Let's go people!" Pearl screams, turning her attention back to Ebony and Ajay as they're rolled in side by side.

Ebony is overcome with emotion and has to be sedated, though she doesn't want to be. She begs her mother and mama Jo, who had just come in, not to let them take Ajay away from her side. They tell her he has to go to surgery. Pearl administers a sedative through her I-V to help her calm down while mama Jo talks to her.

"Ebony I need for you to relax," Jo says, "He'll be fine but not if he thinks you're not. You and the baby are who he's fighting for in there, okay? Calm down baby. He's gonna be okay. He's my baby and I wouldn't tell you anything but the truth. You know that right?"

"Yes ma'am," she cries, "I need him, mama Jo. I'm so scared."

"He's gonna fine," Jo says, "Calm down so he can relax back there. He's going to hear that you're upset and he won't be able to relax. Okay?"

The sedative kicks in and Ebony falls into a deep slumber. Pearl orders her
263

to recovery where Ajay will be when his surgery is done. Soon after, Pearl learns that a wealthy business tycoon and Cincinnati alum, Mr. Parkwood has arranged for Ajay to have a private suite. Parkwood orders a special bed which is considerably wider and longer than the hospital beds but it works the same way. After all, Ajay *is* a blue chip athlete. His supporters and alum will spare no expense when it comes to his care and comfort and Ebony's too. Parkwood had already promised Ajay the use of his private jet for when Ebony gets closer to the delivery date. That way he can get home at a moments notice or anytime he needs to be home right away.

For now, Ebony is sleeping and Ajay is in surgery with weak vitals. He isn't out of the woods, just yet. But his doctors feel confident they can get him basketball ready in a few hours. Parkwood told them they'd better make damn sure they do, if they want to practice medicine in Ohio.

June was shot in the leg. Kilo was hit in the arm. Tim receives 16 stitches plus bandages. That's just from his fight with Ajay. The 3 of them are treated in the emergency room. They'll be released after the police question them or whenever the police permit them to leave. Roger was shot twice in both legs. The owner of the blue and white Regal and Craig's 1st cousin, Carl is critically injured. Him, Ajay and Roger was rushed to surgery immediately. Craig was pronounced dead at the scene.

Back out at the U, the police try to take statements but no one cooperates. They do recover 2 guns near Craig's apartment. The younger crew are still at Ajay's waiting for word on him, June and Kilo. The police question all of them once Rena, Anna and Debbie, Sam Sr, Archie Sr and Greg Sr are there accompanying their minors. The police still get nowhere. Nor do they find any other weapons. They search the apartments of all the participants. Wayne and Arthur are long gone with the crew weapons. The police found the 2 guns near Craig's place and that was it. Tim's posse had gone to the hospital with him, Craig, Carl and Roger. Roc is still at their apartment with their baby and some female friends but they have nothing to tell either. The police take shell casings and any other evidence they can find. They see no one is willing to cooperate so they soon wrap up and head for the hospital.

That scene is a mad house with what the press is calling, *"Rival gangs being treated simultaneously."* Before leaving the hospital, Parkwood orders that headline ripped from the news before the breaking news is done running. He leaves 1 of his top assistants with Al to insure Ajay and his family are treated with the best care possible. The police have a full time job just keeping the 2 groups separated while trying to question them all.
264

TIME TO GROW-RELOADED-TIME WILL REVEAL 2

The news *initially* reported it as a gang turf war. But that headline has been modified to *Overzealous Spring Breakers, Gone Wild*. Credit Parkwood for that change as well. He doesn't even want Ajay or his family questioned in the presence of the staff and others at the hospital. So the police tell everyone they're going to be held for questioning. They order them to report to the precinct as soon as they're released. Nina refuses to leave her brother and best friend.

She says, "I'm not leaving Ajay and Ebony. I'm not leaving them."

The female officers are threatening to put cuffs on her. Still she's stead fast. Pearl and Jo come to her aid and assure the officers, they'll all be more cooperative once they know the outcome of Ajay's surgery. Parkwood's assistant takes over from there. He calls the chief of police.

Minutes later, the police take them outside to get statements. They'll question Ebony and Ajay later. Pearl tell them, both Ebony and Nina are pregnant. The police say the mother's to bring them down later.

Ebony is still sleeping in recovery. Her heart rate has been stabilized and her pulse is normal again. Prior to Ajay's surgery, Pearl had been sure to tell the surgeons and her coworkers to take special care of him.

"He's my son-in-law and the father of the baby my only daughter is carrying. He's like a son to me," she had said. Which they all knew that already. "And he's a future pro ball player."

They know he's the outstanding basketball player from Cleveland, who has gone on to be a star for the University of Cincinnati. Even if they didn't know it before. They knew after the big flux of media attention at the hospital, following the shooting. But on the insistence of Parkwood, the media are kept at bay. And the staff had already been warned to take extra precautions with Ajay. Many feel that Parkwood is the Jeb Baker of today.

Most of the guys are given test for gun powder residue. Kilo and Roger are tested in the hospital. Ajay isn't charged initially. Neither is Kilo. Ajay didn't fire a weapon. June, Roger, Carl and Craig did but Parkwood made sure none of his athletes were bothered. His assistant has Al to alert George Wheeler and have him come down too.

Ajay is still in surgery when the crew's legal team arrives. With Jo and Al's permission, they'll perform the gun powder test on Ajay while he's still in post op. Which will prove to be a very intelligent move.

Tim and Roger head to the station when they're released from the hospital. That's where Tim gives *this* statement.

265

"Ajay started the whole incident," Tim says.
Of course the crew's story is different then his. They have the *true* story. *"Tim had instigated a fight with Ajay because he wants Ebony. Craig started shooting first. Some of them may have fired back in self defense. None of the younger crew was involved."*

That was their story prior to leaving the scene and all of them told the same one. It's the same story the police got from the younger crew at the U. Roc and the other females offered no admissions. They hadn't seen how the fight started and couldn't give the police an accurate account.

Carl dies on the table and is tested post mortem. It's determined he had fired a gun. The police seemed determined to get someone. They arrest Chill, Jr and Rob. They ask Jo and Pearl to bring Rich, Tank and June to the station. Roger, Tim, Justin and several more from Craig's posse are arrested as ballistic results come back. That's when the police make a major discovery. They determine that the 2 guns they recovered from Craig's apartment were the same ones used in the drive by shooting of Chill and Renee. They charge Carl and Craig because the guns were found near the property they share with Tim. However, Craig died at the scene and Carl has just been pronounced dead. For some reason Tim is never charged. *Case closed.*

While they clear some cases and open new ones, Ajay's surgery is finally complete. He's taken to recovery where Ebony is still resting. The doctors emerge to tell the family the diagnosis.

"He's going to be fine," they say, "We removed the bullet from his back. The one in his leg went straight through. We got him patched up. He'll need time to recover. Maybe a week or two. But he's in great shape. He's going to make it. He's a strong young man. He should be just fine."

"Thank you God. Oh thank you God," Nina whispers as her, Jo, Al, John and Pearl go back to see Ajay and Ebony while the crew wait.

Ebony wakes up as they're coming in and begins to hyperventilate. The staff calm her down. Pearl and Jo tell her she's right next to Ajay. She turns to see him sleeping and wants to go to him. They help her down off of her bed. She goes to Ajay's side and kisses him immediately.

"I love you baby," she whispers in his ear.
He seems to smile slightly, as if he can hear her.

After an hour in recovery, he's moved to his private suite with the larger bed. Ebony climbs into bed and lays as close to him as she can, so he can feel when she breathes.
266

Earlier, mama Jo had asked her to do this, so he can smell her scent and know that she's near. She sleeps in the bed with him at the hospital, all night. Jo, Pearl, Nina and Tank stay in his room too. John and Al go with Renee and Wheeler's team to secure bail for Chill, Jr and Rob.

Ajay wakes up just past midnight. He's groggy from anesthesia but he's even more pissed that he's been shot. He's pleased to see the bed he's in and Ebony in it with him. He notices Jo and Pearl are asleep in his room. He can see Tank and Nina cuddled up on 1 of the 3 fold out couches. He tries to nudge Ebony but it's difficult for him to move. Eventually, sensing a change in his breathing pattern, she wakes up to check on him and looks directly into his eyes.

"Baby," she says smiling as her eyes well up, "You're awake."
Grimacing, he tries to adjust his body to lay closer to her and give her a half smile. He whispers, "Hey."

"Hey yourself," she whispers back and smiles, "Anthony are you okay?"

"I've been better," he says trying to be humorous.

"Don't you ever scare me like that again," she demands, "I thought I was gonna lose it. I couldn't feel you breathing."

"Sound to me like you did lose it," he says, "You got sick?"

"You could hear me?" she asks.

"Ebony. Anytime we're in the same time zone," he says, "I know what you're up too, okay? I could hear you *before* I got shot. Kilo was trying to hold you back. I thought he was gonna let you go because you kept screaming for him too."

"I had your gun," she reveals, "I was about to mess up. Bad."
"How?"

"I was coming to shoot Tim," she says, "I wanted it over before this happened. I thought about Stoney and I couldn't let that happen you."
She's crying, "I've never been so scared in my whole life, Anthony."

"I know. I heard you baby," he says, "And I'm sorry."

"I thought about the baby and I tried to be calm," she says, "But I couldn't. Not after you stopped breathing. Baby I can't do this by myself."

"You won't have too," he says, "I promise."

"Can we get out of the game?" she asks.
He smiles and says, "You're not in the game. And we're on our way out. It's just not an overnight thing, baby."

"I need for you to be out of it," she cries, "I don't wanna lose you baby. You're my heart, remember? I can't live without my heart."
267

"I won't make you have too," he tells her, as he slides his left arm under her and adds, "Come closer."

She does and he about to kiss her. Then he ask, "Does my breath stink?"

She kisses him, laughs and asks, "Do you want me to get your toothbrush and help you brush them?"

"I take that as a yes," he says, trying to smile.

"Well you've been out for awhile," she say as she giggles, "We *was* eating pizza before all of this happened."

She gets his toothbrush and toothpaste and helps him brush and gargle. Then she brings him some cool water to drink. He was parched.

"Thanks baby," he says after they're done. Then he says, "Now kiss me *for real*."

She does. Over and over. She cries while thanking God for having her man alive, safe and in great shape.

The following day

Bre, Lynn and Jb fly in from Atlanta, early this afternoon and come straight to the hospital. When they arrive, Ajay is awake and talking with Ebony, Bruce, Kim, Brittany and Reaper. Jo and Al have gone home to shower. Tank and Nina have gone to the U while Pearl is still on duty.

"Hey lil bro. How are you feeling?" Lynn ask as her eyes well up with tears.

She has worried a lot over her little brother, after hearing he'd been shot yesterday. She leans over the bed rail and gives him a hug.

"I'm straight. Just ready to get up *outta* here," he grumbles.

"I'm ready to kill a muthafucka over this," Lynn says, "Don't nobody mess with my lil brother but *me*."

Ajay smiles at her. His oldest sister has always been his protector. She's ready to go to war for her only brother.

"It's not gonna be enough of them left to spread on a *Ritz cracker,* sis," he say as he tries to laugh but the pain makes him choose otherwise.

"I'll take that then," she says, "But you just had surgery. You're not going anywhere. Not anytime soon."

"It's gonna take a lil time, cousin. Just take your time," Bre says, "You'll be outta here soon. I'm sure of it."

"Not soon enough for me. I'm ready now," he groans.

"They got cops all over the place. I missed a real one," Jb says.

"Not as real as it can get," Ajay offers.

He's a soldier. He isn't even completely out of danger and already, he's
268

thinking about the next battle and ready to get on the streets to handle his.

"What went down, crew?" Jb asks.

"That bitch Tim tried to flex," he answers, "He got hot because his girl was over by my crib talking to me and Ebony. So by the time Tank and Nina showed up, he had *had* enough liquor to get brave. He hollers out, *'Tell Ajay if he let me fuck his bitch I'll let him fuck mine.'* I had to get him."

"So that nigga thought he wanted some?" Jb asks.

"That nigga was full of liquid courage and got his ass whooped," Ajay answers, "I just wish I could've finished him."

"Ebony is beautiful, brother," Lynn says, "You're gonna have that problem a lot. Plus guys and fools can see that she's loved."

"Get use to it, man," Jb says, "I deal with that shit every other week. We all do."

"I'm not about to get use to it," he says, "Get use to me protecting mine."

"So what's up on crew? Are they still locked up?" Bre asks.

"Yea they was trying to hold them for arraignment, last night. But our attorney's are getting them out, as we speak," Ebony says, "My girls went back with Tonya, Jan and Renee to the jail, to pick them up."

"You know I'm celebrating my big *two one*, right?" Lynn asks.

"You're finally old enough to drink?" Ajay asks as they all laugh.

"I *am*," Lynn says, "But I'm in training, all the time, nowadays."

"You're going to the Olympics, sis," Ajay says with a smile.

"True that, bro."

"I'm fixing to get up with the brothers," Jb says, "See how this shit is gonna go down. It's spring break now, *homie*. I got all week to work something."

"Hell yea. It's spring break," Ajay says, "I can't be laying up in this muthafucka, all week."

Ebony tries to convince him to stay until the doctors are ready to release him. But Ajay isn't listening to her or anybody else. He wants to be released, ASAP! He contacts his biggest, best and surest insurance policy. He calls Mr. Bert Parkwood.

All of the crew have been bailed out by Saturday evening. A court date is set for Monday morning. Several of the crew have to go, along with members of Tim's crew. Ebony goes with Nina to give their statements. The police try to coerce Ebony to say Ajay started the incident. She knows he didn't and she sticks to her story. Their attorney's take it from there but this case is far from over. The police are always anxious to pen something

269

on Chill and his crew. In their haste to do so, they usually ignore proper procedure. Just as they have done in this case.

Attorney George Wheeler has already gotten most of the evidence barred or tossed. And many of the charges have been dropped. However, some of the crew are charged. Some are going to face penalties and/or go to trial. Just who it will be, is still not clear. Neither are all of the charges. The crew have Bert Parkwood on their side and George Wheeler as their lead attorney. With those odds, they could run a wheel in Vegas.

Ajay is released on Tuesday morning. Much sooner than his doctors wanted to release him. Parkwood had the power to sway the Chief of staff. He wants Ajay under the care of his physicians in Cincinnati, for his post-op.

Upon Ajay's release, there are 2 detectives there to charge him with 2 counts of 1st degree murder and 1 count of attempted murder.

"You know this is some bullshit," he says, "I didn't fire a gun."
Ebony calls Wheeler and the police know to wait for him to get there.

When he arrives, Bert Parkwood is with him, fresh from his home in Cleveland. He states to the detectives that he's here to insure that Ajay is released from the hospital and goes back to school immediately.
Attorney George Wheeler whispers to Ebony, "According to the residue test conducted on Ajay, the day he came in, he didn't fire a weapon. We submitted discovery over the weekend. If they indict him. It's a mistrial."

"It'd better be," she says, "He needs to be out today, alright? I don't want him in jail. He's still recovering from the surgery."

"I don't either. If these fellows want to try to railroad him, like I don't know my job," he says, "Then they're going to have to pay him."

"Yes. Or me," she replies as she walks over to Ajay to get his valuables and give him a kiss.

"We'll meet you down there, Ajay," Wheeler says.
Ajay wants to get upset but he knows Mr. Wheeler has been down with the crew for longer than he's been alive. No one has ever done any serious time. He goes quietly with the 2 detectives.

****

In Shaker heights, the crew are outraged when they get the news of Ajay's arrest. They all know he didn't fire a weapon. Chill explains to them how Ajay being charged, is a good thing. And it's a move that will prove to
270

be a game changer for the crew while leaving them untouchable, as well. "They're charging Ajay but he didn't shoot no gun," Chill says, "We all know this. But watch how Wheeler handle them. He's gonna have this shit down to nothing. Maybe an assault charge, if anything. Which is all Ajay did. Y'all do recognize he's got Cincinnati Alumni behind him too, right? Wheeler is getting funds sent to him from *all* over. Ajay is taking one for the team, right now. Once they see they can't get a conviction, then they have to let it go and not even charge him. Then if they try to come after another one of Wheeler's clients, one of *us*, Wheeler's gonna bury 'em with some type of malicious prosecution accusation," he says. "Remember, Ajay Jackson is a superstar. Those alums are gonna protect him. Wheeler's got a team and a plan. Always have. I haven't seen him lose yet," he ends as he chuckles.
After hearing it broken down by Chill, the crew settle down and wait for Ebony to come back from bailing him out.

While in central lock up, Ajay is placed in the tank with the rest of the, *in the right place at the wrong time,* stragglers. He had requested to go to general lock up and not segregated population. One of the unlucky inmates is Joe from the Westside. The Joe from the *H-town Rat's* rape episode. He had gotten jacked up before daylight. He was caught with a small sack of herb, on paper, with no real homies to look out on him. He spots Ajay when he walks into the cell and comes to him immediately.

"What's good, Ajay?" he asks.

"Definitely not this here," Ajay responds.

"I hear you," he says, his voice lowering as he starts to tell Ajay his saga.

This is the second time he's been locked up, this week. He says he was brought down on Friday night, for assault on his girl. He was in the very same cell with Tim and his fellows. He tells Ajay how they were talking smack, all evening. Talking on how they had to check some niggaz who be handcuffing they ho's because they ho's really want to get with them.

"I knew they was full of shit when they was talking that shit about Ebony. Everybody knows how the foursome get down," he continues, "They ain't trying to fuck wit nobody."

"Where is this shit going, man?" Ajay asks impatiently.

"I already know you're in here on bullshit," he whispers, "Them stupid first timers was wolfing, all night. Talking about they was gonna get out of their situation on a crew ticket. You know what I'm saying, dude?"

"Talk to me," Ajay says with very little patience left.

"They're gonna try and sell y'all out man. And anyway, that old

271

red bone ass *nigga*. He's five oh," Joe says, "He a straight poe poe."

"*Snitchin* and shit?" Ajay asks.

"Nothing but a *see eye*. Anybody that's been in this bitch as much as I have, knows it. He's the one who got Dre busted on that campus robbery," he adds, "But he was buying up all the loot that came through. Then when his ass got popped, he snitched."

"So man, why are you coming at me wit all this? What you want?" Ajay asks, recognizing and respecting the jail house hustle.

"I'm trying to get out of here too, man. But I never forgot the crew for not rolling on us about them hood rats," he confesses, "And them niggaz was the same ones who rode down on big Chill and his wife."

"Oh really?" Ajay plays along.

"Man, they confessed to the whole thing, right up in here. That's how I knew you was on the way. Then they told five oh, you shot them two niggaz that died. And plus you beat him up because he had fucked your girl. Then he said you've been threatening his girl for awhile too."

"*Anthony D. Jackson!*" the correctional officer yells from the end of the corridor.

Ajay walks slowly to the cell door. He has made bail within the hour.

"I'll see what I can do for you, dude. Stay up," he says to Joe as he walks out.

"I appreciate it, Ajay," he says.

Ajay is out and on his way home with Ebony. He knows Tim will need to leave the area soon. He has violated every damn thing Ajay told him not too. As he was beating his ass, he specifically told him he didn't want to hear, "*Absolutely no more degrading talk about my girl or your ass is going to meet your maker.*"

Tim hadn't abided by that. Thus he won't be safe anywhere in the area of the University apartments. The crew are going to *drop some change on him* and they'll do that as soon as Ajay gives the word. Of course, he relays Joe's information to the crew as well. Tim and his clique had been against them and out to bring them down, all along. But who sent them?

Chill sends a bondsman to get Joe out. They feel good having the information about Tim's clique being allied with the now deceased murderers of Stoney. But they already know it goes deeper. They're going to see to it that the remaining *living* members of that squad get dealt with. Unless they leave, immediately. The crew have many young soldiers vying for a position with them. Many young men in the Cleveland area, who are already doing dirt and just want to work for the crew. They have done

272

work, called it auditions and pledged their loyalty to Chill and his crew. Only Chill is yet to employ them.

In the midst of all the turmoil going on this week, the crew still have their spring break. Lynn's 21st birthday celebration, the following Friday, is off the hook. MLK's spring break is the next week. The foursome are going to Cincinnati with their guys.

However, on Saturday their guys are preoccupied with the potential trials plus the beef with the CSU squad. The foursome are feeling ignored. They want to do something to occupy their time, so they go out cruising. There isn't anywhere they can ride to in Cleveland without potentially running into problems because they're crew. They decide to hop on interstate 90.

"Let's go somewhere different," Rebbie suggests.

"We should. Since everybody's doing they're own thing and we're left stuck until tomorrow," Ebony adds.

"Okay. The next major city sign we see, we're going there," Nina says, "How about that?"

"We've got paper. Let's do it," T-baby adds and laughs.

Ajay call Ebony's cell phone and she talks to him for a few minutes. When he ask her where she is, she says, "Out riding with my girls."

He says be careful and he'll see her later. She says okay and they hang up. The foursome talk and clown a lot while on this road trip.

In less than 3 hours, they're in Pittsburgh. They're excited that they've gone to another state, on their own. It's *even more* exciting because nobody else knows. They find a place to eat and take in the sites.

At some point during the trip, unbeknownst to Ebony, Nina turns off her phone. She did it so they wouldn't have to answer about where they are and why it would take so long to get back. Especially if Ajay calls and wants Ebony to come immediately. They have a great time and really bond in Pittsburgh.

It's well after midnight when they head back. That's when Ebony notice that her phone is off. She turns it back on and checks her messages. Each of their guys have left several.

"Who turned my phone off?" she asks.

Nina admits she did because she didn't want anyone to stop them from going on their trip. Ebony figures it's going to be trouble.

By the time they get just inside of Mentor, Ajay calls and Ebony answers.

"Where the hell are you *at*?" he asks, sounding worried.

273

"On the shore way."

"Why was your phone off?"

"Nina turned it off," she says, "I didn't know she did. I just noticed and turned it back on and we got all the messages. I was just about to call you back."

"Come see me," he demands.

"Okay. We're on our way," she says.

It's 4 am. He sounds pissed or so she feels. She tells her girls that their guys are at the U waiting for them and they're upset too.

"Well it's about time," T-baby says.

"They didn't have time today. But they all mad now because we caught out," Rebbie adds as she giggles.

"Well let's go see what's up," Nina says as she laughs too.

Ebony doesn't laugh. She just looks at Nina.

"Are we gonna tell them where we went?" Rebbie asks.

"Hell yes. I am!" T-baby says.

"We got souvenirs, girl. How are we *not* gonna tell them?" Nina asks as she continues to laugh.

"Alright then. I guess we're gonna tell them," Ebony says, "I know I'm gonna have to hear this shit for awhile."

Her girls giggle at her for being nervous about having to tell Ajay. They think he'll be angry about the trip. But they have it all wrong about who is going to be the *one's* angry.

They arrive at the U, just before dawn. June is on the balcony of Ajay's apartment. He see them when they pull in and park. Rebbie hops out first and goes to him. His first words are about where she's been. She tells him and why she hasn't returned his calls.

"*Pittsburgh*!? Y'all done lost y'all damn *minds*?" he screams.

But Ajay doesn't fuss with Ebony at all. They retire to his room, almost immediately. He's just happy she's back and safe too.

"I guess you got bored waiting around here all day, ha?" he asks.

"Yes I did," she says, "But we wasn't trying to be sneaky. We just wanted to go riding and we knew it wasn't safe to ride around the city. Not with all the beef going on."

"Alright. I'm not tripping. But you know better though," he says with a smile. She's at a lost for words. "Come on and lay down over here with me."

He's lying on his king sized bed, still bandaged from the surgery and sore too. She joins him. They watch *Sportscenter* while listening to the other 3 couples argue. Eventually, everyone gets quiet or at least they aren't
274

arguing anymore. But it's still quite noisy in the 2-story apartment.

"I bought you this shirt and this money clip while I was there. Do you like them?" she asks.

"Yes indeed," he says, "I always love the gifts you get for me. But I don't like you going on the highway like that, baby. Anything could've happened to you."

He speaks in a soft tone. Before she can respond, he begins to kiss her. He rubs her breast and between her legs. She's turned on but he's slow about mounting her. Recognizing that he's still sore and needs to reserve his strength, she slides out of her own clothes.

"I know you're real sore and can't move a lot," she explains, "So you *have to* let me do the work until you heal."

"My pussy be *real* hot since you're pregnant, baby," he says, "That's what it is. You can't wait on me these days. I'm moving to slow."

He chuckles as he observes her actions. He likes that she's taking the initiative and he tells her so. She doesn't respond. She just removes his clothes too.

"Hell yea, baby girl. Bring it on," he says while still smiling seductively.

He's kissing every part of her body he can come in contact with. While she's undressing him. She truly can't wait for him, any longer. She rolls over on top of him and places him inside of her.

"Yea baby girl. Take control of yours," he says with a smile, while recognizing why she has taken charge.

He's totally turned on by her aggressive move *this* morning. They make love for the next 25 minutes. No pain. *All gain.*

Sunday, the foursome leave with their guys for Cincinnati. It's mid April. They had helped Lynn celebrate her 21st birthday. Their crew in Columbus have a birthday, as well. They stop to visit Jackie and her family. They give Chaundra money for her 11th birthday which will be on the 28th. She shows them a letter and a card she'd gotten from lil Kenny. They like that and think it's cute. They hit the road, on time and arrive in Cincinnati by 3:00pm.

All 4 couples hang out at the house with Jan and Rob. They play cards and party for awhile too. Ebony ask Ajay about inviting the ladies basketball team over this week, so her and T-baby can see them again and T-baby can play ball with them. He stalls on her request and never gives her a reason why. Nor does he invite them over. Not tonight and he's not going to invite them over, later in the week either. Ebony and Nina go to bed early. Ajay insist Ebony needs her rest. But he wants her in bed for
275

other reasons too. When he does come to lay down he's buzzing. He wakes her up with soft kisses on her nipples.

"Ouch baby!" she say as she rolls toward him.

"That hurt when I suck on 'em?" he whispers.

"Yes."

"Okay. I'll have to be gentle then," he offers, "They're big. Your breast *and nipples* are changing but I love it," he chuckles as he continues to arouse her with very stimulating foreplay.

She's eager to have sex. She finds that she enjoys it, even more, now that she's pregnant. She's also better able to handle his size. Well, better than before the pregnancy. But she still can't handle him.

"Your pussy is so hot," he whispers as he enters her, "It's like standing next to the oven."

He loves it more than ever, as he says, "If I would've known it was gonna be this good. I would've tried to plant a seed a long time ago," he admits.

He looks into her eyes and smiles a sly smile. They make love several times before going to sleep.

Sex with Ajay gets better every time, in her opinion. She notice how much wetter she gets with the pregnancy and how much more he sweats. She also notice he never mentions the ladies team again. She wonders what problem he has with them but she doesn't ask. It's not a priority to her, at this time.

The next day Kim calls and talks to Jan and the foursome. She tells Ebony some news on Angel that she's heard during spring break. Angel is coming to Cincinnati to see Ajay. She had tried to visit him while he was in the hospital but Jo and Pearl put a stop to her efforts. Ebony tells Ajay about her plans to visit him. He has her to hang up with Kim and he calls Cleveland. He tells Angel not to come. She's upset but she knows Ajay means what he's said. She tells him she wants to come later.

He says, "We'll see," and hangs up before she can object.

The next day after class, they all go shopping for baby things. Neither Nina or Ebony know the sex of their babies, so they keep it simple.

"We can get t-shirts and diapers," Nina says.

"And sleepers too," Ebony adds.

Ajay and Tank let them pick what they want and they pay for it. Then they go to dinner.

On Thursday, Ebony and T-baby visit with coach Sanders at UC. They take the visitors tour and meet with the existing players again. This is the second time for Ebony. She doesn't notice any tension from the females. Not particularly. Or anything noticeable that would make Ajay see them as
276

not worthy of her company. But there is 1 player that seems stand offish with her. She takes a mental note. She's not the Ajay type at all. She's stocky and bullish. She has a lesbian look but it's apparent she likes men because she has a *Tupac* fetish. Much like any other female who's into boys. Her name is Katrina. Her parents own the campus gift shop and she's labeled as a spoiled rich girl. T-baby isn't impressed by her and neither is Ebony. As long as she isn't trying to fuck their man, they don't see a need to label her anything at this time. They dismiss it immediately.

"We're coming here next year," T-baby says.

Ebony is still offered a scholarship despite being pregnant. Coach says she can red shirt her freshman year. She's attending in the fall. Nina and Rebbie are coming on scholarships for the dance and cheering teams. Nina has 1 for Academics and she won't have to forfeit either of them. They talk about how much colleges are willing to waive when you have stars in your family. Cincinnati has high hopes for Ajay. Like another NCAA birth and possibly a Final Four appearance or better. They're expecting the same from Ebony and T-baby.

On Friday, they're joined by their parents as the foursome sign their scholarships. Then their parents take them out to dinner before they head home. The crew celebrate for the remainder of the weekend. Rob and the foursome leave for Cleveland, late Sunday night.

By the 2nd week in May, there's a warrant out for Ajay's arrest. Attorney Wheeler, UC coach Booker, Bert Parkwood, Al and Jo go with him to turn himself in. Attorney Wheeler will get the 2 murder counts dropped for lack of evidence and discovery from his defense team which proves Ajay didn't shoot a weapon. The police had determined that the slugs taken from Craig's body where from a 357 magnum. Ajay owns a 357. It's registered to him and was left to him by his deceased paternal grandfather, Allen Jackson Sr. The police have known about the gun he inherited for about 8 to 10 years. That's the evidence they used to bring the charges. They want the gun turned over. Wheeler has another road block for them. The gun had already been reported stolen, years ago. Wheeler gets the DA to look up the report and they surely find it. Al and Jo had filed a police report when their van had been broken into in early 1989, while they were at work. They reported the gun stolen because it had been in the van prior to the burglary. When they filed the police report, they truly thought it had been stolen. They only found out different, a year ago. Ajay had taken it out of the van and had it in the safe at his uncle Brad Sr and aunt Deb's home. But Al left the report on file, on the advice from Wheeler.
277

In the event there was a case similar to this one. Great advice.

"There is no way you're gonna railroad my client with this," George Wheeler says to the DA, "His three fifty seven was reported stolen over five years ago. You got something else? If not, then I do."

He shows them the results of the gun firing test performed on Ajay while he was in recovery.

He says, "He didn't fire any weapon. Now unless you've got something to hold him on, my client will be going back to college today."

The prosecutor has to save face, so he keeps the assault charge against Ajay filed by Tim. The police are still trying to find someone from the crew to charge with the murders of Carl and Craig. But they're back to square one. They had considered charging the whole crew but there was other's from Craig and Carl's clique who was shooting as well. Including Craig and Carl. Plus weapons was discovered on their property. There is really no way to prove who had fired the fatal shots. Especially without a murder weapon. The murder charges against Ajay are dropped. UC alumni are paying for the best legal team money can buy to protect Ajay and his crew. Ajay knows T-baby fired his 357. And even though they aren't on the best of speaking terms, at the moment, he's going to protect her until the end. That's the way the crew do things. *Loyalty over anything.*

On Saturday, Ajay sees Angel at *Gordon park*. She shows up with her posse. At the first opportunity, she makes her way over to where he's standing with his crew. She tells him she's attending UC in the fall also. He doesn't care and tells her so, as he says, "I think that's a bad idea."

"Why?" she asks.

"Because Ebony is gonna be there," he says, "We're gonna be living together. That's gonna shut everything down."

"Maybe we can manage to see each other," she tries.

"I don't think so. I'm *her man so* I understand why *she's* coming," he says, "I don't know why you are. I really wish you wouldn't."

She ask him why. He doesn't offer an answer and he leaves her standing there alone and goes back to his crew. If she can't figure out why she shouldn't come to UC, then that's her problem. He's perturbed by her. Still she can't catch his drift. She hangs around in the park, hoping to get more conversation with him. He leaves without another word.

Later, she comes through Shaker Heights while the guys are in Chill's yard. She doesn't stop. She sees Ebony outside with him. The whole crew are outside getting ready to go to their club. Ebony and Nina aren't going. They're babysitting CJ, Brad III and Destiny. Nina and Ebony get

278

the 3 babies and bring them to papa's house. They're staying with him until the crew leave the club. Ajay and Tank help them get the babies inside. They speak to papa, then head to *The Chill Spot.*

Angel shows up at the club alone. She has gotten dropped off and wants to talk to Ajay. She ask Arthur if he'll do the deal for her. Reluctantly, Arthur passes the word on to Ajay, who is even more reluctant to go outside to talk with her. But he finally does. The first words out of her mouth is her asking if they can hook up. He says no. She starts to cry as she begs him to give her some of his time.

"Get in the car," he says, "I'll take you home, this time. But don't ever get dropped off nowhere that I am again. Or you'll be stuck there."
He doesn't even want to look at her. He keeps his head straight as she gets into his six four. He's hearing Ebony's voice in his head, asking him, *"Why do you have to mess with her?"* And this time he hears himself telling her, *"The only girl I have to see is you."* He's going to keep his word to the girl he loves. She's with him 100%. He made a promise to her and gave her a ring. It's time he kept his word to her as well. His shooting and trial had brought them even closer together. He loves where they are, at this point.

Angel sits comfortably, then closes the door. He barely gives her time to adjust herself in the seat before he lays down the law.

"We're done," he says suddenly, "So if there's anything you need to say to me. Say it now."
He starts up his car and pulls away. He leaves the music off so she can say her final words to him.

"I love you, Anthony-"

"Don't *ever* call me Anthony," he snaps, "Never in your fuckin' life. No one calls me that but Ebony."

"I love you, Ajay," she offers.

"Get the fuck *outta* here wit this bullshit," he says in disgust.

"I do and I wanna be with you," she says, "I wanna be with *just you* and nobody else. But you act like you don't want to see me no more."

"I don't," he says.

"Why not?" she asks, "I did everything you ask me to do."

"I told you I have a girl," he says, "I told you that, from jump."

"You want even give me a chance to show you that I can be-"

"Look here. I need to tell you this," he says, "I'm about to be a father. Ebony is my girl and I'm about to marry her. I won't be fuckin' with you, even if I wasn't getting married. Because I'm not feeling you, like that. Besides, she already knows about you and she's gonna be on top of it. I'm not interested anyway, so it's done."
279

"You're just gonna dog me like *that*?" she ask.

"I'm trying to tell you in the nicest way I can. Don't come to Cincinnati to be with me. Or get dropped off to meet me. Because I'm not going to see you. Not anymore."

All of a sudden, she reaches over and slaps him so fast he doesn't have time to react. But after he regains his composure, he slaps her back. Then he pulls his car over on the shoulder.

"Get the fuck out," he says calmly.

"Please Ajay. I'm sorry. I-" she tries.

"Get your *muthafuckin ass* outta my car!"

He reaches across her and opens the door. She's stalling. He shoves her out of his car, closes the door back and drives away.

He turns his music up loud so he can calm down before going to papa's to pick up Ebony, Nina and the babies. He takes CJ and Brad III to Jr's, where Bre and Tonya are waiting. He takes Destiny to Chill's house where they meet Tank. The 4 of them go to his apartment for the night.

Ajay returns to college the following week. The semester is over but he has to do summer weight training. He also has to get the keys for the even bigger alumni spot where he will live, starting this summer. The Cincinnati alumni have leased it to him for his extended family. They want to keep their star players comfortable plus give them peace of mind. They'll have plenty of room in this huge mansion when the 2 babies are born. The alum wives have already hired a nanny to help the young couples too. Pearl and Jo like that the University has taken such a vested interest in the welfare of their grandbabies. But the soon-to-be grandmothers plan to keep the babies in Cleveland. Ebony and Nina haven't agreed with them on that issue. Neither have Ajay and Tank, But they're going to leave it be, for now.

"Let them say whatever they wanna say," Ajay tells to Tank, "And we'll deal with them later."

"True that," Tanks answers.

Ebony and Nina have appointments this Friday. Ajay and Tank come home for the weekend so they can go with them. For Ebony, this is her 2nd appointment. Ajay goes with her. Their pregnancy is progressing normally. She's about 8 weeks. Nina has appointment seven She goes every 2 weeks. She's doing very well too. Her and Tank have their ultrasound and find out they're having a girl. They're going shopping immediately after leaving the doctors office. Their due date has been changed to the 28 of September. They're both excited to know they're having a girl. Tank spends $1000 at the baby store and still didn't get all of the things he wants.
280

Nina convinces him to wait and they can get more, at a later date.

Out of high school

The foursome's high school graduation is next weekend. The ceremony is Saturday, May 28. Nina is the Salutatorian while Ebony, T-baby and Rebbie finish with high honors. The May celebration honors the graduates, Memorial Day and the birthdays. Kim turns 15. Pam turned 12 on the 5th. There's a lot of talk and anticipation of Ajay and Tank's, soon-to-be fatherhood.

Jr teases Ajay, saying, "Finally got someone to call you daddy, cousin."

"And give Ebony a break," Chill adds as all 3 of them laugh.

Everyone knows Ajay thinks of himself as a Mack. He always had some girl calling him daddy or mister. 1 of those girls was Angel. But he has already told his guys what happened with Angel, a couple of weeks ago. They know she's over. Chill is especially pleased about that. He's always on Ajay more so nowadays, about his player ways. Especially now that Ebony is pregnant. He wants Ajay to be completely faithful to her.

"Look at what she's willing to give up for this baby, man," Chill had says.

They both realize Ebony is going to miss out on her freshman season at UC and she'll have to go a 5th year if she wants to play for 4 years.

"Today is not only her graduation but it's three years since that nigga tried that shit in Houston," Ajay says, "She didn't even remind me of it this year."

"That's a good sign," Chill says, "She's got some more positive stuff to think about."

"But she don't wanna get married," he says as he laughs.

"That shocked me the most," Chill says, "I thought she would've been pushing you to get married. Pregnant or not."

"She wants to marry me," he says, "But just not now. She wants to wait until she's done with college."

"So what are y'all gonna go?" Chill asks.

"We're going to the justice of the peace, the third week of July," he says, "That week before we move her things to the Natty house. We decided on July seventeenth. I'm looking forward to it, actually. I haven't fucked with nobody but her, this whole year."

Ajay realizes the sacrifices she's making for him and he's really making a great effort to show her the respect she deserves. They're inseparable these days. And now that she's out of school, they're together daily. When he's home she stays at the U. When he goes to Cincinnati, she goes with him.

281

TIME TO GROW-RELOADED-TIME WILL REVEAL 2

All of the crew are home again by *Father's day* weekend. The Father's day and June birthday celebration will be on Sunday. But on Saturday, Ajay goes out to the park with the guys. The foursome are at his apartment making dinner. While they're in the kitchen, the phone rings and T-baby answers it. It's Angel calling for Ajay.

"Hello," T-baby says.

"Is Ajay there?"

"Who the fuck wanna know?!" she yells into the phone.

Angel doesn't leave her name. She hangs up when T-baby starts to curse her out. But she calls back many times. Until Ebony figures out who it is. She calls Ajay's cell phone. It's obvious Angel doesn't know *that* number.

Ebony tells Ajay, "Angel keeps calling the apartment and hanging up."

He tells her he'll take care of it. Then him and Chill go to Angel's mother's apartment. He tells her once and for all, not to call his apartment anymore. She says she understands. But as soon as they leave, she calls again. This time she ask to speak to Ebony. Ebony puts the phone on speaker, then she says, "This is me. What do you want?"

"You think you can keep Ajay from me, bitch?! You outta yo mind. He's gonna be with me. Whether you like it or not! I'm gonna take your ass out when I see you again, bitch! You and your fuckin' baby!" she yells into the phone.

Then she hangs up and leaves her phone off the hook, as if the foursome would even call *her* back. But now they're heated over Angel's threats. Ebony wants to beat her ass but she knows no one is going to allow her to fight while she's pregnant.

They call Renee and tell her what was said. Renee tells them Angel will get hers and she's going to see to it. Ebony hates that her and Nina aren't going to be allowed to fight. But she knows the crew are going to handle it in the best way possible. They'll have to catch her at the club or at 1 of their parties. What they fail to take into account is that Angel is aware of how tight they are. And that they'd most likely be gunning for her.

The foursome get back to their cooking duties after hanging up with Renee. They discuss the things they'd like to do to Angel and her posse. They have their meal nearly done when their guys get back.

"You've got it smelling *good* up in here, baby girl," Ajay says as he strolls into the kitchen and hugs her from behind.

"Thank you," Ebony says with a bright smile.

"Oh *excuse me*. But Ebony isn't the only one cooking?" Nina says.

"Baby you've got it going on too," Tank say as they all laugh.

"We all do," T-baby adds and Rebbie agrees.

282

"What are y'all cooking in there?" June asks as he flops down on the sofa, "Cause *it is* smelling good. My stomach is growling like crazy."

"Country food," Rich offers.

"Big mama got my girl right," Ajay says, "She learned how to cook down there in Houston."

He kisses her on the cheek, then ask if she's okay. She says she is, as she smiles at his compliments.

"What's for dinner," June asks.

"Macaroni and cheese, chopped steak, rice, gravy and cornbread," Rebbie answers.

"And Chocolate cake," Ebony adds.

"All from scratch," T-baby offers.

"Straight home cooking," Nina adds and Ebony laughs.

"See that's what these babies need," Tank says.

"I'm going to take a shower," Ajay says to Ebony, "You wanna come with me?"

He starts out of the kitchen. She accepts his invitation.

"Nina can y'all watch the food while I take shower," she ask as she follows Ajay to the bedroom.

"Y'all can't take no shower in there," June yells and Ajay laughs.

"We've got to get some clothes," Ebony tries.

"I don't know what for. You're not gonna use them," Rebbie say as they all laugh again.

"Don't hate," Ebony says with a giggle while her and Ajay retreat to the bathroom.

When they're safely out of earshot, her girls tell the guys about the threatening phone call from Angel.

"That bitch is just pissed off because Ajay won't fuck with her tramp ass, no more," Rich says.

"She's lucky he didn't shoot her ass that night," Tank says, then he wishes he could take back his statement.

Ebony nor her girls know Angel had hit Ajay. Ajay hadn't told Ebony about it yet. He wasn't going to tell her until later, if necessary.

"What night, baby?" Nina asks.

"What happened?" Rebbie asks.

The guys have to tell them the story. They do and swear them to secrecy.

"That bitch put her hands on my brother?" Nina asks after she hears what happened.

"Hell yea. But he slapped the taste out of her fuckin' mouth though," Rich says, "And that ain't even like Ajay. But he hit *her* back."

283

"I'm gonna do it too," Nina says but Tank gives her a negative shake of the head. She corrects herself "Well my girls can. Since I'm pregnant."

"He put her ass out on the highway and left her there," June say as he cracks up laughing.

"When did this happen?" T-baby asks.

"When her and Nina was at papa's house, babysitting," Tank says.

"Damn. Do Ebony know this?" T-baby asks.

"No and don't tell her. *Please*," Rich says, "If he wants her to know, he'll tell her."

"That's why that bitch is mad," T-baby say as she laughs.

"I know she's history, *fasho*," Nina says, "Ajay don't play that."

"Ajay will never mess with her again," Rebbie says, "You notice you don't see her around anymore. He's gonna get her."

"He probably already did," Nina says and no one seconds her.
Now the girls are wondering if Ajay has already said he was going to kill Angel. The guys offer no answer. They change the subject to lighter conversation or they try too. But the girls keep coming back to Angel.

Ebony and Ajay finish their shower, then rejoin them for dinner. Ajay sits down at the table while Ebony goes into the kitchen to fix their plates. Nina makes him aware that the 3 of them know of the slapping incident, without alerting Ebony. She has gone back into the kitchen to grab her plate.

"I'm about to tell her, right now," Ajay says.

"Tell who, what? Me?" Ebony ask as he grabs her plate and places it at her seat while Ajay pulls her chair out.

"Yea. Sit down. I've got something to tell you," he says as she sits down next to him.
He tells her about the incident. She's instantly angry and he can see it on her face.
She says, "How's a bitch gonna be putting her hands on *my* man?"

"Whoa, baby girl. My baby will not be born cussing," he says trying to make a joke and calm her down, simultaneously.
But she wants to rant, as she says, "No Anthony look," she says calmly, "I don't hit you. She's not going too either. And no other girl or woman is going to be putting their hands on you. No way."

"I know but she's through anyway. She's out of the picture, okay," he says as he continues, "She's been buggin' me. I told her not to come to Natty for school. So even casual conversations, I broke it all off that night. That's why she got mad and that's why she was calling here today. She
284

knew I wasn't here. She had just saw me at the park, playing ball. But she don't have my cell number and she's never had it. She probably figured out you was here because she didn't see you with me. She's ass out. She know it's a wrap."

"She threatened to kill me and the baby," Ebony tells Ajay.

He's silent as he stares at her. It's as if the words she had just said are channeling through his mind. He continues to stare right through her. Nobody says anything for at least 60 seconds, as they wait for his reaction. They can see his lip quiver. They know he's angry. He takes a deep breath.

"I see it's time to put a real end to this shit," he says.

He doesn't have much to say, other than the obvious.

"She's not gonna fuck with my babies. If she do, she'll have to take me too. She's history."

They all agree, then enjoy their dinner. He's still slightly perturbed, though he tries to appear cheerful. He doesn't want Ebony to worry about the threats from Angel but he isn't going to let it go.

After dinner, big mama calls to check on her expanding and elevating eight. Ebony tells her she has fixed a home cooked meal.

"That's how you get you a husband, baby," big mama says with a chuckle, "And that's why mama taught you to cook, like that."

"I have one already," Ebony tells her.

"Oh I know," big mama says as she giggles.

Then they both laugh. Ajay thanks her for teaching Ebony to cook, *"like you"* and assures her that the good cooking is only 1 of the things which keeps him around. Big mama talks to all 8 of them. She's pleased to know they're all back together and getting along great.

CHAPTER 21

NOT *QUITE* AN ANGEL

The very next weekend, all of the guys help mama Jackie, Chaundra, Charlotte and uncle Jason plus his niece Justine, move into their new home in Cleveland. Jackie had been planning to move back since shortly after Stoney was killed. She wants to be closer to CJ, Bre and the crew families. The crew want to be closer to her and Stoney's sisters too. The house she purchased is almost directly across the street from the house which Jr and Tonya live in. Jackie's house is right next door to Mrs. Green. After getting her settled, the crew have a barbeque and sell plates at *The Crews House of Soul Food,* as a homecoming. They raise lots of money and give Jackie and Jason a housewarming fund to help smooth their transition.

The crew have 4 legitimate businesses and all of them are turning in really good profits. April 1980-they had opened *Crew Details,* a car wash and detail shop. In March 1991-*The Chill Spot nightclub* was opened. In June of 1992 they opened *Crew Cuts & Styles*, a hair salon and barbershop. Then in March of 1993 they opened *The Crews House of Soul Food*, a restaurant and catering service. All of these business are holding their own, so the crew feel they're ready to launch another venture.

On June 20 1994, they have the grand opening of *Granny's House,* a nursery and daycare center. They name it appropriately after Pearline "granny" Brown. It's located in the strip mall with their other businesses. It's right next door to *Crew Cuts and Styles*. It seems every time there's a discussion about the strip mall, a different story of how they came to own it is told. This time the story is the strip mall had been owned by Chill and Ajay's grandfathers and some of their business colleagues. When colleagues fell on hard times and wasn't able to pay debts owed, they sold their shares to the grandfathers until they eventually owned it outright. The crew guess it was during this time when the state had tried eminent domain and took possession. Either way, when their grandfathers died it passed on to Chill's father Paul and big Al. When Paul was killed Al became sole owner. He put it in Chill and Ajay's names when they was still minors and all the parents kept up the property taxes and maintenance over the years. They've rented some of the spaces out to others during the years. But Al always said whenever the guys were ready to go into business for themselves, they could have it. The crew are certainly making good on their dreams. Every member of Chill's crew will have their own business for their family. That's the goal they are dead set on reaching, so before long they can be totally legitimate. No more drug deals and weapons exchanges. *Totally legit.* Only *Time Will Reveal* if they achieve this dream.

Ajay, Tank, June and Rich go back to Cincinnati on Monday. June and Rich have to continue football practice while Ajay has summer weight training and conditioning. Tank has track meets to compete in. Ebony stays in Cleveland this week to work her summer job at *Granny's House daycare* with Jackie, Brenda and Anna. Sandy helps Nina and Tonya run the salon along with Justine, who's uncle Jason's niece from Columbus. Archie Sr, Sam Sr and Greg Sr help out with the barbershop and the nightclub. The restaurant and catering services are handled day to day by Belinda, Rena, Debbie and the grandparents. Brian Sr and Rich Sr have always worked with the crew, managing the detail shop. The crews parents are very proud of them for doing so well for themselves and the family. Some of their parents who had started out helping them part-time, are now full time in their family owned business. When the crew finish college they'll all have profitable businesses to run, with at least 1 business per family. Their business ventures are far from over. They want to be a totally self contained unit as well. It's like they had said along time ago. Instead of Cleveland, the maps will read: *CrewLand.* They had a vision way back then, when they came up with that name for their area and turf. That's the very name that's chosen for the strip mall. *The CrewLand Mall!* Roll on crew!

Ebony enjoys her 1st week at the daycare center and she likes having a job. She thinks it's good practice for motherhood too. She loves the kids who attend their daycare. Her and her girls have lunch together daily and discuss their workday. All of the crew are working within the mall. Jan, T-baby and Rebbie work in the restaurant, waiting tables. Opening the restaurant in the spring proves to have been the best season. By summer, their clientele has tripled. They have most of the crew at home to help out. The high school and grade school crew help out too.

It's Friday June 24th and the restaurant is packed. All of their businesses are bustling. *Crew Cuts N Styles* is packed with folks getting ready for the June birthday bash at *The Spot,* tomorrow night. *Crew Details* is busy with folks getting their cars cleaned up for the club scene. In its 1st week, *Granny's House* opens with 27 kids on it's daily roster. Included are Brad III, CJ and Destiny. They are equipped to handle 50 kids with ages
287

ranging from preemie to Kindergarten. They know they will fill up soon.

Nina and Ebony are going to doctors appointments at 4pm. Ajay, Tank, June and Rich are on their way home. Jan isn't due back to school until early August. She decides to stay in Cleveland and work at the restaurant until then. Jb, Lynn and Bre are back in Atlanta and already planning to open businesses there, in the near future.

Nina and Tank drive the Tracker to their appointment while Ebony and Ajay follow them in the six four. On the way, Ebony and Ajay talk about how her week has been without him.

He asks, "How are you doing?"

"I'm doing fine. How are you?" she asks.

"Tired of having to miss my girl," he say as he smiles.

"I miss you too," she says, "I tried to stay at the apartment because I can smell your scent on the pillows. But it's to lonely out there without you, Anthony. So I brought your pillow to my room at mama's."

She laughs and he looks at her and smiles. He likes that but makes a funny.

"You can't cheat with my pillow either," he says as he chuckles, "So that's why you didn't stay there last night?"

"Yes I stayed at mama's but Jesse got on my last nerve," she says.

"What did he do?"

"He kept wanting to touch my stomach," she says, "And it's not even big yet. He knows I'm having a baby so he's doing dumb stuff just to worry me."

"He's excited about being an uncle."

"He don't do Nina like that," she tries.

"Because Tank made him leave her alone," he tells her.

"Well he needs to leave me alone too," she says as she pouts.

"I'll talk to him about it alright?"

"Okay," she smiles.

"That's all you wanted, ha?" he asks as he tickles her and she giggles. Then he says, "You know I got you baby," he says and laughs.

"I know," she says, "I couldn't wait to see you."

"I just left Monday," he tries.

"It's Friday now," she says and they both laugh again.

They talk about how all of the missing each other will be over as soon as the fall semester starts.

"But it'll start again when you go to the NBA," she says and smiles.

"Yea but you'll have a big ass house and some kids to keep you from getting lonely, then," he says and they both laugh again.

288

They arrive at the medical complex and go in to see Dr. Weston for their appointment.

Rebbie and T-baby are thrilled when they see June and Rich walk into the door of the restaurant. They seat them immediately, then take a break.

"How was your trip home, baby?" Rebbie asks June.

"It was fine because I was looking forward to seeing your beautiful face," he answers.

"For real man," Rich adds, "That's the reason I deal with that boring ass ride, so I can see my sexy ass lady."

"I'm glad you deal with it," T-baby say as she smiles.

They sit at a corner booth and talk while waiting for their friends to return from the doctor and join them.

Nina and Ebony finish their appointments and the 4 of them head straight to the restaurant to meet T-baby, Rich, Rebbie and June for dinner. Afterwards, Ebony and Ajay go to his apartment alone. Nina isn't feeling well. Her and Tank go to Jo's house for the night.

Rebbie, June, T-baby and Rich are at Rob's with him and Jan. Rich feels like he needs to talk to T-baby in private, so they go into the bedroom to be alone. He needs to open up and he does.

"Trisha I've been wanting to tell you something for awhile now but I didn't know how to tell you."

"Just tell me, baby. What's going on?" T-baby asks with a smile.

"You remember when we was going through all of that fighting, cheating and shit?"

"Uh huh," she says.

"I was using drugs," he admits.

"What?" she asks as she's stunned by this revelation.

"I was snorting powder in high school," he says, "And I almost lost my scholarship when I failed my drug test, last summer."

"I never knew," she says.

"I didn't tell anybody but the guys and my parents. That's why my dad put me in that program," he admits, "I was blowing it out in Mentor. You use to think I was drunk but that was the powder."

"I didn't know," is all T-baby can say.

"I was too embarrassed to tell you," he says, "I think about the shit now and I can't even believe it myself."

289

She gives him a hug and kiss and says, "I will always be here for you."

"I know that now. But then, the drugs had me feeling like you and everybody was against me," he says, "When I went in the circle that changed a lot of shit for me. Having my own family whoop my ass, that was an eye opener. Plus when I saw you with that nigga that's when I knew I had to get my shit together."

"And you did," she says, "You have, baby. Big time."

"I had too," he admits, "I didn't wanna lose you, Trisha. We had lost our baby and that was the last straw. I decided to get clean and try to stay clean and that's what I'm doing. I've been clean for six months and eight days. I haven't had no cocaine since the night you miscarried."

She holds him and eventually, they cry together. Then they make love several times before falling asleep. Wrapped tightly in each others arms.

At Ajay's apartment, him and Ebony are sound asleep. After a late night run to *Taco Bell* for nacho's and salsa for her, they turned in early. It's nearly 3am and Ajay's house phone is ringing.

Ring!!! Ring!!!! Ring!!!!

"Hello," he says, waking from a deep sleep.

Ebony squirms to stay close to him as he reaches for the phone.

"What are you doing?" Angel asks.

"*Bitch* didn't I tell you to stop calling me?" he snaps.

Angel tries to get in another sentence but he cuts her off.

"I heard what you said to Ebony. You fuck with her and I'm gonna kill yo ass. Do you understand me?" he snarls.

"Ajay. I'm sorry-"

"Yea I know. You're a sorry muthafucka. Don't fuck with my girl. Do you understand me?" he ask, "And don't call me no muthafuckin more. Do you understand?"

"I understand," she says.

He hangs up and she doesn't call back.

They next day, all of the crew work at their mall. The food for the June bash is prepared at the restaurant. Later, the party is crunk. All of the crew, their friends as well as the usual unwelcome guest are there. Even Angel has the nerve to show up. But she stays outside in the car and out of sight. She's just hoping for a sighting of Ajay. She sits in the car talking to herself and thinking of new ways to threaten Ebony, the entire night.
290

She's a fatal attraction, if ever there was one. Ajay doesn't realize what he's got on his hands.

Chill is 25 and June will be turning 19, tomorrow. Ally wants to go to June's party. Ally is Rebbie's sister. She's only 11 years old. Rena won't allow her to attend the party because she isn't old enough. She ask Rebbie to sneak her out.

"You've got two more years, kid," Rebbie tells her before leaving for the club, "I only got to go early because my girls are older than me. You've got to get you a clique."

They both laugh and soon, Rebbie leaves for the party.

Angel waits in the car the entire time that Michelle and Alana are in the club. She's actually afraid to let Ajay or any of his crew see her. She knows how down they are for each other. She also knows if she's seen, then she'll surely have a beat down coming or worse. She thinks of ways to get even with Ebony while watching her and Ajay come out, go to her car and leave. She wants to follow them but she isn't driving. Michelle is still in the club. When *The Spot* closes for the night, her and her friends go to Arthur's apartment. While there, she asks him to go and get Ajay. He doesn't even waste time backing her down.

"Bitch you're *psycho*," Arthur says with a chuckle, "You don't know Ajay at all. Ajay will bleed you out, girl. Let me tell you a little something about him. He don't play no *goddamn* games. He says exactly what he means. Unlike a lot of other guys, who will lie just to kick it wit girls. He don't do any of that type shit. He's straight and to the point. You chasing a dream. That man don't want you. He's with Ebony, one hundred percent. You was a piece of ass. *Period*. Then you had the nerve to *threaten Ebony?*! Let it go, Angel. You're gonna fuck around and Ajay is gonna end up killing you. Then the crew *and me* are gonna make things rough for everybody that knows you. Because Ajay would be loosing out on the NBA and going to prison," he warns. Then he gives her advice.

"You'd better leave the shit alone and move on. Ajay don't play fuck shit. I done told you. You're messing with the wrong dude."

Then he tells Michelle she has to take Angel home immediately. He tells her not to be in her presence, if she expects to be with him. He doesn't want the crew to find out Angel is at his apartment. Not after what she'd threatened to do to Ebony. Michelle takes her to her mothers apartment and severs ties with her, right then and there. Then she heads back to Arthur's place, satisfied that she has removed 1 obstacle for her man's life.

On Sunday, only the restaurant is open. Ebony can spend all day

291

with Ajay before he goes back to Cincinnati, in the morning.

"I like my job but I miss going to Natty with you," she says.

"You'll be coming in August, for good," he says, "I want you down there but I know you wanna work. We'll get married and then August is right around the corner. Our mama's don't want you traveling a lot while you're pregnant either."

"I know. They told me that too," she says, "So did big mama. But August isn't that far. I can't believe you're okay with a shotgun wedding, baby. I understand why but I always dreamed of a big wedding."

"You can still do it big," he says.

"It's not enough time," she says, "And if we wait, I'll be big."

"Then do the wedding later," he says, "I just want to be married before my first child is born."

"Okay and I know you wanna keep your word to my dad too."

They smile as they lay in bed watching TV. Before long, Nina, Tank, Rich, June, Rebbie and T-baby come over to spend the night.

The next morning, Ebony and Nina are slow to rise. They got extra sleep for the babies. The foursome make breakfast for their guys, then send them off to Natty around 9am. Nina drives the Tracker to work. Rebbie and T-baby hitch a ride with her. Ebony doesn't have to be at work until noon. She stays behind and cleans the apartment after everyone leaves. She's happy her morning sickness has subsided. She sips orange juice and watch video's on Black Entertainment Television.

At 11:30 sharp, she leaves for work. She doesn't notice the gray car in the visitors section of the parking lot. But as she's leaving, the gray car follows her. It's still following her as she gets onto Cliff Ridge drive, heading to *The CrewLand mall*. She drives through the winding road and finally notices the gray car as it speeds up behind her. She dismisses it, thinking *somebody is in a hurry*. Suddenly, the car smashes into the back of her Accord causing her to spin out and slide. She regains control. She's hit again just as she's entering a hair pin turn. Her car leaves the road, goes through the guard rail and over the embankment. She plummets 40 feet or 4 stories down the side of the cliff. The gray car continues around the curve.

Noon!

The mothers at the daycare center are use to Ebony showing up early. Her shift is for noon today and she hasn't arrived. Brenda calls the salon to see if she's over there.

292

"Nina is Ebony at the salon?" Brenda asks.

"No ma'am. She was suppose to be there at twelve," she answers.

"She hasn't shown up or called," Brenda says, "Can you call her and tell her to come on in or let us know if she's not feeling well."

"Okay," Nina says.

She hangs up and dials the apartment. She lets the phone ring at least 10 times but there's no answer. She hangs up and calls Ebony's cell phone and gets no answer there either. She calls Pearl's house. Jesse answers.

"Lil man is Ebony there?" she asks.

"Call me Jesse," he orders.

"Jesse is she there?" Nina asks, losing patience.

"No she's not home," he answers, "She stayed over Ajay's."

"If you hear from her, tell her to call me at the shop. Okay?"

"Okay," he says.

Nina begins to worry. It isn't like her best friend to go off and not tell her girls where she's going.

I know she didn't go to Cincinnati with Ajay.

She even thinks about calling his cell phone but she thinks better of it.

If he hasn't talked to her, then he's gonna stress about where she is too.

She decides not to call him. But she tells Tonya she hasn't shown up for work. Tonya tells her, she should go and look for her, right away. Nina goes and gets T-baby and Rebbie to ride along. They're in the middle of noon rush but after Deb finds out crew is missing, she tells the girls to go on.

"Call me when y'all find her," Deb says.

Everyone know Tim's crew still has beef with them. Even though they've moved from the area. Still they aren't ruling them out. Not to mention the recent threats Angel made. They aren't taking either scenario lightly. Nina, Rebbie and T-baby leave the mall heading to the U.

They arrive and there's no sign of Ebony. Her car and her daycare uniform are both gone.

"She left here, going to work," Rebbie says.

"Where the hell is she?" T-baby ask as she starts to worry.

"We're gonna find her, kid," Nina offers, "Let's trace her route." They head back toward the CrewLand mall.

As they approach the curves of Cliff Ridge drive, the traffic is stalled and the police are present.

"What's the deal?" T-baby asks from the passenger seat.

"We just came through here," Nina says as she pulls the Tracker

293

over to the shoulder of the road so she can get out and check out the scene.

"What are you doing, Nina?" Rebbie asks.

"Let's go see what's going on," she says, "I got a real bad feeling." Immediately, they jump out of the jeep and run toward the 1st police officer they see.

"Hold on, ladies. I can't let you up there," the officer says.

"We're looking for my cousin," T-baby says, "She didn't show up for work."

"We got a serious accident up here," the officer says.

"Can you tell me if a blue Honda is in the accident?" Nina asks. The officer doesn't answer her but he does ask them to come with him to his car. They do. He gets a thorough description of Ebony and her car.

"What was she wearing?" the officer asks and they tell him what she should have on.

"Is she the basketball star from MLK?"

"Yes sir," T-baby says.

"She is too," Rebbie says pointing to T-baby.

"I knew you looked familiar," the officer says to T-baby, "Okay. I need for you young ladies to wait here while I check it out." He walks up the highway about 20 yards to the scene and exchange information with the lead officer.

"At least now we know who's down there," the lead officer says, "Where the hell is rescue already! We've got to get the highway opened up so they can get on through here. We need to get down there, guys." The Cleveland community knows of Ebony from her basketball success, her huge family and their contributions to the city. Many of the crew are local celebrities, nowadays. Knowing it's an upstanding kid from their district, the police step it up another notch as the fire and rescue team arrive.

"Let's get the rescue team through here. ASAP," the lead officer says on his radio. They direct the trucks through the traffic and to the scene. They set up in record time. The lead rescue officer is repelling down the cliff almost immediately. The 1st officer goes back to the girls.

"Will you ladies come with me please," he asks. This makes them more anxious as this time, they follow the officer to the staging area. They don't see Ebony's car. They only see skid marks. Long skid marks which run up the right lane, across the center line and back to the right lane. Then through the guard rail..........................,

"Oh my God!" Rebbie screams as she notices Ebony's car down the embankment, "That's Ebony's car!"

294

The other girls notice it after Rebbie does and they all become instantly hysterical. The 1st officer tries to reassure them, they're doing all they can.

A female officer who has been assigned to them says, "Rescue is here. We'll get to her, okay? But please. I need for you young ladies to calm down and work with me."

She starts by getting all of Ebony's contact information. But before she can finish the interview, Brenda comes tearing through the crowd. She runs up to where the girls are standing with the officers. There are 2 more officers with them now and the rescue team is already in position.

"What's going on?" Brenda asks.

The girls try to explain but they're too incoherent. The female officer gives Brenda the details. Then Brenda calls Pearl at the hospital.

"Pearl I'm looking at the car," she says, "She went off the cliff."

Pearl panics on the other end of the phone. The lead officer tells Brenda they have an officer at the hospital who can bring Pearl out to the site. Because Pearl is definitely in no shape to drive. She's upset. She hangs up and calls John to inform him. He's near Jackson Mississippi.

"I'll take my truck to the station here and get a flight," he says, "Call me the minute you get to where she is."

Pearl's assistant covers her rounds, as she says, "You go check on your daughter. Let us know how she is and when they're on the way with her."

"She's sitting at the bottom of a cliff, Joyce. I don't know-" Pearl starts to cry again.

"She'll be alright, Pearl," Joyce says, "That kid is a fighter. We all know that."

Joyce and the entire nursing staff give words of encouragement as Pearl gets a page. It's the officer at the hospital contacting her. He's ready to take her to the scene. He soon locates her and takes her to his patrol car.

Brenda calls their daycare to inform Anna and Jackie. Every available person there, leaves heading to Cliff Ridge. Tonya stays at the salon but Jr, Jan, Chill and Renee go to the scene.

"Tonya don't call Ajay yet," Chill says, "Let me check things out first. Then I'll call him."

2 hours later from Natty.

"Hey auntie Anna. Where's my baby at?" Ajay asks.

"I'm not sure," she answers, not knowing what to say.

"I called her cell phone *and* the apartment," he says, "I didn't get her. I know y'all ain't got my baby working so hard she can't even call me."

295

"You're in Cincinnati already?" Anna asks, trying to appear calm.

"Yea. Yes ma'am. We just got here. Is Ebony at work?"

"No she's not here, right now. Umm let me ask Jackie-"

"What's going on?" he asks, sensing something is wrong.

It's obvious his aunt is stalling. Ebony usually calls him once she gets to work and she hasn't. He has already figured out that she's unable to call him and unable to answer her phone. He just doesn't know exactly what's happened or why she can't call. Jackie takes the phone, just as Belinda walks in. She's coming over to see if they have any news. Anna gives her the be quiet gesture, by putting her index finger in front of her mouth. Jackie tries to give Ajay some kind of explanation without telling him about the accident. She thinks it's best they wait until they know what her condition is before even telling Ajay that she has been in an accident.

Chill, Jan, Jr and Renee are at the scene. They're very impatient with the police. They want to know if anyone has gotten to her and if she's responsive.

"Has anybody talk to her?" Chill asks.

"We got four guys down there securing the car so we can hoist her up," an officer says, "We'll know something shortly."

"Have they at least checked to see if she's alright?" Renee asks.

The lead officer gets on his radio.

Ajay had given up trying to talk to Jackie and hung up. He knew she was hiding something. He tries Ebony's cell phone again.

Ring! Ring! Ring!

"Hello," rescue officer 1 says.

"Who *the hell* is this and where is my girl?" Ajay asks.

"This is officer David Jacobson of Cleveland Fire and Rescue."

Ajay quickly identifies himself before barraging him with questions.

"Where is Ebony and why are you answering her phone?"

Jacobson knows him as the all-star basketball player at UC, formerly of MLK, as he identifies his position. Ajay questions him thoroughly. Jacobson assures him that he's there to help her. He tells him the situation as best he can and per his job limits. Ajay presses him.

"Tell me how is she?" he asks, trying to stay calm.

"Give me a second, okay? I just got down here to the car. It's mangled pretty bad," Jacobson says.

296

"Can you see her?" Ajay asks as he holds his breath.

"Oh yes, son. I can see her."

"Tell me how is she?" he probes, "I *need* to know, man."

Jacobson reaches through the broken windshield and puts his fingertips to Ebony's jugular to feel for her pulse.

Hello?" Ajay says.

The line goes dead. In the seconds it takes for him to press the #2 on his speed dial and wait for the connection, his whole life flashes before him. His palms are starting to sweat as Jacobson answers again.

"Hello Ajay. The signal down here is not too good," he says, "I've got a pulse. Hang on a second," he says as he radio's back up to the lead officer. *"I've got a weak pulse here. She's alive and we have to get her out of here now. Right now!"* he yells as he gets his men in position.

The lead officer sends down the stretcher as they let the crew, who are waiting at the staging area, know that she has a pulse.

Pearl is on the scene now and very distraught. Brenda calls John and tells him the rescue team has gotten to the car and that she's still alive.

"Oh thank God," he says pushing out a gust of air.

"They're sending down a stretcher to put her on, John. She's got four guys down there with her," Brenda says.

David Jacobson talks to Ajay, who now has more information on Ebony then those who are at the scene. Jacobson keeps him calm.

"Ajay?" Jacobson says with question in his voice.

"Yes sir," he answers.

"She's alive, son," he says, "But you've got to let me get to work, alright? It's imperative that we get her out of this vehicle as soon as possible. Because it's not stable enough to work here. I'll give you my number. I know you're in Cincinnati and you're worried."

He gives him his cell number so he can call him back if they lose the signal. It's the only way he can get him to hang on and stop asking questions. The stretcher is there and the 4 officers are ready to remove her from her car.

Jacobson says, "Let's be very careful with her, guys. She's a basketball star and she's pregnant too. That's the expecting father, Ajay Jackson on her cell phone. He's listening to make sure we do a good job."

He lays her cell phone on her chest so Ajay can hear. The signal dies. She starts to respond as they're putting her on the stretcher.

"She's waking up, guys. Hold on," Jacobson say as he takes vitals on her and the baby, then radio's back up to the crane operator.

"Let's go! Right now! Let go *now!*"

297

They pull the stretcher up and Jacobson stays with her as he promised Ajay he would do. He discovers her phone had lost the signal again as the EMS techs load her into the Ambulance.

Meanwhile in Cincinnati, Ajay informs Tank, Rich and June of the accident. Then he calls his coach and tells him.

"Ajay let me get a hold of Parkwood," coach Booker says, "He has planes and jets. He can get us up there in under an hour, if all's clear."
The guys grab what they need to bring and head to Coach Booker's home.

"She's alive, right?" June asks Ajay to break the silence.
Ajay tells him yes. Tank doesn't ask or say anything. He just wants to get home and check on his twin. Rich drives them in Ajay's car and the entire ride is silent. They arrive at coach Booker's house, just as he's finishing his call with Mr. Parkwood.

"We can leave in twenty minutes," he say as they head to the airport and Ajay calls Jacobson back.

"Hello."

"This is Ajay. I talk to you earlier on Ebony's phone," he says.

"Yes Ajay. She's in the ambulance. We're leaving with her now."

"Is she awake? Y'all taking her to East General, right?" he asks.

"No sir and yes sir," Jacobson says as he lets him know, no she isn't awake and yes they're going to East General.

"Is she gonna be okay?" Ajay asks, "Just tell me that. *Please.*"
Jacobson can hear the desperation in his voice. Ajay is sincerely worried about his future. As he talks to Jacobson, he refers to Ebony as his wife. The urgency is evident in his voice when he says, "She's my good luck charm. I need her to be okay. That's why I asked you to stay by her side. Just until I can get there. Please keep her alive for me."
Jacobson feels a cold chill, just listening to him speak. It's obvious to him that Ajay cares for this young lady he's just pulled from a deadly wreck. They're both basketball players, just like his own daughter.

"I think she has a very good chance of making it through this Ajay," he says, "Once she survived that drop, I'd say anything is possible."

"Is my baby alright?" he asks.

"It's really to early to tell and I have no expertise in that area. When she gets to the hospital, they'll be able to check her out thoroughly," he says, "Just get here as soon as you can, son."

"Okay. I'll be there within the hour."

"Okay, Ajay. I'll be at the hospital when you get there."

"I'd like that, sir."

"Oh Ajay?" Jacobson starts.

298

"Yes sir," he says.

"I thought you'd like to know. She did wake up while we was taking her from the car," Jacobson says, "She called out for you."

Ajay has tears in his eyes as he says, "Will you tell her I'm leaving the airport, right now. Tell her I need her very much and I'm coming to take care of her. I'll be there in the hour. Will you tell her that for me?"

"I'll tell her."

They hang up.

Mr. Parkwood gets departure clearance and they're in the air, in 15 minutes, on their way to Cleveland. Ajay, Tank, Rich, June, coach Booker and Mr. Parkwood make the trip. He sent an assistant to East General to make certain Ebony's accommodations and care are up to par. He talks to Ajay in flight and reassures him that he's in charge.

"She's going to have the best care possible," he says, "I've never seen you look stressed before. Not even when *you were* lying in the hospital."

"She's *way* more important than that," is all Ajay says.

He's only thinking about getting to Ebony and his unborn child. Mr. Parkwood pats him on the back, hugs him and assures him that he's there and he'll spare no expense making sure she's taken care of.

Ebony arrives at the hospital, unconscious with weak vitals. After x-ray's, the staff are working double time to save her and the baby. Dr. Weston checks the fetus and gets no positive responses.

"We need to get her to surgery," she tells Pearl.

"How is the baby?" Pearl ask as the others listen.

"It doesn't look real good but you know we'll do everything we can," Dr. Weston says.

Dr. Stansfield, the lead surgeon, remembers Ebony from 3 years ago when she removed her cast. Her and Weston tell Pearl and the crew the extent of the injuries from her x-rays.

"She suffered multiple injuries in this accident," Stansfield starts, "She has four broken ribs, her left leg is broken at the femur and tibia. Those are the only broken bones visible from the x-rays."

"She has a massive amount of blood in her abdomen. As far as we can tell it appears to be from the fetus. It's in distress," Weston adds as she tears up.

"She was wearing her seatbelt which is wise. But I feel the airbag deployment force is what caused the broken ribs. She doesn't appear to have any major organs punctured," Stansfield says.

299

"Is she gonna be alright?" Renee asks.

"I think she'll be fine. But she's going to be in a lot of pain for the next few days and the weeks, following the surgery. Not only physical pain but mental as well. We don't think the fetus will survive," Stansfield says and Weston concurs.

"Where's Ajay? In route?" Weston asks.

"Yes," Renee says, "He's in the air, right now."

"I'll talk to him when we come out," Weston says, "I'll help however I can. I know this isn't going to be easy for any of you. You know these girls are like my own kids. The foursome was some of the first babies I delivered for this huge family."

They take Ebony to surgery as Dr. Weston continues to fight back tears.

Chill is with officer David Jacobson in the family recovery waiting area. He calls Ajay's cell phone.

"Hello," Ajay says on the 1st ring.

"How are you, man?" Chill asks.

"I don't know. How's my wife?" he asks.

Chill tells him the extent of her injuries and that the baby may not make it. He tells him she's in surgery.

"Is *she* gonna make it, Chill?" he asks, knowing Chill will tell him the truth. The others on the plane wait for his reaction.

"Oh yea, bro. She should be fine," he answers.

While they're on the phone, Jo comes running into the waiting room. Nervously she asks, "How are they?"

Renee tells her the injury report. She also gives her the details she has on the accident. Then Jo tells her that Al has gone to meet John.

"I talk to Ant, a lil while ago," she says, "He's in the air. Allen's meeting John at the airport."

Then papa comes in with Jesse. They're both understandably upset.

Papa asks, "Has anybody called lil John or Eloise and Percy?" he asks.

Brenda tells him they're waiting for the outcome of the surgery before they call Atlanta or Houston. "How did this happen?" papa asks.

They don't have a lot of information on the cause of the accident. The lead officer from the scene is there at the hospital. They call him in to give them the latest details about the wreck.

"Just judging from the skid marks, there was a second vehicle involved," the lead officer says, "We've got investigators out there now." He's still taking statements from everyone to help build his case.

From the air

300

Mr. Parkwood calls the chief of Detectives, there in Cleveland. The chief is a personal friend of his, former classmate and fellow alumni. He doesn't waste any time getting to the point. He tells him he wants him to put a blood hound detective on this case and he wants this accident investigated fully and solved to his satisfaction.

"I'll put my best guy on it, Bert," the chief says.

"Make sure you do," Parkwood says, "She's future alumni."

"I know that and I'm on it," chief says.

"We need to give Ajay some peace of mind," Parkwood tells him.

"And we will." chief says, "We sure will."

"My man," Parkwood says and they hang up.

At the hospital

Papa demands this investigation be a priority and judging by the reaction so far, it is.

"She's an upstanding kid with a bright future. Whoever did this and left her to die, I want them prosecuted to the fullest extent of the law," papa Brown says as he phones George Wheeler immediately to represent his family.

Then he notifies Percy and big mama and doesn't wait until surgery is over. "Percy says all of you must want him to shoot first and speak later," papa says, "He ain't in the mood to wait on information about his oldest granddaughter."

Poppa and big mama was upset that they hadn't been called as soon as it happened. They're her grandparents and they need to know how she's doing, immediately. Papa has Renee to call Jb and the girls in Atlanta as well. Once Wheeler's on the case, the crew get faster results.

The police know about Tim and his clique and also of Chill, Renee and Ajay's shootings. 1 angle is that this could be retaliation. They also know about the threats on Ebony's life made by Angel Taylor. They send teams out to interview all of the potential suspects.

Tim and his clique moved from the University apartments, shortly after Ajay's shooting, to avoid another confrontation with the crew. However, the Cleveland police department was able to get a lead on Tim, Justin and Roger and their alibi's are solid. They are in Cincinnati and has been there working jobs since Cleveland State University dismissed for the summer. All 3 have summer jobs and they were on the clock at the time of Ebony's accident. That's when the police decide to thoroughly investigate their contacts in Cleveland.

301

Alana, Michelle, Tameka and Angel are among the females, they had contact with while in Cleveland, who knew of Ebony.

"Tameka Robinson is currently incarcerated. We can scratch her name off," 1 officer says.

"This Angel Taylor's name has come up twice. We'll seek her out first. Then work the other two," the 2nd officer says.

At the same time they're seeking to make contact with Angel, 2 officers are arriving at her mother's apartment to question her. She's missing in action. Her mother's live-in boyfriend answers the door.

"I thought y'all was here to tell me you found my car," Tony Mangrove says. He's her mothers boyfriend, this month, "I reported it missing this morning. "

"No sir. We don't have any information on your vehicle, at this time," the officer says.

"I'll need a full description of it," the 2nd officer says.
Tony gives him all the information on his car. A 1979 Chevrolet Caprice Classic, 4 door. Color, gray. Tony and Angel's mother tell the officers, Angel is probably with her friends Alana and Michelle, at the mall or something. After questioning Angel's family, they go question Alana next. Michelle will be the third contact they'll question.

Alana is uncooperative at first. Until the officers warn her that she could be charged with obstruction of justice and accessory after the fact. Then she tells them she knows Angel had gone to the U, earlier that morning, to visit their friend Michelle at Arthur's apartment.

"I don't know how she got there though," she lies.
The 2 officers head to the University apartments to question Michelle.

When they arrive and knock on the door, Arthur is nervous initially. He sends Michelle to answer and he sits on the couch within earshot. So he can hear what's going on before they see him. The 1st officer asks Michelle about Angel and when is the last time she'd seen her.

"She was here this morning, at about ten thirty," Michelle says, "We made her leave at eleven and we went back to bed."

"You *made* her leave. Why?" 1 officer asks.

"I don't hang with her anymore. Because she was a problem for his friends," she says as she points to Arthur, who's heading to the door now that he knows what the officers are there for.

"What kind of a problem?" the other officer asks.
She tells them Angel had threatened Ebony, so her family and friends didn't want her around anymore.

"She came here the other night with me," Michelle says, "But my
302

boyfriend told me she wasn't welcomed here. So I took her home and told her that I was no longer gonna hang out with her. Because I got love for him."

"How did she arrive here?" officer 2 asks.

"She was in her mama boyfriend's car," Michelle answers.

"Do you know if she came in contact with Ebony Brown while she was out here?" 1 officer asks.

"I don't think so. They don't get along," she says, "They was *kind of* dating the same guy."

"Ajay was *never dating* Angel. *Never,*" Arthur interrupts in an agitated tone, "She was a side piece and he broke off everything with her for good, last month. He's with Ebony, *exclusively.* One hundred percent."

"I heard that this Angel threatened harm to Ebony," the 2nd officer says, "Do you know anything of the threats, like what was said?"

"Yes," Arthur says, "She called Ebony at Ajay's apartment and told her she was gonna take her and the baby out the game. Like taking them out. You know?"

He's curious as to why they're questioning them about Ebony and Angel. He inquires and the officers tell them about the accident. Arthur excuses himself immediately and calls Chill, who's still on the phone with Ajay.

"Hold on, Ajay," Chill say as he takes the call from Arthur, "Money shot, what's up?"

"Chill, what up man?" Arthur asks.

Chill fills him in. Then Arthur tells him about this mornings occurrence with Angel.

"She was out there about the time Ebony was leaving?" Chill probes.

"Hell yea, she was," he says, "Now that I'm hearing about the accident. I think she could've been out here just to wait for her. You know what I'm saying, man? Because Michelle cut ties with her Saturday. When she took her home. She told her to stay the fuck away from her, after I told her what the bitch said to baby girl. Still she showed up here this morning. Michelle said she was driving a gray Caprice Classic, if that helps out any. Man you know I'm out here. But that's all I got, for now. But I won't stop."

"Alright, money shot," Chill says, "That's a lot crew. A whole lot. I got Ajay on the other line."

"How is Ebony?" Arthur asks.

"She's in surgery," Chill says, "Ajay's on hold. Let me get back with you later," he says and they hang up.

Arthur tells Michelle to head home. He's going to the hospital to check on
303

Ebony. She tells him she'll try to find Angel. He insist she find her before she contacts him again.

"You'd better find her before Ajay does," Arthur warns, "If she did this shit to baby girl, he's gonna *kill* her muthafuckin ass. I'll do that bitch myself before I let Ajay miss out on the NBA. I don't give a fuck about Angel and never did. But I don't want that for Ajay and Ebony. Find that bitch and turn her in."

Michelle leaves heading to Alana's, who she feels can lead her to Angel.

Ajay and company land and take a car service directly to the hospital. When he arrives, Ebony is still in surgery. Chill fills him in on the information he has gotten up until this point. Ajay is very angry but he isn't leaving the hospital. Not until he sees his girl.

"That's cool, man," Chill says, "I'll be here with you."

Another 2 hours later!

Michelle goes to Darlene's apartment and starts to bait Alana from jump.

"I think Angel did it," Alana volunteers.

"Why do you say that?" Michelle asks.

"She *said* she was gonna get her," Alana admits, "I didn't believe she would actually do anything but-"

"Girl, her muthafuckin crew is gonna fuck all of us up behind this shit," Michelle says, "Arthur is gone to the hospital, right now. You know by now they all know she was out there. How long do you think it'll take before they start looking for you and me? Alana, do you know where Angel is?"

"I think so but I didn't tell the police anything. Because I didn't wanna rat her out," she admits.

"Alana you don't need to be involved in this shit with the crew. You know how they are," her aunt Darlene Casey warns, "They'll kill our asses, just for being somebody Angel knew."

She's been listening.

"I'm not involved, auntie," Alana tries.

"Bullshit if you're not." Darlene says, "You knew she was planning it. You knew she was going after her *today*. I heard y'all talking about it, Alana. Then you didn't tell the police the truth. I'm not close to Ebony. But I wouldn't have tried to *kill her* over Ajay. What if that girl dies?"

Alana thinks about it for a minute. She still likes Tank a lot. She knows if she helps Angel, Tank will truly consider her an enemy.

304

"Alana, Tank isn't speaking to you now," Michelle says, "You know he's gonna fuck you up if he finds out you knew something about his little sister and you didn't tell him. So if you know how to find Angel, you should start with that."

Alana says she'll tell Tank what she knows. Darlene decides to drive the girls to the hospital.

At 5pm, Ebony is taken from the surgery unit and wheeled into recovery where she'll stay until she wakes up. Dr. Weston and Stansfield come out to brief the family. Weston sees Ajay and goes straight to him with her arms extended.

"Hi, Ajay. How are you, sweetheart," she gives him a hug, "How are you holding up?"

"How is she?" he asks.

"She made it through just fine," Stansfield says, "We got her left leg set in traction. We got her rib cage patched up. But like I said before the surgery, she'll be in a lot of pain for the next few days."

"What about the baby?" Jo asks.

"I'm sorry, Ajay," Weston says tearing up again "We couldn't save the baby. I think it was a little girl but she was very early in her gestation."

He puts his face in his hands and tries to fight back his tears but to no avail. He drops down to 1 knee. Rich comes to his side.

"I know how you feel, cousin. I know, man. I know," Rich says as he remembers the lose of his own baby.

Nina, Rebbie and T-baby are visibly shaken. Pearl can't hold back tears.

"Can I see her?" Pearl asks Stansfield.

"Yes but two or three at a time. Five minutes please."

Ajay regains his composure and gets to his feet. Weston pulls him, Pearl and John to the side. She needs to talk to them in private. Al and Jo go on back to see Ebony while Ajay and her parents talk with Weston.

"She had some damage to her uterus and we repaired it very well. But," Weston becomes choked up as she tries to continue, "She may have some difficulty getting pregnant and baring children."

"Oh Lord God! Please have mercy," Pearl prays as she leans against John and cries, "Please God. Don't take her ability to be a mother."

"I didn't say she couldn't. But she'll definitely need to wait awhile. When and if she becomes pregnant again, she'll need to have adequate prenatal care," Weston says, "She's anemic but we already knew that. She's got some sickle cell traits and we're going to keep an eye on her with that, as well," Dr. Weston concludes by saying to Ajay, "I'm so sorry."

He hugs her again and thanks her for all she's done.

305

"I'll be checking on her while she's in here. You know I will," says Weston.

She inquires about Destiny, CJ and Bradley III from Jr, Chill and Renee. They're still seated in the waiting room. Chill is on his phone with Kilo. They're trying to track down Angel. She's ghost but they aren't going to give up. Kilo and Arthur have contacts all over the city of Cleveland looking for Angel Taylor. Chill tells them to inform him of anything new. He's going to be at the hospital, keeping his eye on Ajay.

Ajay, Pearl and John visit Ebony together. When mama Jo comes out with Al, she's in tears. Pearl, Ajay and John stand at Ebony's bedside. Ajay becomes more angry after seeing her laying in the hospital again. Her face and head are swollen *so large* that she looks like another person. Her mid-section is bandaged and bloated. Her entire left leg is in a cast, hanging in traction. Her left arm is swollen battered and bruised. Same as most of her other visible areas. Him nor John can take it anymore. They go back out to the waiting room. Pearl stays in recovery. Nina, Rebbie and T-baby go back and can't get Pearl to come out with them when they do leave. She isn't leaving Ebony's side.

"She's not out of danger," Pearl says, "I'm not taking my eyes off of her until she is."

All the crew visit. Even coach Booker and Mr. Parkwood go back to see her. Parkwood had them to get her special room prepared while he was out in the lobby. Ajay meets David Jacobson, face to face.

"It's good to finally meet you," Jacobson says.

"I wanna thank you for answering that phone and talking to me," Ajay starts, "I was going crazy because I knew something was wrong. I talked to her while I was on the road, headed back to Cincinnati. She had just told me she was about to leave for work. She said she would call me back when she got there and got a break. But she said I had to let her know that I made it back to school. She would usually still call me as soon as she gets to work before she starts her shift. It was two hours passed noon and when she didn't call at the time she usually does, I called her. I didn't get an answer anywhere, at first. So *I* called the daycare. They didn't wanna tell me but I knew something was wrong. She keeps me informed about her whereabouts. Because she knows I'm somewhere worrying about if she's okay or if somebody's hurting her or bothering her."

"You're the person she called out for when I was pulling her from the car," Jacobson says.

"When you answered her cell phone, I thought you was a kidnapper" Ajay says as they smile briefly, "I knew something wasn't right.
306

I know what I got man. A princess. She's my baby and I love her, so much."

"She's a fighter too, man. I've got to give her that," Jacobson says, "When I first got a view of the car. I thought *there is no way* anybody survived that drop. I saw her in there but I was sure she was gone. I didn't want to have to tell you that. So when I checked for a pulse and found one, I was relieved."

"*You. Man.* You made my life when you said *she's alive, Ajay,*" he says as his eyes tell Jacobson that he had been more afraid then his words can describe. He says, "Because I wasn't breathing that whole time I was waiting for your answer. Then the phone hung up. *Man.* She's a superstar too, so Cincinnati is gonna lay out the red carpet for her."

"I know her, Ajay," Jacobson says, "I know all of you. My daughter played for Smith. Her name is Shantel. Shantel Jacobson."

"Oh yea. She's good. Didn't she sign with UC too?" he asks.

"Yes she did. And me thinking of her, is what made me move so fast when I saw that young lady in that car," Jacobson says, "I hope someone would have that same compassion if that were ever my Shanny. I called her a little while ago and told her about her future teammate. She's coming down to see her later. I told her there are already so many people here and that she should wait until all of the family visits."

"Well you and her are our family now. I want y'all to be apart of our lives, from now on," Ajay says, "And I know we'll be seeing a lot of you in the future. At the games, right?"

"All the way to the final four, I hope," Jacobson says, "Or farther." Him and Ajay finish their conversation as they go back to visit Ebony together.

As soon as they're out of sight, Darlene arrives with Alana and Michelle. Renee is just about to leave to go help Tonya close up the shop when she sees them come in.

"What do y'all want here?" she asks as she's not in the mood for any groupie type behavior.

Especially not while Ebony's life hangs in the balance. Jan is standing near Renee as is T-baby, Nina and Rebbie.

"Renee, I think my niece has some information that might be useful," Darlene says, "I wouldn't have come here, otherwise."

"Yes. What is it?" Renee asks as she looks at Alana.

Tank and the others gather around them while Alana reveals what she knows.

"I don't know for sure if she had anything to do with the accident because she had a knife when she was at my house," Alana says in 1 breath,

307

"I don't know if she caused the accident or not. I can't say, for sure."

"She who?" Renee asks.

"Angel," Alana says, "She said she was gonna stab her."

"Why didn't you say something to me," Tank asks.

"How? I can't get in touch with you. Plus she said y'all already knew she was gonna get Ebony. I just didn't think she was serious."

"With all of our businesses that you go too," Tank says, "And you didn't think to call one of them? The daycare or nothing?"

Alana is dumbfounded. Her daughter Olivia is at *Granny's house* as they speak. So she has to know that number. She didn't call and her excuse is she didn't think Angel was serious.

"Well I guess now you know she was, ha?" Nina says as she gives her an evil stare and says, "I could kick your ass, right now."

"I'm really sorry this happened-"

"Right," Tank says before he grabs Nina's hand and walks away.

Chill thanks Darlene for bringing Alana. He *tells* her she's going to take her to the precinct.

"Let me get detective Hardin for you. So you can talk to him," he says, heading to the pay phone.

Detective Hardin is the detective hand picked by the chief of police at Mr. Parkwood's request. Hardin tells Darlene to bring Alana in to see him this evening and she agrees to do so. As her and the girls are about to leave, Ajay exits recovery and spots the 3 of them heading to the elevators.

"*What*? Where's the bitch at?" he asks, approaching them swiftly.

He figures Angel's involved when he sees Alana. Chill catches his arm and quickly explains why they're there. After hearing they're here to help, Ajay says, "I still don't give a fuck. You could've called and told somebody what that bitch was up too. She took my first baby. *Fuck* you and her. Go get the bitch and bring her to me, if you want me to believe you're trying to help out." He walks away.

John comes back up to the waiting area. He's been to the scene with papa and uncle Greg. They have some more information from the investigators eye witness accounts.

"She got rear ended by a gray Caprice Classic," John says to Chill and Al, "But they haven't found the car or the driver yet."

"Damn! Angel did it," Chill says as he goes after Ajay and brings him back to hear the latest.

There's no doubt Angel had tried to kill Ebony. She did kill what would've been Ebony and Ajay's first born.

Another hour later. Ebony is still under sedation and her mother is

308

still by her side, as John comes in to tell her the latest news.

"Angel Taylor ran her off the road," he says.

"Who is Angel Taylor?" Pearl asks, "That name is familiar."

"Some girl that still likes Ajay," he says, "He had broke things off with her, a while back. She threatened to get my baby girl because of it."

"I'll bet it's the girl who tried to see him when he was in here for surgery, back in April," she offers. Then she recalls it and says, "Yes. That was her name. Me and Jo shut that down before it could ever get cleared. He didn't want her in here then, John. I remember her. *Lord.* Even when the boy tries to do the right thing, Ebony ends up half dead."

"Pearl this is not his fault," John says immediately.

"I know that, John," she says calmly, "And I don't blame him. I know he loves our baby. I know with all of my heart that she loves him too. One more thing I know to be true is. If Ajay finds this girl before the police do, he'll kill her. I don't want that to happen, John. Baby girl needs him to be out here with her. If he kills Angel Taylor, he'll go to prison for the rest of his natural life. He will lose his future and we'll loose him and our daughter, for sure. I don't want what happened today to destroy the rest of their lives. Nor any of the rest of my family. *Do not* let Ajay find this girl. Not any of them or you either. Not anytime soon. I want you and Al to talk to him and all of their crew. You fathers. Y'all have to do that, real soon. Talk to Ajay today."

"We will. We talked on it before today," he says, "We're gonna keep an eye on him because he's gonna get in some trouble behind this, if we can't keep him calm. I can't even say I don't feel like killing her, myself. But it's a safe bet to say Ajay has plans on her not living another day. The same fate she dealt to his first child."

John has a good bead on Ajay. He couldn't have been more correct.

At 11pm Ebony wakes up. She cries out. Pearl and Jo comfort her.

"Mama, what happened?" she asks as the head nurse comes in.

"Baby you was in a bad accident but you survived, sweetie. I need you to try and calm down," Pearl says as Jo rubs her face.

"You're okay, baby girl," Jo says, "Ant is out in the waiting room. I'm gonna get him for you."

The nurse takes Ebony's vitals. Then she leaves the room immediately. Jo leaves to go and get Ajay. The family feels it's better that he tells her about the lose of their baby. Ajay comes back into the recovery room.

"Hey, baby. You're finally up, ha?" he says with a smile as he tries to be brave.

309

"What day is it?" she asks.

"It's still Monday," he says.

Pearl and Jo leave. Leaving them alone in recovery. Ebony has questions. She still isn't sure of what day it is or how she got here or why.

"You came back home?" she asks.

"What do you think? You was in a car wreck," he says, "You don't think I'm suppose to come and see about you?" he asks with a smile.

"It must've been real bad," she figures but can't recall it yet.

"Yes baby. It was pretty bad," he answers, "Your car is totaled."

"My car? It is?" she asks, stunned.

"Yes."

"How?" she asks recollecting her thoughts. She says, "Oh I went off the cliff, didn't I?"

"Yes."

"I remember a car pushing me from the back," she recalls, "I hit the side rail and the airbag came out. It must've knocked me out because that's all I remember."

"You've been unconscious since noon," he says, "It's eleven o'clock at night, right now."

"Is everything okay? Is the baby okay?" she asks.

She searches his eyes for the answer. But he can't look at her. She thinks the worst.

"Why do you look so sad, Anthony. Am I paralyzed?" she asks, looking sad.

"No baby. You're leg is broken and some ribs. But-" he says as he tries to smile.

"Is the baby okay?" she asks again.

He stops smiling. Then he shakes his head negatively. She screams immediately as tears well up in his eyes. He knew this would be the hardest thing he's ever had to tell her. She's crying and screaming frantically. He can only hold her and plead with her to calm down.

"It's okay baby. It's okay," he tries.

"*Our baby's gone*?! *Anthony*?! *No!*" she screams, "*Oh God no! Why*?! *Why*?!"

She can be heard out in the waiting area which gives her family a haunting chill. Some of them start to cry too. Ajay cries harder as he tries to console her, as he holds her as best he can.

"Baby please don't do this. It's gonna be okay," he pleads, "Don't do this. *Please*. Ebony it's okay. It's okay," he says still trying to hold her.

"*Why*?!" she screams, "*Why did they take our baby, Anthony*?! *Oh God! Why?! No!*"

310

"Baby. Doctor Weston tried everything she could and *you know* she did," he says, "But it was nothing she could do. Our baby died before you got to the hospital. She couldn't save it."

She starts to grasp the situation slowly. Still she cries hard and so does he.

In the waiting area, T-baby and Rebbie are crying again and so is Renee. She has come back with Tonya after closing the salon and meeting Darlene, Alana and Michelle in detective Hardin's office. Before Ebony had screamed out, her and Tonya had made the crew aware of the information Alana and Michelle had given to Hardin.

"What the bitch have a knife for? She was gonna cut the baby out?" June asks, "Is that what they said?"

"That's what Alana said she told her," Tonya answers.

"So what did Alana have to do with it?" Rich asks, "Cause we can go on and get her ass now."

"From what we can tell," Tonya says, "She knew Angel was going to the U but she didn't go with her."

"She can die with her," Rob adds and they all cosign him.

Back in recovery, Ebony's slowing her breathing and becoming somewhat calmer.

"What was it?" she asks.

"Doctor Weston thinks it was a little girl but you was barely twelve weeks," he says, "She couldn't survive."

He's wiping the tears from her face and his. "I'm so sorry," he says as he kisses her face, over and over.

"Anthony this is not *fair*," she says.

"I know, baby girl. I know. I'm sorry, baby. I'm so sorry this happened to you. To us and our baby girl. I'm so sorry," he says, "I need for you to be alright, baby. So I can be," he says managing to calm her.

"Somebody bumped me and ran me off the road. Do they know who did it yet?"

"No they don't know. But they'll find out, okay? Or I will. You know your crew is gonna handle this like always. Right?"

He doesn't want to tell her about Angel because she doesn't need to worry about loosing her baby to Angel's threats. Not now. No way! Not when she's stuck in traction for at least another 3 weeks, knowing she has lost her 1st child. The last thing anyone wants to do is to tell her that Angel did it. He'll tell her when she's stronger, up and around. When she's out of the bed and able to move around on her own. When she's healed and the swelling is down. When he has taken care of Angel Taylor, once and for all.
311

2 weeks have passed and Ebony is getting stronger by the day. She's able to get out of bed briefly to go to the bathroom, go down the hallway and then back to her room and back in traction. Ajay has bought her the new *Bone Thugs n Harmony* CD. Jb brought her a new CD from a new group out of Atlanta named *Outkast*. She has many visitors. All of the crew and family have visited her many times. The Atlanta crew came in on the weekend following her accident. By last weekend, the 4th of July, all of the Houston crew had come too. Ron and his crew, including April and Yolanda have come and gone back by now. Big mama and poppa however, are still in town. Big mama is leaning more and more towards moving back to Cleveland. Shantel Jacobson and her daddy visited, several times. Her coaches and teammates from MLK and coach Sanders, her new coach from UC, has been in to see her, several times too. Dr. Weston still visits her daily. She receives many calls, gifts, cards and flowers from well wishers. Even coach Hightower from Smiley high in Houston and every officer involved in her rescue, have all either visited, sent flowers or both. She had been moved to her private room on the Wednesday following her accident and her girls had arranged all of her gifts in her room. Pearl sent or had taken most of her flowers home to care for them. She had too many to keep in her room and there are more arriving daily. Ajay has brought her flowers for every day she's been in the hospital. Today is his 20th birthday. She wants to go home but he assures her, he'll be at the hospital with her. She feels he wants to celebrate turning twenty. Or at least she thinks he would prefer to party and bullshit. Rather then sit at the hospital. She suggests he have a party. He quickly dismisses the thought saying,

"It's not gonna be much of a celebration for me, if you can't come, baby."
She doesn't bother him with her party thoughts anymore after that.
"We can celebrate it when you get out of here," he says.

"Happy birthday, baby," she says.

Now 3 weeks after her accident and she still doesn't have a clue that Angel had caused it. The bandages are removed from her mid-section today. She's progressing at record speed. Her ribcage has healed properly. The cast on her leg has to stay on a few more weeks. She's just eager to be discharged. Her and Ajay have already decided she's going back to Cincinnati with him. And though they hadn't waited for their parents opinions, their parents agree with them on this one. Al and John give their opinion on it. Pearl and Jo agrees with them all.

"I'd rather she go with Ajay, Al," John says, "I know he'll guard

312

her like I would, if I could be here. And I need him to be in Cincinnati."

"As long as he's able to see her and know she's not in harms way," Al says, "Then he'll be able to get his training time in and keep his schedule down there. He has to be ready to compete in the preseason."

"I want him to be ready to play, so that's a bet," John says, "He's going high in the draft when he declares. I just don't have a guess yet on *how high* in draft he'll go. But he'll go high, for sure. By the time he's a senior or whenever he declares. But he won't if he stays round here and catch up to that-" John shivers and shakes his head unable to finish his thought.

"As long as he's in Cincinnati," Al says, "He can't be here killing that lil bitch. I finished it for you."

Him and John aren't off of the idea of doing it themselves. They would do it in a heartbeat to save Ajay and Ebony's future. They're not the only ones in that line either.

Ebony is finally released from the hospital on July 25th. Ajay is there to drive her home.

"Today would've been our eighth day anniversary and our next appointment for the baby," she says to him.

Nina calls to tell her that her and Tank are going to the doctor and they'll hook up with them later. Ajay is staying in town for the July celebration. Then Ebony is going back to Cincinnati with him and the guys. Al and the fathers are attending the celebration and any other event Ajay attends while in Cleveland. John is back on the road and he left strict orders, not to allow Ajay to find Angel anytime soon. The celebration is going to feature some hometown stars and the fathers feel certain that Angel will show up.

The celebration does go on but not until the 30th. Ebony attends with cast and all. Their hometown group *Bone Thugs N Harmony* performs at *The Chill Spot,* for the celebration. Surely, everyone who is anyone is there. Ebony was never going to miss seeing them perform live, that's for sure. She has loved Bone since the days of their talent shows. When the foursome would always loose to them. She knew they would blow-up and they sure have. Their EP, *Creepin' On Ah Come Up* is flying off the shelves. Rob has a moms and pops record store set up inside of the detail shop. He can't keep their CD's or tapes in stock. The club is booked solid. The Bone brothers had promised Chill they would come back home and do a show for him when they got on. They kept their word. Tonight is standing room only. Everybody's here. People have come from neighboring towns to see *Bone Thugs n Harmony*. All of the crew's friends and even some of their foes are in attendance. All that is except one.

313

Angel still hasn't surfaced but the police did find Tony's car. It was found banged up and abandoned in Pittsburgh and looking like it had been in a accident. There was cobalt blue paint on it, as well. The perfect match to Ebony's Accord. Ajay hears the new information and he's still trying to figure out where he can find her.

Where is she? Is she in Pittsburgh too? If so, who is she staying with?

What he doesn't know is detective Hardin is on the case. He has reviewed all of the evidence and statements they've gathered, thus far. He has paid very close attention to Angel's contacts here in Cleveland. All of her family and friends. Her family has no apparent ties in Pittsburgh. He was almost at a dead end but not for long. He knows Alana is a friend of Angel's. The closest friend she has in Cleveland. He has also found out that Alana and Darlene have family in Pittsburgh. He knows Darlene is sweet on Ajay as well. So she wouldn't be helping Angel out. Alana is sweet on Tank but who are her loyalties too? She had come in and offered testimony against Angel and is the best witness he has, too date. But was she completely forthcoming? This is his line of thinking. He's had all of Alana's known family watched for 2 straight weeks. They saw no signs of Angel. However, he's good at what he does. He'll work every angle to get a lead. But will Angel get away or will he bring her in? Can he get to her before Ajay and his crew do? That is the question and only time will reveal the answer.

The crew have their August celebration and going-away party for the college bunch. This fall there are 13 crew members attending college. Tonya is going to grad school at CSU. Lynn and Jb start their senior year at Tech where Breanna is a sophomore. Ajay and Jan are juniors at UC. Tank, June and Rich are sophomores and the foursome are freshman in college. They love that the alumni in Cincinnati have really laid it out for Ajay and them. The 9 Cincinnati crew are sharing a huge 7 bedroom mansion, *quiet as kept* and their receipts will show it's being paid for by *CrewLand Enterprises*, their family umbrella.

Ebony has her 6-week follow up with Dr. Weston, this morning. She'll have her cast removed in another 2 weeks. Her and Ajay go to the appointment together. They talk more about the likelihood of them ever conceiving another baby. Ebony talked with her about it many times while she was still in the hospital. Dr. Weston gives her and Ajay the same advice today.

"The longer you wait, the better your chances will be of carrying

314

to full term," Weston says, "It wouldn't be wise to try again *too* soon."

"I know but how long should we wait?" she asks.

She wants a baby now more than ever. Ajay hasn't talked about his feelings on the subject, much. He knows Ebony aches to be pregnant again but he wants her to take the pills. The ones Dr. Weston had prescribed for her while she was in the hospital. Some days he had to put them in her mouth and make her swallow them. He ask Weston to help him out.

"Ebony, I think you should wait at least a year, sweetheart," Dr. Weston advises, "Now that's my professional opinion. I don't think it's a good idea for you guys to try anytime soon. You know I wouldn't steer you wrong, don't you? Ajay was the very first baby I delivered, in my private practice. So I've been looking forward to the day that I deliver his first child. That will be full circle for me. I have a vested interest in your family, as a whole, sweetheart. I am going to see you two through this. I promise you. I will tell you as soon as I think it's safe to try again. But not *anytime* soon. I just don't believe the embryo could survive a month."

Ebony is disappointed with this advice but Ajay is fine with it. He'll talk with Ebony about it more than a few times in the coming months. She isn't going to give up on having their baby. Not after she had come so close. Plus prepared her mind for it and for a shotgun wedding. And they had their parents approvals, on top of that. She's not going to give up.

Lynn and Bre joined the ROTC programs at Tech when they entered as freshmen. They're planning a career in the military when they finish school. But before she left for Tech this fall, Bre and CJ had gone out to the California State penitentiary to visit Stoney's father. He was very pleased to meet his granddaughter. He wasn't even aware that his son had been killed. He apologized to Bre for not keeping in touch with Stoney. She told him she would like for CJ to know him and he promised CJ that he wouldn't loose touch with her.

CHAPTER 22

THE TRIALS OF AJAY

By early September, the foursome are settled into their college agendas and practices. It's past the Labor day weekend. Ebony had her cast removed 2 weeks ago. She's into her preseason practice schedule and weight training.

One evening, the foursome and Jan are sitting around the house in *Natty* talking and reminiscing about their lives. Nina and Tank have gotten engaged but have decided to wait until after their daughter's birth to get married. John nor Al like this plan but it's their decision. They're going home for a doctor's appointment, this coming Friday. Surely they'll have to hear another discussion or 2 about it. But Nina isn't open to getting married while she's pregnant and she isn't going to back down. She's totally focused on their daughter's birth.

"I'm going *every week* now," she says, "Today was my original due date."

"I miss being pregnant," Ebony says.

"Me too," T-baby adds, "You know my baby would've been born by now. If,… you know," she stops talking when she notice Ebony's sad expression.

"I want this little girl to be *all* of ours," Nina says.

"She's *going to be* all of ours," Rebbie says and Jan agrees.

"She's gonna be here with us, everyday," Jan says.

"We're all gonna have to help raise her," Ebony adds.

"We can't do this without all of your help either," Nina admits.

"You know we got your back, cousin," Rebbie says as she smiles.

"I know y'all do," Nina says and they all laugh.

It feels good to be able to talk about babies without crying for a change.

Ebony never thought she would be able to accept not having her baby inside of her. But as the days, weeks and now months roll by, it's becoming a little easier to handle. Besides, she has to be supportive of *twin*, Nina and her little niece who's due in a few weeks.

Early Friday morning, Nina and Tank leave for Cleveland. They have a 4pm appointment with Dr. Weston.

Rebbie has an appointment with her counselor at 10am. In the meeting, she finds out she's been accepted into the School of Performing Arts. She is ecstatic. She's always dreamed of mixing her love for dance with acting and singing. It's definitely possible now. She hurries back to the house to call her mother at *Crews House of Soul Food*.

"Alright, baby! This is so *wonderful*!" Rena yells, "I'm so happy and I'm so proud of you!"

Her and Rebbie talk for more than an hour before they hang up. Then Rena shares the news with all of the crew at the mall. They're going to include Rebbie's accomplishments in the September celebration.

"An actress," Archie Sr says after hearing his daughter's news.

"Or maybe Broadway," her grandma Annabelle offers.

They're all happy for Rebbie and very proud.

Michelle is working her *own* plan. Her and Alana go visit Tameka in prison the following Thursday and tell her what Angel had done to Ebony and Ajay.

Tameka isn't able to handle doing time. She's been beaten up a few times. The rumor is, the crew put a hit out on her. No one has admitted too or taken credit for such a hit. But the crew are very deep, all over. Not only on the streets. They have loyalty in the penitentiary also. From guys and girls as old as papa and granny, who are still locked up from the days of *the Black Panthers, the San Francisco 8, The Angola 3* and the whole *Black Power Movement.* They're still loyal to the crew. The 1st crew had created a strong hold in Cleveland, from the start. Each of it's generations just got stronger. Each new generation continues to look back to the first one for wisdom. The present crew, with Chill at the helm, may not live within the law, all the time. But no matter what they do, right or wrong, their elders support them and get them passed it by showing them the best way. That's the strength of family. The older generation has never sugar coated anything with the next one. They started out honest and always will be honest about what they endured. And the struggles they had to surpass to get to where they are now. They didn't allow either crew to falter when it came to upholding the family honor either. That was 1st and foremost. For *either* crew. The Matrons and Matriarchs passed the history on. They told their offspring about the days when they broke laws. Only in their day, the laws were unjust. Those were *Jim Crow Laws.* When breaking the law was something as simple as sitting down at the front of the bus. Or trying to use the public restroom on a road trip. Or going into a diner to order lunch. They told their offspring about their loyal comrades who will live out their
317

lives in the penitentiary. But they've never forgotten them or lost touch. So for Tameka to go into a Cleveland facility, after having done harm to a member of the crew, it was unspoken but known that she would have some jailhouse justice to endure. It's often times worse than street justice. Those brothers and sisters who are doing time from the Jim Crow era, the elders call prisoners of war or the exiled. Like Rebbie's maternal grandparents. Many of them went to jail for the same things the 1st generation had to do to make it to Cleveland. *Teaching their offspring how to get their own.* Jackson-Jones Revue use to travel the *Chitterling circuit.* There are many stories of them being chased out of towns by angry mobs of white men, just for being outside at night. The groups were called lynch mobs. Groups of klansmen who's only reason for being infuriated with them was the color of their skin. Bigotry and racism was a fixture during their growing years. From the 1930's to the 1960's, which was still the segregated era. That was only one of the things *Dr. Martin Luther King Jr* marched and fought to overturn. He encouraged all good Americans to stand and speak out against those unjust laws which forced Black people to be 2nd class citizens. This generation of crew use to find it hard to believe that granny and big mama wasn't able to eat wherever they wanted to eat. But the Matriarchs gave them a little more history each and every time they questioned their past.

"*This is why we had to learn to cook at a young age and why we always cooked big meals,*" big mama had explained, "*We had to take plenty of food on the road. We packed lunches with enough food to last for days. Because we wasn't gonna be able to get a meal along the route.*"

"*Not until we got to the town where we was performing,*" granny had said, "*And they always had a spread of food. That's where Sunday meeting came from. We all, as Black folks, had to be family. We had to stick together and take care of the other. That's lost on today's black people.*"

"*That's right. We all had to count on each other,*" grandma Sally had said, "*And now blacks don't even speak to each other.*"

"*We had a system where we communicated,*" grandma Annabelle added, "*All along that circuit they knew who was coming down the line.*"

"*And they looked out for us,*" papa had said, "*They put us up for the night and everything.*"

"*We traveled in large groups too,*" poppa had said.

"*We told our kids, your parents, those stories. Thinking we was protecting them. But they heard those stories and it angered them,*" grandpa Joshua had said.

"*They rebelled hard. They was determined that if a bigot put his hands on them,*" grandpa Charles had said, "*They was gonna kill him.*"

318

Ultimately, the priority for the past generation of crew was to see to it that the next crew was successful in life. That was their only goal. They give Chill and his crew the space to find their own way. But the parents and grandparents are always paying attention. Even if it seems like they aren't. So whether or not someone had sent a kite down the line to do Tameka harm, wasn't even necessary. Just the other inmates knowing she had violated crew, left them with the feeling of *"protecting the family."* Just like they had done it back in the days.

Michelle is on a mission today. Her and Alana finish their visit with Tameka. Before they leave, they put some money on the book for her. They leave the prison and hit the highway, heading back to Cleveland and talking along the way. Michelle know Alana's time with her is short. So she's going to see what she can do to help Arthur, before she ends it with Alana. The same way she cut Angel off. They talk on how rough Tameka is having it. They talk about Angel and what she may be doing. All of sudden, Alana breaks and asks, "Do you *wanna see?*"

"What do you mean do I *wanna see?*" Michelle asks.

"Just like I asked. *Do you wanna see?*" Alana asks again, as she flashes her a devilish smile.

"Yes," Michelle answers, thinking she's playing a trick and trying to bluff her but the next comment makes it all too serious.

"Then take that next exit. I got the gas," Alana says as she instructs Michelle to take the Pittsburgh exit.

She does so, reluctantly. Still thinking Alana just wants to use her to go and visit her folks, like she has a reputation for doing. That's where her 4 year-old daughter Olivia lives, full time. Now that crew won't allow her in their daycare. Michelle thinks maybe Alana is feeling maternal for a change.

Ebony and T-baby are in the sports arena playing pick up games with other players and students. Ajay and some of his teammates come in to watch them. Ebony is acting as if she wants to favor her leg, too much. Ajay stops the game and speaks to her on the sideline.

"What's going on?" he asks.

"My leg feels funny," she lies.

"Does it really?" he asks, knowing she's lying. She smiles. "Is it *really*, baby girl?" he asks again.

She can't stand on a lie. Not with him. She never could. He know she's still playing it up for sympathy and he isn't going to allow her to do that. He wants her to be strong and play strong, at all times.

"If you don't feel like playing today. Sit down," he says, "But don't half ass
319

play. That's not even in you, baby. We're winners and we go hard."

"I know. It bugs me that you know me so well," she says as she laughs, "The rest of them was falling for it."

"Play ball or sit down," he says, "You have two options."

"I don't yield the court unless I lose," she says, "And I don't lose."

"Well play some damn ball, then," he says and he isn't smiling.

She excuses him from the court, laughs and goes back to finish the game. She turns it up as he sits courtside. He cheers her and T-baby on. They win their 3 on 3 games by overwhelming margins. Until they're done playing for the day.

"I wish you would've came in, five games ago," T-baby says to Ajay, "I wouldn't have had to play so hard."

They laugh as they head for the mansion.

Michelle and Alana arrive in Pittsburgh. They don't go to Alana's grandparents house. Instead, they go to her stepbrothers apartment. No one knows this guy as Alana's stepbrother. He's the son of a man her mother had dated when Alana was little but they never married. This is probably the reason Hardin hasn't sniffed him out yet too. At this apartment, Alana uses her own key to open the door. They go inside and there's Angel, sitting on the sofa watching *Jerry Springer*. Michelle feels shock and betrayal, all at the same time. Alana has known where Angel was all of this time. Michelle doesn't like this situation she's in. Not one bit. But she's going to play the game. At the same time, she's going to beat Alana at it. She knows Alana and Angel are secretly jealous that she has a real relationship with Arthur. Plus the crew hasn't held any grudges against her because she has proven to be someone who can be respected. But Angel and Alana don't get that part. They don't know that she's aware of how they schemed and plotted against her and tried to get her in trouble with Arthur either. But Arthur had told her what they was up too and swore her to secrecy. She passed his test and they've been cool every since. Today, Alana has played another dangerous game of trying to make her apart of helping to hide a damn fugitive from justice. Michelle has no desire to share a cell with *what's left of* Tameka. Nor either one of these two. She's going to show them she's better at playing the damn game. *The loyalty game,* that is.

"Angel! What's up, girl?!" Michelle plays it, giving her a hug.

"Nothing much," Angel says, "I'm sick o' hiding out. This shit is for the birds."

"Are you okay? How are you surviving?" Michelle asks.

"My girl's been looking out on me," she says referring to Alana.

320

Alana receives benefits from the state. She gets them for her daughter, through her grandmother. She's sharing the benefits with Angel and her stepbrother. Food stamps, Aid to Dependent Children and even money she gets when she sleeps with men. Whatever she can do to come up on some cash, she has been doing it while helping Angel stay hid. Michelle doesn't approve of what Alana is doing. Further, she knows she isn't going to be a part of it. She's vying for the title of Mrs. Money Shot. Something she know these 2 wouldn't be able to stand. She's going to fool Angel into believing she has missed her. It's already working. Michelle could care less about anyone who would try and make her an enemy of Arthur's or the crew. But for now, she has to play the game. She doesn't want to alert either of them but she isn't willing to keep this a secret. She's going to tell Arthur as soon as she gets back to Cleveland. They visit with Angel for 4 hours. Alana only visits her daughter for 1 hour.

After 5 hours in Pittsburgh, they're back on the road to Cleveland. Michelle feels like she's been in the twilight zone. She tries to make Alana feel bad for not letting her help with Angel's needs. She plays it cool.

When they get back to Cleveland, Michelle gives Alana $50.00 to send to Angel, the next time. This way she knows Alana will send money at least once more. Michelle is hoping this will be long enough to keep Angel in place so she can help Arthur and the crew get that trace on her. And if possible, catch Alana up at the same time. Michelle is more loyal to Arthur than anyone could've known. She drops Alana off and goes directly to the U to see her man.

Michelle lets Arthur know what happened in Pittsburgh. Arthur gets on the phone and calls Chill immediately.

"Money shot. What it do?" Chill answers, knowing Arthur is always calling with new info on something the crew is passionate about.

"What up gee?" Arthur asks.

"Chilling with my lil family."

"Who's hangin' wit ya?" Arthur asks.

"I got Bruce, Reaper, Greg, Jesse, Jr, Rob and Sam. What's up?"

"Y'all down to ride?"

"What's up?" Chill asks again.

"I know where your girl at," he says.

"*Angel*?" Chill asks, turning down his stereo and sitting up.

"Yep."

"Talk to me, bro," Chills says, feeling excitement for the 1st time in weeks.

Arthur gives him the information he got from Michelle. Chill tells him to

321

give him a little time to come up with a plan. A *sure fire* plan. They hang up and within minutes, Chill has a plan. He calls the house in Natty.

"Hello?" Nina answers.

"What up, sis?" Chill asks.

"Hey big Chill. What's going on?" she asks.

"I need a favor from you," he says.

"You got it."

"I need Tank to ride with me," he says.

"Okay. On what and do I get to come too?" she asks.

"No, baby. You can't ride right now and you know it," he says and laughs.

"Alright," she says and laughs too. "So what's the deal?"

He tells her the plan. She doesn't like the contact Tank has to make but she's willing to overlook it for the crew. She says okay. Nowadays, she trust Tank completely. She gives him the phone and lays back down next to him.

Chill tells Tank the plan. He doesn't like the contact either but he's down to ride with Chill for Ajay and twin. Tank and Ebony always tell people they're twins, only because they're 11 months apart and are the same age for 1 month out of the year. He reminds Chill that him and Nina have to be in Cleveland, every Friday now, for doctor's appointments. They can kick it into overdrive on their next visit.

This Friday, all of the crew are coming home. The September celebration is this Saturday, the 17th.

Tonya had made 23 on the 13th, Bre made 20 on the 9th. Shannon, known as Reaper, will be 15 on the 24th. Brad III has turned three and his birthday party will be at *Granny's House*.

The celebration is great as usual. This time when Michelle and Alana show up, they're actually invited. Tank asked Alana to come via a phone call from Cincinnati, on Thursday night.

"You *want me to come*?" she had asked in disbelief.

"Yea, girl. You didn't hear me or something? I just said meet me at the spot," was his response to her.

He was playing the game. She was just excited to hear from Tank, after so long. When she arrives at the celebration, she's hesitant to approach him. So him and Chill step to her. Tank plays the role, telling her he wants her to meet him at Arthur's. She is to leave the club with Michelle and meet him there. Nina leaves early and goes to Ajay's apartment with her girls. 3 of the foursome are in on the plan. Ebony still doesn't know about it and Ajay has to fill her in. But before he gets around to it, she overhears him talking

322

to Chill about Angel and where she is, when they're still at the club. She had gotten angry with him, for even mentioning Angel's name. She left the club without him. When he does make it to his apartment, she's in the their bedroom ready to confront him.

"Why was Tank talking to Alana and why are you worried about where *Angel* is?" she asks.

"Angel ran you off the road," he says without taking a breath.

She's stunned, angry and upset, all at the same time. She can't even form her words. She doesn't know where to start. But when she's able to speak coherently, she has plenty of questions.

"What did you just say to me? I know you didn't just tell me that Angel killed my baby. *Our baby.* You *knew* that?"

"Yea. I found out when you was in recovery," he admits, "I didn't tell you then because I didn't want you to worry. No one knew where she was, at that time. Baby, she did this because she knew it was over. It's been over since I gave you the ring and my word," he says, "That's why she slapped me. That's why she threatened you and that's why she caused you to have the accident. Because she knew it was over. I've been living in a silent hell for all of these months because I want her dead. And now I know where she is and I'm going to get her. I'm gonna end this shit, once and for all. I want that ho's skull as a trophy, like *Predator*."

She's still upset. However, she understands his reasoning. That would've set her off. And it probably would've affected her recovery as well as their relationship. For sure it would have. For her to know she had lost their baby at the hands of her man's ex whore, who had threatened to do *that harm*. If she had been told that Angel did it and at the same time, have to deal with the lost of her baby, it would've been massive and very damaging.

"Anthony I'm upset that you kept this from me. But thinking about it now, I understand why you didn't tell me *then*," she says, "But it's been almost *three months*."

"I know. But I wanted her to be caught *first*," he tries, "At least then, you would have the satisfaction of knowing she didn't get away with it. That is what's been tearing me up inside. I had no idea where to find her. Sit down. I'll tell you everything. Including the plan to bring her to justice. Or hell, one."

He tells her the story as he knows it. She recalls on her memory of that morning. She remembers the gray car following close to her.

"She was at the U when I left for work?" she asks.

"Yes," he says, "And you was suppose to be looking out for stuff like that and you wasn't suppose to be alone. We've been on your girls case

323

every since, for that. While trying not to alert you, at the same time. She was serious about her plan to hurt you."

"I want her dealt with Anthony. I want her out of my life, for good," she says, "And I don't care how she goes. She took our *babies life*. She was *trying* to take mine."

"Yea and when I catch her ass," he says, "I plan to take hers." With that comment, she know she has to change his mind immediately. *I'm not losing my man to the prison system for that worthless bitch!*

She know he's sincere enough to do just that but she doesn't want *him* too.

"Ajay-"

"You don't call me Ajay, baby girl," he insists.

She sighs heavy and says, "Anthony, baby you can't do it. Period. No." she tells him, "They're gonna know you did. You'll go to jail."

"Well-"

"No. Not well," she says, "I don't want anybody from the crew to mess with her. If anything happens to her, right now. They're gonna think it was us. *Automatically*."

"Baby I can't just let her pass when she killed my baby," he says.

"Do you wanna sentence me to living the rest of my life out here," she says, "Waiting on visiting day, so I can see you?"

"No. No I don't."

"That's what it would be like, if you kill her," she says, "You're not gonna do any such thing, as big mama would say. You're gonna make sure *she* goes to prison. That's what I want to happen. Okay?"

"Okay, baby," he says, "All I want is for you to be satisfied with wherever the outcome is."

"So do you know where she is now?" she asks, secretly thinking about doing it herself.

"Yea. And get this. She's in Pittsburgh. Staying with Darlene's folks. Alana's stepbrother," he says, "Those ho's knew where she was, from day one. And no baby, you can't do her either. If I can't. You can't."

"Yea okay."

"I'm serious, Ebony," he says, "I don't want that sentence either."

"Okay but didn't you tell me they came to the hospital?"

"Oh yea. I wanted to fuck them up, then," he says "But they was acting like they was there to give us some information and shit. Chill was holding me back because when I saw them. I saw blood."

"I got it now. So that's why Tank was talking to Alana?" she asks.

"Yep," he says, "We're gonna get her, *ourselves*."

324

"And Nina knows about this?"

"Yea. She knew before Tank did."

She's still angry and she wants revenge. But she certainly doesn't want Ajay to cross paths with Angel. That would definitely not end well.

"So what's the plan?" she ask and he fills her in.

"And Nina is *alright* with this?" she asks in disbelief.

"Yep. I'm telling you. Chill told her first. On the phone."

"I don't know none of y'all, anymore ha?" she ask as she laughs.

"Baby, Nina agreed to do this for you and me," he starts, "She knows Tank's not interested in that bitch. Or nobody else but her. Just like I am with you. He's just putting in work for the crew. It's the same shit y'all was doing with them bitch niggaz that use to live out here. Remember?"

She remembers the plan her and her girls had to follow when Chill and Renee was shot by Tim's crew. Even though she's tried to forget it.

"Okay," she says, "I get it. So what is he doing with her tonight?"

"Setting the trap. He's got to get her to trust him again."

She understands but still she has a terrible feeling about this whole plan. She knows Anthony's emotions. How he puts it all in for whatever *he perceives* as justice.

"Baby, you know you already have court on the twenty sixth for the fight with Tim," she says.

"I know and I'll beat it."

"But you don't want another charge on you-"

"I'm not worried about that, right now, baby," he says, "I'll be careful. That's all I can promise you. But I'm gonna get the bitch who killed my first born. And nearly killed the love of my life. That's all I see."

For him, the subject is closed. The plan is already unfolding. Ebony couldn't stop it now, even if she really wanted too. But she doesn't. Nor does she want to lose her man or her family, in the process.

"Baby, promise me you won't go to prison," she pleads as her eyes well up with tears.

He thinks about it as he looks into her eyes. Eyes that already have tears in the wells because she knows the extent he'll go to, to protect her, their love and their relationship. He can see in her eyes how afraid she is for him. Not for Angel, Alana, Darlene or Michelle. She's afraid for Ajay and what he's capable of doing if he lays eyes on Angel.

"I'll go to hell before I go to jail," he says. *"Case closed."*

Tank won't have sex with Alana. He can't act that well. However, he does let her perform lip service on him. That isn't a part of the plan

325

either but he's seeking a little revenge of his own. There's no way he can forget the trouble she caused him in his relationship with Nina. Simply because she wouldn't keep her mouth shut. She couldn't accept the position she was given in his life. A piece of ass. Plain and simple. In his defense, Tank had told Alana then that he wasn't single. But she wanted to woe him with her dick sucking ability. She was so confident in her ability that she had guaranteed him she could make him leave his girl for her. When he didn't, she played foul. Tonight, she thinks he's single. He tells her that him and Nina have broken up. Only because this is a part of the crews elaborate plan to catch Angel. Still tonight, she begs to show him her skills. So he allows her too perform oral sex on him. He chokes her repeatedly with his dick. In his mind, the entire time, he's thinking of how much he despises this bitch. And how he would really like to bash the top of her head in. Until nothing's left but her neck bone. She is none the wiser.

Michelle is down with Arthur. Arthur is down for the crew. So her actions in this situation, just might prove to the crew that she isn't as shady as they once thought. She's about to get their respect. For Michelle, that's something she has wanted since day one. She might have the crew's respect. But not their trust. Never that. Or at least, not yet. Time will reveal if that ever happens.

The UC crew head back to Cincinnati on Sunday night. Ebony is still nervous about the plan. But she's more focused on her man's upcoming court date. He has to be back in Cleveland next Monday for court on the assault charge filed by Tim. His court date is the 26 of September. Ebony is nervous about how the trial might go. Ajay isn't on paper. Nor does he have any other charges against him. She still doesn't trust the system. Not when it comes down to justice for her man, her or her crew. They all feel like Tim's assault charge is bullshit. She feels like he only pressed charges on Ajay because Ajay had beat his ass. Ajay figures something totally different. Tim is a snitch! He's helping the police do exactly what they've been wanting to do for some time. Get a charge against the crew that will stick. Ajay even knows more about why Tim and his crew sought out their girls at the mall that day. In his experience with the justice system, he has known them to do just about anything and use any approach to get to whatever their ultimate prize is. It wouldn't surprise him if they had told Tim to go after Ebony because they know from her letters and visits to him in state school, that he was sweet on her. But he knows it's more than that.

As they all sit around the crew house in Natty, Ebony watches how

326

the other couples vibe and compare them to her and Ajay. She tells him, she thinks the 2 of them have grown a lot more than the other couples.

"They still argue over petty things," she says, "They have more confrontations than we do."

"It's always been like that to me," he says, "You know daddy don't play that talking back."

The both chuckle. He was being silly but he agrees with her on her point. Their relationship has become the example instead of the problem. They're looking toward their future together and hoping their best friends will get there too.

In Cleveland, the next generation of the crew are in full effect. They are running MLK high school. 16 year-old Bruce is the most popular junior or person on campus, for that matter. Much like his older brother Jr had been. He is an all-star football player and has many girls after him. Kim is constantly getting into fights, just like Tonya had done during her tenure at MLK. Kim is the only girl from the crew, at the high school, this year. When she fights more than 1 girl, Bruce plus Reaper, who is in 9th grade, have to help her. The 3 of them have already been suspended from school and this is only the 2nd week. They roll thick and just like the crews before them, they have *Juice*. Most of the students at MLK like them and want to be down. With every new generation of crew, comes new challenges and new situations. With Bruce's crew getting older, even the tone of the crew celebration parties have started to change. There is a lot more wilding out and a lot more envy too. Bruce is the subject of hate for he is crew and a star player. But Chill thinks Bruce's crew is too flamboyant. Too reckless. He talks with all of them about being so flashy.

"It's all good that you got money players. But don't flaunt it," he says, "Y'all like the flashy jewelry and designer clothes. That brings heat."

He tells them to pull back on all of that because that brings too much attention to the crew. Bruce had already given the Sentra he'd gotten from his sister-in-law Tonya, to his girlfriend Kim. Though she isn't allowed to drive it yet. He had gotten himself a Cutlass for his 16th birthday. It's similar to Jr's but his is a 1992 with a soft top. The next generation works at the businesses with the rest of the crew, so Bruce makes legal money. Chill refused to put them up on the other game because they already think *the show off game* is where it's at. And it's because of their flashy ways which already attracts too much attention, that Chill won't include them in street business. He's right and very smart not too.

Reaper's a football player and quite good. But he's more into music

327

and spends a lot of time with Rob at the studio and record store. He also wears a lot of flashy jewelry and *dope boy gear*. The record store which is still located within the detail shop at *The CrewLand mall* hasn't been officially named as another crew business but it will be in the near future. Reaper has 8 songs recorded. Rob is in the process of getting his 1st single edited for the radio. Reaper's dream is to get signed to *Bone Thugs* new label, *Mo Thug records*. The crew supports his dream. He's always performing at *The Spot* and in talent shows around Cleveland.

Kim is a sophomore basketball captain and football cheerleader captain.

Brittany is a track star for the 8 grade and she loves to sing. Greg Jr plays on the 8th grade football team. Jesse is a football player and good in track like Tank. Sam Jr is on the track team with him. Erica is in 8th grade also. She's following in Nina's footsteps as a cheerleader. The 8th graders now are going to be the biggest class of crew graduates ever but not until 1999. There will be 5 of them. The family call them *the 99 crew*.

Pam and Ruthie are both on the track team for the 7th grade. Pam is following in Lynn's footsteps. She's fast on the track already. Steven, Chaundra and Ally are 6 graders. Ally cheers like her big sister Rebbie. Chaundra favors track and field while Steven plays football and basketball.

Kenny or Lil Chill is in 5th grade. He wants to play football and run track so Chill works with him daily to get him ready. Charlotte, Stoney's youngest sister is in 4th grade. She wants to be a cheerleader.

Archie Jr, Rebbie's baby brother is only in 3rd grade but he loves basketball and wants to be like his mentor and crew cousin Ajay. June's youngest siblings, the James twins Brina and Brandon, are in 2nd grade. Brina wants to be a basketball player like her cousin Ebony while Brandon likes track and basketball. This is the next generation of the crew. Eighteen strong just like the generation before them. The crew will go on forever it seems. But for now Erica is the youngest member of the active crew and Ruthie or Roo, Rich's only sister, will be 13 in December. They have already started to form relationships like their older siblings. Bruce and Kim are a couple and so are Reaper and Brittany. Greg Jr and Erica like each other as do Jesse and Ruthie who still isn't ready for crew parties. Sam Jr like Pam and she likes him too. Even Ally and Steven have plans of being a couple. They can't wait until they get crewed up.

It's Monday September 26 and Ajay has Court. He's acquitted on the charge of assault against Tim. The judge rules this way for him because as the judge stated, *"He was shot during the altercation and he didn't fire a weapon."*

328

The judge does however slap him with a fine for reckless endangerment for all of the gunfire that was let off that day. Ajay pays his fine and goes back to college. He has the support of a lot of prominent people in Ohio because of his ability to play basketball. The UC alumni are with him at every turn. Pulling strings, calling in favors and funding certain projects. Ajay has it made right now. He needs to be smart and use his head and not do anything stupid. However with Angel on the lamb and him knowing where she is, it's only a matter of time before he'll need another string pulled. That becomes more evident to the crew now that the court date is behind him. Chill knows they need to get some reciprocity for him before he heads off on his own. They can put their plan against Alana and Angel into action now that his court docket is clear. They will execute this weekend.

Friday September 30 Phase 1 of the plan!

It's time for some action. The crew have been feigning for a chance to get at Angel while getting Alana caught up in the process. Ebony is going with Nina to her doctors appointment today instead of Tank which is also a part of the plan. However what isn't part of the plan is Nina not returning to Cincinnati. Those are Dr Weston's orders. Nina is 2 days past her due date and Dr Weston has ordered her to stay in Cleveland until after the baby is born. Tank is more nervous then ever but he still has to go along with the plan.

"Nina boo, baby you better not go in labor while I'm gone to Pittsburgh," he say as he smiles, "Or you're gonna blow the whole thing." Him and Alana have a double date tonight with Arthur and Michelle. All of the crew are in on the plan by now. Alana and Tank have been in constant contact since the celebration 2 weeks ago. Alana has bitten hook, line and sinker on the crew's bait. She truly believes Tank and Nina are split up and why wouldn't she? She has been to Chill's house. She had even kicked it with the crew last weekend at the club and no one had threatened her nor had they come after her on Nina's behalf. Not even Nina herself, so why wouldn't she believe she's all in?

Arthur drives his 1990 Riviera to pick up Michelle and Alana. They meet Tank at Ajay's apartment. Ajay is there with Ebony. Alana is nervous when she sees Ebony initially but Ebony is cordial to her. She smiles as Alana walks in the door and that is something Alana is definitely never had the benefit of.

"Hi Alana," Ebony says.

329

"Hi Ebony," Alana says.

"I guess we're gonna have to learn to get along, ha?" Ebony says.

"I never had anything against y'all," Alana tries, "I just like your brother, is all."

Ebony smiles again before she goes back into the kitchen. She frowns and kicks the refrigerator. She's having a hard time playing *this* game. Ajay comes into the kitchen to check on her. He comes up from behind her and puts his arms around her waist. He kisses the back of her neck.

"Are you gonna make it?" he whispers with a chuckle.

"I don't know," she says, "I just wanna bash her head in."

"Maybe later," he says and they both laugh.

He places his chin on her left shoulder and continues the hug her from behind. Alana walks into the kitchen and startles them.

"I'm sorry. Can I have something to drink?" Alana asks.

"Yea, you can. You can go back and sit down," Ajay says, "She'll bring you a coke or something."

"Okay. A coke is fine," Alana says as she heads back to the living room, already taking her new found *freedom* for granted.

Ebony pushes Ajay away from her and says, "Baby, I can't do this."

"Do it for my baby, then. Okay?" he asks, almost pleading, "I need to get that bitch back here and Alana's the glue."

"You'd better stay out *here,* for me too," she says, "And not only for our lost baby. But for our future babies too. You got me?"

"Yes ma'am," he says as he smiles.

She rolls her eyes at him as she giggles. She gets Alana a coke and a glass and take them to her.

"Thank you," Alana says.

"Welcome."

Ebony goes into the bedroom. She's happy it's time for phase 2. The sooner it's done. The sooner all of this fake shit can be over with and her crew can get back to normal.

Phase 2!

For this part of the plan, Ebony and Ajay have to fake an argument. Then she has to demand that he take her home, *after* the fake argument. They simulate an argument which could've fooled the *Oscar committee!* Even Tank is starting to think they have gotten angry for real. Ebony demands to leave, "Now! Right now! Damn it!"

She enjoys the opportunity to curse in front of her man too. She's milking
330

this plan for everything its worth. She figured she may as well get some instant gratification out of it too.

Her and Ajay leave. Instead of him taking her home, as she had pretended to demand, he drives his car out of his parking area. But he doubles back and goes around to the back of the building and lets her out.

"Be careful, baby. And remember your word," she says, "You're coming home to me and remaining a *free* man."
She gives him a sweet kiss. Then she hurries to Rob's apartment and hooks back up with her girls.

When Ajay and Ebony had left Ajay's apartment, Tank started to casually mention the daughter Alana has and how much he has secretly wanted to meet her. If Alana bites, he is to ask her if he *can* see her. If she says yes, then he'll insist they go today.

"So where is my daughter at?" is how Tank goes into it.
Alana looks at him in shock, then she smiles. She know Olivia isn't his. But she's willing to lie, if he wants to claim her.

"She's staying in Pittsburgh with my folks, so I can go to school."

"I really do wanna meet her," he says, "I couldn't say that to you while I was still with Nina. But I wanna see her *bad*. You don't know how much it bothers me to have a kid out there that don't even know me."

"You can meet her. I want you too. You'll like her, Jeremy. She's a sweetheart," she says, "A really good kid."
She must've taken after her father. Whoever he is.

He goes in and out of his personality. He had no idea this plan would be so hard to act out. He's faked interest in lots of girls in his nearly 20 years of life. But this is proving harder to fake, then the others. This girl assisted another in trying to kill his only sister. His twin. He can manage this.

"Call me Tank. Not Jeremy. Let's go see Olivia," he suggests.
"She's in *Pittsburgh*."
"*And*? That's only a couple of hours away," he says.
"You wanna drive there?" she asks.
"We can," he says, "I've gotta go back to school. It can't wait until I come back. Not after you said it's okay. I can't hold that." He laughs and she does too. He says, "If Arthur don't mind, we can drive over there and see her tonight. On our date." Alana bites on all of it. She wanted him to be her daughters father from day one. "We should go today, anyway," he adds, "Because I have to be back in Natty tomorrow, for way too long."

"She's in Pittsburgh, though. That's a drive," Alana stalls.
He tells her it isn't a problem. He really doesn't want to hang around
331

Cleveland with her, right now. Because he doesn't want to run into Nina.

"As soon as she know I'm here, she'll be looking for me," he says, "You know what I'm saying, right? *Naggin* me about something."

Alana feels that and agrees they should take a road trip to avoid trouble for him, with his *baby mama*. He calls Arthur on the speaker phone and tells him the plan, as if Arthur doesn't know it already. Arthur gets into his role.

"Why don't we take that ride, man. I don't have nothing up for tonight," he says.

They agree. Tank, Alana, Michelle and Arthur will take a trip to Pittsburgh to visit Olivia.

Ajay is at Arthur's apartment waiting on his queue. They have to work him into this trip. Shortly after Tank and Arthur hang up, Ajay returns to his own apartment. He goes into his bedroom and slams the door, simulating that he's still angry from the argument with Ebony. Alana figures it must've really gotten heated as he drove Ebony home.

"He's pissed at your sister?" she asks, "I've never seen that."

"You know him and Ebony are not gonna stay together," Tank offers, "She hasn't been right with him since she lost the baby. They don't even get along at school. He was talking to me about hooking back up with Angel. I told him that would be cool if she was still around. But she's not. So I'm gonna help him find a girl. He thinks Angel really loves him and she disappeared because she couldn't stand seeing him with my sister."

"Angel *is* missing in action. But I know she would be game for that," Alana says, "If she was around, that is. She was so in love with Ajay but she said he didn't want nothing do with her when Ebony got back."

"Hey. Since Ajay don't have shit to do. He may as well hang out with us, ha?" he suggests, "You don't have no friends in Pittsburgh?"

"You know my aunt likes him," she says.

"He's not gonna fuck wit her. She swung on his mom," Tank says, freeing up a lie at will, as he continues, "He's not gonna mess with her. I know that already."

"Well tell him to come with us and maybe he can meet one of my cousins while we're there," she suggests.

Bingo! Ajay is going on the trip and Alana actually thinks it's her idea. This plan is working too well. It's time to roll out.

After Ajay takes a shower and gets cleaned up, he suggest they use one of Chill's Blazer's.

"Arthur, this fucking Riv don't have enough room for six people," he says, "Cause you know I'm gonna get up on something."

332

Chill lets them borrow the 1992 Blazer. Even more than that. Him, Jr, Wayne, Kilo and Rob get in on their part of the plan. They decide to come along in the 1989 Blazer as Chill makes the case for all of them going.

"The crew rolls thick. Especially outside of our set," he says, "Y'all don't know what sets you'll roll through and may not be welcomed in."
With that, the road trip is underway and phase 2 is looking well.

Back at The U!

"Damn! I can't just sit around here and do nothing," Ebony says.
"I know this shit better work." T-baby adds.
The foursome are just about a minute away from getting anxious, when Nina starts to complain about discomfort.

"My back is hurting me badly," she says as she goes to lay down on Rob's couch.
Ebony props pillows behind her and asks, "is that better, Nee Nee?"

"Yes. That's a little better," she says, " Thanks, kid."

"You can't go into labor until Tank gets back," Rebbie says as they all giggle.

"Don't we have another phase of the plan to do?" T-baby asks.

"Ebony does, first," Rebbie says, "And if they get her back here, then we get it in, for *real*."

"Ebony, when are you suppose to call Ajay?" she asks.

"At eight O'clock."

"Cool," Rebbie says, "We only got fifteen more minutes."

Phase 3!

Ebony calls Ajay. The argument continues because he's not at home. He goes off on her, on the phone. Right in front of Alana. After hanging up on her, he hints of hooking up with Angel.

"I should've just kept fucking with her, anyway," he says, "If I would've known this shit wasn't gonna work out, I would've."
Alana thinks she's down and the crew are down with her. She takes them to her favorite club and they get her fucked up. She slips up and tells Ajay that she can get in touch with Angel, *if he* really wants to get with her. He says he wants too. The 2 Blazers head to her stepbrothers apartment.

Phase 4!

333

Alana has no idea the crew are aware that Angel is the 1 who caused Ebony's accident. She feels like they had suspected she had, at one point. But now that they're all kicking it with her, she figures they've given up on Angel as a suspect. They arrive at her stepbrother's apartment. Alana opens the door. In the apartment, on the couch, is *Angel*. This is when the *real* acting takes place for Ajay. He has to keep his composure. He's hearing Ebony's voice in his head, saying, '*You're gonna make sure she goes to prison. That's what I want to happen.*'

"Hey, what's up?" he asks as he hurries to her and gives her a friendly hug.

Inside, his natural impulse wants to strangle the life out of her ass. But he still has to play the game. Angel is caught off guard. Alana has kept her informed over the last couple of months. She'd told her that her and Tank are cool again. She'd also called from her grandmothers to tell her that Ajay was with them and he had been talking about hooking up with her. Angel's guilt told her he wouldn't come. But now that they've shown up, she's all for it.

They all kick it at the apartment until Chill suggest they go to an after hours spot to get some breakfast. This is the clincher of the entire plan. They have to get Angel to leave with them, voluntarily. She's reluctant, at first. But Ajay's charm wins her over. He's pinching her nipples and pretending he's in the mood for her. Then he moves away from her and says, "Lets go crew. I'm hungry. She ain't wit it. We may as well go eat and head out." Then turning to Angel, he says, "I thought your girl said you was down for me. My bad. I won't bother you again."

He heads out the door, leaving everybody inside. Angel doesn't want him to leave. She puts on her shoes and says, "I'll go and eat with y'all, if Ajay don't go home. If he stays and kick it with me, I'll go."

"Hell yea, he's gonna kick it with you," Kilo says, "W*hy the hell* you think he came over here? He's pissed off now. That man don't beg nobody for shit."

Tank gets in on it and says, "He done rode out, asks you to go with him and you *trippin'*."

"Okay. I'll go," Angel says, "I said I'll go."

"Then go tell *him* that," Chill says and Angel leaves out the door.

A few minutes later, Ajay comes back inside and tells Chill to come on. They all load up in the Blazers and ride out.

In the 1989 Blazer, there's Chill, Jr, Kilo, Ajay, Angel and Wayne. In the 1992 Blazer, there's Arthur, Michelle, Tank, Alana and Rob. Chill and Arthur are the drivers. In the 89 Blazer, Angel is trying to serve Ajay

334

but he doesn't allow her too. He's no longer playing any fucking game. He just wants to get back to Cleveland and back to the U. Where Angel sat and waited on his girl, so she could take her life and did kill his first baby. Angel slides up under him like they're on a date. His body tenses up from the urge to harm her. She's kissing on his chest and trying to give him head.

"Not right now," he says, "I've got something for you though. I thought you didn't want me to share you. Slow your role."

Instead of going to eat, Chill and Arthur get on the interstate and head to Cleveland. Angel doesn't know where they're going. Initially, she thinks maybe they're just joy riding.

In the 92 Blazer, Alana learns what has *really* been happening these last few weeks. This is the part of the plan where Michele gets to shine.

"The day we went to see Tameka and you told me *you knew* where Angel was," Michelle says, "I was so pissed at you, Alana. You know Arthur is loyal to this crew. And you know I'm loyal to Arthur. Did you really think I was gonna *help* you cover this up? On top of that, I already knew you and Angel tried to salt me up with Arthur. That's low down."

Tank tells Alana the whole truth. He says, "And my girl Nina, Ebony, the whole fuckin crew is riding on this one. We planned this shit good, didn't we?" He chuckles first, then he flat out laughs. The others chuckle at his tone of voice. Alana is more afraid than she is angry. Not 1 of them give a damn. She can't imagine what Angel is going through at this very moment.

But in the 89 Blazer, they're still riding along on the plan. No one tells Angel anything. It isn't until Chill takes the Cleveland exit that she starts to feel like something is wrong.

"Where are we going?" she asks Chill but he doesn't respond.

She asks Ajay and he gives her a death stare. The same look he had that night when she slapped his face. She starts screaming, instantly. He hits her in her face with everything he has. She's knocked unconscious. Kilo reaches over the seat and hits her to wake her up.

"I don't want this bitch to get brain damage," he says.

They laugh. All except Ajay. He hits her again. Kilo pulls her into the back seat with him and Wayne to protect Ajay from a murder charge. It's a job just keeping him off of her during the 3 hour ride back to Cleveland. He has hell fire in his eyes and the love for his girl in his heart. But the pain of losing his 1st baby is at the forefront of his mind.

Phase 5!

After a few hours, they arrive at the U. They take Alana and Angel

335

into Arthur's apartment. Rob heads to his apartment to get the foursome. The rest of the crew are at the club. They'll all hook up after *phase 6*.

When the foursome come to Arthur's apartment, Alana and Angel know they've been had, for sure. The 1st thing Ajay and Tank do is plant a sweet kiss on Ebony and Nina. Then Rob brings in a tape recorder for Angel's confession. Which they plan to get, 1 way or the other. Ebony can barely contain herself but she's more concerned about her man. He's pacing the floor. She's so proud he had kept his word to her and hadn't killed Angel along the highway. She has no idea of how hard it was to make sure he *kept* his word. She can see that he's stressing. So she goes over to him and puts her calm and loving hands on him. He stops pacing and stands with her. But he never takes his eyes off of Angel. He wants her blood spilled.

Chill starts, "Angel, I guess by now you know why you're here."

She stammers for a response, "No. Not really," she mumbles.

"Bitch!" Ajay yells, "Play wit it and see what you get!"

"Hold on, Ajay," Chill says as he holds him back.

Ebony is quivering with anger, just to be in the same room with Angel. A safe room, at that. A room with her crew in it and hopefully, willing to let her have her revenge. She's about to have it. Rather the crew are willing for her too or not.

Chill continues, "Why did you feel like you needed to fuck with my family?"

"I didn't-"

"We already know you did it. The only thing that remains are the terms," he goes on, as if she wasn't speaking, "You bitches just *think* you got nuts. Y'all ho's never had enough game to get shit by *my* crew. We know about the gray Caprice Classic. *Tony's Chevy?* We know Alana hid you out? Michelle gets my respect for this one. She brought it all home. We got you and your home girl. That's all we need. Now I'm gonna ask you *one* more time. Why did you feel like you needed to fuck with my crew?"

"I just wanted Ajay to talk to me," she admits.

"So you kill my lil girl, bitch?" Ajay says softly, "My *first* kid."

His voice is trembling. Ebony is finding it harder to keep her composure. She can hear it in his voice. He wants to cry. He's reliving the day of the accident. The murder and the attempted murder. He's remembering the sorrow and hurt that poured out of her when he had to tell her their 1st baby had been killed. The struggle it took for him to calm her down and at the same time, suppress his rage, confusion, concern and grief. This angers her, immensely.

"I didn't know she was gonna go off the road," Angel tries, "I was

336

trying to make her stop the car and get out. So we could fight for Ajay."

"So you could cut my baby out, right?" Ajay asks but Angel doesn't respond.

"But she did go off the road. She went off the cliff," Chill says, "And you left her there to die. Then you ran off."

"My baby did die, bitch," Ajay says softly, "And so will you."

"Ajay, I love you-"

"Bitch, *please!*" Nina says before Chill motions for her to stick to the plan.

"Go on, Angel. Tell your side while you're breathing," Chill says.
Ajay fires up a blunt, passes it to Ebony and says, "Get right."
He's already in the zone. Ebony shares the weed with Rebbie and T-baby, as Chill sends Nina into the bedroom.

"You don't need to be in here anyway, baby," Tank says as he kisses her again, passionately.
In sight of Alana, so she can see that they're still *very* much a couple.
Then he escorts her into the bedroom as she still complains about her back pains. She wants 1 of his famous massages.

"My back's been hurting me, all day," she's telling him as they walk out of the living room.

"Come on and lay down," he says, "so I can rub it for you."
Alana is left in the living room. Tank's part of the plan is done.

In the living room, Ebony and Ajay are most impatient as Angel starts again with her reasoning.

"Ajay, I'm still in love with you," Angel says, "All I wanted was for you to spend some time with me. You was my first and then you just dogged me out. Shared me with your friends."
Ebony looks on and listens in disgust. Ajay has no comment yet.
"You put me out on the highway at four o'clock in the morning to walk home. You had sex with my friends, in my face-"

"So what, bitch? You had sex with my crew, in my face," he offers.
"You told me too."

"And you did it, ho," he says, "You know I didn't want yo ass. I told you that, from jump. I told you I had a girl and who she was. *Period.*"
He turns to Ebony and says, "Baby, have I ever shared you with anybody?"

"No and you're not going too," she says, "You are my one and only and you know that to be true because we grew up together. Right next door to each other. I'm not like this liar here, who claims to have been a virgin. But she's got sex history. How do you do *that*?"
She never takes her eyes off of Angel.
337

"Damn straight, I'm not," Ajay says, "I love *you*. You're the only girlfriend I've ever had and the only one I've ever wanted to have. I don't share my girl with no muafucka. I told you and every other bitch that I was ever around, that Ebony was my girl and that shit wasn't gonna change."

"So, Angel," Chill says, "Basically what you're telling me is you tried to kill baby girl and you *did* kill my young crew, because you got *played by* my crew and couldn't lie your way into my homeboys heart? Is that what you're saying here?"

Angel doesn't answer. Chill looks at her with an expression of impatience. "I guess so," she finally answers.

"Well if you want her. Here she is," Chill says, "If you can finish the job. Then you can have Ajay."

"No the fuck she cant have me. And she ain't gonna fuck with my woman either," Ajay offers.

Angel knows this is a set up. Ajay doesn't even try to play it off.

"I don't have anything against Ebony, personally," Angel admits, "We're just in love with the same man."

"Well I've got something *personally* against you," Ebony says unable to hold back anymore as she unloads on Angel.

"You killed my baby. You almost killed me. Now it's just you and me. It's time to do this shit, yourself. No cars and no knives. Because I *hear* you had plans of cutting my baby out of me. Well here I am, bitch! With no interference."

She starts to punch Angel and they begin to fight, 1 on 1. Angel and Ebony. Ebony is commanding the fight. Angel does get in a body blow, every now and then. Until Ebony slams her to the floor and climbs on top of her. They continue to fight as Angel almost manages to roll her. But Ebony pins her down with her knees and continues to punch her in her face and head. Nina and Tank come back out of the bedroom.

"I wouldn't miss this for the world," Nina says, "Labor and all."

Ebony continues punching. Angel, not ever respecting a fair one, reaches up and grabs her hair.

"Let my hair go, bitch!" Ebony screams.

She manages to free her hair from Angel's hand as she continues to punch her. Angel is clawing and scratching at her chest and neck. Ajay looks on. He can barely resist the urge to kick Angel in the head. She rolls Ebony over and tries to punch. But Ebony holds her by the wrist. Angel bites down on Ebony's hand and Ajay loses it.

"Hell no!" he yells as he snatches her up off of Ebony and starts wailing on her.

338

He's punching her so fast, he's already hit her 8 times before Chill and the guys can react and pull him away. Then Ebony jumps up and lights into her again.

"I heard you hit *my man*," she screams and rams Angel's head into the side of Arthur's island counter. She falls backwards and lands in the recliner, "Hit him now, bitch! I wish you would!" she yells as she pounces on her.

Angel is reaching for her pocket. She's going for a knife. Ajay notices and pulls Ebony away. He starts beating Angel, mercilessly. It takes every person in the room to get him off of her, this time. They finally pull him free and into the kitchen. That's when Angel and Alana make a break for the door and run outside. T-baby and Rebbie run out behind them but Kilo and Wayne are already outside waiting. They was out there, watching through the window. Just in case the girls managed to escape. They grab Alana, then Angel.

"Y'all ho's ain't going nowhere," Kilo says.

"No where but to *fuckin'* jail," Wayne adds with a chuckle.

T-baby and Rebbie get in a few licks on both girls, for good measure. Suddenly Ajay, who had managed to shake the crew off of him inside, comes tearing out of the apartment and grabs Angel again.

"You tried to run from me, bitch? Ha? I thought you *loved* me. I thought you *wanted* me, so much. Why you *runnin*?" his voice is chillingly calm.

He starts to choke her with 1 hand while punching her with the other one. Angel is damn near unconscious when they pry him off of her, this time. Chill tells them to bring the girls back into the apartment. Kilo and Wayne do the honors. They get them back inside and close the door. Tank and the others work on calming Ajay down again.

Then Chill asks Ebony, "Are you done?" as Ajay yells, "I'm not!"

"Bro, this is not for you," Chill says, "She attempted murder on baby girl. She killed the baby girl she was carrying."

"That was *my* baby," Ajay says.

Chill can feel Ajay's anger as he turns his eyes back to Ebony but stays in front of Ajay.

"Ebony needs to tell me what she wants to do next," he says as Ajay reluctantly backs off.

"Call Hardin," Ebony says, "I want her arrested for murder and for attempted murder. And they can take Alana down for obstruction of justice and aiding a fugitive."

She says this while staring at both the girls. "Oh, I guess y'all ho's didn't

339

realize I know the law. I do. And both of y'all are about to get familiar with it too."

She does know her law. She's had enough experience with her crew, in her lifetime, to know about charges.

"You want Hardin on it now. Then you need to call him," Chill says, "But first, we're going to Ajay's apartment so Arthur can fix his shit back up," he finishes with a short laugh.

They all go to Ajay's place leaving Arthur and Michelle behind to straighten things up. Michelle has witnessed the entire incident. She's amazed at how tactical the crew are.

"Them muthafuckaz don't be bullshitting, do they?" she asks.

"That's what I was trying to explain to you, that day you told me you knew something about this whole thing," he says, "You don't wanna cross the crew. *My* crew."

Then he goes over the statement with her, which she'll give to the police. She understands it, perfectly.

The crew get to Ajay's apartment. Before allowing Ebony to call the police, Chill tells Angel to give her confession, "Right now and you can live. Bullshit with me and you won't. Simple as that."

Rob starts the tape recorder. Angel gets her composure together. She looks directly at Ajay as she tells what she had done and how Alana had assisted her. For good measure, they have Alana to give her confession too.

Phase 6!

Ebony calls Hardin and tells him they have Angel and Alana in custody. They have both confessed on tape to what they had done to her. And that her and Ajay had fought with them both. Hardin says he'll be right over. They hang up. Then her, Ajay, Chill and Rob. Nina, Tank, T-baby and Rebbie wait for the police to come. Kilo and Wayne head to *The Spot*.

Hardin shows up in 15 minutes with 2 uniform officers. He takes Angel and Alana into custody. They call an ambulance for Angel. She has been beaten, black and blue. Hardin and the officers leave with both girls. Then Chill, Rob, Rebbie and T-baby go to the club to meet up with their mates. Ebony, Ajay, Tank and Nina stay at Ajay's. They're waiting on the completion of phase 6. They realized when they initially came up with this plan, that somebody might have to get dirty. They were right! Phase 6 will take awhile to complete. Because less then an hour later the police are back
340

to arrest Ajay and Ebony for assault. They cuff them and take them to the central precinct for booking. Tank and Nina leave and go to *The Spot* to tell the others. Arthur and Michelle take Arthur's car and follow them to the club.

Ebony has never been to jail before, so she's a little frightened. Actually, she's a lot frightened. She's really afraid to be in the jailhouse, let alone being under arrest. There is a lot of noise from the out of control inmates and convicts. And this is just the people in booking. She wants to go home to the comforts of her own room. Or 1 of the rooms she shares with Ajay. She looks around at the other suspects and it's amazing to her how comfortable they seem to be in this hell hole. The décor is awful and so is the smell. The loud talking, doors slamming, books hitting desk and voices of authority yelling to be heard over all of the other chatter. makes for a very intimidating occasion. Watching police strong arm and intimidate suspects, isn't something she's ever wanted to witness. And although she's heard about how it goes down at the jail, she's never wanted to be a witness to it. She wants to go home. But she doesn't know if and when that's going to happen.

Ajay could've gone to private lock up or holding. They don't do it because Parkwood, Hardin and Wheeler are his representatives. He asks that they put Ebony in segregated population and is pleased to find out that Hardin was going to do that anyway. After they get Ajay secured in his private area, Hardin goes in to visit Ebony. He doesn't ask her any questions. Nor does he put her on the defensive. He keeps her company, basically. He has brought her some hot cocoa because she had complained about being cold. He keeps her in an interrogation room and not even in a cell. He assures her that he'll make sure the charges don't stick on her. But for Ajay, because of his priors, things will be hard to lose and he will get the hardest charge of the 2 of them. Ajay had just been acquitted on an assault charge and it was yet to be adjudicated. Plus he was shot as the result of a neighborhood brawl where 2 people lost their lives. His crew has been rumored to have participated or have their names mentioned in cases of unlawful situations. However, none of that has panned out. But tonight is going to be a little murkier. This time, Ajay is charged with felony assault. He had assaulted Angel in 2 states. Plus if they push for it and they're planning to, they can charge him with interstate kidnapping. A federal charge. But Ajay has weight. He has wealthy Alumni who do favors *for the DA* and are owed favors *from the DA*. Either way, Ajay isn't worried. He has done what he promised *himself* he had to do. Make sure Angel was in
341

custody. He has done that and the rest will have to work itself out.

Ebony could've been charged with felony or misdemeanor assault. But she isn't. She doesn't even have a bond by the time Hardin is done. But she does have a fine that she'll have to pay. He filed hers down to disorderly conduct. He isn't going to pursue the charges, so Ebony is pretty much, *Scott free.*

George Wheeler is on the scene, shortly before 10am. He arranges for them to be released on their own recognizance and Ajay is able to bail out by 2pm. Their parents and crew are waiting for them. Pearl and Jo are visibly upset but they aren't angry. They're upset at seeing both of their children in jail. But they're happy they had gotten Angel and Alana and no one was killed in the process.

Later, their representatives and matrons get together. Wheeler, Hardin, papa, grandpa Charles, grandpa Joshua, Mr. Parkwood and with Poppa on the phone, are going to see to it that Ajay and Ebony's charges go away. It'll take a lot of pull and favors to get Ajay's dropped. He had done some real serious damage to Angel. Or at least, that's how he had told it to the police.

"Ebony and Angel had a fight. A typical *girl fight.* Punching, clawing, scratching and biting," he had told them, "But me, I whoop that bitch to sleep. She killed my unborn child. I want her dead," he had said to Hardin.

Wheeler is going to try a *crime of passion* defense if this makes it to court. Which with Parkwood on the scene, he doubts that it will. He has Michelle as a key witness to say the 2 girls had left Pittsburgh with the crew on their own. Willingly and as a matter of fact, the trip to Pittsburgh had been Alana's idea. Wheeler has all of the crews statements as to what had happened. He has Alana and Angel's confessions implicating each other and themselves.

"We got a good case?" papa asks.

"Pretty damn solid," Wheeler says.

"That's what I need to hear," poppa says as Joshua and Charles cosign him.

Later, Alana is released on bond. Angel is remanded to custody for being a flight risk. It's not even so much that she will run away, that caused Wheeler and the reps to ask the Judge to deny bail. They don't want her out on the streets because of Ajay. He has already assured them that he
342

isn't doing anymore assault charges. Misdemeanor or felony.

"The next charge I get will be a murder charge. Angel's," he had said before him and Ebony left the precinct.

Wheeler nor their representatives want that and neither does Ebony. At least, not for Anthony, her or any her crew.

Time Will Reveal

THE END OF PART TWO-RELOADED!
COPYRIGHTED SINCE 2003!
© True's Relate Publishing/LTBrown®

Join us at:
Black Coffee's Crew Nation-The Movement
on Facebook now and let me know what you think of this title!"
-Black Coffee
FAN PAGE on Facebook: Time Will Reveal fan page or Black Coffee's Books
Websites: www.truesrelatepublishing.com
www.blackdollone.com

On Twitter: Lovely T. Brown @AuthorBlkCoffee

If you were charged more the $25 [US dollars] and shipping wasn't included in that price, contact us at the following websites, immediately.

MY website: www.blackdollone.com
www.truesrelatepublishing.com
Join us on FACEBOOK for the discussion questions:
Black Coffee's Book Club and Black Coffee's Crew Nation

http://twitter.com/AuthorBlkCoffee

All books except AJAY, available in print and eBooks
Nook and Kindle

Also available by Black Coffee:
The entire Time Will Reveal Series
Time To Learn- RELOADED-Time Will Reveal part 1
Time To Love-RELOADED-Time Will Reveal part 3
Time To Know-RELOADED-Time Will Reveal part 4
Time To Feel-RELOADED-Time Will Reveal part 5

(Time Will Reveal, short stories series)
#1 MORE THE 4 ADMIRERS-RELOADED
#2 MR. WRONG AND THE RATS-RELOADED
#3 THE CREW'S PRIORTY [TBA]

And more of the Time Will Reveal series!
The Making of AJAY- Every Man- RELOADED (PRINT ONLY)
Time To Show-Time Will Reveal part 6 [Late Fall 2013]
Ajay and Ebony 1-Time Will Reveal 7-Time To Give [TBA]
Ajay and Ebony 2-Time Will Reveal 8-Time To Live [TBA]

[future releases]
The Foe, The Friend-Poetry [print & audio]
All By My Lonely-The Organization-part one
Still By My Lonely-The Organization-part two

344

www.ingramcontent.com/pod-product-compliance
Lightning Source LLC
Chambersburg PA
CBHW061322170626
46817CB00001B/276